Playing God
in the Nursery

Playing God in the Nursery

JEFF LYON

W·W·NORTON & COMPANY

NEW YORK   LONDON

Published simultaneously in Canada by Stoddart, a subsidiary of
General Publishing Co. Ltd, Don Mills, Ontario.
Printed in the United States of America.

The text of this book is composed in Baskerville.
Composition and manufacturing by The Maple-Vail Book Manufacturing Group

FIRST EDITION

Library of Congress Cataloging in Publication Data
Lyon, Jeff.
    Playing God in the nursery.
    An outgrowth of a series of articles written for the
Chicago Tribune in 1983.
    Includes index.
    1. Neonatal intensive care—Moral and ethical
aspects.   2. Infanticide—Moral and ethical aspects.
3. Medical ethics.   I. Title.
RJ253.5.L96   1985   174'.24   84-25457

ISBN 0-393-01898-9

W. W. Norton & Company, Inc., 500 Fifth Avenue, New York, N. Y. 10110
W. W. Norton & Company Ltd., 37 Great Russell Street, London WC1B 3NU

1 2 3 4 5 6 7 8 9 0

To my parents and my brother, Mike

"How small, of all that human hearts endure,
That part which laws or kings can cause or cure!"
—Oliver Goldsmith

Issues to be covered

for life

Sanctity of life

for death

Cost

Quality of life

Contents

Foreword

Few events can be so devastating for parents as the birth of a child with severe disabilities. This is especially true in our culture where perfection is a cornerstone of the American Dream.

While medical technology has eradicated the majority of dread illnesses, the sad fact remains that disability and disease cannot always be conquered. Certainly we are able to sustain many infants who, even a decade ago, would have died. It has become painfully apparent, however, that in many instances heroic medical intervention does little more than prolong the act of dying. In less clearly defined cases, critically ill infants may be the unwitting beneficiaries of a compromised existence, void of the cognition and participation we value as the parameters of meaningful life.

Who decides whether medical treatment is appropriate, or if it is inhumane, has become an important moral dilemma—one that has generated intense and often heated controversy since the case of Baby Doe in Bloomington, Indiana, in 1982. Debates on this issue have extended beyond physicians and family to the arena of the courts and regulatory agencies. Regrettably, the solutions sometimes rendered there have been founded on the premise that *all* life—no matter how compromised and miserable—must be maintained if that is technically possible.

Life is indeed sacred, but it is not absolute. Society's acceptance of this fact more frequently has allowed our chronically ill elders to die with dignity. Yet in the cases of so-called Baby Does—grievously ill infants with life-threatening disabilities—and, far more frequently but less noted, for infants whose premature births jeopardize survival, decisions to withhold life-sustaining treatment have been compounded by the fact that infants are unable to articulate what would be in their best interests. Since the case of Baby Doe, the responsibility for making these admittedly difficult treatment decisions has been hanging in a balance, weighted by government and the courts at one end and parents and health-care providers on the other.

In the text that follows, Jeff Lyon has sensitively probed the complicated needs of seriously disabled infants and their families. He has succeeded in painting an incisive portrait that, for the first time since the issue of Baby Doe captured national attention, brings into focus the overlapping implications of the treatment vs. nontreatment question—medical, legal, ethical, emotional, financial, psychological, and social. Lyon's nonprejudicial account offers no specific recommendations; it does, however, lend support to the medical community's position that treatment decisions in the best interest of the life-threatened infant do *not* rest with the courts or with government.

It would appear also that the issue is not an exclusively medical one. If I can draw one conclusion from Mr. Lyon's thought-provoking text, it is that the treatment of Baby Does is a societal responsibility and must be considered in that context.

The parents of seriously ill newborns and the physicians responsible for their care are intellectually able to render decisions on necessary treatment. In those cases where decisions to forgo treatment are considered, however, outside counsel is often required. Although parents ultimately bear the burden of a seriously ill child, we must recognize that even good parents can and do make bad decisions. This can occur without any malice on their parts and may result from shock, confusion, fear, or anger at not having a "normal" child.

Most physicians and hospitals agree that the most equitable process to ensure responsible care to disabled infants is review by a community-based multidisciplinary panel composed of local representatives of medicine, clergy, law, ethics, social work, and disability groups. These committees, recommended by the President's Commission for the Study of Ethical Problems in Medicine and recognized as a viable arbiter of these cases by the Department of Health and Human Services, lend support to the family, physician, and hospital during the process of reaching appropriate treatment decisions.

One significant impediment to allowing society to address the complicated issue of Baby Does without federal intervention is the government's erroneous contention that medicine's role is to do everything possible to save life even when life itself, for reasons beyond our control, has irreversibly slipped past our ability to restore it. Jeff Lyon has more accurately perceived and presented the definition of "medicine" in his recognition that there are limits to what we can and ought to do.

I urge everyone concerned with the future of Baby Does, irrespective of their stance on the issue, to reexamine the three roles of medicine denned in the Hippocratic Oath: doing away with the sufferings of the sick, lessening the violence of their diseases, and refusing to treat those who are overmastered by their diseases, realizing that in such cases medicine is powerless. In spite of modern technology, there are limits to what we ought to feel obliged to impose on dying patients and on those whose futures are overmastered by futility.

M. Harry Jennison, M.D.
Executive Director
American Academy of Pediatrics

August 14, 1984

Acknowledgments

Brevity may be the soul of wit, but it is inhospitable to gratitude. Far more people and institutions have assisted me in the course of this project than I could ever thank in the space I have. But in no way does that diminish my debt to them, for without their assistance this book could never have been written.

I must, however, extend my special appreciation to a number of individuals, particularly those who read parts of this manuscript and offered valuable advice and criticism. They are Dr. Marvin Rosner, of Northwestern Memorial Hospital; Dr. Thomas Gardner, of Evanston Hospital; the Reverend James Bresnahan, of Northwestern University Medical School; Drs. Ira Salafsky and Carl Hunt, of Children's Memorial Hospital; and Sonia Ringstrom, Ph.D., of Loyola University.

A number of others were exceedingly generous with their time at various stages of this work. They include Dr. Godfrey Oakley, Jr., of the U.S. Center for Disease Control; the March of Dimes Birth Defects Foundation and its chief of research, Richard Leavitt; Columbia-Presbyterian Medical Center, in New York, especially Drs. Michael Katz, L. Stanley James, and William Heird; the University of California, at San Francisco, particularly Drs. Roderic Phibbs, William Tooley, and Peter Budetti, and Albert Jonsen, Ph.D.; Children's Memorial Hospital, of Chicago, notably Drs. Susan Luck, Farouk Idriss, David McLone, Joel Charnow, and Jerome Schulman, as well as the hospital president, Earl Frederick, and the ombudsman, Nancy Neir Wachs; Evanston Hospital, of Evanston, Illinois, particularly Dr. John Hobart, Carol Ceithaml, Ph.D., and Martin Drebin, vice-president; Northwestern Memorial Hospital, of Chicago, especially Drs. Richard Depp, James Brown, Ruth Deddish, and William J. Burns, Ph.D.; Dr. Rosita Pildes, of Cook County Hospital, Chicago; Dr. L. Joseph Butterfield, of the Children's Hospital, Denver; Dr. Bernard Towers and

Acknowledgments

Prof. Norman Cousins of the UCLA School of Medicine, Los Angeles. Also Lee Dunn, Jr., J.D. of the firm of McDermott, Will, and Emery, Chicago; Carol Amadio, M.S.W., J.D., and Gary Morgan, of the Illinois Department of Children and Family Services; Dr. Edward Lis and Eugene Bilotti, of the Illinois Division of Services to Crippled Children; Joel Kleinman and Mary Grace Kovar, of the National Center for Health Statistics; Thomas Murray, Ph.D., of the Hastings Center's Institute of Society, Ethics, and the Life Sciences; and Dr. Max Harry Weil, of the Chicago Medical School, North Chicago, Illinois.

Finally, I must express my heartfelt thanks to my editor, Kathleen M. Anderson, for her skilled ministrations and, above all, her patience; to my agent, Peter Shepherd, for his timely and perceptive advice; to my manuscript editor, Otto Sonntag; to Walter Reed and Ruth Moss for their encouragement; to the editors of the *Chicago Tribune* for granting me the leave time necessary to produce this book; and most of all to my wife, Bonita, for more reasons than I can ever enumerate.

Preface

This book is an outgrowth of a series of articles I wrote for the *Chicago Tribune* in 1983. It is an attempt to provide a framework for discussion of one of the most troubling moral issues of our time—whether it is ever justifiable to withhold lifesaving medical treatment from a child with severe birth defects. The subject has received considerable publicity of late. The decision of several couples to let their damaged newborns die was followed by strenuous efforts on the part of the United States government to ensure that all handicapped babies receive lifesaving care regardless of the parents' wishes. As events unfolded, it became clear that at the heart of the matter were profound and vexing questions, which many of the finest minds in government, the law, philosophy, and the medical profession have been unable to resolve satisfactorily. Is death sometimes preferable to a life of extreme disability? Can parents make that determination for their child? Is it an expression of compassion to let a sick baby die—or is it, as some contend, murder?

The ultimate arbiter of these and other questions must be society at large, but few accounts of recent Baby Doe cases have given the public enough information with which to judge the merits of the issue. This volume attempts to fill that need by analyzing as many sides of the question as possible. It places the nontreatment of infants in a historical context and examines the practice from a legal and ethical point of view. Beyond that, it addresses the issue's disturbing social and economic implications, taking, for example, a long look at the impact defective children have on their families. It puts particular emphasis on the government's failure to back up its concern for handicapped newborns by approving the necessary programs to sustain them later in life.

Finally, there is the ongoing fight against birth defects. We still do not know what causes most abnormalities, yet medical science has made encouraging progress in treatment and prevention—particularly in the area of prematurity and low birthweight, which are major contributors to disability. I have included an extensive discussion of these medical details, for no understanding of the broader moral issue is complete without an appreciation of how handicaps come about and the limitations medicine faces in repairing them. One last note: I have relied throughout the book on case studies to illustrate various points. In many instances, the names of the principals have been used; in others, I have used pseudonyms at the request of the parties involved.

It is hoped that the factual material presented here will enable the general public to reach some conclusions. Just as war is far too important a matter to be left to the generals, so the treatment of impaired infants is too important to be decided by doctors and lawmakers alone. It is also hoped that this book will provide some comfort to parents suddenly faced with the momentous decision of how to proceed mercifully on behalf of their defective newborn. There is no interest group for such parents, and they are badly in need of one.

Jeff Lyon

September 1984

Playing God
in the Nursery

1

"Baby Doe"
Two Children and a White House Crusade

The town of Bloomington lies just beyond that point in Indiana where the land turns with improbable suddenness from the flat monotony of the north to the rolling beauty of the south. All at once, the rivers seem to quicken and you are in hills thick with elegant oak and hickory trees. It is shy country, green and dark, where the bridges wear head shawls and lovely ravines drop away and out of sight. Everywhere is the gentle warning that the road is guest here, now and always.

Bloomington, itself, has lost some charm in recent years. The town's most picturesque features—a rugged 19th-century courthouse and the ivy-clad campus of Indiana University—coexist cheek by jowl with shopping plazas, auto-parts stores, and junk-food emporiums designed to woo the student trade. But if some of its scenery has changed, the essence of the town has not. It remains as peaceful and serene as the encircling countryside, a tightly knit, homespun community that is protective of traditional values and tolerant of the liberal university population it hosts.

Then, in the spring of 1982, this tranquillity was disrupted by a shocking and tragic episode. A Bloomington couple allowed its infant son to die of a treatable birth defect. The child, who succumbed while surrounded by willing rescuers, has become known to the world as Baby Doe, his identity sealed by the courts to protect his parents. We will continue to respect their privacy by not naming them in this book.

Though Baby Doe's whole existence was compressed into a matter of days, it left more of a mark on the nation than lives of far greater duration. The impact of his death was felt in the White House and in virtually every hospital nursery in the United States, and it triggered a nationwide debate that shows no signs of fading.

But the most immediate effect of the Baby Doe case was on the people of Bloomington, who were painfully divided into two camps by the issue. The parents found themselves supported by some of their neighbors and reviled by others. The child's doctors nearly came to blows over him, and one threatened to kidnap the boy on the night of his death. His nurses subsequently required psychotherapy to overcome their sense of guilt. And today, almost three years later, the community's scars have not completely healed.

Good Friday, April 9, 1982. The afternoon light was dying as Dr. Walter Owens, a large, slightly rumpled man with a graying goatee, hurried into the rear entrance of Bloomington Hospital, where one of his patients had just gone into labor. The hospital, a sprawling, limestone-block structure, stands on a rise on Bloomington's east side. Its essentially military appearance is only slightly relieved by a few architectural flourishes, such as a greenhouse-style entryway and some incongruous-looking columns and smoked-glass windows. It is the only hospital in a town of 52,000 people.

As Owens strode through the antiseptic halls on his way to the maternity ward, he had no way of knowing what an emotional hurricane would be unleashed during the next few hours. His thoughts were confined to the clinical details of the birth that lay ahead. The mother, a petite woman with closely cropped hair, was 31 years old. Her pregnancy had proceeded quite normally, and she had previously given birth to two healthy children. There was no reason to expect anything other than a routine delivery.

Owens was pleased to be involved in the case. He was genuinely fond of the parents, a pair of former schoolteachers who had given up the classroom several years earlier—she to raise her children, he to become an executive with a Bloomington firm. Owens found them to be pleasant, conscientious people with a straightforward manner. They had been married for seven years and were both looking forward to the birth of their third child. The father, a dark, heavyset man of 34, seemed to be brimming with delight. He had taken Lamaze natural-childbirth classes with his wife and was eager to coach her through the delivery.

Scanning the medical chart, Owens noted only one indication that something might be wrong. It had manifested itself when the woman's amniotic sac burst, 45 minutes after her admission to the hospital. She began to pass amniotic fluid of an abnormal greenish color. This "staining" of the fluid signifies that the child is giving off a fetal waste product known as meconium, which is sometimes, but not always, an SOS from the fetus, suggesting that it may not be getting enough oxygen.

In the absence of any other warning signals, however, Owens was not overly concerned. At about 7:30 P.M., with labor progressing nicely, he made his way to the doctor's lounge and slipped into his hospital garb. Then, after carefully scrubbing up for the birth, he joined the parents in the delivery room, the smallest of three such units on the hospital's second floor. The room is a stark and utilitarian place, with dull gray walls and a speckled tile floor. No platoon of backup personnel was bustling about, as one might see in the large teaching hospitals of the great cities. The only other person present as Owens began to deliver the baby was the nurse Dana Watters. Childbirth is an intimate arrangement in most of Middletown America.

Over the next 40 minutes, everything went smoothly. Owens could not have asked for a more uncomplicated birth. Buoyed by her husband's encouragement, the mother bore down again and again until the baby's head began to emerge. Swiftly, Owens inserted a rubber bulb syringe into the tiny mouth. The idea is to suction out secretions from the child's pharynx before the infant has a chance to take its first breath. The technique is designed to combat a serious birth peril—meconium aspiration pneumonitis—which can mean respiratory crisis and even brain damage if any meconium swallowed during labor is inhaled into the lungs.

This task completed, Owens returned to shepherding the child on its journey from the uterus to the outer world. Within moments, the couple became the proud and vocal parents of a six-pound baby boy. The time of delivery was logged at 8:19 P.M., and it was at that instant— as he placed the infant on its mother's abdomen—that Owens saw he had a catastrophe on his hands.

The baby was as limp as a rag doll. Blue from lack of oxygen, it lay scarcely breathing, its small heart pumping raggedly, like an engine that won't turn over. Its initial Apgar score, a rating system used by doctors to evaluate a newborn's physical state, was an abysmal 2 out of a possible 10.

But Owens observed something else in the small, flaccid body that lay before him, something that made his heart sink. He saw the telltale signs of Down's syndrome, the mysterious realignment of the 21st chromosome that consigns a child to a life of mental retardation. The doctor's eyes collided with those of Nurse Watters. She had noted it, too.

The mother must have seen something in the child's face as well. "You look beautiful," she crooned, stroking the infant on her belly. "You look different from my other two, but I love you anyway."

The father eyed his newborn son uneasily. "His color's not too great," he remarked in a thin voice. "He seems kind of blue."

Dr. Owens kept his eyes riveted on the child. He felt helpless for a moment, knowing that he would soon have to convey the truth about the child's condition. Is there another profession besides obstetrics, he wondered, that can take someone so quickly from exultation to despair?

But there was no time to ponder. The child needed help to breathe. Owens tried flicking its tiny chest with his fingers to stimulate respiration, but it responded weakly. He nodded at Mrs. Watters, who whisked the baby to a nearby radiant warming table, where she set to work. First she dried the boy vigorously with blankets, then began feeding him oxygen via a hose from the wall. A minute went by, then two. At last the infant began to breathe normally, and his color brightened. Mrs. Watters gave a thumbs-up signal to Owens, who was delivering the placenta. The veteran obstetrician relaxed somewhat.

With practiced hands, Mrs. Watters took up what is known as a DeLee trap and threaded it into the child's esophagus. Her intention was to suction out the stomach, removing amniotic fluid and meconium, which could potentially back up into the windpipe. But as she slid the slender tubing down the throat, she felt it suddenly stop. She tried again. It wouldn't budge.

"I can't pass the catheter, Dr. Owens," she murmured anxiously.

The two of them peered at each other over their masks. They both knew what that meant.

"Esophageal atresia," thought Owens grimly, sliding over to the warming table to see for himself.

Atresia is a medical term meaning "absence" or "abnormal closure." An esophageal atresia is a condition in which the baby's esophagus fails to develop normally during the months of pregnancy. It ends in a blind pouch, then may resume farther down, so that the net effect is that of a washed-out bridge. No food can reach the stomach.

Very often the defect occurs in tandem with a complication known as a tracheoesophageal fistula, in which the lower, or stomach, end of the interrupted esophagus may hook directly into the windpipe. The child will have trouble breathing, being unable to rid itself of mucus, and eventually its lungs will be "digested" by its own stomach juices backing up. Owens suspected the child had a fistula as well.

The mother's face seemed to cloud over as she waited for Owens to stop examining the baby. He was taking forever, much longer than he should. "What's wrong?" she asked, alarmed. Her hand, swollen from pregnancy, tightened around her husband's.

Mrs. Watters bit her lip. "We seem to be having some difficulty getting the tube down into his stomach," she replied. She did not elaborate.

The father, his impassive-looking surgical outfit concealing the apprehensive man inside, kept his wide eyes focused on the doctor. His color had turned pale.

"Is . . . he going to be all right?" he stammered.

Owens lifted his surgical cap and passed a hand through his gray-streaked hair. "We're going to have to see," he said solemnly. Believing a second opinion was in order, he asked the father who their family doctor was. Their general practitioner was Dr. Paul Wenzler, the man replied, but where their children were concerned, Dr. Wenzler consulted with Dr. James Schaffer, a prominent Bloomington pediatrician.

Owens told Mrs. Watters to get Schaffer on the phone immediately. By chance, Schaffer was already in the hospital making rounds. He agreed to examine the baby in the special-care nursery.

Wasting no time, Mrs. Watters bundled up the infant and set off on the trip down the hall. As she rushed out of the room, the father looked imploringly from her to the face of his son. Then he buried his head in his hands.

James Schaffer is one of those harried, shirt-sleeved baby doctors whose offices are always overrun with kids and who seem to pad around happily with a stethoscope permanently affixed to their necks. He studied the infant's upward slanting eyes, its flat nasal bridge, its small, rounded head, and its stubby fingers. There was little doubt that it had Down's syndrome.

Next, he, too, tried to pass a catheter down the baby's esophagus. Just as before, it would not go down. Schaffer was not surprised. Down's syndrome is frequently accompanied by other malformations. He ran his expert hands along the child's limp body, and soon he noticed something else amiss. There was a weak pulse in the child's leg, a symptom of a constricted main artery. Sure enough, when the chest X ray came back, it seemed to show that the heart was abnormally enlarged. This did not surprise him either. Cardiac defects occur in

40 to 60 percent of all Down's children, which is one reason why 20 to 40 percent of them die before the age of 10. While Schaffer was examining the infant, Mrs. Watters returned to the delivery room. She found Dr. Owens explaining to the baby's mother and father that their son appeared to have serious birth defects. Both parents were crying. The discussion lasted only a few moments before it was time to wheel the exhausted mother down the corridor to the postpartum recovery room. As is her custom when a child is born with defects, Mrs. Watters assigned herself to stay with the couple for the rest of the evening. She feels people should not be handed off to new nurses at such an emotionally delicate time.

Moments after the couple left the delivery room, Schaffer appeared and began to confer with Owens. Joining them was Wenzler, who had just arrived at the hospital. Their discussion was brief. The basic facts of the child's handicaps seemed clear enough. All that remained was to outline for the parents what the treatment options were.

The three doctors filed into the recovery area, where the mother lay in silence, the only patient occupying the four-bed room. Her husband was pacing the floor at the foot of her bed. As gently as possible, the physicians began to explain the prognosis for their newborn son.

Schaffer spoke first. In his opinion, the child needed an immediate transfer to James Whitcomb Riley Children's Hospital in Indianapolis. Riley was equipped to surgically repair the boy's esophagus and trachea; Bloomington Hospital was not. Without an operation, Schaffer explained, the child would die. Furthermore, Riley could give him the battery of sophisticated tests necessary to ascertain what other malformations he had.

Dr. Wenzler concurred. The child should make the 40-mile trip, and it should be undertaken as soon as possible. Without the operation, the boy would not be able to eat or drink. Anything he took by mouth would cause him to suffocate.

Then it was Owens's turn. The parents stared expectantly as he began to speak. "It was right at that moment," Schaffer later recalled, "that everything went to hell."

Owens could simply have joined Dr. Wenzler in seconding Schaffer's recommendation. Had he done so, a chapter in American moral politics might never have been written. But he chose not to. Owens is an earnest, direct man who, in the parlance of the baseball diamond, calls them exactly as he sees them. And that night, he saw things a different way. The operation, he told the parents, could indeed save the child's life. But there was more to consider. He explained that it was a rigorous procedure, generally accompanied by a significant amount of pain, and that it frequently required follow-up surgery over several years. Above all, he reminded them, it could do nothing about the Down's syndrome. The child would still be mentally retarded for the rest of his life.

"However," he informed the parents, "you do have an alternative."

What they could do, he explained, trying to choose his words carefully, was in effect do nothing: simply refuse consent for the surgery, in which case the baby would die of pneumonia in a few days as the digestive juices attacked his lungs.

Having said his piece, Owens fell silent.

In retrospect, some might consider his behavior paradoxical. Why would a doctor whose entire career had been devoted to bringing babies into the world now raise the option of letting one die? Owens later ascribed it to an experience he'd had years before, an event involving his own family. His nephew's wife had given birth to a malformed baby, among whose defects was one requiring major surgery. It was performed at once, at the pediatrician's recommendation. When numerous bouts of pneumonia subsequently afflicted the infant, the same pediatrician vigorously treated them.

"But the child has never been normal," Owens explained. "It learned to walk at the age of four, and it has never learned to talk. It is, at times, aggressive and destructive. My nephew and his wife are very strong people and have handled it. But they've had no more children. She has essentially devoted her whole life to caring for this retarded child.

"Obviously, this has colored my thinking on the survival of such children. I believe there are things that are worse than having a child die. And one of them is that it might live."

The pediatrician who had recommended surgery for Owens's grandniece, and who had treated her pneumonias so vigorously, was none other than Dr. James Schaffer.

It was 9:30 in the evening. In the hospital's special-care nursery, the child lay in an incubator, oblivious to the debate being waged over his fate. Down the corridor, huddling together in the recovery room, his parents seemed in danger of buckling under the weight of the choice they had to make. The doctors suggested they take some time to weigh their options. The emergency was not so critical that they had to decide on the spot. The couple nodded. Moments later, the husband walked to the visitors' lounge, where their best friends—his boss and his wife—had been waiting. He brought them back to the recovery room and the two couples remained closeted for more than 20 minutes, trying to sort things out.

In the interim the three doctors sat drinking coffee at the nurses' station. A chill had descended upon them since Owens had suggested nontreatment. They did not speak.

At almost the stroke of 10 P.M. the father appeared in the doorway. He looked drained but maintained his composure.

"We've reached a decision," he announced softly.

For a moment he seemed to have trouble with the words. But at last, with a glance at Owens, he said, "We have decided that we don't want the baby treated."

Schaffer looked shocked. Immediately, he began to remonstrate with the father. Didn't they understand that the baby would die without surgery and that with it, he would be all right? Yes, they did understand, the man said. But they were nevertheless withholding consent.

With his colleagues looking dumbfounded, Owens leaped up to congratulate the father. "You've made a wise and courageous choice," he told the man. "I didn't want to say this before, because I didn't want to influence you. But here's how I look at it. If you let the baby die, you're going to grieve a little while. But if you go ahead with this surgery, you're going to grieve for the rest of your lives."

Chagrined by the turn of events, Schaffer stalked out of the room. A few minutes later when Owens entered the special-care nursery to check on the baby, he found Schaffer speaking by telephone with the chief physician on duty at Riley Hospital's neonatal intensive-care unit. Schaffer's voice rose as he apprised the Indianapolis doctor of what was going on. Then he turned to Owens.

"I want you to talk to this man," he said, tersely.

Owens took the receiver. Right away, as Owens remembers it, the doctor on the phone became threatening. This was infanticide, the physician said heatedly, and there were laws against such a thing. "There's going to be a court order to take control of this child," he warned Owens. "You can be sure of it."

Owens recollects that Schaffer, too, became intimidating. "He kept threatening me and the parents with criminal action. He was convinced that surgery was the only way to go."

In reply, Schaffer denies that he ever got abusive. He says he maintained a professional demeanor at all times. "But," he admits, "I did tell Walter that he could get his ass in a sling."

The parents continued to cling to each other in the recovery room. The father had closed the curtains that ran on a track around his wife's bed. Having been forced to make this decision, they now had to contend with the negative reaction it elicited. Feeling a sudden need to explain themselves to someone, they turned to Mrs. Watters.

"The things they said satisfied me that they were kind people and not monsters," she recalls. "They told me they just didn't want their baby to suffer. At that point they were convinced they were doing the right thing. But a few minutes later, Dr. Schaffer returned to talk to them some more. When he left, I went in there again and found the mother crying and confused. Dr. Schaffer had continued trying to change their minds. He kept stressing they were making the wrong choice."

Through choking sobs, the woman told Mrs. Watters that she had her two other children to think about. And then she asked the nurse for her advice.

"I told her I had three kids and that if it were my third child, I'd have to look at all options, too, just like them. We continued talking until my shift was over, at 11:30. They kept asking how the baby was doing. Was its color better and so on. It wasn't self-centered at all. I felt they loved that baby."

Saturday, April 10, was the lull before the storm. Owens, in consultation with the parents, drew up the infant's treatment order. The order stipulated the following: (1) hospital personnel might feed the child orally if they wished but they should be advised that it was likely to result in aspiration and death; (2) intravenous feedings were positively forbidden; (3) the child should be kept as comfortable as possible and given sedation as needed.

The treatment order was taped to the side of the baby's Isolette. That accomplished, the couple had a second unhappy piece of business to attend to: talking to an attorney. There had been threats of legal action on the night of the birth, and now the hospital was acting strangely. An administrator had begged them to take the child home, and when they had refused, he had asked them to sign a release absolving the hospital of responsibility for the baby's death.

The father's boss suggested a lawyer named Andrew Mallor. A few phone calls were made, and Mallor agreed to take the case.

One can hardly blame the hospital for being nervous. A child with a treatable medical condition was being allowed to die in its special-care nursery. Aside from the many humanitarian questions involved, there was the issue of legal culpability. If the baby died on the hospital's grounds, while technically under its care, could the institution be held criminally liable?

After having discussed the problem with the hospital administration all day Saturday and into the evening, the hospital's attorney, Len Bunger, came up with what appeared to be the perfect solution—a judicial hearing. A judge could order the parents to send the child to Riley. And a judge could take custody of the day-old infant away from them if they refused. At the very least, Bunger reasoned, it would take the responsibility off the hospital's shoulders. Even if the judge approved the parents' choice—and how likely was that to happen?—there would then be legal sanction for the child's death.

Having buoyed hospital officials with these arguments, Bunger set about arranging a hearing. In a town as small as Bloomington, this is a rather simple affair. There are only four judges in the entire Monroe County court system. Bunger's first call was to Circuit Judge James Dixon, who would normally hear such cases, but Dixon was unavailable. The next name on the list was that of Judge John Baker, of the superior court.

Baker, 35, was at home coloring Easter eggs with his three young children when Bunger's phone call came. A tall, boyishly handsome individual, Baker had earned his law degree at Indiana University and had spent five years practicing real-estate law in his uncle's firm before being appointed a judge in 1975.

Bunger apologized for the late hour—nearly 10 P.M.—but stressed that it was a matter of extreme urgency. Baker listened as the attorney explained the details of the case. If the child was not operated on soon, Bunger said, he would suffer irreversible physical damage.

Baker agreed to call an immediate hearing. "But where do you want to have it?" he asked.

"How about right here?" Bunger suggested. "At the hospital."

Attorney Andrew Mallor was just walking in his front door when the telephone rang. He had spent the evening attending a ballet recital with his daughter. Picking up the receiver, he was surprised to hear the angry voice of the baby's father.

"We've just been informed," the father said, "that they're going to hold a hearing at the hospital in 10 minutes."

Mallor was nonplussed. Ten minutes was not enough time to prepare a case. And he was even more perplexed to find out that someone from the hospital had apparently told the father that the parents need not be present.

Mallor asked the man to meet him at the hospital as quickly as he could. Then he hurried out again into the calm spring night.

The site of the hearing was a storage room on the hospital's sixth floor. With the rest of the medical complex undergoing extensive remodeling, the room had been pressed into service for conferences. Ordinarily, the sixth floor is a utility area, which, on a late Saturday night, imbued it with an eerie quality. The elevator doesn't even go that high; one has to get off at five and walk up a flight of stairs.

Baker gaveled the hearing to order at 10:30 P.M. Actually, *gaveled* is the wrong word. Baker had no judicial accoutrements whatsoever—

neither gavel, robes, law books, nor legal briefs. As he began to consider whether the child lying four floors below should be allowed to live or die, his only tools were a note pad and an open mind.

The questions to be resolved were of a significance strangely out of proportion to the surroundings—the makeshift conference room with its ring of chairs. At issue was nothing less than whether parents ever have the right to refuse lifesaving treatment for their children and whether a life of handicap is so abysmal as to warrant its termination at birth.

Only rarely in American jurisprudence had such questions been raised. On the few occasions on which they had, the courts had almost invariably ruled against the parents and in favor of life. But in those instances the doctors had always been lined up *against* the parents.

In Bloomington, however, it was a different matter. There existed a strong—one might say vehement—difference of clinical opinion as to what the best course of treatment was. An experienced and much-esteemed physician, Dr. Walter Owens, was willing to go on record with the medical judgment that the child was better off dead.

Even so, nobody in the room seriously expected Baker to deviate from the usual legal finding that a handicapped child, like any other citizen of the United States, is protected by the Constitution's guarantees of life, liberty, and property and that no one—be it court, doctor, or parent—could abrogate those guarantees.

Gathered in the room was a diverse group of some of Bloomington's most prominent citizens. Owens was there, of course, along with Drs. William Anderson and Brandt Ludlow, his partners in an obstetrical clinic a block from the hospital. Also on hand were Drs. Wenzler and Schaffer and another Bloomington pediatrician, Dr. James Laughlin. Seated near them were Len Bunger and Andrew Mallor, the attorneys, and Gene Perry and Maggie Keller, administrative vice-presidents for the hospital. Finally, there was the father, looking grim and tired. He had come alone. His wife, he explained, was still too weak from childbirth.

Walter Owens was the first witness. He ran through the events of the night before and explained that when Schaffer and Wenzler had begun to propose all-out surgical intervention, it had set off something inside him. Believing it wrong to allow the parents just that one option, he had insisted on "giving the parents a choice." Owens then offered his professional opinion of the child's future. He said he felt certain the boy's level of mental retardation would be so severe that he would never enjoy even a "minimally adequate quality of life."

The testimony began to swing around the room. Starting with

Schaffer and then Wenzler and Laughlin, they all declared that the only "acceptable" course of medical treatment was to send the infant to Indianapolis, where, as one of them put it, he could receive a "full-court press."

Laughlin disagreed with Owens about the prognosis for a Down's syndrome victim. He said he had personal knowledge from his own practice of three Down's children who had a "reasonable" quality of life.

Judge Baker's pen made scribbling noises as he took notes on his legal pad. Then he called on the father.

John Doe, as the man was referred to in the court record, seemed in remarkable possession of himself for someone who, in the span of 30 hours, had gone from being a happy expectant father to being a defendant in an infanticide hearing. Speaking clearly and calmly, he tried to explain the couple's position. For seven years, he told Baker, he had been a public-school teacher. In that time, he'd had occasion to work closely with handicapped children, including children with Down's syndrome. These experiences had left him with the opinion that Down's children never lead very good lives, an opinion that his wife shared. Faced with a Down's child of their own, they had decided it would be wrong to subject him to a life of such an inferior kind. There were also their two other children to consider. A severely handicapped child would place a tremendous burden on the family as a whole. For all of these reasons, the father said, he and his wife had chosen to allow the baby to die.

It was almost 1 A.M. when the testimony finally ended. All eyes fell on the judge. Baker announced that he was going to leave the room for a while to consider his decision. Thinking back on it in a later interview, he said that he never had any doubts which way to rule. "The issue was pretty obvious," he recalled. "I knew what I was going to decide while it was still being argued. The problem was I just didn't know how to say it."

It was no more than 30 minutes before Baker reentered the sixth-floor conference room. The participants hurriedly took their seats, their drawn faces betraying the lateness of the hour and the unhappy business at hand. As he settled his long, youthful frame into the chair, Baker looked curiously vulnerable, sitting there within arm's reach, shorn of his judicial raiments.

Baker cleared his throat and began to read. Since there were two divergent medical opinions, he said, it was his conviction that the Does had every right to select one of the two. It was not for the court to decide which one they should choose. Whereupon he directed the

hospital to follow Dr. Owens's treatment plan; the child would be permitted to die.

Owens patted Mr. Doe on the shoulder. The father's face seemed
to melt with relief. Schaffer rose slowly from his chair. He was utterly
astonished.

Easter Sunday, April 11. The special-care nurses revolted, threatening to walk off the job if the baby wasn't removed from the nursery.
His presence among women whose every professional and human
instinct was to nurture him was like an open wound.

Linda McCabe, head nurse in the unit, vividly recalls coming to
work that weekend and seeing the child lying in its incubator with a
"Do not feed" order taped to the side. "I felt like they had a lot of gall
asking me to do that. I thought, 'Over my dead body.' "

Maudleine Starbuck, chief nurse of the obstetrical floor, found the
mother to be a caring person who was very concerned with how the
nurses felt about her and the decision she had made. "I told her we
were trying hard not to be judgmental, but we had to move the child
off the floor. It was very hard on my nurses. They felt they were
literally killing the baby."

To quell the uprising, the hospital hastily transferred the child to a
private room on the fourth floor. The Does found themselves forced
to hire private nurses from an outside nursing service, which created
yet another problem. The private nurses could watch the child around
the clock and comfort him. But they were not allowed, under hospital
rules, to give him drugs. Only the fourth-floor nurses could administer the morphine shots and phenobarbital prescribed to keep the baby
calm and pain-free as his life slipped away. One of them, Teleatha
McIntosh, says she found the task devastating emotionally. "Without
a doubt, it was the most inhumane thing I've ever been involved in,"
she recalls. "I had all this guilt, just standing by, giving him injections,
and doing nothing for him." But even nurses who raged at the parents for their decision had to admit they were attentive and loving to
their child, frequently visiting the bedside and cradling him in their
arms.

Early on Monday morning the Does, who are Catholic, had the child
baptized. The sacrament was performed by their regular parish priest,
who had indicated support for their decision. They named the child
Walter, after Dr. Walter Owens.

By this time, pressure on Judge Baker was beginning to build. Local
right-to-life organizers, who had heard of his decision through their

highly efficient grapevine, were bitterly assailing him, particularly for
his failure to appoint a guardian ad litem (a legal advocate who speaks
on behalf of a child or other incompetent) at Saturday night's hearing. To answer such criticism, the judge appointed the Monroe County
Department of Public Welfare guardian ad litem and asked its Child
Protection Committee to review his decision. The committee is a
standing entity charged with investigating child abuse. It included
among its six members a parole officer, a housewife, and the director
of the county welfare department.

The committee hearing was held on Monday night in the same hospital storage room. Just as before, the proceedings were held at 10:30
P.M. on very short notice. Owens, rousted from bed, had only 15 minutes to make it to the hospital.

The hearing was a replay of Saturday night's, with one exception.
Owens had, on the spur of the moment, invited the parents of a child
with Down's syndrome. In poignant detail they described the difficulties, both practical and emotional, that they had encountered in raising the youngster.

After 45 minutes of deliberating, the committee announced that it
found no reason to disagree with Judge Baker's ruling.

Walking wearily out of the building, the father turned to Mallor,
wanting to know whether the ordeal was finally over.

"Yeah, that's it," Mallor replied confidently. "I can't imagine anything more."

The next morning, however, in the aging courthouse in the center
of town, events were taking place that would prove him wrong. The
county's young, aggressive prosecutor, Barry Brown, and his deputy,
Lawrence Brodeur, were offended by the progress of the case. To
Brodeur, it seemed to create a frightening new precedent permitting
parents, if they didn't like their child, simply to end its life.

The two of them brooded over how they could best overturn Baker's judgment. They had already ruled out criminal action against
the Does. Everything the couple had done was with the court's approval,
and prosecuting them would serve no purpose in any event. But there
was another option. They could have the child declared neglected
under Indiana's Child in Need of Services (CHINS) statute. Joining
them in this petition was Philip Hill, a local attorney who had been
asked to enter the case by Dr. James Laughlin, his former college
roommate. Following the Child Protection Committee hearing, Hill
had requested that Baker appoint him guardian ad litem for the child.

Since Bloomington's regular juvenile hearing officer happened to
be Hill's wife, it was necessary for her to disqualify herself in favor of
a substitute, the local attorney C. Thomas Spencer, who agreed to act

as judge pro tempore. This is a frequent arrangement in Bloomington, where the courts are chronically shorthanded. Spencer had often
sat on the bench on a pro tem basis, receiving the standard $25 fee.
But these cases had involved lesser concerns, not matters of life and
death.

For the third time that week, a hearing was held on virtually a
moment's notice. This time, Owens literally had to leave one of his
patients undressed to make it to the courthouse on time.

Spencer was not faced with the broader questions that Baker had
been forced to address. His purview was the narrower issue of whether
the child was being neglected or abandoned. Whether it was because
he didn't want to overturn Judge Baker and the Child Protection
Committee or because, as he stated, the Does were following "a medically recommended course of treatment for their child," Spencer ruled
that there was no violation of the CHINS statute. "[T]he Court finds
that the State has failed to show that this child's physical or mental
condition is seriously impaired or seriously endangered as a result of
the inability, refusal, or neglect of his parents to supply the child with
necessary food and medical care."

Even as Spencer sat reading his decision at 8 P.M. on Tuesday night,
the infant lay in his incubator, dying. His body weight had dropped
from lack of nourishment. He was crying from hunger, and his lips
were parched from dehydration. His ribs were sticking out, the result
of respiratory strain caused by the tracheoesophageal fistula. That
afternoon, when the stomach acid started corroding his lungs, he had
begun to spit blood.

The nurses did what they could. They turned him over, gave him
back rubs, and put glycerin-soaked swabs into his mouth to ease the
dryness. They also diligently suctioned the blood from his throat.
Despite their best efforts, however, it was clear he had less than 48
hours to live.

Again the father asked Andrew Mallor whether Spencer's ruling
was the end. He and his wife were walking an emotional tightrope.

"Yes, that's finally it," said Mallor.

Instead, there began a series of frantic, last-ditch efforts by the
opposing side. At eleven o'clock that night Attorney Hill sought and
failed to get a temporary restraining order from Judge Baker authorizing intravenous feedings. The next day, a National Right-to-Life
Association lawyer from Terre Haute named James Bopp entered a
petition on behalf of Bobby and Shirley Wright, an Evansville couple
eager to adopt the child. Appearing in court for the parents, Mallor
angrily replied that the Does were withholding surgery from the child
not because they wished to be free of it but because they thought it

inhumane to make it go through life with Down's syndrome and other defects. To grant an adoption petition would be tantamount to saying they were abandoning the child. The petition was denied.

Brodeur and Hill, meanwhile, pursued the matter Wednesday in higher courts. First, they tried the Indiana Court of Appeals, which rejected their request for an immediate hearing. Then they carried their appeal to the Indiana Supreme Court, in the form of a petition for a writ of mandamus. Such a petition is an emergency maneuver that asks a high court to exercise its discretionary control over a lower court. In this case, the justices were being asked to force Baker to order medical treatment for the dying child. Without a word of explanation, the supreme court turned them down, voting three to one to do so.

But the action before the supreme court had one unintended consequence. For five full days, the media had been unaware of the drama unfolding at Bloomington Hospital. This press blackout inadvertently came to an end Wednesday afternoon. By coincidence, the Indianapolis district attorney had a case coming up before the supreme court that same afternoon. The pack of reporters that always tagged after him showed up early and decided to hang around the chamber until the case was called. In the meantime, Brodeur had begun to argue his case, which was listed in the docket as *In re: The Guardianship of Infant Doe* v. *John and Mary Doe, et al.*

The reporters stayed long enough to get an earful. Then they ran to call their city desks. In no time at all, the story was going out over the national wires.

That night the Does got very little sleep. The phone rang incessantly as newspapers and press associations clamored for comment. The parents resolutely refused to talk, a silence they have maintained until this very day.

Journalists covering the story were careful not to publish the parents' names. Nevertheless, the town being as small as it is, the Does' identity quickly got around. The result was a torrent of crank calls and threats. A neighbor had to sit on their porch all night with his dogs.

Thursday began as Lawrence Brodeur, at his own request, succeeded Philip Hill as guardian ad litem. He was about to play his final card. Accompanied by a constitutional expert from Indiana University, Brodeur booked a flight to Washington, D.C., where he planned to file an emergency appeal with the U.S. Supreme Court.

But time was running out for Baby Doe, as the press had christened him. He had begun to hemorrhage freely, the blood oozing from his nose and mouth. Three times Thursday afternoon and evening he had stopped breathing, only to fight his way back. His physical limpness had increased to the point where he had lost all muscle tone.

Nurse Bonnie Stuart, who was working the 3-to-11 shift that day, recalls seeing Mrs. Doe looking troubled. "I never saw the lady cry, but she looked like she hadn't slept much. She'd ask me if I thought it would be much longer, like she was hoping it would be over soon. Then she'd stare into space. I never replied. It was not a friendly conversation. I wish I'd never seen the woman."

Stuart says the mother left early in the shift, which particularly upsets her. "I feel the parents could have been there for the death," she says bitterly. "I'm angry at them for involving me and then backing out, making me take care of him."

As the hours continued to pass that evening, Dr. Schaffer came in a number of times to look at the infant. He would shake his head and walk out.

It was after dinner that Owens began receiving what he says were "peculiar" telephone calls from the hospital, asking him why he had ordered no food for the baby. Suspicious that he was somehow being "set up," he immediately drove to the hospital, where he posted himself next to the child's incubator.

Within a few minutes there occurred one of the most bizarre episodes in the history of American medicine, an episode that saw one doctor guard a dying baby from another doctor who was threatening to try and save its life.

According to Owens's version of events, while he was sitting next to the child, Schaffer walked in with Dr. Laughlin and announced, "We've come to take charge of the baby!" Schaffer then said he was going to take the child down to the special-care nursery and start feeding him intravenously. Owens asked him whether he had a court order. "I don't need it," Schaffer replied.

Owens grew menacing. "If you do anything to that child," he growled, "you're putting yourself at peril." Whereupon he dialed Andrew Mallor, who got into a heated exchange with Schaffer on the telephone.

At that point Schaffer left, Owens says, but came back a few minutes later with another pediatrician, Dr. Carol Touloukian. Touloukian examined Baby Doe and declared that the child had already deteriorated beyond the point of resuscitation. She persuaded Schaffer to leave with her.

Within a short time, however, Schaffer reappeared in the doorway with an IV bottle in his hands. Owens says there is no doubt in his mind that Schaffer intended to "kidnap" the child.

Schaffer's version differs very little, except that he says he never actually told Owens he was going to remove the baby from the room. Schaffer recalls, "I told Dr. Owens that we were going to start an IV, that the chief of staff of the hospital, Dr. Alan Somers, had asked me to. The hospital was paralyzed, you see. It didn't seem to be able to act. On the other hand, I could. But if I'd just barged in there they probably could have got me on a kidnapping charge."

In seeming contradiction, however, Schaffer admits he went so far as to place a telephone call to Riley Children's Hospital, asking whether they would send a helicopter for the baby if he resuscitated it with an IV.

Schaffer's ambiguity extends to whether he would have tried to overpower Dr. Owens to get at the child. First he says he doubts it. But then he adds passionately, "I probably would have started that IV, yessir. And I don't think it would have been advisable for anyone to try and stop me. I'd have gone past anyone who tried to interfere with my treatment of a critically ill baby." He knew that had he begun an IV, he might have been held in contempt of court. "I didn't care," he says, "because we have a judge in town who needs another job, and maybe when the next election comes, he'll get one. Why not subvert a judge's decisions? It depends [on] what's right and wrong."

Schaffer says he also had a "sadistic" reason for showing up, "to see Walt sweat a bit. I told him, 'Walt, what are you trying to prove by this?' He had been hovering over the baby for days like a mother bird, afraid somebody would come in and do something to it. That kind of behavior bothers me. I've hovered over a baby trying to save it. But why hover over it to make sure no one touches it?"

Whatever Schaffer's intentions may have been, while he was standing in the doorway with the intravenous bottle and tubing in his hand, the entire matter became academic.

At exactly 10:01 P.M., six days after his birth, Baby Doe died with the two doctors looking on. Cause of death: chemical pneumonia, due to the regurgitation of his own stomach acid.

An autopsy was conducted by John Pless, the Monroe County coroner. Dr. Pless discovered that there had been no enlarged heart; the X rays had been wrong. Nor could he find any direct evidence of brain damage caused by oxygen deprivation. But the child did indeed have a tracheoesophageal fistula. The coroner says he has no doubt the child was, in medical vernacular, "a bad baby."

Pless, a pleasant, meticulous man, maintains an office on the first floor of Bloomington Hospital. He sits behind an oversized desk, where a large gray microscope and a desktop computer are the primary tenants. Forensic books are stacked all over the office, and as he discussed the autopsy one recent afternoon, he idly played with a human clavicle. It belonged to a young man whom the coroner's office has been trying to identify ever since his body was found in a state forest in 1975. More of the man's bones— his ribs and a hipbone—occupied a cardboard box on the floor.

"The baby," Pless said, "received oxygen immediately after birth. It just didn't breathe very well. That's crucial in this case. It suggests it was not a good baby. It was blue for at least two minutes; then it was very limp even after it pinked up.

"It doesn't surprise me that I didn't see brain damage. It could have been there without my finding it. I suspect there may have been some. Many doctors will tell you they can resuscitate blue babies and there won't be residual brain damage. But they are talking about kids who are otherwise healthy, not Down's children with tracheoesophageal fistula. This baby just wasn't put together very well."

On the night of Baby Doe's death, Lawrence Brodeur was in the Atlanta airport, awaiting a connecting flight to Washington. He had to turn around and come home.

No single event in years had so galvanized American social reformers as the death of Baby Doe. There was immediate pressure on the conservative administration of President Ronald Reagan to do something.

Various organizations representing the disabled were especially up in arms. There seems to be an abiding fear among handicapped people that society will someday turn on them as having low social value, that at some point, perhaps when they are old, they will not be afforded medical care. Couldn't an attitude that condoned nontreatment of handicapped babies be easily expanded to include adults as well?

The disability-rights groups got on the phone to the White House, seeking some assurances. Paul Marchand, chief lobbyist for the Association of Retarded Citizens, called Michael Uhlmann and Stephen Galebach, two of Reagan's legal policy advisers. Well-connected board members of the association took their case even higher, right into the President's inner circle of James Baker and Edwin Meese III.

Meanwhile, Americans United for Life, the legal arm of the U.S. prolife movement, was conferring with U.S. Rep. Henry Hyde, the movement's chief spokesman in Congress. It was AUL's suggestion that perhaps Section 504 of the Rehabilitation Act of 1973, which prohibits recipients of federal funds from discriminating on the basis of handicap, might somehow be applied. Hyde agreed to get the message to the President.

Then, within days of the death of Baby Doe, another handicapped baby boy was reported to be languishing without lifesaving treatment in Robinson, Illinois. His birth defect was myelomeningocele, the most devastating form of spina bifida, in which the spinal cord fails to seal over with protective tissue during gestation and instead protrudes in a membranous sac through an opening in the lower back. Unless victims receive prompt surgery to enclose the cord, they face a high probability of early death from infection. Even with the operation, they are subject to severe handicaps, including paralysis, incontinence, and, in some cases, retardation.

Following an informant's tip that the parents had refused to authorize surgery in the Robinson case, an investigation was launched, and once again the nation's press splashed the affair all over its news pages. However, the investigation ground to a halt when arrangements were made for a Chicago pediatric neurosurgeon to treat the child. The infant was later given up for adoption.

By this time, the Reagan administration had acted to appease its right-to-life constituency. On April 30, a mere five days after the birth of the Illinois child, Reagan sent a memo to Richard Schweiker, then secretary of the Department of Health and Human Services (HHS). The memo directed him to notify all federally supported hospitals that they were in violation of federal law if they withheld from handicapped citizens, simply because they are handicapped, "any benefit or service that would ordinarily be provided to persons without handicaps." The law in question was Section 504 of the Rehabilitation Act of 1973, the statute suggested to Henry Hyde by Americans United for Life. The President continued "Our nation's commitment to equal protection of the law will have little meaning if we deny such protection to those who have not been blessed with the same physical or mental gifts we too often take for granted."

In response HHS subsequently sent a "Notice to Health Care Providers" to the 6,800 medical institutions in the United States that receive federal monies, warning them that they faced the loss of those funds if they denied treatment or nourishment to handicapped babies. Dated May 18, 1982, and signed by Betty Lou Dotson, director of the Office of Civil Rights, the directive read, in part, "[I]t is unlawful . . . to withhold from a handicapped infant nutritional sustenance or medical or surgical treatment required to correct a life-threatening condition if: (1) the withholding is based on the fact that the infant is handicapped; and (2) the handicap does not render the treatment or nutritional sustenance medically contraindicated."

The warning was instantly attacked from several quarters. The University of Wisconsin pediatrics professor Norman Fost interpreted it as requiring heroic treatment in every case except where the handicap itself ruled it out. But what if, he wrote, a child is born blind, deaf, and totally without mental function, and what if he also has no kidneys? Did the directive mean it was unlawful not to keep the child indefinitely alive with a kidney machine?

Chief Justice Richard Given, of the Indiana Supreme Court, who had voted only weeks before not to intervene to save Baby Doe, declared, "There's no need for any legislation. . . . We can't legislate miracles. We can't pass a law saying doctors have to save every child that's born." And Carlton King, the Robinson, Illinois, hospital administrator whose hospital had come under fire in the spina bifida case, was quoted as saying, "We take it for what it is—a non-binding opinion."

The White House, however, was by no means finished. The right-to-life movement and the disability groups continued to press Reagan to give the warning more teeth. Helping their cause was Dr. C. Everett Koop, the veteran pediatric surgeon whom Reagan had appointed surgeon general of the United States. Koop is a flamboyantly outspoken antiabortionist whose abhorrence of reproductive choice runs so deep that he has called amniocentesis, a procedure by which fetal disorders can be detected in the womb, "a search-and-destroy mission." He has on many occasions fulminated against the medical practice of letting severely malformed babies die. In fact, Koop once helped produce a movie entitled *Whatever Happened to the Human Race?* The film, which Koop wrote, narrated, and starred in, opens with a shot of a conveyor belt carrying baby dolls across the screen. When a doll without legs comes along, a large male arm appears and tosses it in the garbage. The film's narrator, meanwhile, inveighs against infanticide.

Under the approving eyes of Koop, HHS set out to enlarge upon Betty Lou Dotson's directive. The project was carried on in great secrecy all winter; then, on March 2, 1983, the agency unveiled what became known as the Baby Doe regulations.

The regulations were released in the form of an "interim final rule," which is bureaucratese for a regulation that goes into effect immediately. To the intense chagrin of physicians throughout the country, the rule required hospitals receiving federal funds to post "conspicuous" warning signs in delivery rooms, maternity wards, pediatric units, and nurseries. These warning signs were to read, "DISCRIMINATORY FAILURE TO FEED AND CARE FOR HANDICAPPED INFANTS IN THIS FACILITY IS PROHIBITED BY FEDERAL LAW."

The posters were also designed to urge anyone with knowledge of a handicapped infant being denied "food or customary medical care" to call a "Handicapped Infant Hotline," with the 24-hour toll-free number 800-368-1019. They said the identity of callers would be kept confidential.

No one in the administration made any bones about it. It was meant to be a "snitch" rule. Its target was the large number of nurses who Margaret Heckler, the incoming HHS secretary, insisted were out there, bursting to inform on infanticidal doctors but afraid of retribution.

Hospitals were given until March 22 to implement the regulations. That happened to be the day before a Jimmy Carter–appointed commission on ethics in medicine had scheduled the release of its report criticizing such doctrinaire approaches to handicapped newborns. Many people saw the Reagan administration's timing as an attempt to upstage the commission.

Opposition to the regulations was immediate and widespread. They were a monumental blunder, critics said, representing an unprecedented invasion by the state into medical decision making and family life, and rendering couples answerable to bureaucrats about their own flesh and blood. The implication seemed to be that doctors and parents are inherent child abusers and that Washington, not mother, knows best. There were other concerns as well. The regulations appeared to empower HHS to do very little other than to take hospitals' funding away, a retroactive punishment that would not compel treatment in an ongoing case. Hence, agency investigators would have no real role in the operating room other than as meddlesome bystanders. The toll-free phone line opened the floodgates to anyone, from a hospital janitor to an outright crackpot, to question medical judgment. Finally, the regulations seemed based on the philosophy of vitalism, which contends that all life should be preserved in all circumstances, regardless of its quality, hardship, or ability to sustain itself independently. Infants who were dying or in pain might thus have their suffering prolonged.

In reply the government said only that someone had to defend the rights of sick infants. And on March 22, as scheduled, the telephone bank in Washington opened shop. Callers heard a voice on the other end greet them with the words "Baby Doe hot line."

Over the course of the next three weeks, the hot line fielded 572 calls. Most were requests for information, wrong numbers, or crank calls. Only 16 involved actual complaints about infant care, and of these, only 7 were found worthy of investigation. None were deemed to have involved a violation. In other words, the hot line had uncovered not a single bona fide case of infant abuse despite the surgeon general's claim that infanticide was a practice much more widespread than commonly believed.

In the meantime, critics charged, the regulations were actually doing harm. One case that was investigated involved Siamese twins that were admitted to Strong Memorial Hospital in Rochester, New York. The call had come in on March 29 from an unidentified individual who had read about the twins in the newspaper and had apparently just assumed they were not receiving care.

On the basis of such a flimsy report, the full mechanism of the regulations was set in motion. Almost instantly, a "Baby Doe squad," as the agency called it, was dispatched to Strong Memorial. Two investigators came from New York and one from Washington, D.C. The first action taken by the investigators was to demand the twins' medical records. Immediately, according to affidavits, they began to quarrel over whether the New York or Washington office should be in charge of the records. Late that night they arranged for a neonatologist to fly in from Norfolk, Virginia, to examine the children. But the doctor left the following morning, after he learned that the team had neglected to get parental consent for the exam. As he was leaving, he expressed approval of the way the hospital was treating the children—they were receiving full intensive care, including mechanical respiration, antibiotics, and nutrition.

The parents, meanwhile, already reeling from the birth of grotesquely deformed infants (the children had two heads and one torso and could not be surgically separated), now had to cope with the trauma of being investigated. On top of this, press reports of the HHS probe caused other parents to begin doubting the quality of the hospital's care. Two days after the arrival of the Baby Doe squad, a family reportedly removed its critically ill child from the institution before treatment was completed, in the belief that the hospital intentionally hurt children.

An even more discouraging incident occurred at Vanderbilt University Hospital in Nashville, where, according to a caller's remarkable claim, 10 children were simultaneously not being fed or given adequate medical treatment. The Baby Doe squad arrived at 9:30 P.M., on March 22, along with a neonatologist from St. Louis. A meeting was instantly convened with the attending physicians for each of the 10 babies, the chief of pediatrics, the chief pediatric resident, and the associate nursing director. The meeting ran until midnight, after which the group made rounds to review each child's case. The investigators spent the next day examining medical records and interviewing nurses and other hospital personnel. At the end of this scrutiny, the neonatologist from St. Louis announced that the children were getting good medical care in every respect.

But the effect of the investigation on the hospital was completely disruptive, according to reports. The chief of pediatrics worked with the investigators for 8 hours, the chief resident for 10, and the associate nursing director for 18 hours—time that would have been better

spent caring for youngsters. The need to get charts back from the
Doe squad caused a delay in moving children to surgery. Lab reports
had to be reordered. Six nurses were unavailable for patient assignment because they were being interviewed. Afterward, the hospital
determined that the call to the hot line had come from a disgruntled
employee.

A Baby Doe squad also spent three days in Coos County, Oregon,
investigating whether a child born in Coquille Valley Hospital with a
hopeless congenital defect should receive intravenous feedings. The
child had an encephalocele, in which the brain bulges out of an opening at the base of the skull. The doctors and parents argued that the
defect was inoperable and terminal and that the baby girl, who had
no swallowing reflex and thus could not eat, should be allowed to die
naturally. Oregon Right-to-Life insisted that the child's life be perpet-
uated as long as possible with an IV. The furious parents had to stand
by helplessly as Right-to-Life, with the HHS investigators looking on,
took the matter to court. An early court injunction that mandated the
feedings was later rescinded, but the child died before the feedings
were withdrawn. She was 10 days old.

Hospitals and physicians throughout the nation breathed a collective sigh of relief when on April 14, 1983, U.S. District Court Judge
Gerhard Gesell struck down the Doe regulations. He acted on a legal
challenge brought jointly by the American Academy of Pediatrics, the
National Association of Children's Hospitals, and the Children's Hospital National Medical Center in Washington.

If there was any judge in the country who knew something about
the treatment of congenitally abnormal newborns it was Judge Gesell.
He is the son of the late children's specialist Arnold Gesell, of Yale, a
world-famous pioneer in the study of children with birth disorders.
The jurist had literally grown up with the problem.

Judge Gesell was not at all impressed with the need for the Baby
Doe regulations. He called them, by turns, "arbitrary and capricious"
and "hasty and ill-considered," and he threw them out on a technical-
ity, noting that HHS had not allowed affected parties enough time to
comment before they were implemented.

Not content merely to strike them down, he used the occasion to
try and drive a stake through their heart. He declared that HHS had
not addressed the issue of whether the termination of painful or
intrusive medical treatment might be appropriate "when an infant's
clear prognosis is death." And he said that the regulations had little
meaning beyond their "in terrorem effect"; in other words, they would
not produce more compassionate medical care but would instead

frighten doctors into treating every case as heroically as possible, without concern for the suffering generated by the treatment itself.

Deeply stung, the Reagan administration fought back. On June 27, 1983, it released revised regulations. Although not substantially different from the first version, the new ones stressed that they did not compel "impossible or futile acts or therapies" that would only prolong the dying process for a terminally ill child. What HHS was seeking to stop, explained Dr. Koop, was "starving a child to death. In anybody's law, that is homicide."

Dr. Koop also denied that the HHS investigators had caused chaos at hospitals, insisting they conducted themselves "in as gentle and kindly a manner as they could." He blamed the large number of wild-goose chases on callers phoning in "spurious reports" designed to "jam the system." When I asked him who might have been so mischievous, he said, "Spoilsport physicians trying to sabotage us."

The new regulations allowed 60 days for public comment. In those two months, 16,739 expressions of opinion flooded the HHS offices. Some 97 percent backed the administration.

Following that deluge, a mysterious silence descended on the agency. For many weeks there was no indication of when, if ever, the revised regulations would go into effect. Everyone in the medical community relaxed.

Then, as autumn began to deepen, a new tragedy captured the headlines. On October 11, 1983, a baby girl was born on Long Island, New York, with a combination of birth defects, any one of which would have been considered calamitous. These included a myelomeningocele of level L-3 to L-4, meaning that the spinal cord defect was situated between the third and fourth lumbar vertebrae; microcephaly, an abnormally small head; and congenital hydrocephalus, a condition in which cerebrospinal fluid builds up within the cranial vault, inflicting pressure on the brain. The higher on the patient's back that a myelomeningocele occurs, the greater the number of nerves leading to the lower body that are adversely affected. The Long Island child's lesion was high enough to indicate she would have substantial paralysis of the legs and would possess no control over her bladder and bowels. Her head circumference was only 31 centimeters, well below average. This measurement, which indicated that she had a serious shortage of brain mass, would have been even smaller had it not been for the fact that her skull was somewhat distended from hydrocephalus. Hydrocephalus is a frequent postnatal consequence of myelomeningocele, but when it is already in evidence at birth it is considered an ominous sign that brain damage has occurred. An ultrasound examination revealed that fluid had caused a "moderate" dilation of three of the four compartments of the child's brain. Together, the microcephaly and hydrocephalus made it extremely probable that she would suffer from severe mental retardation as she grew older.

In addition to these abnormalities, the child had a condition that prevented her from completely closing her eyes or from using her tongue properly to suck. Moreover, she had spasticity of the upper extremities, a thumb abnormality that indicated she would not have full use of her hand, and a prolapsed rectum.

Dr. Arjen Keuskamp, a pediatric neurosurgeon who examined the infant shortly after her birth at St. Charles Hospital in Port Jefferson, New York, recommended that she be transferred immediately to University Hospital in nearby Stony Brook. Surgeons there could repair her herniated spinal cord and implant a shunt in her brain to drain off the excess fluid. These corrective procedures promised to extend the girl's life span considerably, but they could do nothing to cure her anticipated paralysis and retardation. The child's parents, a 30-year-old building contractor and his 23-year-old wife, initially signed a consent form approving anesthesia for the corrective operations. But after consulting with more doctors, and with religious advisers, a social worker, and members of their family, they reversed themselves. They decided to forgo surgery. Instead, they authorized a "conservative" course of medical treatment, which consisted of feedings, antibiotics, and hygienic care of the baby's exposed spinal sac. The Stony Brook doctors supported the parents' wishes.

Not everyone on the hospital staff concurred, however. One of them spoke confidentially on the telephone to a Vermont right-to-life attorney named A. Lawrence Washburn, informing him that the child was being denied "life-preserving surgery." Washburn, 48, has for many years instigated lawsuits in various jurisdictions on behalf of fetuses and handicapped babies. He has a reputation for single-minded zealotry, even among his fellow prolife activists. When Washburn heard what was going on at Stony Brook, he was outraged. In spite of the fact that he had never seen the baby, talked to the doctors, or met the parents, he filed suit in the New York courts to compel the surgery.

"No matter what the child's condition is, she still has the same right to live that you and I have," Washburn explained in an interview. "The constitution is not self-enforcing. It takes someone to stand up for a helpless person; otherwise there would be violations all over the place."

On October 19 and 20 an evidentiary hearing was held in the Long Island courtroom of New York State Supreme Court Justice Melvyn Tanenbaum. The interests of Baby Jane Doe, as the child was referred to in the petition, were represented by a court-appointed guardian ad litem, the local attorney William Weber.

Controversy centered on the issue of the infant's prognosis. If she was operated upon, what were her prospects of survival and what kind of life would she lead? Dr. George Newman, one of the child's neurologists, testified that without surgery, she had virtually no chance of living more than 2 years. With surgery, her life span might exceed 20 years, he said, but her existence would be a grim one. "It would likely consist," he said, "of lying in bed, being fed probably by bottle, possibly by nasogastric tube. . . ." Newman predicted that the child would suffer from epileptic seizures, beginning at the age of three months. Moreover, due to her incontinence, she would have a constant and intractable bladder infection, which several times a year would travel to her kidneys, producing fever. Eventually, the condition would develop into chronic renal failure, which was apt to lead to death. The child would also be subject to painful bedsores on her legs, lower back, and elbows, Newman said, and he speculated that her prolapsed rectum—a condition in which part of the rectal mucosa protrudes from the body—would become dehydrated and cause her additional pain.

The neurologist testified that Baby Jane would enjoy few, if any, positive experiences to offset this physical discomfort. "On the basis of the combinations of the malformations that are present in this child, she is not likely to ever achieve any meaningful interaction with her environment, nor ever to achieve any inter-personal relationships, the very qualities that we consider human. . . ."

Q.—"In your professional opinion, could this child experience joy?"

A.—"No."

Q.—"Sadness?"

A.—"No."

Q.—"Any other such emotion?"

A.—"No."

Q.—"Reaction to heat?"

A.—"Yes, I believe she would respond to heat, fever, cold."

Q.—"Reaction to painful stimuli?"

A.—"Yes."

Q.—"What other cognitive skills might this child be able to develop, in your professional opinion?"

A.—"It's unlikely that she is going to develop any cognitive skills."

In light of this prognosis, Newman said, Baby Jane's parents had decided that it would be "unkind" to allow their daughter to undergo surgery. He reaffirmed his conviction that "all of [the parents'] behavior has been totally and completely out of concern for the child."

Testifying next was Dr. Albert Butler, chief of neurology at University Hospital. Butler concurred in Newman's assessment that the child would be "severely retarded," with or without the surgery, but he took a less dismal view of her future.

"[I] think we have to reasonably expect," he said, "that this child might be able to sit up, look around, be aware of parents or good friends, be somewhat apathetic as far as the face is concerned. . . . [F]or want of better words, we say a lack of personality. . . ."

Weber, the guardian, tried to establish that the child's head measurement of 31 centimeters was within the normal range (in fact, only 3 in 1,000 full-term girl babies have heads that small) and that there was no proof that she had any brain damage. Butler resisted, explaining that microcephaly is a reliable indicator that parts of the brain have not formed correctly.

Q.—"Would it be a fair statement to say that at this very moment we really don't know the full extent, if any, of brain damage?"

A.—"Precisely, no."

Q.—"That the microcephalitic condition in and of itself does not necessarily mean brain damage, is that correct?"

A.—"The association of microcephaly with brain malfunction is so high that one could say with a reasonable degree of medical certainty that because microcephaly is there, brain malfunction is there. . ."

Butler was asked whether he believed the decision by the parents not to have the surgical repair was a medically reasonable and acceptable one.

"Yes, sir, it is," he replied.

The father then briefly took the stand. In order to protect the shreds of his privacy, he was obliged to testify behind a screen, as if he were a Mafia informant. In a hesitant voice, he told the hearing that he and his wife, who were referred to in court only as Dan and Linda A., had been married for less than a year, and that this was their first child.

Q.—"Did you make a decision on the 11th as to whether or not the surgical procedure that was being outlined to you would be done?"

A.—"Yes, I did."

Q.—"Was that decision to have the surgery at that time?"

A.—"We could not give our consent to perform such surgery at that time."

Q.—"Could you tell this Court . . . what faith are you?"

A.—"I'm a Roman Catholic."

Q.—"And your wife?"

A.—"The same."

Q.—"Did you talk to any of the sisters, Catholic sisters at the hospital about your decision?"

A.—"Yes, yes, I did. . . . [W]e had a sister come visit us basically every day since our admittance into the hospital, and the sister gave me a lot of strength, and she also was pretty supportive of the decision that I had made."

Q.—"In reaching that decision, could you tell me if you took [into account] what the effect of that decision would be on your baby daughter?"

A.—"Absolutely."

No one in the courtroom pressed the father for an explanation of *why* the couple had chosen to withhold surgery. It was a curious omission, but it seemed to reflect a reluctance to cause the man further discomfort. He was excused without cross-examination.

In his closing statement, the parents' attorney, Paul Gianelli, said that his clients had reached their conclusion "after soul-searching, after thoughtful inquiry, and after getting the best medical advice available to them." He used the occasion to lash out at Washburn for bringing the lawsuit. "I find it ludicrous that Mr. Washburn . . . would have the right to ask this Court to interfere in this most painful personal decision that a human being could ever be asked to make. He comes into the Court and asks the Court to act, and then he leaves, and my clients will have to live with his actions for the rest of their lives."

Weber was remarkably succinct, saying only, "Judge, if you're going to make a mistake in this case, make it on the side of preserving the life; that's all I ask."

After a night of deliberation, Tanenbaum delivered his ruling. He decreed that the child must undergo surgery. While expressing sympathy for the parents, who "have obviously suffered a profound disappointment," he said, "It is clear to me . . . that the infant is in imminent danger, and that the infant has an independent right to survive; that right must be protected by the state. . . ."

Gianelli immediately appealed. Late that night Justice Lawrence Bracken, of the appellate division of state supreme court, stayed Tanenbaum's order pending a hearing by a three-judge appellate panel. The panel heard the matter the next day, October 21, and promptly reversed the decision of the lower court, finding that "concerned and loving parents have made an informed, intelligent, and reasonable determination based upon and supported by responsible medical authority."

The court continued, "The record confirms that the failure to perform the surgery will not place the infant in imminent danger of death, although surgery might significantly reduce the risk of infection. On the other hand, successful results could also be achieved with antibiotic therapy. Further, while the mortality rate is higher where conservative medical treatment is used, in this particular case the surgical procedures also involved a risk of depriving the infant of what little function remains in her legs, and would also result in recurring urinary tract and possibly kidney infections, skin infections, and edemas of the limbs."

As in the case of Bloomington's Baby Doe, a medical strategy that essentially involved not treating the child was being elevated, in court, to the status of a treatment plan. "Conservative" treatment, impressive though the phrase might sound, was in actuality a euphemism for a course of action likely to result in death. Unlike Bloomington's Baby Doe, however, this child was being fed. Moreover, she was receiving antibiotics to counteract a meningitis infection. To this extent, steps were being taken that could enable her to survive; but even this threatened to have an undesirable consequence, as the Washburn faction repeatedly pointed out. Without a shunt procedure to relieve the progressively worsening hydrocephalus, Baby Jane might survive with even less intellectual function than she would have had if she had been operated upon immediately.

Seven days later, October 28, the state's highest court, the New York Court of Appeals, upheld the appellate court's decision, but on different grounds. It found that, because the petitioner, Washburn, had no relationship to the family and because he had not followed the established procedure of contacting the state child welfare agency, which has primary responsibility for initiating child-neglect proceedings, there was "no precedent or authority" for the lawsuit.

"There are overtones to the proceeding which we find distressing," the court of appeals said. "Confronted with the anguish of the birth of a child with severe physical disorders, these parents . . . have been subjected in the last two weeks to litigation through all three levels of our State's court system. We find no justification for . . . these proceedings."

During the hearing, several justices exhibited strong displeasure at Washburn's role. One of them asked whether third parties should be allowed to intrude on private matters like "a medical vigilante squad," and another asked, "How come a perfect stranger can interfere in the family decisions in a tragic situation such as this?" In their ruling, the justices irately denounced the "offensive" activities of outsiders, contending that to permit someone like Washburn to exercise control over Baby Jane "would be to recognize the right of any person to institute judicial proceedings which would catapult him into the very heart of a family circle, there to challenge the most private and most precious responsibility vested in the parents for the care and nurture of their children."

Out of court, Washburn declared he had the right to step in on behalf of the infant. "It's like the good Samaritan," he said. "Maybe I'm trying to redeem lawyers by stopping by the wayside."

While the case was climbing up the legal ladder, the Reagan administration was becoming involved. Goaded by complaints from the American Life Lobby, a prolife organization, the civil rights division of HHS petitioned University Hospital to make available for inspection all of Baby Jane's medical records. The purpose was to run a sort of paraffin test on the institution to determine whether it was discriminating against the child because she was handicapped, presumably a violation of Section 504. The hospital, which is operated by the State University of New York at Stony Brook, refused to honor the federal agency's repeated requests, and on November 2 the U.S. Justice Department sued in federal district court to obtain the records.

From the Justice Department's point of view, it was an almost ideal case to test the principles behind the Baby Doe regulations. Here was a child being denied surgery that could clearly prolong her life. That her life would be miserable, at best, was immaterial. What mattered was that surgical procedures normally performed on myelomeningocele victims were apparently being denied to Baby Jane Doe solely because she was destined to be retarded. The timing of the case suited the federal authorities as well. A favorable court finding would give great momentum to a reissuance of the regulations. Furthermore, the case was being heard in New York, which afforded a chance to make an end run around Gesell, whose jurisdiction was in Washington.

To some, however, it seemed a mismatch. The immense power of the federal government was being used to bully one lonely couple, already engulfed in personal sorrow.

"For someone to walk in and invite the rest of the country into our house is a terrible intrusion into our lives," Dan A. told an interviewer in the couple's ranch home in Smithtown, a community on the north shore of Long Island. The A.'s had added two rooms to the home in anticipation of their daughter's birth.

The parents tried haltingly to explain why they had decided against surgery. "We were told she would have no control over her bladder or rectal functions," the father said. "And we were also told that she probably had brain malfunction . . . that the part of the brain that controls much of our awareness was either missing or not entirely formed."

"We are not talking about a spina bifida child," Linda A. added, "one who could perhaps walk someday with braces. They are showing these kids on television when they discuss our case. She will be an epileptic. Her condition for future life is to be bedridden, and she would not have use of her hands.

"We also know that as she grew older, she would always be an infant. She would never know love. And while she might feel sorrow and joy, her overall condition would be pain."

The conservative *Wall Street Journal* was furious at this invasion of family privacy by the state; it called the government "Big Brother Doe." The *New York Times* fumed that it wasn't the severely retarded little girl the government cared about; it was "the *idea* of her."

Indeed, Dr. Koop declared on national television, "We're not just fighting for this baby. We're fighting for the principle of this country that every life is individually and uniquely sacred."

On November 17, U.S. District Court Judge Leonard D. Wexler, sitting in Uniondale, Long Island, handed down his judgment with respect to the government's suit. Wexler dismissed the contention of the parents and hospital that Baby Jane's records were protected by the right to privacy and by the rules of physician-patient confidentiality. Nonetheless, he denied the government access to the medical records. He held that the hospital had not violated the antidiscrimination clauses of Section 504, because it stood ready to perform the surgery if the parents gave consent. Nor were the parents at fault, Wexler said. "The papers submitted to the court demonstrate conclusively that the decision of the parents to refuse consent to the surgical procedure was a reasonable one based on due consideration of the medical options available and on a genuine concern for the best interests of the child."

The Justice Department had taken a calculated gamble and lost. However, the government reasoned, if it was in for a dime, it might as well be in for a dollar. An appeal was filed with the U.S. Court of Appeals for the Second Circuit.

In early December the Washburn faction appealed the state appellate court ruling to the U.S. Supreme Court. The high court tersely refused to hear the case.

On February 23, 1984, the U.S. Court of Appeals handed down its verdict, affirming Wexler's judgment by a two-to-one vote. The line of reasoning that the court employed was devastating to the Reagan administration's position, for it declared that Section 504 was intended to assure the disabled equality in such areas as housing and employment and not to compel medical treatment of handicapped newborns. "Our review of the legislative history has shown that Congress never contemplated that Section 504 of the Rehabilitation Act would apply to treatment decisions involving defective newborn infants when the statute was enacted in 1973, when it was amended in 1974, or at any subsequent time." The court said that until Congress rewrites the statute, "it would be an unwarranted exercise of judicial power to approve the type of investigation that has precipitated this lawsuit."

Not only did the ruling deny the government access to Baby Jane Doe's medical records; it also dealt an apparent deathblow to the revised Baby Doe regulations, which had at last been issued on January 12, 1984. These new regulations, written personally by Dr. Koop, took a more lenient approach than did their earlier incarnations. Most notably, they bowed to a recommendation that HHS encourage, but not require, hospitals to set up infant care review committees, or so-called "ethics" committees, "to assist the health care provider in the development of standards, policies, and procedures for providing treatment to handicapped infants and in making decisions concerning medically beneficial treatment in specific cases." These committees, once in place, would apparently obviate the need for so many on-site investigations by Baby Doe squads and would put medical decision making back in the hands of the hospitals. Yet watered down as the new regulations were, the appellate court judgment seemed to doom them.

The government responded by asking the U.S. Court of Appeals to reconsider the ruling *en banc,* that is, it sought to have all the justices in the circuit vote on the question. In late May the court rejected the request. Just a few days later, on May 24, U.S. District Judge Charles L. Brieant, of Manhattan, announced that the revised Baby Doe regulations were "invalid, unlawful, and must be set aside," declaring that he was "controlled" by the U.S. Court of Appeals decision. Brieant acted in a lawsuit filed by the American Medical Association and several other medical societies challenging the legality of the regulations. In reaction, the government indicated that it might take the issue as high as the U.S. Supreme Court.

Notably absent from the AMA's lawsuit was the American Academy of Pediatrics, which a year earlier had initiated court action against the first round of Doe regulations, causing Judge Gesell to strike them down. Preferring negotiations to further litigation, the academy had signed a compromise agreement with prolife and disability rights forces in November 1983; it stated that decisions regarding treatment should be based solely on medical criteria and not on the child's intellectual or physical potential. But the agreement broke down in April 1984 when a set of guidelines drafted by the academy was rejected by the cosignatories of the compromise as placing too much emphasis on "quality-of-life" considerations. The sticking point was that the guidelines, which called for 10-member hospital ethics committees to review all cases in which parents and doctors proposed to forgo life support for an infant, failed to envision putting a "special advocate" for the infant on such committees, and that the guidelines did not seem to encourage decisions in favor of treatment. Expressing surprise at the collapse of the agreement, Dr. M. Harry Jennison, the academy's executive director, said, "There will be an ample number of people on the ethics committees who serve that function of being an advocate of the child. A separate ombudsman really is not necessary."

Meanwhile, two efforts were pursued in Congress to make it a statutory requirement that disabled newborns receive all necessary medical treatment. In the House of Representatives, a bill was passed in February 1983 that would withhold federal grants for the prevention of child abuse from states that do not establish procedures guaranteeing the medical rights of handicapped children. The vote was 396 to 4. A similar, but more explicit, bill was hammered out in the Senate in June by a remarkably diverse group of lawmakers who included Sen. Alan Cranston, a liberal Democrat of California, and Sen. Jeremiah Denton, a conservative Republican of Alabama. The bill redefined child abuse to include "the withholding of medically indicated treatment from disabled infants with life-threatening conditions," and it obligated hospitals to provide such treatment or face action by state child protective services. The state agencies were to create a network of designated individuals at each hospital to act as watchdogs. These representatives would report suspected cases of nontreatment, enabling the state to institute legal proceedings on behalf of the child. The bill did, however, contain a number of loopholes. For example, it said there would be no obligation to make heroic efforts to save a baby's life if the child were "chronically and irreversibly comatose"; if such efforts would merely "prolong dying, not be effective in ameliorating or correcting all of the infant's life-threatening conditions, or otherwise be futile in terms of the survival of the infant"; or if, by being futile, "the treatment itself under such circumstances would be inhumane." With its strong bipartisan support and the unwillingness of members to vote against purported "child abuse" in an election year, the bill passed the Senate by a vote of 89 to 0 on July 27, 1984. House and Senate conferees later met to iron out differences in the two bills, and the finished measure was signed by President Reagan on October 9, 1984. It was expected that the American Medical Association would in due course initiate a constitutional challenge on the grounds that the government was again interfering in private therapeutic matters.

At the time of this writing, with so many things happening on so many fronts, the ultimate outcome seemed very unclear. But it appeared quite possible that the issue would, in one way or another, find its way to the U.S. Supreme Court sometime in 1985 or 1986.

Ironically, the Baby Jane Doe case itself became moot in early April 1984. Dan and Linda A. announced that they had allowed doctors to perform a shunt operation on their daughter to relieve her hydrocephalus. The child, whom they said they had named Keri-Lynn, had been experiencing increasing discomfort in weeks prior to surgery as the fluid accumulated within her brain. Her myelomeningocele, meanwhile, had healed over with tough, leathery skin, making future infection improbable. The child was considered healthy enough to go home from University Hospital.

Both parents seemed to have come to terms with their situation. "I feel like a daddy now," the father was quoted as saying.

However, Dr. George Newman, the infant's neurologist, said he saw no reason to revise his earlier prognosis. "Her head measurement by any usual standard indicates rather severe microcephaly," he said. "She will still be severely retarded and, I still think, bedridden all the days of her life."

All of this came about because one small town doctor on a Good Friday evening decided to give two grieving parents a choice. It is likely to be years before the issues that were raised that night in Bloomington, Indiana, are settled to society's satisfaction. What do those who lived with the Bloomington case for six terrible days have to say about it in retrospect?

Lawrence Brodeur, the assistant prosecutor, continues to bristle over Judge Baker's use of quality-of-life criteria as justification for not treating the Doe child. "Who," asks Brodeur, "can make a decision as to what is minimal quality of life? Very simply, no one can. Nobody is qualified to do that. Maybe the child will be happy. Maybe it won't. How can you know? So you have to go back to your basic tenets of law."

Dr. James Schaffer says he still cannot believe it happened. "It was like a comedy of errors," he says, "one step after another. A judge decides that a family has the right not to have its baby treated. The child protection agency backs him up. But when a child comes in with a bump on the head the whole welfare department gets up in arms. This is an organization designed to protect children in the community from certain things. It seems to me dying is one of those things.

"The quality of life for a Down's child doesn't have to be bad. I have a dozen kids in my practice with Down's, and some of them are pretty damn bright. There was no way to look at Baby Doe and know how he would turn out. The point is, there may very well have been more wrong [with the baby] than Down's. But they didn't allow it to be sent to Riley for more tests to find out. Was it so important for the baby to die to prove a point?"

Dr. Walter Owens says he has never doubted the wisdom of the parents' choice. The reason he advised them not to send the child to Indianapolis for more tests was that he felt they would "lose control" of the situation outside of their home community. "Their feelings would have been overridden. They would have had no say, and if they demurred at all over the course of treatment, a sympathetic judge would have been found to take the child away from them."

Owens says the parents are now doing "wonderfully well, considering. They are the salt of the earth. If you were killed in an auto accident, they are the kind of parents you would want to raise your kids. They are people with strong values. Decent, very ethical people, who love their other children very much and had enough love for this child that they didn't want to see bad things happen to it—repeated major surgeries with a doubtful outcome, and not much chance of a good life even if they were successful."

Judge John Baker also says he has not changed his mind. "I've never had second thoughts," he says. "I've thought about it from every angle, but I've never come to another conclusion."

Baker explains, "I think Indiana law is clear. When there are two medical opinions, each in conflict, which to choose is up to the parents. There were two sides here. One side said, Let's do a full-court press, let's do everything medically possible. The other side said the child's opportunity to bring joy and be healthy was very limited and that once they opened the baby up, there was no pulling back. They'd have to correct all the abnormalities, and in so doing they might cause the child to be strapped to the bed forever. I couldn't subject the child to this."

The judge says he's received a huge volume of mail. "Some say they wish they'd been allowed the same alternative with their children. Others say they wish I'd been hanged with the rest of Hitler's exterminators."

As for the Does, Judge Baker says, "They've resented comments about their moral character. They had a tragedy on their hands. It was their baby son who died, after all."

Teleatha McIntosh, one of the nurses who watched the Doe child die, found the whole affair extremely traumatic. "I feel that a terrible injustice was done," she says. "I couldn't sleep for a long time afterwards. Every time I closed my eyes, I'd see that baby lying there bleeding, and fighting for breath. It was hard to get it out of my mind."

Bonnie Stuart, who also worked the fourth floor that week, says she, too, had insomnia. "It still seems like a nightmare to me. I still can't believe it happened in today's society. I said 'This is wrong,' 50 times a night as I was taking care of him. He wasn't limp like they said. When I'd give him a shot of Demerol, he'd flinch. He'd open his eyes when I stroked his head. He looked like a perfectly normal little boy. Yes, he did have the eyes of a Down's child, but other than that he looked normal."

Dr. John Pless, the county coroner, says he personally feels the Does had a right to make the decision they did. "It took me a long time," he says, "to develop ideas of what I'd do if it was my child. I'd find it difficult to do what those parents did. But I feel they had the right to do it, and it's wrong for third parties to come in and say they made a bad decision afterwards."

The parents' attorney, Andrew Mallor, says the Does have never once regretted their action. "People get the image of a healthy baby lying in a crib starving and evil parents trying to do it harm. They don't understand this was a very, very ill baby, and in such cases it might be better to let nature take its course. They are as good a couple as you'll ever meet and the question of what it was like to be confronted by this horror in what was to be a joyful moment has never been considered properly."

Nurse Dana Watters wrote a letter to Mrs. Doe after the episode. "I told her how badly I felt for them. She wrote back to say how much they appreciated my concern and to tell me how much it hurt to wake up in the middle of the night expecting a baby to cry and then to find no baby there."

In the more than two years that have passed since the Doe child died, a number of things have happened to the people who fought over his fate.

Lawrence Brodeur took the case to the U.S. Supreme Court, arguing that although the child was dead, the issue of whether his life should have been ended needs to be resolved because it will come up again and again. In the autumn of 1983 the Supreme Court declared it a moot case and refused to hear it. Barry Brown, the Monroe County prosecutor who tried so vigorously to have Judge Baker's ruling overturned, was subsequently defeated in his race for the state legislature. He and Brodeur now share a private practice.

The nurses McIntosh and Stuart required several months of psychological counseling following the episode. The hospital provided it free of charge.

Judge Baker has a reelection campaign coming up in 1986. He believes his decision in the Doe case may harm him at the polls. He and Dr. Owens have become very good friends, to the extent that he recently brought his children over to Owen's house for a hayride. Dr. Owens has also become quite close to the Does. When his own son died tragically many months ago, they were the first people to come by to console him.

The Does have continued to remain very private people. Thus far they have not publicly revealed their feelings about what they went through to anyone. In April 1984 Mrs. Doe gave birth to another child. It was a healthy baby girl.

2

Infanticide
An Overview

The Does' decision to let their baby die contained nothing especially novel. Parents, good ones and bad, have been consigning their offspring to death for thousands of years.

The new idea was the Reagan administration's—that virtually all babies, however grievous their handicaps, must be kept alive at any cost.

Until a few years ago, nobody would have seriously advanced that argument; it would have seemed quixotic in the extreme. Even though theologians had long upheld the principle that human life is sacred, in regard to severely impaired infants it was an academic point; the vast majority were doomed to early deaths because doctors quite simply lacked the power to heal their afflictions. No litany of pious pronouncements could alter the fact that nature, not medicine, was in the driver's seat. Even the administration's most avid proponent of rescuing handicapped babies, Surgeon General C. Everett Koop, admitted in a 1974 issue of the journal *Pediatrics* that only 50 percent of infants with Baby Doe's defects survived surgery.

Tremendous strides had been made in virtually every other field of science and technology before medicine made any substantial breakthroughs in saving the lives of imperiled newborns. One can almost date the watershed at 1960. By the time we had made any headway against myelomeningocele, the first nuclear submarine had already been at sea for several years. We were literally streaking through space before we figured out why a premature baby couldn't breathe. In short, there was no hue and cry over denying infants medical treatment in those days because there was precious little treatment to deny them.

Even now, with all our newfound know-how, we can do very little to actually prevent birth defects. In the United States alone an estimated 260,000 children were born with a physical or mental abnormality in 1982. That amounted to 7 percent of the 3.7 million registered live births. In the United Kingdom a 1972 study reported that 8 percent of all British youngsters had mental or physical disabilities, and the figure would have been far higher, the researchers said, if learning and psychiatric difficulties had been included.

When discussing birth defects, one is really speaking of a large and diverse group of conditions that have been lumped together for convenience. They are sometimes called congenital anomalies, *congenital* meaning "present at birth," and *anomaly* meaning "abnormality." There exist several thousand different physical malformations and genetic disorders, such as those of the two Doe children. Other examples include clubfoot, faulty heart valve, cystic fibrosis, and Tay-Sachs disease, and even such ailments of later life as Huntington's chorea. Also in this category are various forms of mental retardation and seizure states. In addition there is a group of defects resulting from the ravages of low birthweight and extreme prematurity. Finally, there are the crippling birth injuries, such as those due to asphyxia or head trauma. But while these misfortunes are widely dissimilar in cause, they are very much alike in their detrimental, sometimes devastating effect on the victim.

In a sense, birth defects are a great leveler. They refuse to play favorites, striking across every ethnic and geographic line. Anencephaly, for instance, a malformation in which the newborn lacks all or most of a brain, occurs approximately once in every 1,600 births in countries as disparate as Israel, Hungary, and New Zealand. Britain, meanwhile, has the same rate of esophageal atresia as Norway and Spain. Some countries fare well in regard to one defect, only to be besieged by another. Finland's rate of anencephaly is low, just one occurrence in every 4,500 births. But it has by far the highest known rate in the world for cleft palate, one case in every 885 births. In 1980 Japan recorded the world's lowest rate of hydrocephaly, or enlargement of the head due to excess cerebrospinal fluid; yet its rate of reduction deformity, an absence or underdevelopment of the limbs, was 20 percent higher than any other country's.

Similarly, no race or economic class is immune. A study by the University of California at Berkeley recently found that black and white infants one year of age had an identical rate of severe birth defects. And a federal study showed only a small difference in the anomaly rates among mothers with and without a college education, the usual measure of socioeconomic status.

Clearly, the problem of birth defects is not an isolated one. On the contrary, it is of great international magnitude, affecting millions of families per year. Yet it is a problem largely excluded from public dialogue, primarily for reasons of faintheartedness. People tend to block out the thought of damaged babies, and of the handicapped in general.

The enduring silence on the subject during the era of medical helplessness obscured the fact that medicine had developed its own system for dealing with the most severely deformed infants. Not all of them died on their own. Sometimes it was with a little gratuitous help from the obstetrician who, in order to minimize suffering for the child and its parents, would place a blanket over the tiny form. More often, the parents would be quietly consulted, and a joint decision would be reached to "let" the baby die by providing it minimal care, and in some cases no care at all.

Such benign neglect may sound cruel, but it pales before the wholesale slaughter of children, both healthy and otherwise, that fills the historical record. Many different cultures and peoples have condoned infanticide for every reason from family planning and religious ritual to improvement of the breeding stock.

The apple doesn't fall very far from the evolutionary tree. Scientists are amassing chilling evidence that animals in the wild frequently employ infanticide. Among gorillas, an invading male will kill the helpless young of a defeated rival, hoping thereby to force the widowed females to mate with him. Wild stallions do a similar thing. The Harvard anthropologist Sarah Blaffer Hrdy has hypothesized that animal infanticide fulfills a variety of complex societal functions.

The practice may be in our nature, too. Excavations of human burial sites from the Pleistocene age suggest that anywhere from 15 to 20 percent of all live births ended in infanticide. It is thought the motivation was the spacing of children and a need to balance the allocation of scarce resources.

The ancients seem to have killed their young with gusto. Carthaginian necropolises yield the tiny graves of thousands of youngsters sacrificed to the gods. And the Bible makes mention of those "that slay the children in the valleys, under the cleft of the rocks." Among the Greeks it was common to do away with unwanted newborns by leaving them outside to die, a practice known as exposure. This custom was so widespread among the Romans that they made it part of their founding myth: Who were Romulus and Remus but exposed infants saved by a hospitable wolf?

While any child could theoretically be disposed of at the discretion
of the father, whose authority in that era was law, the two most prominent categories of victims were always females and the malformed.
That birth defects were as prevalent in early times as they are today
is confirmed by clay tablets found in the royal library of the Assyrian
king Ashurbanipal, who reigned in the seventh century B.C. The tablets assert that the births of deformed children forecast the future,
and proceed to list 62 known malformations and the specific events
they presage. They state, for example, "When a child is born with no
fingers, the town will have no births. When it is born with no well-
marked sex, calamity and affliction will seize upon the land." So
ingrained were such superstitions throughout antiquity that our word
monster, used to describe a defective infant, comes from the Latin *mon-
strum,* meaning a divine portent.

Plato, in his *Republic,* advocated the selective slaying of deformed
or inferior children, as a means of perfecting society. But it took the
Spartans to transform the idea into law. Under the constitution promulgated by Lycurgus, the lawgiver, ill-shaped or puny children were
to be taken to the Apothetae, a notorious chasm at the foot of Mount
Taygetus, and there disposed of. This was to be done for the well-
being of the state. Good Spartans were to think of their children as
public, not private, property. On the Roman side of the ledger, an
Etruscan king once ordered all monsters killed and burned when
invaders threatened his realm. And during the subsequent empire,
malformed infants were routinely drowned in the Tiber, with the
approval of men no less venerable than Seneca and Pliny the Elder.

The advent of Christianity brought the first crusades against infanticide. Early church leaders denounced the practice as heathen and
vigorously promulgated the view that human life was inviolable.
Nevertheless, some lives were less inviolable than others. In the fourth
table of his vastly influential legal code, the Christian emperor Justi-
nian declared that a father was bidden to destroy his malformed
children.

Infanticide continued unabated in western Europe during the Middle Ages. Though, in the seventh century, the Irish monk Columban
made it a crime, he set such a light penalty for it—a year on bread
and water, followed by two years without meat or wine—that no one
took it very seriously. Moreover, he specifically exempted serfs from
the law, a tacit recognition that the poor had a right to regulate the
number of mouths they had to feed. Famine and hunger were conditions of life in those times, and there was no birth control. In the
later Middle Ages, penalties became much more severe—in Saxony
the prescribed punishment was drowning inside a sack containing a

dog, a cat, a cock, and a viper—but mitigating factors like poverty were always taken into account. Those convicted were almost exclusively unwed mothers, who were no doubt being punished as much for their sexual sins as for murder.

The incidence of infanticide seems to have greatly exceeded the rate of prosecution for the crime. The ambivalent attitude of medieval authorities was partly responsible for this disparity. And the fact that many mothers used a technique called "overlaying," in which they "accidentally" suffocated the child by rolling over on it in bed, made intent difficult to prove. More squeamish mothers farmed their children out to wet nurses, who would discreetly dispatch the child. It is one of history's most striking examples of a double code of justice that wet nurses were never made to answer for these crimes.

By the 18th and 19th centuries, infanticide was epidemic in England and France. A number of historians attribute it to the socially accepted sexual exploitation of female servants and factory workers by their male employers. Killing or abandoning the illegitimate child was often the only escape hatch available to these oppressed women. During the 1860s some 150 dead infants were found in London each year floating in the Thames or lying in streets, ditches, and parks. The sewers of Paris were full of tiny corpses.

Foundling homes were trumpeted as the solution. But these *hôpitaux,* as they were called, soon became so overburdened that the babies perished anyway. St. Petersburg's hospital, in Russia, had 25,000 infant patients by 1830. Only a third of them ever reached the age of six. In France, Napoleon's brainstorm of having turntables put in the vestibules of the foundling homes, so that unwed mothers could drop off their infants anonymously, proved to be a Frankenstein creation. A deluge of waifs ensued. When, by 1833, the number of babies being dumped on French foundling homes had reached the incredible sum of 164,319 annually, authorities concluded that the convenience of the turntables was actually promoting promiscuity. The devices were thereafter outlawed.

Infanticide has been a consistent feature of non-Western cultures, as well. The Eskimos place infants on ice floes when the elders deem them too great a drain on precious resources. Many tribal peoples, ranging from the aborigines of Australia and the Maori of Polynesia to the Yanomamo Indians of Venezuela and the Zhun-twasi bushmen of Africa, have freely exterminated their young. The so-called higher civilizations have not been guiltless either. The Japanese subscribed so openly to infanticide that they even had a special word for it, *mabiki,* whose collateral meaning was "weeding" or "thinning rice seedlings." And the Chinese have been assiduous baby killers, particularly of infant daughters, whose value to their patrilineal society was negligible next to that of sons. Jesuit missionaries of the last century were aghast to find girl babies dumped on the street like refuse, to be collected each morning by sanitation workers. Even in modern-day China, the ancient practice goes on, to the embarrassment of the Communist regime.

Throughout these centuries of carnage, the prime candidate for infanticide was the defective newborn. Often the reason was logical enough: the parents were unable or unwilling to assume the burden of such an infant, who could never contribute to the family. Legally, they were on solid ground, for the deformed were considered nonpersons. The official definition of a freeman in medieval times was one who was not conceived "against the way of human kind, as for example, if a woman bring forth a monster or a prodigy." (This definition was not completely draconian. It did permit a freeman to have "in some small measure though not extravagantly" an abnormal number of fingers and toes.)

Still, when people could find no practical reason to kill a deformed child, they were never lacking for a supernatural one. There was a prevalent view that such babies had the mark of the devil upon them— or that they were the product of debauchery. In 1683 a woman was burned alive in the public square of Copenhagen for giving birth to a child who resembled a cat. Her neighbors were convinced she had cohabited with a feline. Even the scholar John Locke once wrote that women had been known to become pregnant by monkeys, "if history lye not."

All manner of superstition has plagued malformed newborns, abetted at times by the medical community. In 1569, for instance, the physician Jacques Roy interpreted the birth of twins joined at the chest to mean that the Catholic faith would survive the Huguenot movement. And for thousands of years doctors believed that the mental impressions of pregnant women affected the appearance of their unborn. A shock or a fright was said to be particularly harmful. Ambroise Paré, a prestigious 16th-century French surgeon, listed bad maternal image as one of the 13 causes of monstrous births, adding a veneer of science with the observation that it was a concern only in the first 42 days of gestation. In the United States, as late as 1889, Keating's *Cylopedia of the Diseases of Children* had a special chapter entitled "Maternal Impressions."

Medical knowledge has advanced greatly since the time of Paré. However, as recently as the 1940s, one well-known medical text, still found on public library shelves, passed along the specious theory that "mongolian idiots," as victims of Down's syndrome used to be called

owing to their vaguely oriental physiognomy, were an atavistic throw-
back to an ancient racial stock.

It is obvious that until the most recent past, the handicapped child
hasn't had much of a chance—not in a world where even healthy children have been subjected to violence, neglect, and outright homicide.
The notion seems to run deep in our psyche that children are somehow less human than adults, that they are chattel whose fate is subject
to parental prerogative. One is free to condemn this state of affairs,
but it is about as effective as complaining that people have extramar-
ital sex or that they fight wars.

Fortunately, we have laws nowadays to protect children's rights. But
the law has always been powerless to shield impaired children from
death when doctors had no way to save their lives. Then, almost overnight, the picture changed.

It is sometimes difficult to appreciate how far medicine has come in
the last quarter of a century. Like children who assume that television
and computers have always existed, we tend to forget that the current
crop of medical wonders became a part of our lives only a short time
ago.

As recently as 1953 James Watson and Francis Crick solved the riddle of DNA and ushered in the era of genetic engineering and, one
anticipates, the coming conquest of cancer. Incredibly, not until 1956
did Sweden's J. H. Tijo and A. Levan establish that the normal number of human chromosomes is 46. And it was 1959 when the French
geneticist Jérôme Lejeune determined that Down's syndrome was
caused by an extra 21st chromosome. Kidney dialysis, L-dopa, pace-
makers, and the heart-lung machine are all essentially products of the
last 25 years. But even they seem quaint next to laser surgery, in vitro
fertilization, and nuclear magnetic resonance machines.

Suddenly, medicine has been hurtled into the 21st century. Dreams
that have fired our imagination for eons are becoming a reality. Shall
we keep people alive indefinitely? Ventilators make it possible. Shall
we repair exquisitely delicate body structures? Microsurgery is at hand.
What do we do when a whole organ begins to sputter? Take it out
and replace it with someone else's, or even a man-made one, as
pioneering doctors did in Utah with the dentist Barney Clark. And
one day, in the not too distant future, genetic cripplers like diabetes,
cystic fibrosis, and muscular dystrophy may be cured with a little fine-
tuning of the genes.

But all is not unmitigated joy. The advance in technology has
presented doctors with an unprecedented and bewildering array of
ethical issues for which there seem to be no answers. In one of the
most memorable scenes in the classic novel *Madame Bovary,* the insuf-

ferable pharmacist, Homais, cajoles the poor country health officer
Charles Bovary into performing miraculous reconstructive surgery
on a stableboy's clubfoot. Still flush with apparent success, Homais
declares to the local press, "All honor to those tireless benefactors who
go without sleep to work for the improvement or the relief of mankind! Now we can indeed proclaim that the blind shall see, the deaf
shall hear, and the lame shall walk!" But even as the old windbag is
mouthing these words, the stableboy's "cured" foot is turning gangrenous. In a matter of days it will have to be amputated.

Blessed with foresight as well as art, Flaubert recognized 130 years
ago what medical science is only beginning to appreciate today: that
expanded technology provides no guarantee of happiness. Sometimes it is wiser to let the patient alone.

No worthy purpose is served by the strapping of an individual to a
set of exotic machines if the result is merely to keep insensate flesh
alive. Keeping a heart thrumming on into infinity sending blood to a
brain that has long since died is a pointless exercise. By the same token,
keeping alive by heroic means a fully conscious patient whose disease
is hopeless and who is in extreme pain is not only senseless but cruel.
For these reasons, the law permits a competent adult to refuse treatment if he or she so desires.

Some individuals would go further than this and actually initiate
dying. Sigmund Freud, wracked at the end of his life with a grievous
oral cancer, reputedly had his personal physician inject him with morphine shots that brought him blessed death. Euthanasia, or mercy
killing, as it is popularly known, is still a bitterly debated moral issue
and is likely to remain one for the foreseeable future.

Yet the underlying principle, the right of the individual to control
his or her own body against unwanted intrusion by doctors, is well
established and recognized. The issues become less clear, however,
when they involve patients who cannot speak for themselves—that is
to say, the comatose, the severely retarded, and, most notably, children.

Children obviously cannot tell you whether or not they want you to
extend their life by whatever means are available. Such decisions must
inevitably be made for them by third parties. These third parties had
a relatively easy time of it when the range of alternatives was small.
But the unprecedented advance of life-support technology has created a manifold increase in the number of proxy decisions that must
be made on behalf of sick children. That is the heart of the problem.

Beyond any doubt, the most dramatic progress in contemporary
medicine has come in the care of newborns. Babies who almost cer-

tainly would have died five to ten years ago are routinely surviving today. For example, fantastically tiny premature infants—some weighing barely more than a pound—are being saved through the adroit use of mechanical ventilators, electronic monitors, and intravenous fluids, all within the dazzling context of the modern neonatal intensive-care unit. The numbers are remarkable. In 1960 the mortality rate of newborns weighing less than 1,500 grams (3 lb 5 oz) was roughly 70 percent. Today it has dropped to between 30 and 40 percent.

Similarly, some dreaded congenital defects are being forced to yield ground. A case in point is myelomeningocele. As late as the 1950s the condition was fatal 80 percent of the time because of the vulnerability of the spinal cord to infection. Today the numbers are completely reversed. Victims *survive* in 90 percent of the cases.

Anastomosis is the technical name of the procedure used to repair the tracheoesophageal fistulas of infants such as Bloomington's Baby Doe. The two unjoined sleeves of the esophagus are knit together in a rather impressive display of surgical dexterity. It is not a new operation; it was first performed in 1941. But its success rate has risen sharply in recent years.

Gastroschisis is a condition in which the baby is born with its intestines completely outside its body. Time is of the essence in performing corrective surgery, because of the great danger that the child will lose heat through the exposed gut. In 1970 the mortality rate for this condition was 80 percent. Today it stands at 5 percent. The difference is due to hyperalimentation, a breakthrough in intravenous feeding that supplies a child with a complete diet until its viscera have healed enough to digest food, sometimes six weeks or more.

One can go on and on. But what are the consequences of all this Flying Wallenda medicine?

Those who assume that saving a life is an unequivocal act of grace would do well to consider the dismal fate of a disturbing number of "salvaged" babies. The evidence shows, for instance, that many infants of extremely low birthweight go on to have handicaps as they grow older, ranging from learning disorders and poor motor coordination to full-blown cerebral palsy, blindness, deafness, retardation, and epilepsy. A Canadian study found that not one baby in a sample of children who weighed less than 700 grams (1 lb 9 oz) was free of disabilities later on.

Children with myelomeningocele will almost never lead normal lives. At least 40 percent of them will be mentally retarded. Half, if not more, will be paralyzed from the waist down. The majority will have no bladder or bowel control, will require brain shunts to counteract hydrocephalus, and will have varying deformities, including curvature of the spine, a dislocated hip, and a humping of the back. They will be subject, furthermore, to the lifelong threat of kidney disease.

Down's syndrome shortens life spans. A large number of its victims will die before the age of 10, and most will die by the time they are 50. They are subject to heart and other defects, and for reasons not yet clear they face a 20-fold greater risk of contracting leukemia than the general population. Retardation is universal, the IQs averaging between 45 and 55. Although many can be taught to verbalize, dress themselves, and perform a menu of simple tasks, a significant number will be so profoundly retarded that they will never learn to talk or walk and will spend time in such self-destructive behavior as banging their head against the wall.

It is true that many children with less severe forms of myelomeningocele and Down's syndrome proceed to have quite enjoyable, even productive, lives. They can and do bring great pleasure to their families. Nevertheless, it is important to be realistic about these and the several thousand other known handicapping conditions. Many of them have the potential to so incapacitate or humiliate the sufferer as to make existence more a burden than a joy.

Being realistic demands understanding that defects put tremendous obstacles in the path of a child's emotional development. And while many disabled people adjust splendidly or, at the very least, adequately, there are, alas, some who never do; and their lives are doomed to despair.

Being realistic also requires acknowledging the huge strain a handicapped child places on the family. In some cases, the strain defies imagination. One couple of my acquaintance raises its six-year-old son at home. He possesses only primitive mental function and has a form of cerebral palsy that results in wild, uncontrollable movements. He neither talks nor walks, and he is not toilet trained. He must be carried everywhere, cleaned up after, and watched at all times. There are no baby-sitters for a child like him; the parents have to do everything themselves, day in and day out. They haven't had a vacation since he was born. "What we worry most about," the mother says, "is what might happen to him after we die. His general health is excellent, so there's no reason to think he won't live a long time. It is a very difficult thing to realize you're going to have to reach out from beyond the grave to help your child."

Financially and emotionally, such families are drained to the limits of their resources. Yet, they receive little help from society. The very government that compels treatment of handicapped newborns provides scant support for them once they get older. Programs like special education and social services for the disabled are run on a shoestring in the United States, which is put to shame in this regard by more enlightened countries like Britain and Sweden. And what small outlays exist in the United States are continually threatened with the budgetary ax by the same deacons of conservativism who consider it an abomination to let a baby die. Someone once said of the prolife philosophy that it believes life begins at conception and ends at birth. There is a great deal of truth in that witticism.

Divorce is common in families with handicapped children. The relationship simply will not withstand the feelings of guilt and frustration that raising a damaged child unleashes. In some cases, the family unit opts to save itself by expelling the child: such avenues as institutional placement, foster care, and adoption come into play. In other cases, the family unit may stay intact but the child suffers continual neglect and abuse.

Given the negative factors, one might reasonably pose some questions. Should we as a society insist on preserving the lives of the most severely handicapped of these children—those who in former times would have died—only to bestow on them a substandard existence of incapacity, banishment, and pain? And why should a couple's innocent desire for children condemn them to a lifetime with a child who bankrupts them emotionally and financially and perhaps destroys their marriage? Should the act of reproduction be such an awesome roll of the dice? Are we right to demand that doctors use every piece of their mind-boggling technology without exception and to reprimand them when they don't?

The invention of a new tool does not necessarily compel us to use it. Otherwise we should immediately rain cruise missiles upon the Soviet Union, or undertake bacterial warfare against Fidel Castro's regime. Whether we use the tool or not depends on the benefits to be obtained versus the injury that might be wrought. If our instrumentation serves only to confer life that is oppressively limited or to draw out the dying process at the cost of more pain, then it can logically be argued that such instrumentation has no business being used. To conclude otherwise would violate the physician's credo, which not only imposes the duty to save lives but also states, "Primum non nocere" ("First of all, do no harm").

But the mere admission that there are times when the life-support machines are inappropriate does not begin to settle the question.

For example, which constellation of birth defects and what degree of illness justify withholding treatment? And is prognosis such an exact science that we can say for certain that a child will have a dreadful life? The annals of medicine are replete with stories of children who were written off at birth and who ultimately do well.

Equally important, who is to make the choice? Shall it be the par-

ents acting alone? Surely no one has more legal standing than they to
determine what is best for their child. But they have not gone to medical school. Very likely, their child is suffering from a condition whose
name they can't pronounce and have never heard of. How can they
make an informed decision?

Consequently, doctors enter the picture, but their presence creates
additional pitfalls. A serious danger exists that physicians will unduly,
though perhaps unintentionally, influence the father and mother with
their own values and biases. A doctor who thinks most myelomeningocele victims have difficult lives can easily be envisioned steering the
family of such a patient in the direction of nontreatment. The con-
verse is true as well. Furthermore, it is not unknown for doctors to
take off like rogue elephants, proceeding with their own treatment
plan while oblivious to parental desires. In either case, the doctor has
made the whole life-and-death decision alone. Many people, including doctors, find something wrong with that.

What role, if any, do the courts have? They are the traditional arbiter of competing rights, and a rights question is definitely at issue
here: the child's right to live versus its right to die. But consulting a
court every time there is a question of withdrawing treatment is neither feasible nor desirable. A sick baby's needs are immediate; they
will not be put on hold for lengthy legal proceedings. And judges are
no better equipped to make erudite medical decisions than the average parent.

Do bureaucrats have any place in the picture at all? Should they be
careening around a nursery like Keystone Cops, as the Baby Doe regulations empowered them to do? Is it fitting for the government to
intrude on people's personal lives to that degree? Does it not exacerbate a couple's anguish to be threatened by state fiat at such a tragic
moment in their lives?

Suppose the decision is made to withhold treatment and allow the
child to die. What sort of treatment do you withhold? Do you draw
the line at not initiating any heroic measures, such as virtuoso surgery? Do you withhold even ordinary care? If the child has a grave
infection, do you omit antibiotics? Or do you withhold even the barest
essentials of life, including food and water, in the hope of hastening
death? Without surgery Bloomington's Baby Doe could not be fed by
mouth. Yet intravenous feedings would only have served to prolong
his painful state. In that event, one might as well have performed the
operation. It is a double bind, whose troubling solution lay in allowing
the child to starve.

The Doe child took only six days to die. In 1971, however, in a case
that received wide publicity but, owing to a different political climate,

never influenced policy the way the Indiana episode did, a Down's infant was allowed to die even more protractedly at Johns Hopkins Hospital in Baltimore. He had a duodenal atresia, a condition in which the stomach fails to link up with the intestine. The parents, whose identity was never revealed, decided to refuse consent for surgery. All food and water were withheld at their request. In this case, the child took fifteen days to expire. His lingering death, which was later the subject of a film made by the Joseph P. Kennedy Jr. Foundation, demoralized the entire hospital staff.

As one can see, the issue is a quagmire. Discussion seems to generate no solutions, only more questions.

Somehow, though, society is going to have to dredge up some answers from this murky bog. More cases are bound to arise as technology improves. Meanwhile, spreading over the medical landscape is the shadow of another issue: economics. To put it bluntly, there may not be enough money in the health care system to keep all damaged babies alive.

Infant medicine is exceedingly expensive. A study several years ago put the total cost of neonatal intensive care in the United States at $1.5 billion a year. It undoubtedly has gone up since then. The average medical bill for saving a premature newborn of less than two pounds is $40,000. It can, and frequently does, exceed $100,000. A child with severe spina bifida might easily incur several hundred thousand dollars worth of treatment in its first two years of life alone. Obviously, these fees are beyond the means of most, if not all, parents. Society will have to pay them out of its already strained resources. If the strain reaches the breaking point, it may make all ethical considerations moot.

In the autumn of 1973 two pediatric specialists published a paper in the *New England Journal of Medicine* that set the medical community on its ear. The article was entitled "Moral and Ethical Dilemmas in the Special-Care Nursery." Its authors were Dr. Raymond S. Duff, professor of pediatrics at the Yale University School of Medicine, and Dr. Alexander G. M. Campbell, now of the University of Aberdeen, Scotland.

The two doctors revealed that of 299 deaths that occurred in the intensive-care nursery at Yale–New Haven Hospital from 1970 to 1972, a total of 43 had resulted from the intentional withdrawal of treatment—withdrawal that they, as attending pediatricians, had often approved. The diagnoses had included a variety of severe conditions, including multiple anomalies, chromosomal disorders, chronic cardiopulmonary disease, and myelomeningocele.

"After careful consideration of each of these 43 infants," Drs. Duff and Campbell wrote, "parents and physicians in a group decision concluded that prognosis for meaningful life was extremely poor or hopeless, and therefore rejected further treatment. The awesome finality of these decisions, combined with a potential for error in prognosis, made the choice agonizing for families and health professionals. Nevertheless, the issue has to be faced. . . ."

Duff and Campbell made a moving case for an infant's right to die when treatment is only perpetuating its suffering. They told of one patient whose chronic lung disease was so bad at five months of age that even with high doses of oxygen his breathing was still deeply labored. His heart was enlarging from the extra strain of pumping blood, and drugs did not seem to help. "The nurses, parents, and physicians considered it cruel to continue, and yet difficult to stop. All were attached to this child, whose life they had tried so hard to make worthwhile. The family had endured high expenses . . . and the strains of the illness were believed to be threatening the marriage bonds and to be causing sibling behavioral disturbances." Ultimately, oxygen therapy was withdrawn, and the child died in three hours.

Duff and Campbell said some of the hospital's doctors were reluctant to come to terms with the issue. "There was a feeling that to 'give up' was disloyal to the cause of the profession," they wrote. "Since major research, teaching and patient-care efforts were being made, professionals expected to discover, transmit and apply knowledge and skills; patients and families were supposed to cooperate fully even if they were not always grateful. Some physicians . . . commonly agreed that if they were the parents of very defective children, withholding treatment would be most desirable for them. However, they argued that aggressive [treatment] was indicated for others."

They concluded as follows: "Some persons may argue that the law has been broken, and others would contend otherwise. Perhaps more than anything else, the public and professional silence on a major social taboo and some common practices has been broken further. That seems appropriate, for out of the ensuing dialogue perhaps better choices for patients and families can be made. If working out these dilemmas in ways such as those we suggest is in violation of the law, we believe the law should be changed."

An uproar followed publication of the article. Not that anyone in medical circles was very shocked that someone had let sick babies die. Generations of doctors had been doing the same thing on the sly. But here were two doctors openly admitting it.

In the same issue of the *New England Journal,* Dr. Anthony Shaw, a pediatric surgeon at the University of Virginia Medical Center, also bared his soul. Dr. Shaw described eight cases, most of them from his own practice, in which moral dilemmas had arisen in the treatment of critically ill children. In some situations, infants were allowed to die; in others, they were not.

With heavy sarcasm, Shaw mocked the idea that the all-out use of high technology is always in the patient's interest: "Now with our team approaches, staged surgical technics, monitoring capabilities, ventilatory support systems and intravenous hyperalimentation and elemental diets, we can wind up with 'viable' children three and four years old well below the third percentile in height and weight, propped up on a pillow, marginally tolerating an oral diet of sugar and amino acids and looking forward to another operation."

In summation, he wrote, "If an underlying philosophy can be gleaned from the vignettes presented above, I hope it is one that tries to find a solution, humane and loving, based on the circumstances of each case rather than by means of a dogmatic formula approach."

In England, still another respected physician, Dr. John Lorber, had added his voice. Lorber, a specialist in myelomeningocele at Children's Hospital in Sheffield, had gone so far as to devise criteria to use in determining which spina bifida patients not to treat. He called this process "selection," a word that had unfortunate associations with Nazi eugenics. But despite a rather aloof manner that shone through his writing, Lorber left no doubt that he was proceeding from humane motives.

He wrote, "It is unlikely that many would wish to save a life which will consist of a long succession of operations, hospital admissions and other deprivations, or if the end result will be a combination of gross physical defects with retarded intellectual development. . . . We must decide our priorities to ensure that, with all the intensive effort and good will, we shall not do more harm than good."

All four of these men, in one way or another, were writing in reaction to the Great Leap Forward in neonatal technology that had taken place in the 1960s. They were provoked by an attitude that seemed to dictate the use of machines just because they exist. This relentless juggernaut of expertise, they reminded their colleagues, should be tempered with compassionate concern for the future quality of life of the infant and its family.

Elsewhere in 1973, however, events were coming to a head that would ignite the engines of another point of view, one with its own claims on compassion.

January of that year had been one of those rare and fateful months that have enormous and unforeseen consequences for great masses of humanity. President Nixon announced a ceasefire in Vietnam that would "end the war and bring peace with honor." The Watergate burglars pleaded or were found guilty, as negotiations went on behind the scenes to buy their silence. And on January 22 the Supreme Court

of the United States issued its opinion that women have a legal right
to abortions.

The issues of abortion and of not treating impaired babies are inextricably tied. For it it is wrong, opponents reason, to bring about the
death of a child when it is still within the womb, then it certainly must
be wrong to do so when it is a living, breathing creature outside the
mother's body. In fact, abortion and the withholding of treatment
from damaged newborns are often motivated by completely different
concerns. But for the moment, let us assume a tight association.

The high court's landmark ruling, in the case known as *Roe* v. *Wade,*
was seen by many people with strong feelings against abortion as a
serious tear in the nation's moral fabric. To some of the most outspoken zealots, it was the work of the devil. What had been a rather small,
underfinanced band of abortion foes quickly grew into a large,
resourceful, and extremely effective movement, led by some of the
most rigid and tireless reformers this nation had ever seen.

At first the movement's program focused almost entirely on chip-
ping away at abortion; the issue of impaired infants was secondary.
This is understandable for several reasons. There was no Supreme
Court infanticide decision to confront. Also, pressure group tactics
succeed best when they are trained on one issue. Finally, there was
the matter of relative frequency. There are 1.6 million abortions in
the United States every year. The number of babies who die from
terminated medical treatment is vastly smaller.

But a number of things have happened to alter the situation. The
right-to-life movement has made frustratingly little progress with its
antiabortion agenda in recent years. It was time to shift the focus to a
perhaps more productive arena—handicapped babies. More important, a number of well-publicized court battles over the issue of not
treating newborns had created the illusion, if not the fact, of infanticide's wide prevalence.

The death of the Johns Hopkins baby was still fresh in the public
mind when, in 1974, a Maine couple, Air Force Sgt. Robert Houle
and his wife, asked that lifesaving surgery not be performed on their
son, David, born with multiple deformities and a tracheoesophageal
fistula. The hospital sought and won a court order to permit the surgery.

In 1979 a New York couple refused to allow surgeons to close the
open back of their infant daughter, born with myelomeningocele. The
hospital administrator, Frank Cicero, brought suit. The parents said
they wanted to take the baby home and "let God decide" whether she
should live or die. But the judge ordered surgery.

Also in 1979 a case involving a 12-year-old Down's syndrome victim named Phillip Becker made national headlines. Phillip, who was placed in an institution by his parents shortly after his birth, had a ventricular septal defect, a hole between the two lower chambers of his heart. Phillip's doctor said if it wasn't surgically corrected, he would die in his thirties. But the parents, Warren and Patricia Becker, declined to agree to surgery. They were subsequently taken to court by the California child welfare authorities. This time the courts upheld the parents, in a decision that was allowed to stand. Nevertheless, two years later Herbert and Patricia Heath, a couple who had worked with Phillip in the group home where he lived, filed suit to gain custody of the boy. A California Superior Court judge granted their petition, saying they had become his "psychological parents." In the summer of 1983, when the Beckers lost their final appeal, Phillip at last underwent his operation.

Then, in 1981 a Danville, Illinois, couple was actually charged with attempting to murder their Siamese twins, born joined at the hip. It appeared at their birth that surgical separation was out of the question. During the next few days a note appeared on the twins' hospital chart, ordering that they not be fed, at the parents' request. When word leaked out, the county prosecutor responded by introducing criminal proceedings against the parents and the doctor. The charges were later dropped, however.

Again in 1981 a case captured public attention in England, one that was very similar to that of Baby Doe. A girl was born suffering from Down's syndrome and an intestinal blockage that made her unable to digest food. The parents, believing it to be in the child's best interest to let her die, declined to permit corrective surgery. Her doctors obtained a court order for the operation, but when the surgeon who was retained to do the procedure learned that the parents objected, he changed his mind. He said, "I decided therefore to respect the wishes of the parents and not perform the operation, a decision which would, I believe (after about 20 years in the medical profession), be taken by the great majority of surgeons faced with a similar situation."

Thus, a difference of medical opinion existed. The case was remanded to an appellate court, where the family's attorney argued, "This is a case where nature has made its own arrangements to terminate a life which would not be fruitful and nature should not be interfered with." But Lord Justice Templeman, in his decision, countered that the issue was whether the life of the child was going to be so demonstrably terrible that she should be condemned to die or whether her prognosis was so imponderable that she should be kept alive.

Templeman said, "The choice before the court is this: whether to allow the operation to take place, which may result in the child's living for 20 to 30 years as a mongoloid, or whether . . . to terminate the life of a mongoloid child because she has an intestinal complaint. I have no doubt that it is the duty of this court to decide that the child must live. . . . The evidence in this case only goes to show that if the operation takes place and is successful then the child may live the normal span of a mongoloid child with the handicaps and defects and life of a mongol child, and it is not for this court to say that life of that description ought to be extinguished."

Once the media spotlight was being thrown on cases such as these, it began to look as though it was not all that uncommon in America and Britain for parents and doctors to turn away from treating certain babies. Surgeon General Koop commented to the press that while he could not say specifically how often it happened, he could say "that these are not isolated instances."

The prolife movement has therefore assigned great priority to the issue of the treatment of handicapped babies. In this, its adherents are working in concert with a number of national organizations for the rights of the disabled. Right-to-life spokesmen argued vigorously that it was the original Supreme Court abortion decision that has helped bring us to the sorry pass of infanticide. Each step, they say, has sent us that much farther down the "slippery slope" to moral perdition.

These spokesmen are fond of drawing parallels to the Third Reich. They frequently refer to the writings of the Massachusetts psychiatrist Dr. Leo Alexander, who drafted the "Nuremberg Code of Medical Ethics" used in the Nazi medical trials. In a 1949 article in the *New England Journal of Medicine* entitled "Medical Science under Dictatorship," Dr. Alexander wrote that under the Nazis the German medical community became the state's willing instrument of genocide. But the physicians underwent a carefully orchestrated descent into depravity. In its early years, the Hitler regime recognized that it would patiently have to condition German doctors to accept mass murder. It did this, Dr. Alexander said, by first calling for the extermination of those weak members of society whose death could be easily justified on grounds of minimal social value. The initial targets were the chronically ill, the psychotic, the retarded, the epileptic, and the senile elderly. "It is rather significant," wrote Dr. Alexander, "that the German people were considered by their Nazi leaders more ready to accept the exterminations of the sick than those for political reasons."

Alexander emphasized, in words that are undeniably chilling today, "Whatever proportions these crimes finally assumed, it became evident to all who investigated them that they started from small beginnings. The beginnings at first were merely a subtle shift in emphasis in the basic attitude of the physicians. It started with the acceptance of the attitude, basic in the euthanasia movement, that there is such a thing as a life not worthy to be lived."

Could America, God forbid, be traveling down the same path, pro-lifers asked?

It does appear, on the surface at least, that anything which tends to depreciate the value of an individual life threatens to erode our respect for life generally. Yet, there are important distinctions to be made between the origins of the Holocaust and allowing parents the free-dom to let a damaged newborn die. The mass slaughter in Germany had ideological underpinnings; it was both the expression of institu-tionalized bigotry and a calculated attempt to "improve" the racial stock. It is doubtful that parents who elect to forgo surgery or other life support for their youngsters are motivated by any doctrinal con-cerns. Second, extermination in Germany, from its inception, was perpetrated by the state. There is a world of difference between mur-der as an instrument of state policy and euthanasia as a family's pri-vate response to grief. Some contend, however, that the latter could lead to the former, even though this was not the historical pattern in Germany. They fear that acceptance of infant nontreatment will in time lower society's psychological resistance to other, less defensible forms of behavior. But are we so weak, so childlike, that we cannot resist our own darker natures? Is it not possible to permit certain lim-ited forms of mercy death without pitching headlong down the bloody path to Holocaust?

Whatever view one has of the slippery-slope argument, there is no doubt that the medical community freely practices and widely con-dones withholding treatment from severely handicapped babies.

In 1977 the aforementioned Dr. Anthony Shaw published some poll findings in the journal *Pediatrics*. He and his colleagues had two years earlier conducted a survey among pediatric surgeons and pedia-tricians across the United States. The purpose of the survey was to determine the doctors' feelings about a number of troubling ethical issues in children's medicine.

The first question put to the 457 respondents was "Do you believe that the life of each and every newborn infant should be saved if it is within our ability to do so?" The replies showed near unanimity. Some 83 percent of the surgeons and 81 percent of the pediatricians said they didn't believe in saving every child.

The next question was "Would you acquiesce in parents' decision to refuse consent for surgery in a newborn with intestinal atresia if the infant also had (a) Down's syndrome alone, (b) Down's syndrome plus congenital heart disease, (c) anencephaly, (d) [bladder] exstro-phy, (e) myelomeningocele, (f) multiple limb or craniofacial malformation, (g) 13–15 trisomy [lethal chromosomal aberrations], or (h) no other anomalies, i.e., normal aside from atresia?" Sections (a) and (b) of that question virtually describe the condition of Baby Doe.

Among the surgeons, 76.8 percent said they would abide by the parents' wishes if there was Down's syndrome alone, and 85 percent said they would if there was also heart disease. The pediatricians were more cautious. Only 49.5 said they would acquiesce where there was Down's alone, but 65.3 percent said they would if the child had heart disease as well.

Responses for the other conditions varied. Almost all the doctors agreed they would let an anencephalic baby—one with little or no brain tissue—die. Approximately 60 percent of both groups said they would do the same with a myelomeningocele victim. Sixty-three percent of the surgeons said they wouldn't interfere where a limb or craniofacial malformation was concerned. And an astonishing 7.9 percent of the surgeons said they would agree not to operate even where there was nothing wrong with the child but the intestinal atresia alone!

As startling as these figures sound, they are supported by two other surveys. When California pediatricians were asked how they would treat a Down's infant with an intestinal obstruction, 61 percent of the respondents said they would let the baby die if the parents wanted it. And in Massachusetts 51 percent of pediatricians polled said in effect the same thing.

But lest we assume such convictions are limited to doctors, let us look at the results of a 1983 Gallup poll, in which average Americans were asked what they would do if they had a badly deformed baby in need of treatment.

Of 1,540 adults asked, 43 percent said they would ask the doctor not to keep the baby alive. Forty percent said otherwise. Hence, not only do many doctors favor selective nontreatment but the public itself is apparently evenly divided on the issue.

Nevertheless, without a clear mandate, the Reagan administration saw fit to plunge ahead not once, but twice, with its Baby Doe regulations.

This is curious behavior for an administration that was elected on a promise to get the government off the backs of the people; that did everything in its power to cut back federal aid to the disabled; and that tried to push through Congress a reduction in funding for special education—which almost every handicapped baby that survives is going to need. It is also an administration that tolerated a secretary of the interior whose sensitivity to the handicapped was demonstrated by his now-famous remark describing the makeup of his advisory commission as "a black, a woman, two Jews, and a cripple."

Leaving aside any political motives that the administration might have had for placating the prolife movement, one is struck by how much the Doe regulations seem to reflect a mental set once characterized as the "idolatry" of life by the Reverend John J. Paris, associate professor of ethics at Holy Cross College. The Reverend Paris wrote that our modern age had taken life a step beyond being merely sacrosanct. "It is ultimate," he asserted. "Death is not a part of the human condition; it is a failure, a disaster, an absolute, unmitigated evil to be avoided at all costs."

Thus the preservation of biological life by any means, no matter how immobile, insensate, or pointless, has become somehow preferable to the natural act of dying—all of which reminds me of something very troubling. I was visiting the intensive-care nursery at Northwestern Memorial Hospital in Chicago, when I saw an oriental child in one of the incubators. The boy seemed much too big to be still so domiciled.

The doctor explained that because the boy had been many weeks premature, his lungs had been only rough drafts of the finished thing. He had to be helped to breathe; consequently they had placed him on a mechanical ventilator. The problem was that after months of machine-assisted breathing, he had become what doctors call "ventilator-dependent." He no longer could breathe without the machine. The doctors were unable to wean him.

His life had consisted of one medical feat after another. They had to pull him through a siege of osteomyelitis, a serious bone infection. Then they kept him on antibiotics for six more weeks in order to cure two bouts of sepsis, a severe blood infection. And for months they had to fed him intravenously because he couldn't take oral feedings.

The doctor explained that the parents were an immigrant Cambodian couple that spoke no English. She said they were deeply puzzled by the doctors' strenuous efforts to save their son, since in their native land, when a baby cannot make it on its own, it dies. Its death is viewed as the will of nature.

"If and when we can send him home, he's going to need extremely careful attention," said the doctor. "His lungs will be bad for a long time. It worries me. The parents don't understand the instructions we give them. They have absolutely no money. And they can't begin to fathom why he was saved in the first place. In that kind of environment, there's a good chance he will die."

That prompted an obvious question: Then why try so hard to save him?

"I don't have the answer to that," the doctor replied.

3

Born Too Soon
Treating the Premature Baby

A room. Warm and stuffy, barely large enough to walk around in. There are hot lights and blue lights, air hoses and IV bottles, monitor machines stacked one on top of another, their needles jumping, their digital faces glowing ruby red. A furious squawking noise fills the air, a noise like gabbling fowl. It is the sound of the monitors tripping alarms; a heart rate has dropped too low, someone's breathing is dangerously weak. Life is tended in this room as if it were a rare species of orchid.

This is the intensive-care nursery of a large midwestern hospital. Babies lie in long, crowded rows: babies on warming tables; babies in Isolettes; babies rigged by wire and tube to unyielding metal, oily compressors, semiconductors, and pumps; babies that seem to have been patched into some central mechanical mother with a hundred umbilici, all waving like the arms of a Hindu god. The children are dusky red, wizened; blue veins show right through their paper-thin skin. They seem curiously denatured. With a tube down their throat, they don't cry. With an intravenous food line, they don't burp. Their wastes are disposed of immediately by the nurses who stand watch over each of them 24 hours a day. Every heartbeat, every change in fluid balance, every drop of drool is noted and its meaning assayed. Not a gurgle sounds in these infant guts that the doctors don't know about. These are truly technology's godchildren.

One of them, Luisa, is 16 days old. She was born twelve weeks prematurely, weighing only 780 grams. That is just over 1 pound 11 ounces, or about the weight of a carton of eggs. Her limbs are no bigger than your little finger, and her body is the size of your hand.

"Hello, sunshine," a second-year resident says to her. "Can you give me some platelets today?" She is lying on a warming table, an open mattress surrounded by low Plexiglas panels. Radiant heat lamps overhead keep her temperature constant, a must with the premature.

Luisa has been in constant jeopardy throughout her brief life. Her worst problem is a severe case of respiratory distress syndrome, RDS for short, the most common illness in premies. She requires the use of a ventilator. The machine, which is actually an ingenious pumping device, delivers pints of air to her at the controlled rate of 36 breaths a minute. The air can be adjusted for oxygen content. At the moment, Luisa is getting 33 percent oxygen (ordinary room air contains 21 percent).

She has also been ravaged by serious infection and now faces surgery to correct yet another problem, a patent ductus arteriosus. The ductus is a fetal blood vessel linking the pulmonary artery to the aorta. It is supposed to close after birth but in premies sometimes doesn't. When it stays open, or "patent," it lets oxygenated blood that is supposed to go to the rest of the body flow back into the lungs, where it gets oxygenated a second time. These unnecessary trips overburden the heart and can lead to congestive heart failure or a condition called ischemia, in which vital tissues don't get the blood they need. Usually, a drug called indomethacin will cause the ductus to close. But in Luisa's case, the drug, which is still experimental, didn't work. Surgeons are going to have to anesthetize her and operate this afternoon.

"Just a few platelets," intones the doctor soothingly. He needs three cubic centimeters of blood so the lab can test her clotting factors, an essential step before they put her on an operating table.

Luisa is somewhere underneath a tangle of leads and tubes and wires. Two gray leads on her legs and one on her left arm feed into the three-way socket of a Hewlett-Packard cardiac and apnea monitor. A probe on her stomach keeps track of her body heat, and another measures her blood gases—the amount of oxygen actually getting into her blood. In her left arm are two intravenous lines, one for nutrition and one for antibiotics. They are held in place by a "splint"—actually a tongue depressor drafted into service because her arm was too small for regular infant splints. Her head—the size of a tennis ball—is dwarfed by the ventilator valve, which is taped to her face. An air hose leads to the ventilator itself, a small, blue machine about the size of a portable television. Her chest is sunken and her ribs stick out, the result of her respiratory difficulty.

The resident lifts up one of her tiny arms and swabs it with antiseptic. Then, using the smallest needle possible, he attempts to draw some blood, Luisa winces slightly, and her stomach rises and falls spasmodically. No blood comes out.

"The needle's too large," the resident says to the nurse. "Her artery is smaller than the bevel of the needle. I don't know if this is going to work."

He pokes around some more, sliding the needle in and out of the puncture. Each time, Luisa wriggles. Still no blood.

Across from Luisa is Michael. His birthweight was 900 grams, or two pounds. When he was born, two months ago, his mother was in her 28th week of pregnancy. That's only two weeks past the point at which a fetus is generally considered to become viable, or able to live outside the womb. Matthew isn't growing well, nor can he breathe on his own. He, too, is on a ventilator.

A male nurse picks the boy up and starts working his limbs back and forth. "Stimulation hour," he explains.

The nurse is a little depressed this morning. He says that last night they lost a 1,000-gram premie they had been trying to save. "He went into total body failure. We had to boost the breathing rate because his blood gases were low. But he couldn't take it. The ventilator blew out his lungs.

"It's no one's fault," he hastens to add. "The baby just had enough. Part of me actually feels good for him. He's in a better place, free from invasion and pain."

The resident keeps trying to draw blood from Luisa. Her feet kick each time he puts the needle in. Both feet are grossly scarred from dozens of previous blood samples taken from the favored site, the heel.

"It's hard to find these arteries," he says. "They're just so small." He swabs her arm a fourth time with antiseptic and plunges the needle in. At last some blood begins to trickle into the syringe. Slowly it rises. The resident puts his weight on one foot, then the other, and taps his fingers on the warming table, in a burlesque of impatience.

At length he pulls the needle out. "Finally," he says. But squinting at it, he notices that in the time it has taken the tube to fill, the blood has already clotted. It is useless for testing. "Oh, well," he philosophizes. "That proves what I wanted to know, anyway. She's got good coagulants."

One of the most extraordinary medical revolutions of all time has been going on right under our noses.

As recently as 1960, doctors believed that the best way to treat premature infants was to isolate them and leave them alone. You were to feed them and put them in an incubator to keep them warm, but beyond that it was hands off while the heavens considered their fate. "It was so crude it was almost biblical," recalls Dr. L. Joseph Butterfield, of the Children's Hospital in Denver, who was then just beginning his practice.

Premies in those days faced a 40-fold greater chance of dying than normal-sized infants. The vast majority of the smaller ones perished from infections, hemorrhages, and shock, but mostly from RDS, also known as hyaline membrane disease, a scourge that was fatal up to 75 percent of the time. Some who survived were permanently scarred by mental retardation or cerebral palsy. Others did well, it is true, growing up without a trace of handicap, but they were the exception, not the rule.

And then came a knowledge explosion almost unprecedented in the history of medicine—a staccato burst of discoveries that were to knock the dismal statistics into a cocked hat. Pediatric researchers worldwide were experiencing a rare atmosphere of ferment, the unique synergy of minds that always heralds great scientific breakthroughs. Laboring in a dozen countries, cross-pollinating among themselves, they seemed to be announcing new findings as fast as old ones could be inaugurated in the nursery.

In a span of no more than a couple of years, the field of pediatrics made a 180 degree turn. No longer did one let a premie alone. One treated the child as aggressively as manpower and expertise would allow. The results could not have been more remarkable.

Within the past two decades, the death rate for premies has dropped more than 55 percent. But that doesn't begin to tell the story, because the largest gains have involved the very smallest infants, those under 1,500 grams in birthweight. It is these youngsters who have always accounted for the largest number of deaths among the premature.

In 1969, before the most striking progress was made, only half of all babies born weighing between 1,000 and 1,500 grams survived. Today, doctors can save 85 percent of them. In that same year only 20 percent of the babies weighing between 750 and 1,000 grams lived. Now we can save between 50 and 75 percent. Of the smallest babies, those weighing less than 750 grams (1 lb 10 oz), fewer than 4 percent survived in 1969. Today, doctors are able to salvage more than 25 percent.

At some of the best hospitals, those figures are even more impressive. Dr. Roderic Phibbs, director of the intensive-care nursery at the University of California at San Francisco, reports that in 1982 their survival rate for babies under 800 grams was 29 percent; for those weighing between 800 and 900 grams, it was 78 percent; and for those between 900 and 1,000 grams, it was 95 percent. Only one two-pound baby out of 20 failed to live.

Gains have also been made with respect to gestational age, considered a more important factor than birthweight in determining a child's prognosis. Babies that are born before the 26th week of pregnancy, no matter what their size, are on the extreme edge of viability. The survival rate does not markedly improve until one hits 28 or 29 weeks of gestation. But no longer is it the rarity it once was for a 26- or 27-week infant to survive in the better children's hospitals. And the occasional 24- or 25-week infant surprises everyone and thrives.

Another way to look at these figures is to examine the nation's overall infant mortality rate. At the turn of the century, a child's chances of living to see its first birthday were by no means assured. About 100 out of every 1,000 infants born in the United States died in their first year of life.

By mid-century this death rate had plummeted to 29 per 1,000 births. There were many reasons for this, among them the discovery of antibiotics, the development of immunizations against many childhood diseases, and the urbanization of society, which was accompanied by hospital growth and the dissemination of better health care. After 1950, however, the doldrums set in. For the next decade and a half, the mortality rate declined only 1 percent a year. By 1965, 25 children out of every 1,000 born still died in infancy.

Then something truly dramatic occurred. The rate began to plunge again. In 1970 it was down to 20. By 1975 it had fallen to 16. And by 1982, the infant mortality rate, according to the National Center for Health Statistics, stood at 11.2 per 1,000 births. That represents a 53 percent decline in only 16 years!

It would be wrong for Americans to gloat over this. The United States is a lowly 18th in the world in infant mortality, behind such places as Canada, Britain, the Netherlands, Sweden, Denmark, Japan, France, Spain, Singapore, and Hong Kong. Everyone in the industrialized world has made the same strides.

Nevertheless, the improvement is clearly cause for celebration. But why on earth should the rate have fallen so much in such a short time? Why in 1968 did 66,456 newborns die in their first 28 days of life, and in 1978 only 31,618?

The answer is simple: better premie care. Cut premie mortality, and you make a tremendous dent in the total infant death rate. This is because prematurity is by far the biggest killer of newborns. While preterm children represent just 6.8 percent of all live births in the United States, they account for almost 75 percent of the neonatal deaths.

It is easier to talk about prematurity than it is to define it. In 1961 the World Health Organization adopted the following formulation: any child born prior to the 37th week of pregnancy and weighing less than 2,500 grams (5 lbs 8 oz) is considered to be "premature." That sounds plain enough. But it doesn't cover a significant number of full-term babies that, for various reasons, are likewise born too small. They, too, face an increased danger of illness and death.

Physicians therefore prefer to use the catch-all term *low-birthweight* infant. But this has shortcomings of its own. It tells you nothing about the gestational age. To get around these difficulties, a rather complicated system has been devised. Birthweight is considered in tandem with age in assessing a child's risk. Thus, children are either small for gestational age (SGA), appropriate for gestational age (AGA), or large for gestational age (LGA). If a preterm infant is born, say, 34 weeks along, but weighs no more than the average baby of 30 weeks' gestation, then the child is SGA. If the infant weighs what it should for 34 weeks, it is AGA. And so on. For purposes of prognosis, the SGA baby is considered at greater risk than the AGA child because for one reason or another it was not growing well in the womb, an ominous sign.

Any baby, however, that is born before the 37th week is at greater risk of death or serious handicap because its organs have not had time to mature. A fetus grows according to a strict timetable. Each week brings a new milestone. Alveoli, for example, the tiny grapelike air sacs inside the lung through which oxygen and carbon dioxide are exchanged, don't appear until about the 24th week. The brain doesn't begin to develop surface convolutions until the 25th week. Myelin, the protective insulation of the brain's nerve fibers that ensures rapid and efficient transmission of nerve impulses, doesn't begin to form until the 28th week. Body fat doesn't accumulate until the 26th week. The eyelids don't open until the 26th week. Bone marrow doesn't become the main site for blood formation until the 28th week. A fine body hair called lanugo, which protects the fetus from the amniotic fluid, doesn't disappear until the 35th week. The list becomes quite long.

If the fetus is interrupted by birth at any point in this process, the child will be unfinished, like a house that still needs drywalling and siding. Like that house, its body wasn't meant to be lived in quite yet. The baby may have fused eyelids, unformed genitalia, and stiff, balky lungs. It may not be capable of sucking or swallowing, reflexes that develop in the third trimester of pregnancy, and it may have long spells in which it "forgets" to breathe, a condition called apnea. The child will be vulnerable to a host of calamities, including brain damage, respiratory trouble, seizures, infections, hypoglycemia, kidney failure, hypothermia, acidosis, fluid imbalance, bowel infarction, anemia, and circulatory collapse.

Whether the baby survives depends on how much it has already matured, how well it adapts, and how much high technology the doctors have available. The child's body will continue to develop according to the blueprint, but only if the hospital is able to simulate the warmth and nurture of the womb for however long it takes.

Some neonatologists would add a fourth, less tangible factor in survival: the child's innate constitution. There has to be something to account for why some very small premies managed to pull through, long before medicine had any tools to help them. Winston Churchill, for example, was born seven weeks premature in 1873, the dark ages of neonatal medicine. Yet he not only survived but lived to be a galumphing, cigar-smoking old man. Other celebrated premies of the past include Sir Isaac Newton, Charles Darwin, Voltaire, Napoleon, and Victor Hugo, whose most famous literary character was the victim of a grotesque defect of birth.

No one knows why, but girls make stronger premies than boys, and blacks are hardier than whites. Hence, a black female is the best candidate for survival. The average mortality rate at 1,000 grams is 46 percent for a white male, 39 percent for a black male, 37 percent for a white female, and only 31 percent for a black female.

This advantage to blacks is a fortunate accident of nature, because in the United States, at least, blacks are twice as likely to be born too small as whites. This has more to do with sociology than physiology. Women from low income groups tend to have more low-weight babies, a reality that reflects diminished nutrition, less access to good prenatal care, and the higher incidence of teenage pregnancy (adolescent women are more likely to bear premature children).

This socioeconomic link is so strong that during the recession of 1981, when thousands were thrown out of work, the state of Illinois, for example, recorded a sharp increase in the number of low-birthweight births, reversing a 20-year downward trend.

The double doors burst open with sudden force, and a pocket of people come rushing in. They are shepherding something along in their midst, like a scrummaging rugby team.

"Where does he go?" the point man shouts. He is a tall, tired-looking doctor whose white gown floats behind his advancing form. The gown has scorch marks from careless laundering.

"Right here," a nurse beckons.

The protective wedge of bodies opens to reveal the prize, a small Plexiglas case on wheels, moving too fast for anyone to see what's inside. Swiftly, it is rolled into the corner of the intensive-care unit, where a nurse, with sure hands, reaches inside and lifts out two or so pounds of naked red baby. The child, born 48 hours earlier, is gaunt and limp, with eyes that address nothing and limbs that resemble small sticks. It looks incredibly old. The nurse puts the baby on a scale. Then she lays it on a warming table and places a plastic oxygen hood over its head. Another nurse swiftly appliqués its skin with sensors.

"How was he doing on the way down?" one of the doctors crowding around asks.

"Not very good. Grunting a little."

Grunting is a symptom of respiratory distress. Earlier this morning the boy began breathing with difficulty at the small community hospital where he was born. The hospital grew concerned because it wasn't equipped to give sophisticated life support. Wasting no time, it telephoned its sister hospital in the city, which has what is called a level III, or intensive-care, nursery. The city hospital immediately dispatched a transport team to bring the child in by a specially fitted ambulance. The 50-mile trip took 40 minutes.

"Color's not so hot," muses the assistant chief of neonatology, a man named Loggins. "How were his Apgars?"

"Pretty good," replies a second-year resident. "They said he was fine until right before they called. I don't think they know too much out there, though. They struck me as a bunch of yahoos."

"You're a real charitable guy," remarks Loggins.

"Okay. Let's see how old you are, fella," says the resident, whose name is Heineman. He begins to employ on the child what is known as the Dubowitz test in order to determine its gestational age. Such things as posture, nipple size, ear development, and scrotal folds are all clues to a baby's maturity. They are graded according to a scoring system.

"I get 29 weeks," Heineman announces, "más o menos." He makes a waggling gesture with his hand.

Loggins appraises the dusky infant. "I still don't like his color," he says. "He's getting bluer."

Heineman pokes the child's tiny leg. His finger leaves a white spot that doesn't regain hue. "You're right," he agrees. "His perfusion's lousy."

"How are his gases?" Loggins asks a nurse. She checks a monitor. "Dropping," she says.

"You want me to bag him?" the resident asks urgently.

The older pediatrician nods. He is listening to the child's heart through a stethoscope. Heineman quickly takes away the oxygen hood and slips a plastic mask over the boy's face. Then he begins to give him 100 percent oxygen by means of a hand ventilator, a black rubber bladder that is squeezed like a bicycle horn. Heineman looks up at Loggins expectantly.

"Heart rate's still bad," reports the neonatologist from his listening post. "Keep bagging."

For nearly a minute Heineman continues to squeeze the air bladder until, slowly, the child's color begins to return to normal.

"Ah," observes Loggins. "He's pinking up."

"He sure took his own sweet time," Heineman says.

"The kid has definitely got some problems," says Loggins. "I think we better intubate him and get him on a ventilator."

"Right," concurs Heineman.

"Intubation" is the process of placing an endotracheal tube into the child's airway. It is through this tube that air from a ventilator is conveyed to the lungs. Heineman shines a light down the child's throat, taking a sighting preliminary to steering in the plastic catheter. It will be no easy task. A premie's trachea is only the size of a pencil.

"Go for it," commands Loggins, and Heineman begins to slip the tube down. After wrestling with it for a long moment, he pulls it out. "Couldn't quite get it," he says.

The baby's color has begun to go bad again. "Uh, oh," Heineman groans. Once more, he throws the mask over the child's face and begins giving him oxygen, squeezing the bag in and out as if handling the bulb on a turkey baster. The child's stomach pops up and down.

Another 30 seconds pass. At length Loggins says, "All right, his color's coming back. Try the tube again."

Heineman shines his light down the tiny throat and, taking the plastic tube in hand, tries to feed it into the trachea a second time. This time he hits a vocal cord with it and has to pull it out. "Damn," he mutters, disgusted with himself.

Again, the baby is turning blue. Out comes the bag. Woosha, woosha, woosha. Woosha, woosha, woosha. Slowly, magically, the child begins to turn pink. It is as if he were a balloon.

"All right, let me try it this time," says Loggins, holding out his hand. Heineman sheepishly hands him the catheter.

Standing over the child, Loggins asks Heineman, "Do you want me to miss once to make you feel good?" Then he flawlessly slides the tube home.

The modern science of premie care, for all of its phenomenal success, possesses rather curious origins. They may be traced to, of all places, Napoleonic France and the carnival midway.

It has long been known that the archenemy of the very premature is the tendency of their lungs to collapse. But until recently no one knew why.

For generations, premies had been threatened with a gradual and painful death as they fought to get air. Their chest would heave and retract, and their breath would come faster and faster. Eventually the child would turn blue and go into shock. It was a pathetic thing to watch.

Those who recovered were often left with neurologic damage because of oxygen deprivation. But the survivors were few, with mortality running to an appalling 75 percent. On autopsy, a strange translucent membrane would be found lining the victims' alveoli. One early researcher named K. Hochheim erroneously assumed that this membrane was the cause, not a symptom, of the children's troubled breathing. Since the membrane reminded him of glass, for which the word is *hyalos* in Greek, he promptly christened the disorder "hyaline membrane disease." The name has persisted for 80 years, holding its own against a later, more accurate substitute, "respiratory distress syndrome." But whatever alias it goes by, the disease is the number-one killer of newborns, responsible for 30 percent of all neonatal deaths. At one time it took as many as 25,000 lives annually in the United States alone.

The mystery of RDS continued to baffle medicine until the close of the 1950s, even though, in retrospect, the answer was there all along. It had been supplied by two men, separated by 120 years in time.

The first of these gentlemen was the French astronomer and mathematician Pierre-Simon de Laplace, who in the year 1805 put before the French Academy an ingenious theory. Laplace's theory had nothing to do with breathing. In fact, humankind had only learned the purpose of its lungs a quarter of a century earlier, thanks to the chemist Antoine Lavoisier. In 1777 Lavoisier had reported that air in a closed jar containing a bird showed a decreasing amount of life-sustaining gas he called *oxygène* and an increasing amount of a gas that was absorbed by soda lime (later designated carbon dioxide.) Laplace, however, was unconcerned with lungs. The matter he brought before the academy was his theory of surface tension.

Surface tension, for those of us who slept through physics, is the tendency of a liquid's surface to constrict. Why does it do so? Molecular attraction. Imagine a molecule in the heart of a glass of water. It is attracted by all the other water molecules above, around, and below it. Since these attractions are equal, they cancel each other out and the molecule stays in place. But a surface molecule has no water molecules above it, only molecules of air, which attract it very little. Instead, it is drawn to the center of the liquid by the water molecules below.

This is why a bubble pops. The bubble's "skin" is really surface molecules eager to reunite with the liquid. It also explains how a household detergent works. Think of dirt as a prisoner of a layer of grease, whose surface tension won't let it escape. The detergent reduces this surface tension, allowing the dirt to float away—at the same time increasing the life span of millions of tiny air bubbles, which we call suds.

What does this have to do with babies who can't get enough oxygen? It's 1929 now, and our second gentleman, a Swiss tuberculosis specialist named Kurt von Neergaard, has published a paper offering a novel explanation of why lungs expand and contract. He contends that something more than the mere elasticity of the lung fiber is involved. According to von Neergaard's reasoning, each of the alveoli in the lung is constantly bathed with moisture from water vapor in the air. These alveoli sit at the end of the bronchial tree, inflating upon each breath, much like soap bubbles on the bowl of a bubble pipe. On breathing out, said von Neergaard, the wet walls of the alveoli attract each other, and the alveoli tend to collapse. In other words, surface tension is at work.

He went further. It occurred to him that if unchecked, this process would interfere with breathing. The alveoli would fight to stay closed, making it twice as hard to draw air in next time. To appreciate the strength of this bond, try to pull apart two panes of glass separated by a film of water. Von Neergaard decided there must be a chemical agent in the lungs whose job it is to reduce surface tension along the alveoli, keeping them partially open between breaths. Such substances are known in chemistry as surface-active agents, or surfactants.

Unfortunately, von Neergaard was far ahead of his time. His speculations on pulmonary surfactant went ignored for two decades. "As a result," remarked the late respiratory specialist Dr. Julius Comroe, who wrote a fascinating account of this research, "his work, which could have led to saving lives of premature babies in the 1930s, suffered [its own] premature death."

Ironically, when these theories were at last taken out of mothballs, it was under the sponsorship of the Canadian Chemical Warfare Laboratories, the British Chemical Defense Experimental Establishment, and the U.S. Army Chemical Center. As one might guess, these agencies had little interest in the noble cause of salvaging premature babies. What they wanted to know was how to protect soldiers' lungs from the ravages of chemical warfare.

A Canadian anatomist named Charles Macklin, who had been researching lung pathology under a defense contract, was the first to echo what von Neergaard had said a quarter of a century earlier. In a 1954 paper in the British medical journal *Lancet,* Macklin hypothesized that a thin mucoid film covers the walls of the alveoli, maintaining "a constant favourable alveolar surface tension."

The British biophysicist R. E. Pattle was the next to address the subject. Pattle's military bosses were interested in the way a particularly nasty war gas called phosgene does its dirty work. Phosgene kills by causing a bubbly foam to form in the victim's alveoli, bringing on suffocation. It intrigued Pattle that no matter what antifoam he tried in laboratory rabbits, the phosgene bubbles would not go away, as obdient bubbles should. He concluded in a 1955 article in the magazine *Nature* that some "insoluble protein layer" in the lungs is present to "abolish" surface tension.

A year later the scene shifted to the U.S. Army's medical research laboratories in Edgewood, Maryland, where Dr. John Clements was investigating how to counteract nerve gas poisoning. Clements decided to see whether he could actually measure respiratory surface tension, using extracts of rat, cat, and dog lungs. His findings: surface tension dropped dramatically whenever the tissue was compressed, as it would be when the animal exhaled. The inference was inescapable. There was indeed some unknown surfactant in the lungs, and it came into play on the exhale, propping the alveoli open for the next breath.

Into the picture now came a young Boston pediatrician named Mary Ellen Avery, who had herself recently recovered from tuberculosis and was keenly interested in finding out why premies couldn't breathe. She and a colleague, Dr. Jere Mead, decided to adapt all of the above research to the study of babies with respiratory distress syndrome. Was there something different about a premie's lungs that caused them to collapse between breaths?

Working in the pathology lab of Boston's Lying-In Hospital, Avery and Mead compared the lung tissue of 9 children who had died of RDS with that of 47 infants, children, and adults who had died of other causes. Among those 47 were 9 premature infants of under 1,200 grams. What the two researchers found was striking. In every single case the surface tension in the lungs of the RDS babies, and the babies under 1,200 grams, was higher than in the other subjects; it was typically three to four times higher.

The conclusion was clear. A premature infant's lungs were missing something that everybody else's lungs had—surfactant. Without it, a premie's respiration became von Neergaard's nightmare, where, with nothing to break the surface tension, the alveoli deflated with every breath. It was the immense strain of having to force the alveoli open each time that was killing these babies.

Copies of the AMA's *American Journal of Diseases of Children* do not exactly roll off the presses each month to be gobbled up by the multitudes. But no issue of *Time* or *Newsweek* ever had more lasting impact than did the May 1959 *Journal* that carried the Avery-Mead findings. The reaction in the scientific community was immediate, one might even say thunderous. The world of neonatal medicine was never to be the same.

The race began to isolate surfactant and identify its chemical composition. It was disgusting work. Researchers had to wash out beef and sheep lungs and harvest the thick white foam, which according to one of them, "required a big sink and hipboots." But it paid off. By 1962 surfactant had been shown to be a phospholipid, a greasy, natural body substance containing fatty acids and phosphoric acids.

Soon it was found that surfactant, a white, waxy compound with a fishy odor, doesn't even begin to coat the fetus's alveoli until around the 30th week of gestation and that it isn't until the 33d week, only a month or so before term, that it is produced in any major amount. At last, here was the answer to an age-old question: Why does the incidence of RDS suddenly fall off in premies born after the 33d week?

Just knowing these things about surfactant wasn't enough to save lives, however. President Kennedy and his wife had to stand by helplessly in 1963 as their premature son died of RDS. What was needed, doctors proclaimed, was a surfactant substitute that could be added to a newborn's lungs, the way antifreeze can be added to a car.

It would be nice to report that such an elixir now exists. Unfortunately, a long and frustrating research campaign has yielded only spotty results.

The original goal was a synthetic surfactant that could be delivered by aerosol spray. But years of trial and error met with little or no success. Some researchers subsequently turned to naturally obtained surfactants, which appeared to be more promising. In 1978 a team led by Drs. Forrest Adams, Bernard Towers, and Tetsuro Fujiwara at the UCLA School of Medicine showed that lamb surfactant dripped directly into the tracheas of premature lambs prevented RDS. As they were about to test the concept in humans, however, the National Institutes of Health unaccountably cut off their $98,000 grant, and the team had to disband. Fujiwara went back to Japan, where in 1979–80 he successfully injected a mixture of cow and synthetic surfactant into the windpipes of human RDS victims, noting dramatic improvement. A similar experiment was reported in 1983 by a Toronto team led by Dr. J. A. Smyth.

On the other hand, doctors at the University of California, San Diego, have pursued a different tack: using human surfactant isolated from the amniotic fluid of full-term babies. They believe surfactant from the same species lowers the risk of immunological reaction. The experimenters, under the direction of Dr. Louis Gluck and Dr. Mikka Hallman, of Finland, reported in 1983 that their technique had reduced RDS symptoms in eight of nine infants under 1,200 grams. Meanwhile, doctors at the University of California, San Francisco, have never quite given up on synthetic surfactant. They are currently testing an improved version.

Researchers do seem to be closing in on the answer. But the main issues obviously remain to be settled. Which is the best surfactant—human, animal, or synthetic? What are the long-range side effects? How do you administer it, by aerosol spray or by catheter? Does supplying a baby with exogenous surfactant inhibit development of his own? It seems safe to say it will be many more years before these problems are all sorted out.

Though the knowledge gained from Avery and Mead's discovery did not lead to instant panaceas, it did inspire the single most important breakthrough in the treatment of RDS to date: continuous positive airway pressure, or CPAP, as it is called. Throughout the 1960s the standard RDS therapy was to introduce oxygen into a child's lungs only on the inhale. As we've seen, however, the central problem in RDS is the collapse of the alveoli on the exhale. Logic tells us that anything that keeps the alveoli open between breaths would be helpful. Or so it seemed to George Gregory, a young anesthesiologist at the University of California, San Francisco. One night in 1969 Gregory decided to try saving a dying baby by keeping its lungs partially distended with air during the entire breathing cycle. It worked splendidly and the child recovered. Enthusiastic, he tried it again and again on more babies, with the same salutary results. By 1971 Gregory and his UCSF colleagues were able to make the following report in the journal *Pediatric Research:* whereas before 1969 the hospital's survival rate for babies with RDS who weighed under 1,500 grams was only 11 percent, with the aid of Gregory's new continuous pressure system, survival had soared to 83 percent! Hospitals all over Europe and North America stampeded to use CPAP.

CPAP is not mechanical ventilation. It is administered either by a plastic hood over the baby's face or by a nasal or endotracheal tube, and it is designed to facilitate, rather than take over, the baby's normal breathing. For babies so sick they require a machine to do their breathing, CPAP has a counterpart called PEEP—positive end expiratory pressure. The object is the same; to prevent alveolar collapse between breaths by keeping up a positive pressure on the lungs.

These two methods, CPAP and PEEP, have almost single-handedly brought the mortality rate from RDS down from 70 percent to 20 percent—all within the past 10 to 12 years.

How does the carnival midway we mentioned earlier fit in? For that, we have to examine the life of one Martin Couney, who, if you are looking for implausible historical figures, is the genuine article.

Dr. Couney (1870–1950) was an Alsatian physican with a gift for— how shall we say?—showmanship. As was the practice in those days, he started his career as an apprentice, taking up with the great French obstetrician Pierre-Constant Budin, today recognized as the father of neonatology. Budin, in turn, had been the disciple of Dr. Etienne Tarnier, the inventor of the incubator.

The French had pioneered the salvage of sick and premature new-borns, largely in reaction to the vast number of fatalities suffered in the Franco-Prussian War of 1870–71. It was as if every spark of life, no matter how faint, had to be fanned. There was a practical motive besides mere sentiment. The French were only too aware that the hated Germans, who had humiliated them and seized Alsace-Lor-raine, had a bigger population and a higher birthrate. If France had any hope of recovering her provinces, it would be by once again mak-ing herself strong. "France will have but one thought," wrote Victor Hugo passionately, "to reconstitute her forces, gather her energy, nourish her sacred anger, raise her young generation to form an army of the whole people. . . . Then one day she will be irresistible. Then she will take back Alsace-Lorraine."

It is unlikely that Dr. Tarnier had sacred anger on his mind on the day in 1878 when he attended an agricultural show, but he came away so impressed by some new chick hatchers he'd seen that he immedi-ately asked a local manufacturer to build him an incubator for human infants based on the same principle. Three years later he introduced the finished product, with its easily regulated warmth settings. He billed it as a *couveuse pour enfants nouveau-nés*. For the first time in history, medicine had a way to keep premies' body temperature con-stant and perhaps save their lives. French ingenuity did not end there. Other doctors invented a brilliant tube-feeding technique, called gavage, for newborns too weak to nurse.

By the time Couney signed on with Budin in 1891, French nurser-ies were having gratifying success with these new approaches. But Budin was a missionary. He wanted to bring the message to the rest of Europe. In 1896 he therefore dispatched his student Couney to the World Exposition in Berlin to demonstrate the care and feeding of premature newborns. Couney took to his task with relish. He set up his *couveuses* in a pavilion and induced the Berlin Charity Hospital to "lend" him six live premies to put on display. The exhibit, which Couney entitled "Kinderbrutanstalt" ("Child Hatchery"), was a great hit, outdrawing the Congo Village and the Tyrolean Yodelers.

The next summer, Couney took his exhibit to London's Victorian Era Exhibition. But English hospitals refused to lend him any premies. Hard-pressed, he returned to Paris, where Budin arranged to get him babies from a foundling home. A triumphant Couney sailed back across the English Channel with three wicker baskets full of premature infants warmed by hot-water bottles. Again, the public swarmed to see the fragile babies in their futuristic incubators. The exhibit drew 3,000 visitors in a single day. The English medical journal *Lancet* fretted that unscrupulous hucksters might now flock to display miniature infants "just as they might . . . marionettes, fat women, or any sort of catch-penny monstrosity."

Undeterred by such criticism, and clearly bitten by the entrepreneurial bug, Couney took his show across the Atlantic. He turned up in Omaha in the summer of 1898 for the Trans-Mississippi Exposition. Then it was back to France for the Paris Exposition of 1900, and on to Buffalo in 1901 for the Pan-American Exposition. In 1903 he finally settled down in New York's Coney Island. Over the next 40 summers Martin Couney would exhibit more than 5,000 "incubator babies" to a gawking public, making side trips to such places as Denver, Mexico City, Rio de Janiero, and Chicago.

The dubious ethics of displaying premies like so many India-rubber men never seemed to abash Couney. To him, it was public education, though undeniably laden with schmaltz. His barkers, who included a striving young actor named Archibald Leach who later gained fame as Cary Grant, used to end their pitch by shouting, "Don't pass the babies by!" His nurses were instructed to put more clothes on the infants to exaggerate the illusion of smallness. And his redoubtable chief nurse, Madame Recht, is said to have frequently slipped her diamond ring over the babies' wrists to show the crowds how thin the children were. Couney's booth at the Chicago World's Fair of 1933 drew more customers than any exhibit except that of the fan dancer Sally Rand. At the New York World's Fair of 1939 the good doctor managed an operation that included 5 wet nurses, 15 registered nurses, scores of babies, and a U-shaped incubator building designed by the architectural firm of Skidmore and Owings.

But despite his P. T. Barnum exterior, Couney always considered himself a man of science. His methods of newborn care were state-of-the-art, and, as bizarre as it might sound, he played a pivotal role in the development of premie care in the United States. For it was during one of his side trips to Chicago in 1914 that he met a young doctor named Julius Hess. Hess, assigned by the local medical society to oversee Couney's exhibit at White City amusement park, was profoundly affected by the experience. Less than 10 years later he was to found the nation's first premature nursery, at Chicago's Sarah Morris Hospital. Every single innovation that Hess included in his new nursery, he had learned at Martin Couney's knee.

"You want to do the honors?" Heineman, the senior resident, asks.

"Sure. I'm gonna have to learn sometime," shrugs a first-year resident named Kennedy.

On the warming table before them is the premie who was brought in by transport a few hours ago. His condition has worsened, and they have decided to "put a line in him," slang for threading a catheter into one of his arteries through the stump of his umbilical cord. The catheter, a very thin, flexible tube, will be left in place indefinitely to provide the staff with an instant method of obtaining blood samples, taking blood pressure, and administering fluids and electrolytes.

A nurse swabs the child's abdomen with a 1 percent iodine solution and places a piece of tape at the base of the cord to control any bleeding. Then Kennedy begins to tie a ribbon around the umbilicus to make it stand up. It has the color and consistency of an oriental rice noodle.

From a sterile tray, Kennedy takes up a scalpel and the catheter. He must cut the umbilical cord on a bevel, to expose the artery for insertion. It's like preparing electrical wire for splicing.

"I don't cut it there, do I?" Kennedy asks uncertainly.

"Sure. You cut it right there," Heineman replies.

Reassured, Kennedy slices off the top of the umbilicus. So far, so good. Working carefully, Heineman fits a tweezers into the tiny artery opening and by parting the tweezer blades, dilates the hole. "All yours," he says, and Kennedy goes to work. He slides the catheter into the artery, causing the baby to flinch visibly. Slowly he feeds out more catheter, but it goes in only about three inches before it stalls. Kennedy looks perplexed. Withdrawing it slightly, he pushes it forward again. "Nope," he says, "won't go in."

"That's all right. That happens," says Heineman. "Try again."

Once more Kennedy inserts the catheter while Heineman dilates the artery. Again the baby flinches, and again the catheter stops.

"It's okay," Heineman says soothingly. "There's a lot of turns it has to make in there. It's like a drainpipe."

Before he can try a third time, Kennedy must slice off more umbilicus to get a fresh opening to work with. Having done so, he tries again to insert the catheter. "Uh, uh," he moans, frustrated. "It just won't go."

Off comes more umbilical cord. Then Kennedy makes a fourth attempt, and a fifth. Each time the baby tenses. Each time the catheter stops.

On the sixth try Heineman says, "That's it, I think you have it this time." Kennedy feeds the catheter higher and higher into the artery, like a plumber's auger. He wears a look of triumph. But then suddenly the catheter stops. "Son of a bitch," he says.

On the seventh try there is hardly any umbilicus left to cut. Kennedy fails again and gives up in exhaustion. The baby has begun crying bitterly. Tears are streaming down his face.

At this moment, the chief neonatologist happens to come by. He announces that he will show both Kennedy and Heineman an advanced technique for umbilical catheterization. And he indeed works the catheter in almost completely before it once again stalls.

They finally decide to switch to a radial arterial line, a catheter in the arm instead of the navel. It is less desirable but the only option at this point. "We have a saying," remarks Heineman. "If you can't get the procedure done, then he probably didn't need it anyway."

Surface tension, surfactant, CPAP, and PEEP. Amazing as these discoveries about premies were, they would not have amounted to much if there had been no place to put them to use. But in 1961–62 pioneers like Drs. Henry Levison and Maria Delivoria-Papadopoulos, of the Hospital for Sick Children in Toronto, Dr. Robert Usher, at the Royal Victoria Hospital in Montreal, and Dr. Leonard Strang, at University College Hospital in London, began to experiment with the idea of the neonatal intensive-care unit (NICU). Credit for opening the first NICU in the United States is often awarded to Dr. Mildred Stahlman, of Vanderbilt Medical Center in Nashville, Tennessee, who phased in her unit in 1962–63. Other progressive institutions soon followed suit, including Yale–New Haven Hospital, Stanford University Hospital, Boston Children's Hospital, the University of Pennsylvania, the University of California at San Francisco, Hammersmith Hospital in London, and the Johns Hopkins University.

It would be a mistake, however, to think of the openings of these units as clearly demarcated events, complete with luncheons and ribbon cuttings. The transition from premie nursery to NICU was in fact evolutionary, inspired by parallel developments in adult medicine. For all practical purposes, the first adult intensive-care unit had been established in 1959 by Dr. Max Harry Weil at Los Angeles County General Hospital. It was followed in 1962 by the first coronary-care unit, founded at Bethany Hospital in Kansas City. Discerning pediatricians took a long look at these models and said, If the concept works for older patients, why not apply it to children?

For more than 40 years premie nurseries had hewn to the pattern established by Pierre Budin in Europe and Julius Hess in the United States. Highly skilled nurses, such as those trained by Hess's chief nurse, Evelyn Lundeen, had primary control of the units. Doctors were essentially outsiders. The tiny patients were stowed in warm glass incubators and handled as little as possible. Feedings were often postponed for several days after birth because a delay was thought to be therapeutic. The children were kept strictly isolated in fanatically sterilized surroundings that were off-limits to everyone, even parents. But despite these precautions, a distressing number of babies either died or sustained handicap.

Attempts to apply higher technology had produced catastrophic results. In the 1940s and 1950s it became increasingly fashionable to give large amounts of oxygen to premies with RDS. At the same time a mysterious epidemic of infant blindness began to be observed, almost exclusively in the better-equipped medical centers. The new illness was called retrolental fibroplasia, or RLF. Unknown before its description in 1942 by Dr. Theodore Terry of Boston, RLF had by 1950 become the leading cause of childhood blindness in the United States. By 1953 it had blinded 10,000 children, 7,000 of them in the United States.

Investigators tried desperately to find the source of the disease. Then, in 1951–52, a handful of physicians, notably Mary Crosse and Philip Evans, of Birmingham, England, and Arnall Patz and Leroy Hoeck, of Washington, D.C., reported they had traced the disease to an embarrassing cause: medicine's very efforts to keep small babies alive. Evidence indicated that high concentrations of oxygen were damaging the children's retinas. It wasn't until 1954, however, when the results of a national cooperative study among 18 hospitals were tabulated, that oxygen became widely acknowledged to be the villain.

The disease is insidious. Too much oxygen in a premie's first few days of life makes the immature blood vessels of its retina constrict and die. (In a full-term infant or an older person, these vessels are completely developed and immune to RLF.) When the child is later returned to breathing room air, the blood vessels grow back in wild profusion. Swelling and scarring may follow, which can pull the retina loose. If it reaches this stage, irreversible blindness is the result, a complication that can set in as late as adolescence.

Fortunately, only an estimated 25 percent of the cases are that severe. In milder episodes the injury may repair itself, or the child may be left with a wide range of lesser visual disturbances. Vitamin E, given while the child is on oxygen, has been found to ease symptoms, though it has been linked with infant deaths when ' .en intravenously. And new laser surgical techniques can correct some intermediate cases of damage.

When RLF's source was confirmed, it occasioned great breast-beating within the medical profession. Hospitals began turning down the settings on their oxygen tanks. But drastically reduced oxygen levels posed a threat of a different kind: brain damage and death. Throughout the 1950s, premies displayed horrifyingly high rates of neurologic illness. One study of very low birthweight children born in that era found a 60 percent incidence of significant handicap, including retardation and cerebral palsy. How much of that tragic waste was due to anoxia resulting from the administration of too little oxygen has never been precisely ascertained.

In any case, by the year 1963 things were finally coming together. The recent advent of the mechanical ventilator had enabled doctors to provide controlled levels of oxygen high enough to help the infant but not so high as to trigger RLF. Mary Ellen Avery and Jere Mead had identified insufficiency of surfactant as the cause of respiratory distress syndrome. The venerable Dr. Clement Smith, of Boston, had updated his classic text on the physiology of newborns, which had become the bible of the trade. And, entirely by accident, a major cause of brain damage in premies, hyperbilirubinemia, had all but been eliminated five years earlier.

Hyperbilirubinemia is a jaundice condition to which the premature are notably susceptible. Their systems are unable to adequately break down bilirubin, a waste product of the death of red blood cells. If too much bilirubin accumulates in the body, it causes kernicterus, a toxic brain reaction that can result in many disorders, including retardation, cerebral palsy, and hearing loss. One afternoon the nurse in charge of the premature nursery at the General Hospital in Rochford, England, noticed that jaundice in babies faded after they had been lying in direct sunlight. She told her superior, Dr. R. J. Cremer, about it, and he and his colleagues began testing out her observation. First they put children in the sun. The infants' yellowness disappeared. Then the researchers found that it even worked when you put them under an artificial lamp. Laboratory tests revealed that light of a certain wavelength breaks bilirubin down.

Cremer published his findings in the May 1958 issue of *Lancet*. The reaction was striking. With great speed, the gospel of phototherapy spread from the small seaside town of Rochford to hospitals throughout the world. As is true of so many premie breakthroughs, the treatment was put into general use even before adequate controlled testing had been done. Today you can walk into any neonatal ICU and see infants lying under surreal blue lamps, their eyes swathed in bandages to protect them from the intense fluorescent light.

With the emergence of these exciting insights, the NICU was an idea whose time had come. The efficacy of housing all sick babies in one unit, with constant nursing and the latest in specialty equipment, quickly demonstrated itself. From 1968 to 1970 the Royal Women's Hospital in Melbourne, Australia, conducted a study, one of an arguably unethical nature, in which half the infants were given intensive care and half were given routine care on a random basis. More than one-third of the routine-care group died. But less than one-fifth died in the intensive-care category.

By 1973 most of the larger hospitals had already installed NICUs. This dovetailed nicely with a forward-looking piece of social policy that was then coming into its own—the regionalization of health care. In the middle 1970s large parts of the United States and Canada were divided up into a grid, the purpose being to reduce costly duplication of services among hospitals. Each region was to include what was called a level III center, a hospital with a neonatal nursery capable of caring for the most critically ill newborns. Institutions that were less well equipped but could still deal with many neonatal complications were designated intermediate, or level II, centers. Smaller, generally rural hospitals that were geared only to the needs of infants without complications were called level I. Vital to the whole plan was emergency transport, by which the sickest babies would be conveyed by ambulance and helicopter to the level III center. In some western states, where the level III center might cover an area hundreds of miles wide, fixed-wing aircraft were to be used. Today, the Children's Hospital in Denver transports 1,600 babies a year from 10 states to its level III center, utilizing two leased King-Air planes. Does it work? In 1960 Colorado had one of the highest infant mortality rates, ranking 45th among the states. Today it has one of the lowest, ranking in the top 10.

Just as neonatal centers were getting established, certain farsighted practitioners proposed taking the idea a step further. In 1969 Dr. P. R. Swyer, of Toronto, advocated the regionalization of high-risk obstetrical care. Why wait until the child is born, he reasoned, to begin aggressive treatment? If one could identify potential complications prior to birth, one could treat the mother beforehand. She could be brought to the level III hospital weeks in advance of delivery, a far safer procedure than transporting her sick infant by van or plane afterward. Then, during birth, the fetus could constantly be monitored with the latest equipment and given emergency care as it was needed. Once the baby was born, getting it to the ICU would involve only a short trip down the hall.

In 1971 the American Medical Association threw its weight behind such a "perinatal" approach. (*Peri* is from the Greek, meaning "around";

hence *perinatal* means "around birth.") So did the March of Dimes Birth Defects Foundation. At the same time, the Robert Wood Johnson Foundation was supporting a series of field tests to determine whether perinatal regionalization was effective. The foundation, established by General Robert W. Johnson, the power behind Johnson & Johnson, the health products giant, had underwritten demonstration perinatal programs in a number of states. The early results looked impressive. It was therefore inevitable that by 1975 many of the nation's new neonatal centers had reconstituted themselves as perinatal centers. And in 1976, only a decade after having welcomed the specialty of neonatology, the medical establishment certified perinatology as well.

What are perinatologists, and who are their patients? Perinatologists are obstetricians who have taken advanced training in high-risk obstetrics, just as neonatologists are basically pediatricians who limit themselves to newborns. Mothers considered to be at high risk include women with a history of miscarriage or premature labor, women with diabetes or high blood pressure, women carrying two or more children, and women whose fetuses have somehow been compromised in utero.

The tools of the perinatologist are impressive manifestations of technology. Birth defects can be detected and some of them corrected in the womb. A child's vital signs can be monitored throughout labor to guard against birth trauma. And we now possess medicinal agents that can prevent prematurity. The preventive agents belong to a family of drugs called beta-adrenergics; the most widely known is ritodrine. These drugs forestall premature labor by inhibiting contractions of the uterus. They do have side effects, and to work best, they must be given when the contractions first begin. But thanks to a series of scientific coups in the early 1970s, even a short delay of labor may be enough to save the child.

The first of these startling developments was the discovery that one can actually tell, while the child is still inside the uterus, how mature or immature its lungs are, so that now we can accurately predict whether the child will develop respiratory distress syndrome. This became possible when researchers learned that the fetus emits lung secretions into the amniotic fluid. Using this knowledge, Dr. Louis Gluck, of the University of California at San Diego, devised a prenatal lung maturity test in 1971. Gluck knew that until 30 weeks of pregnancy, the amniotic fluid contains more of a phospholipid called sphingomyelin than of another phospholipid, named lecithin, which is a key component of surfactant. From 30 to 32 weeks the two are about equal.

After 32 weeks the lecithin concentration exceeds that of sphingo-myelin. The higher this L/S ratio, the more surfactant a fetus has, and, as we've seen, it is surfactant that prevents RDS.

But Gluck's test was complicated. Wasn't there a simpler way? In 1973 a San Francisco team headed by Dr. John Clements reported that the surfactant level can be determined by just adding alcohol to the amniotic fluid and shaking it up in a test tube. If a foam forms on top and doesn't disappear for at least 15 minutes, then surfactant is present, rescuing the bubbles from surface tension.

This is all ingenious enough. But it doesn't do you much good to know a child has immature lungs if you can't do anything about it. Fortunately, a New Zealander named Graham Liggins remedied that. Liggins was a professor of obstetrics at the University of Auckland. He had long subscribed to the theory that hormones from the fetus's adrenal glands tell the mother's body when it's time to go into labor. This he based on the fact that anencephalic babies—that is, children born without brains—tend to be delivered after their due dates. (The brain is the site of the pituitary gland, and it is the pituitary that pre-sumably would activate the adrenal signal to the mother. Without a brain, there's no pituitary.)

It occurred to Liggins to test his theory out by injecting adrenal hormones into lamb fetuses. He wanted to see whether the hormones, called corticosteroids, would cause the ewe to go into premature labor. What he discovered, in the process, was equally as interesting. When the lambs were indeed born prematurely, they showed surfactant lev-els equivalent to those of more developed lambs. The steroid had somehow matured their lungs overnight!

But would it work in humans? Liggins and his colleague, R. N. Howie, decided to carry out a controlled trial at the National Women's Hos-pital in Auckland. They took 282 mothers experiencing premature delivery, and after slowing labor down, injected them with a steroid called betamethasone. The results? Of babies under 32 weeks in ges-tation, who had received the drug for at least 24 hours before birth, only 12 percent developed RDS. Of the control group, 70 percent acquired the disease. There was no doubt about it: administering ste-roids was like putting lungs on fast forward.

Liggins published his findings in 1972, adding a crucial weapon to perinatology's arsenal. With a simple "shake" test, the perinatologist could now tell which youngsters were likely to develop RDS. Then, by slowing the mother's labor down for as little as 24 to 48 hours, he could speed up the infant's lung growth with betamethasone.

If the 1970s were good to the perinatologist, they also broadened the neonatologist's hand. A new method of intravenous feeding was developed that was straight out of science fiction. Hyperalimentation, as it was called, represented a quantum leap over the quaint glucose solutions of the 1960s. It sought nothing less than the total nutrition of the infant, providing a complete liquid diet of fats, proteins, and carbohydrates, with vitamins and minerals thrown in. The mixture, a sort of amino acid cocktail, is infused via a Silastic catheter that is surgically implanted into the child's superior vena cava, the large vein just above the heart.

Hyperalimentation enables doctors to bypass the digestive tract indefinitely, for years, if necessary. Hence, it has proven indispensable in the fight against a baffling new disease called necrotizing enterocolitis. This life-threatening condition affects 15 percent of low-birthweight children, attacking the intestines, and in some cases requiring the surgical removal of sections of the bowel. The child cannot take any food by mouth for however long the disease lasts.

The past 10 years have also brought refinements in respiratory therapy. Canadian and Swedish hospitals pioneered the use of high-frequency, low-pressure ventilation, in which oxygen is pumped into the child's lungs more than 150 times a minute, four to five times the normal rate. An even newer device is still in pilot form. It works by moving around very small puffs of air, no larger than a cubic centimeter, at a great rate of speed, up to a thousand times a minute. The oxygen is literally swirled into the airway by vibration. The advantage of these techniques is that they place less strain on delicate lung tissues. This minimizes the chance of such high-pressure complications as pneumothorax, in which the alveoli rupture and the escaping air fills the chest, inhibiting further breathing.

Many other developments of the last decade were the empirical result of day-to-day experience in the fledgling intensive-care units. For example, it was only gradually recognized that the best nurse-patient ratio was one-to-one, at least where the sickest newborns were concerned. Similarly, many of the lifesaving techniques and therapies that are commonplace today were the result of trial and error, or perhaps the sudden inspiration of a nurse at three in the morning. Even the sophisticated sensors now in use to measure blood gases, heart rate, body temperature, and the like were dreamed up as research tools, and they worked so well that they were pressed into routine service. It was truly improvisational medicine, with the rules made up as one went along.

Prematurity remains an unknown frontier, however, and just as Dr. Livingstone encountered ever stranger peoples as he pushed on into the African interior, so have neonatologists confronted perplexing new ailments as they have lowered the birthweight threshhold.

There are any number of conditions that are more or less restricted to very low birthweight children. Necrotizing enterocolitis, for one, became common with the improved survival of children under 1,600 grams. But of all these conditions, one stands above the others as the most intractable. It is a primary cause of death and permanent brain damage in the premature, and there is no cure for it. The condition is called intracranial hemorrhage.

Brain bleeds, as they are known, occur in babies of very low birthweight because they have extremely fragile cerebral blood vessels. Most vulnerable is a temporary gelatinous structure in the brain called the germinal matrix. This structure, which is the seedbed of the brain's neurons, or nerve cells, and which disappears around the 35th week of gestation, is rife with tiny, blood-rich capillaries. Adjoining this network of capillaries are the cerebral ventricles, small cavities within the brain that are laid out like Venetian lagoons and that secrete and convey cerebrospinal fluid.

Many things can happen to the brain's delicate vascular system if a baby is born too soon. During birth, complications such as cord compression and detachment of the placenta can produce asphyxia. When the oxygen supply is cut off, not only does brain tissue start to die but the blood vessels dilate and finally burst, causing a hemorrhage and further brain damage. This is analogous to a stroke in adults and is a major factor in cerebral palsy. What can also cause the vessels to rupture is the head trauma of a prolonged vaginal birth. This is one reason so many obstetricians recommend cesarean section for premies.

But the child is not out of the woods after birth. Postnatal hypoxia, respiratory distress syndrome, seizures, and pneumothorax can all endanger the brain's blood vessels. Should the capillaries in the germinal matrix burst, blood seeps into the ventricles, causing what is known as an intraventricular hemorrhage. If enough blood accumulates, the ventricles can swell and blood may infiltrate the brain tissue itself. Grievous brain damage can be inflicted. In addition, hydrocephalus, the dangerous distension of the head caused by an excessive buildup of fluid, sometimes occurs.

Prior to 1976, doctors considered these bleeds to be relatively rare occurrences. Often, unless there is hydrocephalus, the victim shows no outward symptoms. However, studies begun in that year using X-ray CAT scanning techniques showed that bleeds were much more common than had been thought. How common, though, was difficult to say. CAT scanners are bulky, stationary machines, and X-raying every baby's head would have required moving whole NICU populations, ventilators and all, down to the radiology lab, not to mention subjecting already compromised infants to unnecessary radiation. Fortunately, the perfection of portable ultrasound solved the logistical problem. Sonogram pictures could be made right in the NICU, simply by passing a transducer over the child's fontanel, or soft spot. The bleed shows up as white against a gray background.

Ultrasound studies in 1982–83 established the disturbing fact that between 40 to 50 percent of all infants under 1,500 grams have intracranial hemorrhages. The most common are the intraventricular bleeds. The mildest of these are called grade I and II bleeds, and they generally subside without apparent effect. The blood is simply reabsorbed, and the hemorrhage disappears. But the more severe, grade III and grade IV bleeds affect the brain tissue itself and very often—but by no means always—prove disastrous to the child.

A study at the University of New Mexico School of Medicine published in 1983 examined the long-term consequences of intraventricular hemorrhage. A team led by Dr. Lu-Ann Papile started with a research population of 260 infants weighing less than 1,500 grams, 43 percent of whom turned out to have a bleed. A total of 17 percent of the babies with bleeds died in their first year of life compared with 6 percent of those without bleeds.

The Papile team then studied the survivors at the age of one and two years and evaluated them according to standardized neuromotor and intellectual-development scales. Major handicaps were deemed to be paralysis and spasticity (cerebral palsy), blindness, hearing loss, seizure disorder, and serious developmental delay. Such problems as clumsiness or mild disturbances in posture or balance were classified as minor handicaps.

Of children with grade I bleeds, only 9 percent had major handicaps and 42 percent had minor handicaps. Of those with grade II bleeds, 11 percent had major handicaps and 39 percent had minor impairments. This compared favorably, if that is the right word, with the finding for the children who were hemorrhage-free, of whom 11 percent displayed major handicaps and 40 percent minor ones.

But of the grade III children, 35 percent had a major handicap, and 50 percent had minor ones; and of the grade IV children, 76 percent had a major handicap, and 11 percent had minor defects. Almost half had more than one handicap. Although the grade IIIs and grade IVs constituted only 16 percent of the total study population, they accounted for 51 percent of the major handicaps.

Most of these disabled children had received what little treatment is available for hemorrhages, including spinal taps and surgical shunts to drain off the blood. They developed handicaps anyway, pointing up the futility of trying to cure the hemorrhage once it occurs.

Obviously, the answer to this problem is to prevent bleeds before they start. To do this, however, one has to know what causes them, and this is still one of the great mysteries of modern pediatrics.

Some of the most promising research on the subject is being carried out at the Washington University School of Medicine in St. Louis, under the direction of the pediatric neurologist Dr. Joseph Volpe. Volpe has been investigating the role of abrupt changes in the newborn's blood pressure. In theory a sudden rise of blood pressure in the brain could cause the capillaries of the germinal matrix to rupture. On the other hand, a sudden drop in pressure could cause oxygen depletion and bring on a crisis similar to birth asphyxia.

Volpe's team studied 50 infants who required mechanical ventilation to treat their respiratory distress. By measuring the speed of the babies' cerebral blood flow with an instrument called a Doppler flow meter, the team discovered something extraordinary. For the first 12 hours of life, all 50 showed a relatively stable pattern of blood flow. Then 23 of them began to show a markedly fluctuating pattern. These fluctuations corresponded with swings in their blood pressure. As the hours passed, Volpe and his colleagues used ultrasound to test the 50 youngsters for brain bleeds. An astonishing 21 of the 23 infants with the fluctuating blood flow pattern also developed intraventricular hemorrhages, whereas only 7 of the 27 children with a stable pattern did so.

It seemed clear that there was a relation between hemorrhage and fluctuating blood pressure. But what was causing the blood pressure to jump so wildly?

Generally, those with the fluctuating pattern were the ones receiving the most mechanical ventilation. Consequently, Volpe speculated that the ventilator was somehow involved. "We think," he told me in an interview in the fall of 1983, "that it has to do with the way the infant responds to the ventilator. What appears to be happening is the infants are trying to breathe on their own, while the ventilator is trying to breathe for them." It is this breathing out of synchrony, he says, that may bring on the bleed.

To test his hypothesis, Volpe injected pancuronium, a paralyzing drug, into children with the fluctuating blood flow pattern. The drug inhibits their own attempts to breathe. The result: the fluctuating pattern returned to normal in every case. Volpe is now studying whether this results in a decrease in intraventricular hemorrhages.

The Washington University team has made other unsettling discoveries. It has shown that the universal practice of "suctioning" infants on ventilators to remove secretions that might obstruct their airways causes a sharp increase in blood flow velocity in the brain. Hence, it might be a major cause of hemorrhages. They have even found that routine handling of low-birthweight children, just picking them up, for example, causes fluctuations in cerebral flow. It may prove to be a tragic irony that merely a well-intentioned hug may cause a serious brain injury.

Volpe and his research team have also turned their attention to another sort of brain insult, the kind caused by an interruption of cerebral blood flow. It is much harder to "see" brain tissue that has died because of oxygen loss. It doesn't show up on ultrasound, as a hemorrhage does. But using a new technology, positron emission tomography (PET) scanning, the St. Louis team has been able for the first time to measure blood flow to the various parts of the brain. It has found that certain children suffer far more extensive blood loss than anyone had suspected. Volpe says, "It is blood loss, not hemorrhage, that causes most of the brain injuries in children under 800 grams."

The newly discovered prevalence of brain trauma in low-birthweight babies casts a disturbing shadow over medicine's superb achievement in saving their lives. It is a reminder that for every doorway technology takes us through, it presents us with another locked door.

Nevertheless, one of the deans of American neonatology, Dr. William H. Tooley, of the University of California at San Francisco, says medicine has a right to be proud.

During a recent visit that I paid UCSF, Tooley introduced me to a woman whose two sons, both of whom were born prematurely, were being examined in his NICU's follow-up clinic (Tooley believes in following premies until they are 15 years old.) The older boy, Danny, was 10 and suffered from serious learning disabilities. His visual perception was poor, and as a result he could not write well; moreover, he had a very short attention span. The younger child, Steve, was only five months old. Although it was much too early to make a meaningful evaluation, he appeared to be developing normally.

"Both of these children had an almost identical history," Tooley said. "Both were born at 32 weeks, both of them weighed the same. But when Danny was born [1972] we let him stay in utero two weeks without amniotic fluid. We hadn't yet learned to use betamethasone to mature babies' lungs. As a result, he developed a terrible case of respiratory distress and was in the hospital for 15 months. With Steve, it was a different story. He started out with better lungs because of betamethasone. And then he benefited by our improved management of children after birth. We have evolved an approach in which we support them with ventilation immediately, instead of waiting until they obviously need help. You can see the difference 10 years has made. If Danny had been born today, he would have only been on oxygen for two weeks, and I doubt he would have his handicaps.

"If you look at the entire 20 years of neonatal intensive care, you realize we have come very far indeed."

It is evening in the nursery of the big-city hospital. In a secluded corner of the unit, a nurse is putting the finish on a drama that has taken more than a month to play itself out. She is bundling a blanket around the small form of a little girl. Name: none. Weight: 450 grams. Gestational age: 24 weeks.

Her mother, who is 16 years old, had come to the emergency room of a suburban hospital one night, complaining of abdominal pain. Within a few hours, she had delivered a baby. From the point of view of birthweight, from the point of view of gestational age, from any point of view at all, it was a miracle the infant was alive. Somehow it was able to breathe by itself.

The hospital staff took the child to the level I nursery and began to give it supplementary oxygen. Then the mother's parents were called. They were flabbergasted. "We didn't even know she was pregnant," the father exclaimed. When the parents arrived at the hospital to join their daughter, they were disconcerted that the baby hadn't died. "Kids that small don't make it, do they?" the father asked. The chief of pediatrics, whose name was VanKamp, gave a helpless shrug. "I've never heard of one that did," he said.

VanKamp considered himself to be in a serious bind. He knew the child had no chance to survive. It was simply too small, too young. Yet he felt that he couldn't just allow it to die. A week earlier another local hospital had been in the newspapers for failing to give life support to a child with devastating birth defects. The government had come in to investigate and threatened the hospital with a loss of federal funds. Van Kamp now feared the same thing might happen to him.

He decided to treat the baby aggressively. That meant transporting it to the level III hospital in the city, where they had the life-support systems he lacked. He asked the family whether he could send it there.

"No way," the father replied with vehemence. The man explained that they already had an 18-year-old son who was in an institution because of a congenital brain defect. He and his wife were afraid their tiny granddaughter would survive with similar handicaps. "One child like that is enough," the father said. "If she dies, she dies." The 16-year-old mother agreed with her father.

In a quandary, VanKamp telephoned Dr. Taylor, the chief of neonatology at the level III hospital. "What am I going to do? We're

not equipped to take care of a kid that small here. If I don't send her
to you, the feds are going to say I didn't go all-out."

But the last thing Taylor wanted was a 450-gram baby tying up one
of his ventilators. "Look," he said soothingly. "Just keep it warm overnight. A baby that small will undoubtedly die by morning."

But it didn't happen that way. The child was still alive the next day
when VanKamp came to work. The pediatrician was beside himself.
And as the hours ticked by and the child continued to breathe weakly,
he grew progressively more panicked. Finally, he persuaded the baby's
mother to let him send the child to Taylor's hospital for treatment.

Taylor, who had an open bed, had no choice but to accept the baby.
And once he had taken the responsibility, he had to give it maximal
effort. For the next month his hospital kept the child alive by the use
of high technology. In the meantime, it had to turn away larger, more
viable babies because there was no room. On the 31st day, $38,000
worth of medical care later, the little girl did just what everyone
expected she would do. She died.

The nurse has finished wrapping the baby in a blanket. She begins
to make the lonely walk down the corridor with the miniature bundle
in her arms. Is it medicine's duty to try and save such a child?

The nurse passes a large, rather plain-looking woman in a flowered
blue dress who is sitting in a folding chair alongside an Isolette. The
woman pays little attention as the nurse disappears through the doors.
From time to time the woman reaches through one of the portholes
on the side of the incubator and anxiously wiggles the tiny fingers of
the child inside. The boy has been in the ICU for more than two
months. He will have to be here at least a month longer. He has been
through just about every complication a premature infant can experience, but the mother's faith has not wavered.

"We've been trying to have a baby for 20 years," she says. "Last
February I had an ectopic pregnancy [in which the ovum grows inside
the Fallopian tube and must be terminated to save the mother's life],
and then this time my cervix turned out to be incompetent. I think
this is the last chance we're ever going to have. I'm 36 years old."

She caresses the frail baby some more through the Isolette's port-
hole. "Look at him," she says. "He's so small. You can see how much
larger the other babies are. I get jealous of all the other mothers I
know who can hold their babies. But our time will come," she says,
wiggling the child's hand. "Won't it, Steven?"

4

The Dark Side of Progress
Low-Birthweight Infants and the Handicap Rate

The medical profession has received widespread acclaim for its successful campaign to save ever tinier infants. Stories in the daily press frequently celebrate the latest "miracle baby" to be rescued from the clutches of death. But the praise tends to obscure the fact that this triumph has its cruel underside. In spite of the doctors' most careful and sophisticated ministrations—and sometimes directly because of them—a certain percentage of the cases are fated to turn out poorly, even tragically.

Some of the smallest children who have been "saved" will, for the rest of their days, carry scars with them in the form of serious motor impairment, sensory loss, and retardation. Others will remain tethered to machines. Children like these face difficult and, in many instances, pathetic lives. How difficult or pathetic depends on several variables: the extent of their handicaps, their emotional adjustment to those handicaps, and whether they have a warm family unit to love and accept them.

Throughout the 1970s it was the consensus in medicine that keeping smaller and smaller infants alive with aggressive measures was a good thing. Doctors were pleased by the dual joys of extending the gift of life and unleashing their new technological genie. Year after year the birthweight barriers kept falling: now 1,000 grams, now 800 grams, now 600 grams. The temptation to go lower became almost narcotic. On occasion, nervous nellies would raise the specter of handicaps. They would cite low-birthweight statistics from the 1950s showing disability rates of 50 and 60 percent and would repeat the oft-quoted warning of Dr. C. M. Drillien, of Scotland, that the increased survival of very small children would be accompanied by an increased number of handicapped individuals. But these people were patiently humored and then disregarded. The same genie that had banished this specter for larger premies should work for the smallest ones as well.

It was easy to subscribe to this view because there was hardly a shred of evidence to the contrary. No one could cite any handicap data for the lowest birthweights. They simply did not exist. To understand why this is so, one must start by recognizing a few of the verities of newborn medicine.

Suppose a power company wants to build a new dam. It must file an environmental-impact study beforehand. What is going to happen to the surrounding farmland if we proceed with this project? To wildlife? To industry? But if doctors want to begin vigorously treating a whole new class of infant, without knowing the long-range impact of their actions, they have a perpetual green light. And yet they never know the impact.

Why? Because a baby is both enigma and tabula rasa. Unlike the basic mental and physical capacities of any other category of patient, those of a newborn are unknown and aren't scheduled to reveal themselves until well into the future. Even the most primitive accomplishments in an infant's repertoire, such as rolling over, creeping, and voluntarily grasping a rattle, are months down the road. As a result, the neonatologist or researcher is obliged to wait a long time after treatment is given to learn whether the child's faculties have been impaired. And where there has been a more subtle injury—producing, say, a learning disorder like dyslexia—the handicap does not show up until school age, a time lag of five or six years.

When, at the dawn of the 1970s, doctors began saving miracle babies, they were thus pretty much working in the dark. They had no way of knowing whether these tiny bundles they were salvaging would be "quality" survivors or cripples. Yet when caution might thus have been in order, they forged impetuously ahead. What were needed, of course, were follow-up studies of these infants under 1,000 grams. But analysis of this type must wait until the children grow old enough to be tested. If you first learned how to save a 600-gram baby in 1977, you had to wait until 1979 or 1980 to reach any useful conclusions about its mental and physical condition; then another year to collate your findings; and another year to have the paper published. One can see why there's such a gap in our knowledge.

At last, however, the data have begun to roll in. To many people's dismay, they have contained considerable food for thought.

The University of Washington study, for example, which was published in 1982, performed school-age examinations on 25 children who had weighed less than 1,000 grams at birth. The children averaged 10 years old upon testing. A full seven of these 25 children, or 28 percent, displayed one or more major neurological or sensory handicaps. Keeping in mind that some had more than one handicap, the breakdown was as follows: 2 of them had an IQ of less than 70, 2 had cerebral palsy, 2 had hydrocephalus, 1 had a seizure disorder, 3 had hearing impairments, and 2 had visual impairments. Of the group as a whole, 64 percent were in special education and only one-fourth were working at their grade level.

But these results could be misleading. Critics pointed to a flaw in the Washington study. It was based on children who had been born between 1960 and 1972. Since medical care for the less-than-1,000-gram infant had dramatically improved since 1972, it could be presumed that very small premies born later would fare better.

However, a study conducted at the Milton S. Hershey Medical Center in Pennsylvania and published in 1983 was not very reassuring. Here a similar group of infants, born between 1973 and 1976, were followed to the age of 40 months. In this case, 35 percent turned out to be handicapped, 17 percent severely. The severe handicaps included major visual impairment, hydrocephalus, and spastic quadriplegia, a particularly devastating and life-shortening form of cerebral palsy in which all four limbs are spastic.

This study, incidentally, took pains to distinguish between children who had received mechanical ventilation and those who hadn't. Those who had been ventilated had a 72 percent handicap rate, compared with only 19 percent for the nonventilated.

Stanford University Hospital also released a study. Sixty children under 1,000 grams in birthweight were tested at the ages of three and up. Seventeen of them, again almost one-third, had "significant" handicaps, including partial and total spasticity, moderate to profound mental retardation, and partial or total sensory loss. One child born in 1975 was both blind and deaf. Another child born the same year was retarded and paralyzed in both legs by cerebral palsy. A third child, born in the pioneering year of 1968, was blind, retarded, deaf, and partially paralyzed. And a fourth child, born in 1972, was profoundly retarded and paralyzed in all four limbs.

At the University of Southern California Medical Center, 17 percent of a group of young children under 1,000 grams were neurologically abnormal, and 26 percent were developmentally (intellectually) abnormal; there was, however, some overlap between the two groups. Another 30 percent were developmentally "suspect." At the Capital Regional Perinatal Center in Albany, New York, 40 percent of a similar group of children had major handicaps. At Crouse-Irving Memorial Hospital in Syracuse, New York, the figure was 26 percent. At Babies Hospital in the Columbia-Presbyterian Medical Center in New York, the handicap rate was 30 percent.

But the most sobering study of all was one conducted at the Hospital for Sick Children in Toronto, by a group including the noted neonatologist Dr. Pamela Fitzhardinge. Published in the *Journal of Pediatrics* in December 1981, it was entitled "Is Intensive Care Justified for Infants Weighing Less Than 801 Gm at Birth?"

The research team started with a study population of 158 of these very tiny infants, all of whom were born in the period 1974–78. As an indicator of how mortality still reigns, even in the most sophisticated hospitals, 119 of them died—39 from intracranial hemorrhages, 26 from respiratory distress syndrome, and 13 because of infection.

From the small group of survivors, the team was able to follow 37 infants to the age of 18 months. The researchers found that, overall, 49 percent had moderate to severe impairment, including 14 percent who had a major neurological handicap, primarily incapacitating cerebral palsy. Three were blind, 15 had delayed speech, 6 had hearing disorders, and 18 required surgery during the first two years of life.

But the damning news was this: not a single child who weighed less than 700 grams at birth survived without a handicap. The disability rate was 100 percent. Among those in the 700- to 800-gram range, the rate was better, but it remained a considerably high 39 percent.

The Fitzhardinge team concluded that intensive care was "probably not" justified for newborns under 700 grams. (However, Fitzhardinge recently cautioned that all of the children in the study were "outborn," that is, delivered in hospitals miles away and then transported to her NICU, which she feels may have affected the results.)

What are we to make of all these studies? The one thing that leaps out at us is that a significant number of children under 1,000 grams will go on to be handicapped. Overall, the disability rate seems to hover between 30 and 50 percent, and the rate of severe handicap is in the neighborhood of 15 to 30 percent. That means a third to a half have some kind of abnormality, and one out of every four to six has been devastated.

Also, it must be pointed out that what are referred to as "moderate" handicaps in many of these studies are not of the innocuous-birthmark variety. They are called "moderate" or "mild" in order to differentiate them from the incapacitating "severe" or "major" ones. Generally, the researchers construe *moderate* to mean such lesser but still burdensome concerns as partial hearing or sight impairment, the loss of a couple of dozen IQ points, or a touch of cerebral palsy. However, even when a premie's handicap is indeed comparatively mild, it frequently takes the form of a learning disorder—and an inability to learn to read or do arithmetic is a maddening deficit in its own right.

Another fact worthy of mention is that a high rate of neurological handicap among mechanically ventilated children is a consistent finding in many of these studies. Incredibly, considering how widespread ventilation of the newborn is, doctors still don't know for sure whether it is the ventilator that is causing these handicaps or whether children who require respiratory assistance are sicker and more likely to have handicaps in the first place.

Yet another thing to keep well in mind is that the total group of *survivors* below 1,000 grams, both normal and abnormal, is actually quite small. Medicine's vaunted success at these weights is, on close analysis, rather questionable. In 1981 there were 15,935 U.S. babies born weighing between 500 and 1,000 grams, according to the American Academy of Pediatrics. If we assume that the prevailing survival rate for such babies is 50 percent, then we find that only 7,968 survived. Of those, only about 5,578, or about 35 percent of the total number born, were normal survivors. At lower weights, it's even less. The academy doesn't break its figures down this way, but if we make the reasonable supposition that there are 8,000 babies born under 800 grams each year and that the survival rate is 25 to 30 percent, then our projection is that fewer than 2,400 survive. Assuming a 40 percent handicap rate, the number who are normal is no more than 1,440, or 18 percent of all those born.

Such disappointing figures become even more disturbing when we consider how much it costs to treat one of these children. The complete intensive-care package—24-hour, one-on-one nursing, ventilation therapy, blood gas and other testing, and hyperalimentation—gets very expensive.

While children below 1,000 grams in birthweight constitute approximately one-half of 1 percent of all live births in the United States, they account for up to 16 percent of the total NICU costs.

Thus, if the nation's bill for neonatal intensive care came to $1.5 billion in 1978, as Dr. Peter Budetti estimated in a U.S. Office of Technology study, then the price tag for the treatment of these very low birthweight infants was about $240 million. Adjusted for inflation, that comes to $425 million a year today.

Several years ago the economist Ciaran S. Phibbs averaged out the medical bills for low-birthweight infants in six California NICUs over a six-month period. He found that the average hospital charge for a child weighing between 750 and 1,000 grams was $39,504 but that when you divided all the bills incurred by such babies (including those who died) by the number of survivors, a computation called the "cost to produce a survivor," the figure rose to $70,983. For a baby under 750 grams, it was $98,885. In 1984 dollars, it would cost somewhere around $125,750 to produce a survivor of 750 to 1,000 grams, and $175,180 to produce one below 750 grams.

And what does this mean in societal terms? In 1983 a team at McMaster University Medical Center, in Hamilton, Ontario, published a landmark cost-benefit study of neonatal intensive care. Through a series of extremely complicated calculations, they figured out how much of an improvement intensive care represented over the pre-ICU era in terms of (a) additional survivors, (b) additional years of life expectancy gained, and (c) additional years of good health. Taking into account how much more intensive care cost society and what the lifetime expense of caring for the additional handicapped children was, they then balanced it against what society would get back in terms of the survivors' projected earnings. What they came up with was eye-opening. They found that the intensive care of babies under 1,000 grams represented a *net loss* of $7,300 in 1978 Canadian dollars (U.S. $6,402) for each year of a survivor's life gained. This was markedly worse than the $900 (U.S. $789) per year net loss for birthweights between 1,000 and 1,500 grams.

In short, intensive care below 1,000 grams appears not very cost-effective. It is astronomically expensive, yet it produces few survivors and even fewer normal, healthy ones. As a consequence, it comes nowhere near paying for itself in the sense of creating productive, contributing citizens. "By every measure of economic evaluation," wrote the Canadian researchers, "it was economically more favorable to provide intensive care for the relatively heavier infants (weighing 1,000 to 1,499 g at birth) than for those weighing 500 to 999 g."

Given these unpleasant realities, the question becomes evident: Should we be trying so hard to save babies at the extreme low end of the birthweight scale? Some specialists don't think so, among them Dr. Sylvia Schechner, assistant professor of pediatrics at Cornell Uni-

versity Medical College. According to her, "The slightly improved
survival rate in very small infants does not seem to justify the production of a high percentage of neurologically impaired infants. . . . Due
regard must be given to the quality of life of surviving infants and
their families and less emphasis placed on performing technological
feats simply because the apparatus to perform these procedures is
available to the nursery."

Schechner suggests that the "hands off" attitude of the 1940s toward
small babies, which constituted little or no care, should be replaced
with "a more sophisticated hands off attitude during the 1980s."
Emphasizing that "hands off is not synonymous with 'no care,'"
Schechner asserts that children below 750 grams should continue to
be transferred to intensive care. But they should be treated less
aggressively, that is to say, kept warm, given fluids, and supplied oxygen through a plastic hood. They should not be put on a ventilator
unless the parents insist. "This hands off approach has several advantages," says Schechner. "It does not deny the possible benefits of
intensive care to any infant. By minimizing the number of invasive
procedures, it may actually reduce the risks associated with neonatal
intensive care. By leaving the sick infant to itself, appropriate care can
be concentrated on those infants most likely to benefit from intensive
care and best able to withstand the complications of intensive care
procedures."

A similar, if more graphic, opinion was expressed to me recently by
a prominent Chicago obstetrician. "Neonatologists," he said, "are like
greyhounds chasing the rabbit. They see a baby, and they want to do
everything they can to save it, to hell with anything else. They want to
use their new toys. But they don't observe the long-term outcome of
what they do, the substantial neurological deficits, the broken families."

This greyhound instinct appears to be strong. Overcoming the urge
to salvage increasingly marginal babies is difficult. Hence, in early 1983,
when a very low-birthweight follow-up study appeared that seemed
to say that the handicap rate was turning the corner, it was immediately seized upon in some quarters as The Word.

The survey was done at the University of Washington School of
Medicine, the site of some earlier, less optimistic findings. This time,
researchers used as a study population all the babies of less than 800
grams born at their hospital from 1977 through 1980, a total of 95
infants. Of this group, 19 children survived, and 16 of them, ranging
in age from six months to three years, were available for testing. Their
average birthweight had been 730 grams, and their mean gestational

age was 26 weeks, which is the generally accepted frontier of viability. Two children were only 24 weeks along!

Amazingly, the team, led by Dr. Forrest C. Bennett, found 13 of the children to be without any problems greater than cross-eye, near-sightedness, and some mild hearing loss. Only 3 (19 percent) had more serious handicaps, and two of these were manageable—a minimal cerebral palsy and a controlled hydrocephalus. The lone case of extensive disability was a child with significant mental retardation. None of the children had major visual or auditory impairment. None had severe cerebral palsy. And astonishingly enough, the aggregate IQ score was an above-average 106.

But appearances are deceiving. The total absence in Bennett's study of any survivors who had suffered intracranial hemorrhages, seizures, neurological infections, or hypoglycemia—not uncommon events among premies—seemed rather odd. On closer examination, so did his mortality rate. Of the total population of sub-800-gram babies he started with, 80 percent died in the neonatal period, a figure quite a bit higher than the 70 to 75 percent death rate experienced at other major hospitals. What was going on? Bennett offered a credible explanation.

He said it was probable that with decreasing birthweight and gestational age, survival following brain bleeds, seizures, and other "ominous events" grows ever more unlikely "despite vigorous resuscitation and intensive care." He added, "It is also possible that our neonatologists' attitudes and decisions concerning termination of mechanical ventilation for very-low-birthweight infants who manifest serious neurologic dysfunction . . . following severe asphyxia or large intracranial hemorrhage, have been a major contributing factor to our positive results."

In less technical language, Bennett seemed to be saying that the weaker infants already had been weeded out before the study began, partly by Darwinian processes and partly by some judicious help from University of Washington doctors, who were shutting off machines when they felt it appropriate. The handful of babies left for research were the healthiest ones in that weight range and therefore not as prone to handicaps.

However, this questionable sample did not stop Bennett from declaring, "These data suggest that a remarkably hopeful outcome is possible for the few survivors of extremely low birthweight." Unfortunately, this statement encourages the inaccurate view that handicap is an infrequent sequel to therapy and that there is thus nothing wrong in implementing heroic measures to try to save marginal infants.

But what constitutes "infrequent"? For that matter, how much is "too much"? It seems to me the problem doctors have in dealing with this issue amounts to the old perceptual dilemma of whether the glass of water is half-full or half-empty. When is a handicap rate low and when is it high?

A fascinating descent into the eye of the beholder is provided by the Babies Hospital study at Columbia University, published in early 1982, in which the rates of neurologic handicap (17 percent) and of intellectual handicap (13 percent) yielded a total disability rate of 30 percent. These handicaps, not so incidentally, included spasticity in all four limbs, severe degeneration of brain tissue, and developmental delay of unspecified magnitude.

Here is what the researchers wrote: "Compared with previous reports, the *relatively low incidence* of neurologic and intellectual morbidity in these very low-birth-weight infants is *encouraging*" (italics mine).

One can only marvel at the research mind. Some people might be dejected by a set of findings in which 30 percent of a group of children were found to be diminished in their capacity to move and think. But not the Columbia team. Its members look upon it as heartening. Perhaps they were influenced by their own choice of "previous reports" used for purposes of comparison. The three reports they cited were hopelessly outdated ones from the 1960s, when no one had a firm idea of how to prevent handicap in premies and when the disability rate was running wild. It may not have been their intention to put the best face on their own statistics, but that is how it came out.

Meanwhile, the researchers at Stanford University Hospital, who found 28 percent of their survivors to have significant handicaps, including one child who was deaf and blind, another who was retarded and paralyzed, and a third who combined all of these terrible handicaps in one tormented body, had the good cheer to summarize their findings this way:

"These data should answer those critics of neonatal intensive care who feared that it would lead to an increased quantity of survivors by adding only to the number of poor quality survivors. . . . The improved survival rate among an increasing population of [very low birth-weight] infants, coupled with a *relatively low incidence* of significant morbidity, indicates that neonatal intensive care is now contributing a greater number of potentially productive society members relative to the number of individuals who will be a continued expense to society" (italics mine).

The Stanford researchers did concede that the prognosis "remains poor" at birthweights less than 750 grams. But they relieved our anxieties about babies of 750 to 1,000 grams by assuring us, "More than 70 percent of the survivors should be free of significant handicaps and the chances for self-sufficiency are nearly 90 percent. . . ."

Let's put aside their rather optimistic prediction of self-sufficiency for people with retardation and no leg function. Let us only consider the twin assertions that handicap rates of 28 percent and 30 percent are "relatively low."

What would you say if someone proposed a new surgery for heart disease that restored 7 out of 10 people to normal life but that made the remaining people blind, deaf, paralyzed, or intellectually enfeebled? Or how would you judge a new chemotherapy drug that was effective against cancer but whose side effects left 2 or 3 out of every 10 patients confined to wheelchairs, locked in institutions for the retarded, or needing seeing-eye dogs? I doubt that the Food and Drug Administration would approve such a drug, and no hospital would offer such surgery. The cost to those who lost the gamble would be too great to justify the favorable results for the others.

If, to paraphrase Cornell's Dr. Schechner, the improved survival of children below 1,000 grams in birthweight can be accomplished only by the simultaneous production of a certain large percentage of handicapped children, then one has to indeed wonder whether it isn't time for a reappraisal of policy. This is not a game of tenpins or a skeet shoot, in which it might be appropriate to boast that 7 out of 10 isn't bad. We are discussing damaged human lives—lives that must be lived, from moment to difficult moment, for however long they endure. Moreover, these babies must be wrested into existence, like a crop from a barren field. In a sense, then, their handicaps are on our hands, not nature's. If it were up to nature, they would die.

But then what are the alternatives? A total embargo on the saving of all babies below a certain birthweight hardly seems fair, since it forecloses any chance at life for the fraction that turn out more or less intact. If it is hard to justify creating blind paraplegics to obtain a number of healthy survivors, it is equally hard to explain to the ghosts of the potentially healthy that they had to die to avoid creating blind paraplegics.

"What do you do," asks the chief neonatologist of a large city hospital, "take everyone under 600 grams and turn off the oxygen? No, you don't, because you can't predict how each child is going to turn out. I can't apply statistics to an individual baby. Every single baby has a different outlook based on its maternal history, gestational age, and its constitution."

Everyone can point to cases where extremely small babies have done well. Chaya Snyder, the smallest surviving baby on record, weighed only 420 grams (15 oz) and was 26 weeks in gestation when she was born in the Bronx, New York, on August 2, 1979. While she remains small for her age, a common characteristic among premies, she is developmentally normal, according to her doctors. She walks, talks, and has no sensory or intellectual disturbances, they say. Comments her pediatrician, Dr. Cecilia McCarton, of New York City's Albert Einstein Hospital, "Most studies indicate that cases less than 750 grams have a devastating outcome. But Chaya's an example unto herself."

Christie List, who weighed 900 grams and was 26 weeks in gestation when she was born in suburban Chicago in 1976, is in the third grade and, when last observed, was performing quite normally, "although in learning things like reading she tends to wait a little until she feels ready. She's a cautious child," says her mother.

But do the successes justify the failures? The question defies an answer.

It would be ideal, of course, if the disability rate among these tiniest of babies would just obediently decline, as it did at higher weights.

"In the 'old' days," says Roderic Phibbs, director of the NICU at the University of California, San Francisco, "the 1,250- to 1,500-gram infants had a high rate of cerebral palsy and blindness, when they survived at all. Now most of them survive, and while there's still a lot of handicap, most of it is mild. CP is very rare now. It's mostly learning disability and a slight clumsiness. You don't turn off the respirator on a kid who's clumsy.

"It always happens like that when you are lowering the barrier. First, there's a period in which you have no survivors. Then you have survivors with handicaps. Then survivors with fewer handicaps. Sure, there are more handicaps now below 800 grams, but I think that will change, based on past experience. And you'll never improve the technical survival of these kids unless you try."

Dr. Phibbs may well be right. If he and other practitioners had been dissuaded by the chance of handicap when they first began saving children of 1,500 grams, more than a decade ago, they would not have made the progress they have. Unfortunately, improvement of the outlook for premies under 1,000 grams may be years away. These infants, in more ways than their slightly larger brethren, are almost certain to have been born before reaching crucial gestational milestones affecting their respiratory and circulatory systems. This physical immaturity, coupled with their extreme fragility, makes them all the more susceptible to events like asphyxia and intracranial hemorrhage that foreshadow handicap. These factors form a kind of "wall" that must be breached, and this will very likely require a quantum leap in medical knowledge.

The question of whether or not to resuscitate extremely premature infants must necessarily be considered in the context of the family. For the burden of providing for handicapped children once they leave the hospital falls squarely on the parents, whom society then cuts adrift, both emotionally and financially.

Faced with the birth of a very premature child, many parents will wholeheartedly press the doctor to do all he or she can to save it. But what if the child suffers serious setbacks? What if the parents demur when the doctor proposes stepped-up treatment? Suppose they have searched their souls and decided that it is cruel to the infant to continue or that a severely crippled child would impose an impossible burden on their marriage and their other children. Should the doctor overrule them in the belief that it is immoral to let the child die?

Peggy and Robert Stinson have written a haunting book entitled *The Long Dying of Baby Andrew,* which describes the tyranny of healers gone amok. The Stinsons' son was born in December 1976. He was only 24½ weeks along gestationally and weighed 800 grams, poor credentials for survival. Nevertheless, when he started doing badly, he was placed on a ventilator against the couple's wishes. Over the next five months, in spite of their objections, he was forced to undergo the most rigorous high-tech treatments, in the process contracting a chronic lung disease, grueling blood and urinary infections, a gangrenous leg, fractured bones, and seizures. By the end, he was blind and his brain tissue had atrophied, yet the treatment continued. The doctors threatened to get a court order to enforce their right to save the baby. They considered the Stinsons unfeeling and morally suspect for wanting Andrew to be allowed to die a natural death. "What do you want me to do?" one doctor asked them snidely, "go in and hold a pillow over his head?"

Wrote Mrs. Stinson of another doctor: "Carvalho thought I was a bad parent. But it didn't really matter what kind of parent I was because Carvalho had taken over the baby. He would treat the baby according to his ideas about what was right even though he could see that his moral or religious views differed drastically from ours. He could overrule us, could—and did—dismiss what we believe automatically, unemotionally, as if we were beneath notice. Because he has the power."

Myra Orlinsky of Evanston, Illinois, delivered twins in 1977, each weighing less than 1,000 grams. The boy, Brian, was on a ventilator for two months and needed surgery to correct a patent ductus arte-

riosus. He was out of the hospital in three months. Today he is relatively normal, though he has some memory and perceptual problems.
He forgets to write several of the letters when he signs his name.

The girl, Jodie, was another matter. She was born not moving. She,
too, required ventilation and heart surgery, but she also had an intracranial hemorrhage and hydrocephalus, or a swelling of the head.
Doctors had to implant a shunt in her skull to drain the fluid.

Then, when she was about to leave the hospital, she contracted
meningitis. From that day on, any alertness she had shown vanished.
But still the doctors pressed on, performing four more shunt operations and keeping her in the hospital for a total of five months. In all
that time, they never told the Orlinskys she would have lasting damage.

Today, Jodie has no measurable IQ and is totally immobile. She
possesses no vision, makes no sounds, and recognizes no one. She is
entirely tube fed and spends her days vegetating in a beanbag chair
in the institution where she lives. Her only response to the outside
world is to smile when she is held.

"She has the lowest form of existence you can imagine," says Mrs.
Orlinsky, who confesses that recently, when Jodie got pneumonia, she
"was suddenly struck by the whole futility of her [Jodie's] life. Three
doctors were looking at her, taking urine, blood, and everything else,
and I wanted to scream, 'What are you doing?' It was so crazy, all
these big, important doctors looking her over and there is no purpose
to her life."

Mrs. Orlinsky feels very ambivalent about the advanced medical
technology that enabled both of her children to live. "Did the nursery
do Jodie a favor, doing everything to save her?" she asks. "No," she
says, answering her own question. "I think maybe when she had meningitis, that was the time to stop. She is not bringing us any joy. Maybe
she has changed me as a person, but I didn't need to be changed.

"Modern medicine has given me a beautiful son who has great
potential to fully enjoy a good life, and it has also given me a beautiful
daughter whose life will never bloom. I feel like saying, 'Thank you,
modern medicine, and damn you, modern medicine.' "

Physicians are slowly evolving positions on the ethical issues involved
in the treatment of very low birthweight babies. Here is a sampler of
their views from around the country:

Dr. Roderic Phibbs, chief of the intensive-care nursery, University
of California, San Francisco: "I think if a child is not going to survive,
then there's no point in my putting the child through the miseries of
intensive care. There is no law which says you have to treat what you

know you can't treat. But if there's a chance, you always give it to the child."

Dr. Michael Katz, chief of pediatrics, Columbia-Presbyterian Medical Center, New York: "It must be remembered that there are many small premies who turn out to be fine and and independent. One of my colleagues during medical training weighed only 1,000 grams at birth. If anyone in a weight group survives and does well, do you have the right not to try to save the whole group? As for the argument that it costs too much? Well, if you save the little child, you get 80 years out of it. If you save a 79-year-old man with diabetes, you may only get one year. Which is the better investment?"

Dr. Carl Hunt, chief of neonatology, Children's Memorial Hospital, Chicago: "There are babies who have meningitis and hydrocephalus as complications of a hemorrhage, and we know they'll turn out poorly. In such cases, decisions are certainly made to withdraw aggressive support. But there is a whole intermediate group who we know may have a 20 to 40 percent chance of impairment, but also a 40 to 50 percent chance of coming out all right. And we feel compelled to go ahead and do what we can. We feel very uncomfortable deciding to withdraw an aggressive level of support unless the extent of neurological damage is known and is horrendous."

Dr. Bernard Towers, professor of pediatrics, UCLA, and the father of an 880-gram daughter who was on a ventilator for five weeks and is doing well at age three: "Let me say, I believe every newborn of whatever weight should be given a chance to show if it's capable of survival, first of all, and then capable of quality survival. I see no difference in the question of whether to start resuscitation or withdraw it. Some people have an emotional problem. They find it easy to start the ventilator and hard to stop. But I see no difference. As the child's treatment progresses, your intuitive judgment is either confirmed or disproven, and then you have to be open and honest enough to say we tried our best but it wasn't worth it."

Dr. Joseph Volpe, pediatric neurologist, St. Louis Children's Hospital: "You have to be able to know when you've lost the ballgame with these babies. It's when you have people who aren't experienced in evaluating these infants that you run into the problem of salvaging ones who already are too badly damaged. . . . It's very complicated, in terms of talking to families, dealing with the local legal climate, and so on, but certainly withdrawal of life support is something that has to be considered in the forefront if you think there will be a poor outcome. If you have a child of 800 grams with a large hemorrhage and a massive amount of blood within the substance of the brain, we have enough data now to know the likelihood of normal neurological development is essentially zero. In those circumstances, the information has to be conveyed to the family and a decision made. If the family asked me what I would do if it were my child, I'd say I'd want life support discontinued."

Dr. L. Joseph Butterfield, chairman emeritus of perinatology at Denver Children's Hospital: "Once you start playing that numbers game, do you cut off at 700 grams, or 800 grams, it becomes dangerous. Studies are beginning to come in now showing a better outcome for these babies. Maybe when some people say there's no hope for certain infants, it's their care that isn't up to snuff."

Such a potpourri of views reflects the intense ethical ferment that is going on in the specialties of perinatology and neonatology. Hardly a month goes by in which somewhere in the country, at one or another medical institution, a conference or symposium isn't held to deal with the question of withholding treatment from low-birthweight newborns. Yet, in some ways doctors are like so many birds sitting on a telephone wire. They can chatter all day among themselves and never reach any conclusions. They are no closer to defining a policy on this question than they ever were.

Is it even possible to come up with one? The answer is probably not. Hard-and-fast rules do not allow for the vagaries of individual cases. Even in Sweden and Great Britain, where most hospitals already make it a practice not to provide intensive care below 750 grams, the standard is ignored when a child shows particularly good promise or when its parents, who may have tried for years to have a baby, enter a special plea. Nor is it likely that even a negotiable embargo like Britain's would work in the United States. The American doctor seems more sentimental than the British doctor and less autocratic. It is hard to conceive of a U.S. physician being able to let a 600-gram baby die without trying to save it. This emotional factor, together with medicine's current inability to predict how low-birthweight babies are going to turn out, militates against any policy of withholding aggressive treatment at birth. The only area where such a moratorium appears acceptable is below 500 grams and 24 weeks' gestation, where the death rate is almost 100 percent.

Granted that a neat formula probably can't be devised, there are nevertheless some general principles that bear consideration.

(1) If we cannot refuse to *begin* intensive care on a marginal infant, there should be nothing to say we can't stop it. Doctors should not be reluctant to shut a ventilator off or withdraw other technological support if, after a certain period of time, the child's outlook seems poor. What the hand of science sets loose, it can bring to heel.

(2) That outlook certainly ought to take into account quality-of-life

concerns. The issue of not discriminating against already handicapped people is quite different from the issue of not creating *more*
handicapped people.

(3) It is not as difficult as it might seem to determine when the
quality of life becomes unacceptable. Although we may not be able to
describe the precise point at which the level of handicap becomes too
dismal, most of us have an intuitive knowledge of where that point is.
Thus, as Dr. Phibbs said, one doesn't turn the ventilator off on a child
who is clumsy. But one need not feel immoral doing so on a child
destined to be blind and quadriplegic.

(4) We need to surmount the fear of losing the occasional child who
could have turned out well if treated more vigorously. There are surely
going to be such children. However, if we are to embark upon a philosophy that says no human potential should ever be passed up, then
we should begin in the housing projects of our inner cities, where the
same $175,000 it costs to produce one 700-gram survivor could feed,
counsel, and educate dozens of socially deprived children.

(5) Research must be intensified in an effort to better forecast which
low-birthweight infants will have unhappy outcomes. This, as we have
seen, is a complex and time-consuming process. It requires identifying children with intracranial hemorrhage, asphyxia, and other complications and following them to an age when their full potential can
be studied. Such research suffers from a lack of coordination, manpower, and diagnostic equipment. These could easily be provided if
the federal government, which has a strong financial stake in neonatal
medicine, invested in a full-scale national study.

(6) A hospital should not undertake to salvage babies at the extreme
low end of the birthweight scale if its track record with such infants is
nonexistent or poor.

(7) Parents' wishes should be scrupulously observed, except in the
most obviously inappropriate cases. Couples who insist the doctors
continue trying to save a child with a poor prognosis should be heeded,
so long as they understand the consequences. But a similar respect
should be accorded to the desires of parents who don't want further
heroic efforts made.

It is a great mischief for physicians, who will not have to live with
the long-range effects of their actions, to present a handicapped child
to parents who don't want it. As the pediatrician Dr. William Silverman has pointed out, "When parents with marginal financial and
emotional resources are overwhelmed by the survival of a sickly or
malformed neonate, the situation becomes a prescription for disaster."

This view is no mere bugbear. There are solid statistics to back it up. The high incidence of child abuse among the premature is a little-publicized social scandal. A Canadian study reviewed 51 cases of child abuse at Montreal Children's Hospital and found that 24 percent of the victims had been of low birthweight, even though low-birthweight children make up only 7 percent of the Canadian child population. A Washington, D.C., study of 36 battered children found that 28 percent had been of low birthweight. In Indianapolis, the figure was 44 percent. And in Pittsburgh, where a study was conducted in an all-white, middle-class hospital, 36 percent of the victims fell into the low-birthweight category.

Sociologists offer a number of reasons for this peculiar phenomenon. It is thought that the long months of postnatal hospitalization that separate the premie from its family inhibit parent-child bonding. The parents feel alienated from the infant, and perhaps disappointed that it is not the robust, full-term baby they anticipated. The mother may feel a sense of failure; her body couldn't produce a healthy child. Statistically, she is often an unwed adolescent who is emotionally unprepared for child rearing. She also tends to be from the lower end of the economic scale, with all the psychosocial baggage that this brings. Then, once the child is home, it also tends to cry excessively, feed poorly, develop behind schedule, and perhaps have major physical and mental anomalies.

Where there is no violence, a lack of affection can by itself be tragic for the typical premie, who is lagging well behind his contemporaries in height, weight, and mental development and needs all the support he can get. A study at Northwestern Memorial Hospital in Chicago showed that babies with respiratory distress syndrome became verbal at an average age of 25.8 months, compared with 19.2 months for full-term youngsters. After the premies' chronological age was corrected by the amount of their prematurity (compensating for the fact that they started life on the minus side and spent their first months getting back to zero), they still averaged four months behind term youngsters in learning to talk. With such a disadvantage, even premies with no hidden learning deficits may face school problems unless they get a great deal of encouragement from their family.

In view of this larger picture, it would seem imperative that medicine surrender what Silverman calls its "rescue fantasy" and base its treatment decisions instead on a sense of humanity, one that considers the patient within the context of society and family.

The words of a friend and colleague of mine sum it up well. His 640-gram daughter, born two years ago, has only "mild" complications: eye damage, a missing thumb because of a botched IV, and a possible scarred trachea, which may require burning out with a laser beam. "I am still not convinced," he said to me, "that we aren't taking what used to be miscarriages and turning them into lifelong heart-aches for people."

The first thing you notice about Bobby Lee is his eyes. Enormous, like the eyes of a lemur, they dominate his small face. They bulge for unknown pathological reasons. He sits marooned in his crib, with a colorful toy gymnasium suspended in the air in front of him. His eyes never leave you, curious, intelligent, wondrously big. He is 19 months old.

So hypnotic is his gaze that it takes a moment before you notice the hose that runs into his crib through the bars. Ribbed like a vacuum cleaner hose, it is joined to a small tube inserted in his windpipe. This is the business end of the ultrasophisticated air pump called a venti-lator. All his life, with a ghostly hiss, the machine has breathed for Bobby Lee, so that at times it seems it is the machine itself that is alive and the child only an extension.

"This little guy was premature. It's a sad story," says Dr. Rosita Pildes, chief of neonatology at Chicago's Cook County Hospital. Dr. Pildes has paused on a tour of the aging welfare hospital's crowded new-born-intensive-care unit.

She begins to relate the depressing details of Bobby's life: how he was jettisoned from the womb too soon, his organs incomplete; how he would have died without the ventilator; how the price of his sur-vival has been enslavement—all of that mechanical breathing has scarred Bobby Lee's lungs so badly that he needs the machine more than ever. He may never be able to do without it.

There is a name for Bobby's condition. It is called bronchopulmon-ary dysplasia, or BPD. First recognized in the late 1960s, the disease causes the lung tissue to grow thick and fibrous, delaying by months or years the time when the child can be taken off the machine. It affects up to 30 percent of all babies who require a ventilator's help for respiratory distress syndrome. Doctors have not yet determined whether the lungs deteriorate in response to high oxygen concentra-tions or to the constant pounding they endure at high air pressure, but there is no doubt about one thing: BPD is caused by the very technology used to save the child. Such diseases are referred to as iatrogenic, which means "caused by medical treatment itself."

The prolonged ventilator treatment is costing $1,500 a day. This means that the taxpayers have already spent nearly $1 million to keep Bobby alive.

The boy watches his visitors, sucking his fingers. An eager expres-sion forms on his face. Is it a smile? Speech seems to be welling up inside him, but the tube in his throat keeps him from uttering a sound. He can neither laugh nor cry.

"He has no home," sighs Dr. Pildes. The boy's natural parents have turned their backs on him, scarcely visiting anymore. They have made it clear they will not take him in, should he be discharged. As for foster homes, there are none for children who require 24-hour ventilation.

This, then, may be Bobby's world forever: his bed, his nurses, the hospital ward with its other unfortunates, children with spina bifida, children with Down's syndrome, children with God's whole heartbreaking caseload.

The doctor is asked why Bobby Lee is being kept alive. She shrugs gamely. "What are we supposed to do?" she asks. "How can you shut the ventilator off once it's on?"

Bobby Lee's eyes watch as his visitors drift away, a Robinson Crusoe on his wordless island.

The word *iatrogenic* is derived from the Greek, which is fitting, for the ancients were well aware that you could hurt patients while trying to cure them. Writing in the first century B.C. the playwright Publilius Syrus alluded to this when he observed, "There are some remedies worse than the disease."

Iatrogenic illness seems to come with the territory in the neonatal nursery. It is the unavoidable consequence of aggressively applying new or radical therapies on creatures as fragile as china teacups. BPD is far from being the only example. Some brain hemorrhages, according to the current theory, may be brought on by machine ventilation or airway suctioning. Many of the calamities that befell Peggy and Robert Stinson's son, Andrew, were treatment induced, including a grooved palate and gangrene.

More than 30 years ago, doctors discovered to their horror that they were causing their tiny charges to go blind by giving them too much oxygen. Unfortunately, retrolental fibroplasia (RLF) is on the rise again, as more and more very low birthweight infants survive neonatal intensive care. It is thought to occur in up to 4 percent of all youngsters below 1,500 grams, although Beilinson Medical Center in Tel Aviv, Israel, recently reported an incidence as high as 36 percent. In 1979 an estimated 546 U.S. infants were blinded by RLF. Another 1,500 lost part of their sight to the disease.

The recent resurgence of RLF has puzzled doctors because it is occurring despite vastly improved oxygen-monitoring techniques. This fact has led them to suspect other causes, including blood transfusions, apnea, emergency resuscitation, blood infections, and prolonged intravenous feeding. Transfusions are considered particularly likely culprits because the adult red cells in the donor blood carry oxygen more efficiently and therefore may send a damaging dose of oxygen to the baby's retina, even when the oxygen concentration is not especially high.

RLF is a classic example of how human technology can wreak devastating results. It furthermore illustrates the ethical and therapeutic dilemmas facing the neonatologist. If too much oxygen is supplied, the child may be visually impaired. Yet, some children simply cannot survive without oxygen levels that are above the safe limit. What do you do then? Do you save such children at the risk of damaging their sight?

The newborn is truly at the mercy of the physician. Improving the medical outlook for neonatal patients is dependent upon experimentation with unproven treatments. Yet, unlike adults, premies cannot grant their permission for these sometimes dangerous trials. Moreover, it is often considered unethical to assign a baby to a control or placebo group when testing promising new lifesaving measures. "These restrictions frequently discourage careful clinical investigation particularly in the case of new drugs, many of which are used despite warning of insufficient studies in infants and children," write Albert Jonsen, professor of ethics, and his colleague Dr. George Lister, of the University of California at San Francisco.

And there are other ways in which the doctor assumes control over tiny patients unable to protest. In the preceding chapter, I described a recent visit to an NICU during which I watched a first-year resident try unsuccessfully seven times to insert an umbilical catheter into a premie. The baby appeared to flinch each time. At the same hospital, I watched another resident fail three times to force a breathing tube down a baby's trachea. It was all dismissed as "training."

Assault by a host of invasive procedures is the sick newborn's lot. Countless needles are stuck in the child's foot and arms to draw blood. Feeding tubes are shoved down its throat and even into its heart vessels. Are we to assume the premie feels no pain? One author of a book on prematurity recently assured parents, "Since the neurologically immature premie is less responsive to his environment than is a full-term newborn, many of the procedures he will undergo during his first rough weeks of life will cause him less pain than they would cause a term infant or an older child." Do we know that for a fact?

Some time ago these physician notes were reported detailing the "progress" of an extremely premature infant named Mignon, who had been born weighing only 482 grams: "She has been plagued with frequent kidney failures, liver problems that defy textbook definition, and the usual lung problems. . . . [A]t seven months after delivery she is hanging in there. We have kept the [umbilical artery] catheter in her aorta all the way, so her hyperalimentation has been intra-arterial. . . . [S]he can't suck because of the endotracheal tube . . . she has been constantly on PEEP . . . But with no spontaneous breathing, all mechanical ventilation, her lungs are pretty damaged now. . . ."

It strikes me that, in the final analysis, there is a peculiar blind spot with regard to the suffering an infant may incur.

Perhaps the California medical ethicist Andrew Jameton is correct when he says, "I think too often in health care, medical suffering is seen as justifiable suffering. It's natural for doctors to promulgate this view, to ensure an atmosphere in which they can work without guilt. But to the infant who's being worked on, it makes no difference what the doctor's rationalization might be."

In view of all the difficult medical and ethical questions surrounding the care of low-birthweight babies, it would save a great deal of anguish if someone could do something to prevent prematurity in the first place. "Prevention is where the strides are going to have to come," says Dr. Thomas Gardner, a prominent Chicago neonatologist. "In saving smaller and smaller babies there's a point beyond which we can't go because of the lung development factor."

Accordingly, the March of Dimes Birth Defects Foundation is sponsoring a three-year study of women prone to deliver early to see whether teaching them the signs of premature labor results in fewer such births. If women can recognize these signs—which include dull backache, cramping, and a sense of pressure on the lower abdomen—they can contact their physicians, who will prescribe drugs and other treatments to postpone delivery.

The study, funded by a $1 million grant from the foundation, is going on in five cities and should be concluded in the spring of 1986. In an earlier trial in San Francisco, the program dramatically lowered the prematurity rate among 1,150 women, from the national average of 6.75 percent to 2.43 percent. As one perinatologist involved in the study says, "The grant to each participating institution is $70,000 a year. The average treatment fee for very tiny premies is $80,000. Prevent one and you've paid for the study."

5

Birth Defects
A Trail of Ancient Riddles

As thou knowest not what is the way of the wind,
Nor how the bones do grow in the womb of her that is with child;
Even so thou knowest not the work of God.

—Ecclesiastes 11:5

What causes birth defects? For the most part, we do not really know. The frightening truth is that doctors today understand little more about what can damage the fetus than they did 2,300 years ago, in the time of Hippocrates.

"From 50 to 80 percent of the time, when a child is born with a defect, we haven't got the foggiest idea why," admits Dr. Godfrey Oakley, director of the birth defects branch of the U.S. Center for Disease Control. It is Oakley's job not only to count the frequency of birth defects in the United States but also to try to ascertain their cause. The first responsibility is difficult enough, since most parts of the country have no systematic recording procedure. But the detective part of his job is almost impossible. We know that a disturbingly large number of children are born with disabilities every year, and we know that something must be behind this statistic. But aside from a few factors that we have been able to isolate—factors that account for just a small percentage of all congenital defects—we are completely in the dark. It is like some sinister shadow play, in which powerful forces are in constant operation but all we can see of them are vague outlines on a curtain.

We are much more adept at listing the immense variety of birth defects. A complete catalogue would occupy several thousand pages. Things can and do go wrong with the manufacture of every conceivable part of a newborn, from the roof of the skull to the bottom of the feet and from the outer layer of skin to the innermost organ system. The abnormality may be obvious, as in the case of a facial malformation, or it may be diabolically obscure, affecting an infinitesimal level of enzyme. Sometimes the defects occur as lone flaws; at other times, they strike in cruel combination, often congregating in a predictable pattern called a syndrome. Science, that dry, old pedant, has given many of these conditions long, indigestible medical names whose murkiness disguises what the disorders really involve. But nature is under no constraints to be so genteel. The reality of some birth defects is so gruesome as to almost bar description. There are anencephalic children whose heads halt abruptly above their huge, podlike eyes and whose thick, distorted bodies bear a striking resemblance to primitive Picasso figures; cyclopic children with a single eye and long proboscises projecting from their foreheads like the antennae of a mollusk; children born with rudimentary heads that are mere bumps on their shoulders and other children born with heads but no face; and children with the arms and legs of a half-formed twin grafted onto their abdomen.

Fortunately, nature generally compensates for her most grotesque errors by reclaiming the infants within hours of their birth. Even so, that still leaves thousands of disabling and disfiguring conditions that are not automatically lethal. These may range from very mild defects (perhaps an extra finger, which can be easily repaired shortly after birth) to severe conditions (say, profound retardation or skeletal deformities or both) that will drastically inhibit the child for the rest of its life.

The number of babies facing such a destiny is huge. With the earth's population increasing by 82 million people a year—a rate equivalent to adding the entire citizenry of Dayton, Ohio, each day—literally millions of children come into the world with congenital defects annually. Although exact figures don't exist, it is safe to say that worldwide at least 20,000 impaired infants are born every day, or about 800 of them an hour. This incidence occurs with rough uniformity year in and year out, a uniformity demonstrated by four studies conducted in widely separated parts of the United States over a period of three decades.

The first of these studies, published by New York's Sloane Hospital for Women in 1954, analyzed 5,739 births at the hospital over a five-year period. Defects were noted in 7 percent of all babies surviving the first 28 days of life. The second study, examining 1,963 infants through the age of two, was conducted on the island of Kauai, in Hawaii, and was published in 1963. This time 7.3 percent of the children were found to have defects. The third study, published in 1965, was conducted by Sam Shapiro, of Johns Hopkins University. It followed 5,123 children to the age of two. Some 5.5 percent of the youngsters were found to have "significant" anomalies, which Shapiro described as those that would either affect survival or require major educational and medical attention as the child grew. The fourth study was also conducted by Shapiro, supported by the Robert Wood Johnson Foundation. Published in 1983, it analyzed one-year-old children from eight scattered geographical regions. The finding: 9 percent of the children had either a severe or moderate defect; and if mild conditions were thrown in, the total came to 13 percent.

The March of Dimes Birth Defects Foundation believes that the true number of congenital disorders is higher than these studies indicate, pointing out that many defects do not manifest themselves until later in life. Notable examples would be diabetes and Huntington's chorea, a deadly neurological disease that does not appear until middle age. It has been suggested that the actual incidence of birth defects, mild as well as severe, may be as high as 15 percent of all live births. This is in contrast to the assumption prevalent some years ago that only 2 to 3 percent of all children had impairments, an error probably due to a failure to follow children long enough to record defects not readily apparent at birth.

Although birth defects as a group are more common than most people think, the occurrence of each known defect is rather rare. It is the accumulation of all the various abnormalities that becomes significant.

For example, take the chromosomal disorders: Down's syndrome is seen just once in every 800 births; Klinefelter's syndrome, a condition restricted to males and characterized by infertility, the growth of breasts, and often mental retardation, occurs once in every 800 to 1,000 births; Turner's syndrome, which affects females, causing short stature, webbing of the neck, immature sexual development, and moderate degrees of learning disorder, has an incidence of once in every 10,000 births; trisomy 13, a lethal condition causing severe defects of the brain, face, heart, and spinal cord, occurs about once in every 5,000 births; fragile X syndrome, which accounts for up to 25 percent of all mental retardation in males, occurs once in every 2,000 births. Any one of these defects is seen relatively infrequently; but all chromosomal abnormalities combined strike as often as once in every 200 births.

The same is true of nonchromosomal malformations. Cleft palate occurs, on the average, once in every 2,000 births; club foot, once in every 400 births; anencephaly, or absence of the brain, once in every 3,000 births; spina bifida, once in every 1,500 births; reduction deformity, the absence of part or all of a limb, about once in 2,500 births; transposition of the great vessels, a heart defect, once in every 14,000 births; atrial septal defect, another heart deformity, once in every 8,600 births; and tracheoesophageal fistula, once in every 5,000 births. Again, regarded individually they are rather isolated occurrences, but taken together, such structural malformations are seen two to three times in every 100 births.

Although the worldwide incidence of birth defects seems to be relatively constant, within each category of defect there are puzzling variations among nations and ethnic stocks. This strongly suggests that not only gene-pool influences but also environmental factors such as diet, smog, altitude, water purity, background radiation, and local infectious agents play a role in causing abnormalities.

An idea of these geographical variations can be obtained by looking at some figures compiled by the International Clearinghouse for Birth Defects Monitoring Systems, a network of some 26 countries whose purpose is to share data about birth abnormalities. The clearinghouse was established in 1974 at the initiative of the March of Dimes. The following statistics are from the clearinghouse's 1981 annual report, the latest available.

Anencephaly occurred once in every 3,333 births in the United States. But it occurred once in every 575 births in Northern Ireland; once in every 1,666 births in Hungary; once in every 2,127 births in Canada; once in every 2,564 births in England and Wales; and only once in every 8,333 births in Sweden. Even allowing for some differences in reporting accuracy among nations, some hidden factor was obviously at work to produce the huge disparity between Ireland and Sweden.

Or take spina bifida. It was seen once in every 1,786 births by the U.S. reporting station in Atlanta. But it occurred once in every 492 births in Northern Ireland; once in every 900 births in Mexico; once in every 962 births in England and Wales; once in every 1,111 births in Israel; once in every 1,851 births in Canada; once in every 4,348 births in Finland; and only once in every 20,000 births in Japan.

Now consider reduction deformity. The finding in the United States was that it occurred once in every 2,439 births. In Italy, though, it was found once in every 1,220 births; in Northern Ireland, once in every 1,315 births; in Israel, once in every 1,492 births; in Sweden, once in every 1,515 births; in Japan, once in every 1,724 births; in France, once in every 2,380 births; in England and Wales, once in every 2,500 births; and in Canada, once in every 2,941 births.

Finally, let's look at cleft palate. The incidence in the United States was once in every 3,846 births. But in Finland it was once in every 885 births; in Northern Ireland, once in every 1,063 births; in New Zealand, once in every 1,851 births; in England and Wales, once in every 2,439 births; in Canada, once in every 2,632 births; and in Japan, once in every 3,226 births. In the Rhone Alps region of France, it was an incredibly low once in 7,143 births.

Why should Finnish children be so susceptible to palate deformity while the French Alpine children are not? Why should Italian infants be two and a half times more likely to have a limb anomaly than those in Canada? Why does a baby in Northern Ireland have a 40-fold greater risk of having spina bifida than a baby in Japan? Is some vitamin essential to the developing fetus missing in one cuisine and not another? No one knows.

The prevalence of reduction deformity fell sharply in Japan between 1980 and 1981, going from once in every 935 births to once in every 1,724. How does one account for that? Or for the fact that anencephaly increased in South America from once in every 5,556 births in 1980 to once in every 2,500 births in 1981? Did some crucial environmental factor change in these regions over the course of two years?

Northern Ireland had the highest rate of birth defects among all 26 countries in the program. It led in three of the eleven categories— namely, anencephaly, spina bifida, and anorectal atresia, a malformation in which the child has an incomplete rectum or anus. It came in second in four other categories, including Down's syndrome, esophageal atresia, cleft palate, and hydrocephaly. Its nearest competitor was Israel, which led in two categories: omphalocele, in which the abdominal organs protrude though the belly wall, and hypospadias, in which there is an abnormal opening on the underside of the penis. Israel also came in second in two other categories, anorectal atresia and anencephaly. The unusually high incidence of malformation in two countries that are chronically under a state of siege leads an observer to wonder about the causative role of stress.

More riddles. Eastern European Jews are a hundred times more susceptible to a genetic disorder known as Tay-Sachs disease. Its tiny victims lack an enzyme called hexosaminidase A, which results in the accumulation of sphingolipids, or fatty acids, in the brain. Symptoms first appear at six months of age, when an irreversible degeneration of brain function begins. A characteristic cherry-red spot becomes apparent on each retina. Blindness, convulsions, dementia, and paralysis follow, with death coming by age four. Blacks, meanwhile, are susceptible to a hereditary blood disorder known as sickle-cell anemia, in which the red corpuscles lose their round shape and take on a crescent form. The cells tend to hook onto one other, causing the blood to grow viscous and circulation to slow down. The result is chronic anemia, spleen destruction, joint pain, and heart and liver damage. The disease strikes one out of every 400 American blacks, but 10 percent of the black population are carriers of the sickle-cell trait, generally without symptomatology. There also exists an abnormality called beta thalassemia, or Cooley's anemia, a disease of Greeks, Italians, and other Mediterranean peoples. The victim's red blood cells are defective and have a very short life span, leading to anemia, fever, a failure to thrive, and damage to the heart, liver, spleen, and pancreas. Excessive iron from the dying blood cells turns the skin a bronze color, while physical growth and sexual maturity are retarded.

Why should a racial or ethnic group suffer from a particular genetic disorder? In the case of blacks, it has been suggested that sickling of the blood cells provides resistance to malaria and was therefore an evolutionary adaptation to life in Africa. But what possible adaptation could be involved in Tay-Sachs disease? Could the gene, as some researchers theorize, have granted a carrier greater immunity to tuberculosis?

The depressing fact is that we don't have many answers for such questions. We do know, however, why Down's syndrome is more common in heavily Roman Catholic countries such as Spain (the world leader), Italy, France, and Ireland. The reason: older women are more likely to bear Down's children; consequently, countries where birth control is frowned upon and where childbirth continues until menopause are going to have more Down's. Similarly, a high incidence of neural-tube defects—that is to say, spina bifida, anencephaly, and encephalocele—seems to befall working-class people of Anglican and Celtic stock. This is believed by some researchers to be partly a genetic phenomenon and partly an environmental one. It was discovered in England in 1968 that women who delivered babies with neural-tube defects tended to have a deficiency of folic acid, a vitamin contained in green leafy vegetables. Hence, it was theorized that the lack of fresh greens in the British proletarian diet caused genetically predisposed women to bear children with neural-tube defects. Supporting this theory was the knowledge that these defects tend to predominate in northern climes, such as those of Scotland and Northern Ireland, where fresh produce is more expensive, particularly in wintertime, and is thus less available to poorer women. Moreover, the British practice of boiling fresh vegetables destroyed the vitamins in whatever greens the women did manage to buy. In 1980 Dr. Richard W. Smithells, from Leeds, England, published the results of a study in which he tested two sets of expectant mothers who had previously borne a child with a neural-tube defect. These women have a 5 percent greater risk of having another affected child. Smithells gave supplements of folic acid to one set of mothers and not the other. Of the 178 babies born to the treated mothers, one had a neural-tube defect. But of the 260 children born to the untreated women, 13 were so afflicted—exactly the 5 percent expected statistically. In 1981 Dr. K. M. Laurence, of the Welsh National School of Medicine, Cardiff, Wales, duplicated the experiment. This time 44 expectant mothers with a history of neural-tube defects were given folic acid during pregnancy. None of them had a recurrence upon birth. But of the 67 women who did not receive the treatment, 6 proceeded to have children with the defects. It appears from these two tests that folic acid deficiency is indeed the culprit, but further research is being conducted.

The study of congenital defects is known as teratology, from the Greek word *teratos* ("monster"). It is hard to imagine a more pejorative name for a medical specialty, unless one were to rename psychiatry "kookology." No less solemn an authority than *The American Heritage Dictionary of the English Language* defines *teratology* as "the biological study of the production, development, anatomy, and classification of monsters." Such semantic insensitivity reinforces the public's tendency to dehumanize people with birth defects. In recognition of this, several teratologists recently tried to rechristen their field "dysmorphology," from the Greek word *morphe,* meaning "form or shape" and "dys" meaning "abnormal," in an attempt to get away from the medieval aspects of the established name. The effort has yet to catch on, however.

Teratology is at once a very old and a very young science. It is old in the sense that we have been fascinated with explaining birth defects since ancient times. It is young in that it has acquired a firm scientific foundation only in the last 40 years.

For many centuries the prevailing view was that defects were of supernatural or psychokinetic origin. Some held that they were divine portents. Others deemed them evidence of the mother's amorous misdeeds with animals or the Evil One. Still others asserted that they were the result of morbid maternal thoughts during pregnancy. But all was not myth and superstition. Hippocrates understood well the role of heredity and environmental factors. For example, he had this to say on the cause of epilepsy:

> Its origin is hereditary, like that of other diseases. . . . what is to hinder it from happening that where the father and mother were subject to this disease, certain of their offspring should be so

affected also. As the semen comes from all parts of the body, healthy particles will come from healthy parts, and unhealthy from unhealthy parts.

And this on the effect of unwholesome waters:

Such waters then as are marshy, stagnant, and belong to lakes, are necessarily hot in summer, thick, and have a strong smell, since they have no current; women (who drink such water) are subject to edema; when pregnant they have difficult deliveries; the infants are large and swelled, and then during nursing they become wasted and sickly.

Aristotle also wrote with considerable knowledge on the subject and added his belief that uterine injury was somehow involved. In the 17th century, the great English physician William Harvey, after empirical study of chicken and deer embryos, conceived the idea that malformations were the result of arrested embryonic development, in other words, of something that interfered with the normal growth of body structures. Although Harvey was quite correct with this view, it would be more than 200 years before others were to elaborate on it.

With the 19th century came the first real flowering of teratology. There was intense interest in discovering and classifying new defects. In 1843 Dr. William John Little, of England, published his classic clinical description of spastic diplegia, a form of cerebral palsy, and in subsequent years voiced the conviction that the disorder was related to prematurity and asphyxia during birth. In a paper published in 1862, Little employed a literary allusion to drive home the association between prematurity and birth defect, citing the lament of Shakespeare's crippled Richard III:

Deform'd, unfinish'd, sent before my time
Into this breathing world, scarce half made up.

In 1866 Dr. John Langdon Haydon Down, of London, gave a thorough description of a particular syndrome of mental and physical defects that had captured his attention. The disorder was, of course, the one we know today as Down's syndrome. Down chose to call it mongolism, fancying that its victims resembled the descendants of Genghis Khan. He subscribed to the bizarre belief that genealogy could sometimes leap spontaneously across racial lines and that such births seemed to prove "the unity of the human species."

In the same year, an obscure Austrian monk named Gregor Mendel published a treatise that was eventually to have vast influence on the field of teratology but that excited almost no interest at the time.

Mendel was something of an underachiever. He had failed to pass an examination for a job as a high school teacher—ironically, flunking the biology section of the test. Yet by working unobtrusively in his garden, he passed into immortality. Mendel's curiosity was piqued by an oddity: if he bred a round-seeded pea plant with an angular-seeded one, all the offspring would have round seeds. But in the next generation the angular characteristic would reappear in one out of four plants. By carefully observing successive generations of pea plants, this quiet monk formulated the principles that govern genetic inheritance. Not until nearly 40 years later, though, was it recognized that certain human malformations can be passed along like the traits of garden peas.

The 19th century abounded with theories to explain birth defects. Among the most astute thinkers was a brilliant Scottish obstetrician, Dr. John W. Ballantyne, of Edinburgh, who more than anyone else in his era made the connection between prenatal events and birth defects. "There is some experimental proof," he wrote in his classic *Manual of Antenatal Pathology and Hygiene: The Foetus,* "that some poisons reach the foetus and sometimes produce structural alteration in the foetus and placenta." Ballantyne's idea was a fairly radical one for its time, since the opinion of most scientists was that human fetuses were so well protected in the uterus that few, if any, external forces could threaten them. The unborn child was thought to ride out the nine months of pregnancy in an impregnable bunker whose hatch cover was the placenta. This view was rather illogically embraced despite the evidence of a hundred years of experiments showing that environmental factors could induce deformities in chicks and other lower animals. Scientists were convinced that mammals remained somehow immune. The belated dissemination of Mendel's discoveries, in the early 1900s, only served to cement this dogma still further. It became the fashion to ascribe virtually all human birth defects to hereditary, rather than environmental, causes. Genetics was king, a state of affairs that was to last well into this century.

To the outside world the debate was of no interest. People were as cruelly indifferent to congenital defects as they always had been. So-called village idiots continued to be taken for granted and taunted, with no thought as to how they got that way. Carnival goers would rush to see the dog-faced boy, the Siamese twins, and the bearded lady. Parents kept their "strange" offspring in back bedrooms, trying to hide the family's "shame" from the neighbors. And bleak institutions overflowed with unfortunate defectives, who were made to live out their desolate lives under the most appalling conditions. The idea that one might prevent or correct birth impairments never entered people's minds. Why should it? If they were hereditary, there was nothing you could do about them, anyway.

The first chink in the impregnable-womb theory came in 1928, when a Philadelphia gynecologist named Douglas Murphy reported that the X ray, medicine's prized new tool, could severely damage the human fetus. It was common at that time to use pelvic radiation on women to cure "female diseases," particularly cancers, and the technique was performed whether the patient was pregnant or not. Very often, raw radium was placed on the tumor site only inches from the fetus and allowed to remain there for 24 hours. Alerted by some experiments that showed that X rays could cause serious harm to animal fetuses, Murphy reviewed the outcome of 74 pregnancies during which the mother had undergone pelvic irradiation. He found that 25 of the babies, or an alarming 33 percent, were born deformed, most of them exhibiting microcephaly, or abnormally small heads. This rate was more than 2,000 times the statistical probability and caused Murphy to recommend an end to therapeutic radiation of expectant mothers. His findings were brought home even more tragically many years later when pregnant women who were near ground zero during the atomic bombings of Hiroshima and Nagasaki delivered relatively large numbers of children with microcephaly and retardation. Women farther away from the center of the blasts bore children who either were normal or showed less dramatic aftereffects.

Strangely, in spite of the clear implication of Murphy's research that external influences could indeed hurt the fetus, teratologists were not led to rethink their heredity theory. They dismissed the effect of radiation on the unborn as a mere aberration. For the next 10 years the mainstream of the medical community continued to believe that all birth defects were determined before conception, not after. Yet, even as they clung to this presumption, some pioneering clinicians were proving it wrong in the laboratory. Inexplicably, what had been continually lacking were teratologic experiments on mammals. In 1937, however, a researcher named Hale reported that by feeding pigs a diet without vitamin A, he could cause them to have piglets without eyeballs. Then, in 1940, a pair of physicians from the University of Cincinnati Children's Hospital induced skeletal deformities in newborn rats by feeding their mothers a diet deficient in riboflavin. The researchers, a young Austrian immigrant named Josef Warkany and his colleague, Rose Nelson, found that of 164 baby rats, 57 (or 35 percent) had multiple birth defects. "An abnormally short mandible was found in 39 animals," they wrote in the journal *Science*. "A short tail was seen in 12 animals. . . . In 42 of these specimens the lower legs showed reduction in size or absence of the tibia; . . . in 22 there was fusion of the ribs. . . ." By comparison, another group of female rats were fed a normal diet. Of their 216 young, only 1 showed abnormalities. The hidden message in Warkany and Nelson's work was that if rat fetuses were vulnerable to changes in the environment, the same was likely to be true of humans.

Confirmation came quickly and unexpectedly. Epidemics of rubella, better known as German measles, had swept across Australia with a vengeance in 1939 and 1940. As there had not been an outbreak of the disease in that country for more than 17 years, many young pregnant women had developed no immunity to the virus. They came down with it in great numbers. In October 1941 an observant eye surgeon named Dr. Norman Gregg delivered a grim report to the Ophthalmological Society of Australia. He said that in a year's time he had encountered 78 cases of congenital cataract in babies, an incidence he considered so unusually high that he undertook an investigation. He found that 68 of the infants' mothers had suffered from rubella during their first trimester of pregnancy. It appeared, he told his colleages, that German measles could cause birth defects.

Here was further tangible proof that the human fetus was not so safe in his uterine citadel. Gregg's discovery was soon corroborated by another Australian, Dr. Charles Swan, and by later studies in Europe, North America, and Turkey. These investigations identified a number of other defects associated with rubella, including heart abnormalities, deafness, microcephaly, mental retardation, poor motor coordination, and spina bifida.

It was as if a switch had been thrown. All of a sudden teratologists around the world began to concentrate on the environmental causes of birth defects, hunting for other viruses and toxic agents that might be teratogenic (able to produce abnormalities). Over the next 20 years, researchers would isolate a number of substances that can cause malformations in animals, and a few that are harmful in humans. But, oddly enough, society at large still paid no attention. Teratology was to remain throughout the 1950s something of a medical stepchild, its steady progress eclipsed by more dramatic developments like the conquest of polio and the war on heart disease. And then, in 1961, something happened to erase public indifference forever.

On May 4 of that year, a respected young Australian obstetrician named William McBride attended the birth of a baby who had foreshortened arms and an intestinal atresia. Three weeks later he delivered another child with exactly the same abnormalities, and two weeks after that, another one. The limb malformations were of a very rare kind called phocomelia, in which the long bones of the arms and legs are either missing or deformed. Dr. McBride spent a very anxious weekend tearing through every piece of medical literature he could find on congenital abnormalities. At the end of two days, he was convinced the defects had been caused by a new sedative and anti-morning-sickness drug called Distaval, which he had been giving his expectant patients. A little later that year, on the other side of the world, a German children's specialist named Dr. Widukind Lenz was approached by a Hamburg lawyer whose wife and sister had both recently given birth to children with phocomelia. The man wanted to know how such a bizarre coincidence could occur. Lenz agreed to investigate. Over the next several months, his inquiries turned up 50 cases of Hamburg babies who had been born with phocomelic deformities in the preceding 13 months. Municipal birth records from 1930 to 1955 had recorded only one such case in 25 years! Questioning the mothers, Lenz discovered that they had taken a new sedative called Contergan during pregnancy. On November 18, 1961, Lenz addressed the Pediatricians' Association of North Rhine-Westphalia and told them of his fears about Contergan. Less than a month later the English medical journal *Lancet* published a letter from McBride warning of the dangers of Distaval.

Both Distaval and Contergan were trade names for the same drug, a tranquilizing preparation manufactured by the German pharmaceutical house Chemie Grünenthal. The drug's pharmacological name was thalidomide.

Over the following year, it would be disclosed that more than 10,000 babies in 46 countries had been born with deformities caused by thalidomide. The drug is toxic to the embryo during the first trimester of pregnancy, when the infant's limb buds are forming. As a consequence, the child's arms and legs develop incompletely, taking on the characteristic appearance of tiny flippers (*phocomelia* is from the Greek word meaning "seal") The child often has virtually nothing but a head and torso. Hardest hit of all countries were Germany and Britain, which together incurred half the cases. The United States escaped a scourge on a similar scale only because a persnickety Food and Drug Administration officer named Dr. Frances Kelsey refused to approve thalidomide for public sale.

The thalidomide disaster chastened the world in a number of ways. It provided incontrovertible proof that environmental agents can and do cause congenital abnormalities, that poisons can obviously penetrate the barrier of the placenta and reach the developing fetus. And on a deeper level, it seemed to sensitize the public, not simply to the horror of birth defects, but to the plight of handicapped people in general. The photographic image of babies whose hands and feet were attached directly to their shoulders and hips—babies that had been doomed not by the implacable laws of heredity but by a moment's pause at the medicine cabinet—was powerfully affecting to millions of people. Suddenly, the birth impaired seemed less like dehumanized freaks and more like people whose fates had been sealed by ironic and arbitrary forces. It is probably no accident that just a few years later, in 1973, the U.S. Congress passed legislation to improve the lives of the disabled. One might even find in the thalidomide tragedy a major link in the chain of events leading to the legalization of abortion in the United States. The sorrowful trek of an American woman, Sherry Finkbein, forced to go abroad to abort her child after taking thalidomide, received vast publicity and further strengthened the proabortion cause.

Finally, there were two other aspects to thalidomide that directly affected teratology and the medical/pharmaceutical community. First, the manufacturers had never conducted proper animal reproductive studies before placing the drug on the market. But even if they had, as it turned out, little would have been revealed. Subsequent testing showed that the sole effect thalidomide has on pregnant rats is to mildly reduce litter size; it does not cause malformations. Nor did it seem to so affect dogs. Not until researchers tried the New Zealand white rabbit did they find an animal in which physical deformities could be produced. The lesson was that species do not all react the same way to a given teratogen and that animal models are therefore not especially useful in assessing a substance's teratological potential in man. The only sure test is a controlled study on human beings, not always feasible from an ethical point of view. Second, thalidomide dealt the death blow to an old and rickety assumption in teratology, that for something to be strong enough to damage the fetus, it must also produce symptoms in the mother. Thalidomide has almost no effect on pregnant women, other than to make them sleepy or quell nausea. But even a single, minuscule dose, if taken during certain key weeks early in pregnancy, is enough to deform an unborn child. This was not the first time the assumption had been discredited; it was merely the most graphic.

In the years since then, the science of teratology has made steady inroads in identifying still more agents that can injure the human fetus. Still active in the search is Josef Warkany, whose 1940 experiments on rats deprived of riboflavin opened many doors in the study of birth defects. Now an octogenarian, Warkany has made numerous contributions, not the least of which was his book *Congenital Malformations,* an exhaustive compilation of everything known about deformity in man. The project took him more than 10 years. For these and other reasons, the American Pediatric Society a few years ago honored War-

kany with its annual award. On that occasion, Warkany was introduced by a dinner speaker accurately, if with questionable imagery,
as Mr. Teratology.

When one considers the astronomical number of complex processes that go into the development of an infant, it seems amazing
that birth defects don't occur more often than they do. It starts with
a single fertilized egg that somehow differentiates into billions of hair
cells, eye cells, skin cells, teeth cells, blood cells, brain cells, heart cells,
and so on ad infinitum. Some innate directing force, some Cecil B.
DeMille of the body, makes everything happen on signal. But we have
not begun to understand it yet.

Central to the whole affair is a mysterious, gypsylike activity known
as cell migration. Large numbers of cells must move from one part of
the embryo to another within a specified period of time. When for
some reason a cell doesn't get there punctually, a birth defect is the
result. For example, the developing palate is composed of two shelves.
If they don't fuse together during a particular two days of the gestation process, the child will have a cleft palate. A similar thing occurs
neurologically. During the fourth week of fetal life, when the embryo
is no bigger than one of the letters on this page, there forms along its
back a single layer of thick tissue, called the neural plate. The two
lateral ends of this neural plate must fold together like the halves of
a quilt to form the neural tube, which goes on to become the brain
and spinal cord. If for some reason during this crucial week the tube
fails to close at any point along its length, a neural-tube defect, such
as spina bifida or anencephaly, will result. This migration of cells is
not unlike the traffic pattern of airlines crisscrossing the country.
Embryonic cells are perpetually on the move, passing each other on
their way to somewhere else, traveling through pathways composed
of proteins, collagens, and other fibrous substances. For example, tes-
ticular and ovarian cells are thought to originate near the embryonic
head and migrate all the way to the groin. If they don't get there when
they're due to arrive, infertility will be the result, as the British
embryologist Dr. Marjorie England has demonstrated.

Nature invented the idea of quality control long before modern
industry did. Quite often, when a fetus (or embryo, as it is properly
called before the ninth week) is not developing normally, the flaw is
detected and the manufacturing process is brought to a halt. This
mechanism by which gestation self-destructs is called spontaneous
abortion, or miscarriage. Between 15 and 20 percent of all pregnancies terminate in this manner. In former times, miscarriage was viewed
as the tragic loss of a healthy child. Science now knows that 60 to 80

percent of early miscarriages involve embryos so gravely defective that their survival after birth is improbable. Even in later miscarriages, malformations are more common than in babies that reach full term. Thus, instead of seeing spontaneous abortion as a tragedy, one might be better advised to consider it a blessing. Unfortunately, quality control is not 100 percent effective. A certain percentage of malformed fetuses will slip through the screen and be born.

Generally speaking, birth defects can be divided into three loose categories: those that are the consequence of prenatal influences; those resulting from low birthweight; and those that occur because of an injury during the birth process itself. It is the first category that will concern us in this section.

We can break this group down essentially into four subdivisions. There are defects of genetic origin, those caused solely by the genes and chromosomes. There are those inflicted strictly by environmental factors, such as maternal infection, nutritional imbalance, chemical activity, or radiation. And there are those that are multifactorial—those, in other words, in which genetic and environmental influences are thought to have interacted, as in spina bifida, diabetes mellitus, asthma, and cleft palate. There is also a fourth group for which no cause has been identified. These just seem to happen. To the enduring frustration of teratologists, this latter group is far and away the largest, accounting for as many as 60 percent of all congenital abnormalities.

Defects due purely to genes and chromosomes, that is, inherited defects, form a much smaller category than earlier teratologists imagined. All told, they constitute only an estimated 14 percent of all malformations. Those wrought by the genes are called single-gene disorders, and they come about in two ways. Either they are part of a long-standing family heritage, passed down from one's remote ancestors, or they are the result of a "mutation," a spontaneous change in the makeup of a parent's gene.

Genes are the basic units of heredity, and they affect every one of a child's physical and mental characteristics, from its hair color, eye color, and chance of an early heart attack, to whether the child will be a good athlete, scholar, or musician. The basic component of a gene is deoxyribonucleic acid, or DNA. This remarkable substance arranges itself in a double-helix pattern, two strands winding around each other like a braid. Along the strands, a chemical alphabet, made up of just four letters, is imprinted, forming the genetic code. It is the sequence of these four chemicals, which occur in a multitude of permutations, that actually dictates how an individual's body develops. And it is this sequence, conveyed to offspring through the sperm or egg cells, that passes traits along from generation to generation. The code tells the amorphous bloc of cells that is soon to be a child what kind of nose to build, how much insulin to produce, and how many teeth to make. Even a small variation in the code's instructions will cause the cells to manufacture something abnormally. A faulty gene is thus like a misprint in a recipe, equivalent to the omission of the yeast from the directions for bread dough. The misprint is fated to be reprinted over and over. A child born today with a single-gene disorder owes its destiny to ancestors who lived and died eons ago.

Genes are arranged in essentially linear fashion along 23 pairs of larger structures called chromosomes. Each cell in a person's body contains the same genes on the same 23 pairs of chromosomes. A cell from the big toe possesses the identical genetic material as a cell from the ear. In every pair of chromosomes, one chromosome is derived from one's father, the other from one's mother. Twenty-two of these pairs are called autosomes, and they determine a wide variety of characteristics. The 23d pair is known as the sex chromosomes, so called because they determine a person's sex. Sex chromosomes come in two varieties, X and Y. If the embryo receives an X chromosome from each of its parents, it will have an XX configuration in each of its body cells and will be a girl. If it receives an X from its mother and a Y from its father, it will have an XY configuration and will be a boy.

Ordinarily, human cells divide by a process known as mitosis. Each new cell is a carbon copy of the original one and contains the parent cell's 46 chromosomes arranged in 23 pairs. But the cells that manufacture sperm and ova are the only ones in the human body that divide in another way. These cells have devised a special system called meiosis, which gives each sperm or egg only 23 chromosomes, or one of every original pair. This is so that at the time of conception, when genetic material from the mother and father are combined, the resulting fertilized egg will have the proper number of human chromosomes, 46, instead of 92. Right before meiosis takes place, the chromosomes lie down next to each other and exchange long strings of genetic information. The purpose is to shuffle the gene deck a little bit. If this did not happen, the same parental chromosomes would be recycled over and over again; brothers and sisters would be exactly alike.

Genes come in pairs, just as chromosomes do; a person has two genes for every genetic trait. These genes may be either "dominant" or "recessive." A dominant gene is one that makes its influence felt even if it exists on only one chromosome in a pair. Each child conceived by a man with a single flawed dominant gene and a woman with normal genes has a 50 percent chance of developing the abnormal trait. This is because there is a 50 percent chance the father will pass along his faulty gene instead of his normal one. A recessive one, on the other hand, does not express itself unless it is inherited from both the father and the mother. Almost everyone has between four and eight defective recessive genes, but they are "masked" by dominant normal genes. Should both parents carry the same faulty recessive gene, however, the trait can slip around the mask. Each child they conceive will have a 25 percent chance of developing the abnormality, a 50 percent chance of becoming an unaffected carrier, and a 25 percent chance of escaping scot-free. Visualize it this way, where each parent has a normal dominant gene N and a faulty recessive gene f:

	N	f
N	NN	Nf
f	Nf	ff

Here, theoretically, one child inherits both normal genes (NN) and is unaffected. Two more inherit a dominant gene and a recessive gene (Nf), which leaves them unscathed but able to pass the trait along to their children. And one child receives both recessives (ff) and develops the defect. In practice, though, these are only statistical risks. Parents can have 10 normal children or 10 affected ones. Each pregnancy is a new flip of the coin.

Both dominant and recessive genes occurring along the autosomes (chromosomes 1 through 22) can produce birth defects in children of either sex. They are called autosomal dominant or autosomal recessive disorders. A third class of inheritance involves faulty recessive genes carried on the sex chromosomes (chromosome 23). These are called X-linked recessive disorders, and they tend to affect only males. There also exist diseases that are X-linked dominant, but they are very rare.

Examples of autosomal dominant disorders would include achondroplasia, the classic form of dwarfism resulting from a defect in the growth of the long bones, causing the victim to have a normal-sized trunk, a large head, a depressed nasal bridge, and disproportionately short limbs; neurofibromatosis, or the Elephant Man's disease, which is characterized by a proliferation of soft tumors and, sometimes, skeletal abnormalities; and Huntington's chorea, or Woody Guthrie's disease, a degenerative neurological disorder that first appears at about the age of 40 and is invariably fatal. Although these three are quite devastating, most dominant inheritances tend to be less serious than recessively inherited disease. Polydactyly, for instance, the presence of extra fingers or toes, is an autosomal dominant trait, as is adult polycystic kidney, a condition marked by sporadic pain and high blood pressure. Both conditions are entirely compatible with a normal life.

Generally, autosomal dominant diseases are physical abnormalities rather than biochemical ones, and they seldom induce mental retardation. Crouzon's disease, for example, which produces grotesque facial deformities, including a parrot-beaked nose, a towering forehead, and bulging eyes, nevertheless usually leaves the victim with normal intelligence.

Autosomal recessive illnesses, on the other hand, frequently involve an enzyme deficiency, which inhibits the individual's ability to break down certain chemicals. Toxic materials subsequently collect in the body and brain, often causing retardation and early death. Examples of such diseases include phenylketonuria, in which the child lacks an enzyme necessary to break down phenylalanine, an essential amino acid present in many foods, so that an excess of the substance accumulates in the brain and leads to retardation; cystic fibrosis, a disorder of the mucus-producing glands that primarily affects the pancreas and lungs, causing an inability to digest certain foods and the life-threatening buildup of thick, tenacious mucus in the respiratory tract; maple syrup urine disease, a metabolic disorder in which an enzyme necessary for breaking down certain amino acids is lacking, conferring a distinctive maple-syrup odor on a baby's urine and leading to coma and seizures; dysautonomia, a disease of Jews affecting the autonomic nervous system, depriving the victim of the sensations of pain and taste and the capacity to swallow or cry; sickle-cell anemia; beta thalassemia; Wilson's disease, an inability to metabolize copper and its consequent deposit in the liver and brain, with resultant cirrhosis, tremors, muscle rigidity, speech difficulty, and dementia; and Hurler's syndrome, in which mucopolysaccharides accumulate in the tissues, causing "gargoyle" features, dwarfism, clouding of the cornea, humping of the back, severe retardation, and early death.

Some examples, meanwhile, of X-linked recessive disorders are hemophilia, in which the lack of a clotting factor causes excessive bleeding; certain kinds of microcephaly; Duchenne-type muscular dystrophy, a cruel disorder that begins around age 5 and leads to progressive wasting of the leg and pelvic muscles, heart disease, and death by age 20; Lowe's syndrome, characterized by congenital cataracts and glaucoma, a long, narrow head, retardation, kidney disease, skeletal deformities, and poor muscle tone; Lesch-Nyhan syndrome, a metabolic disease marked by severe mental retardation, spasticity, impaired kidney function, and self-mutilation of the fingers and lips by biting; and Bruton's agammaglobulinemia, in which the child lacks immunity to disease and must receive large infusions of plasma or immunoglobulin.

As if the established single-gene disorders were not enough, genes may also mutate spontaneously, as a result of exposure to cosmic radiation or a virus, for example. Such a mutant gene in a parent will then be passed along to the offspring, becoming part of the child's genetic inventory and handed down to his or her descendants in the same manner as any other gene. It has been conjectured that Tay-Sachs disease, an autosomal recessive disorder, began as an isolated mutation in one of the East European Jews who migrated to the Baltic region during the 13th and 14th centuries. Ninety percent of Tay-Sachs victims are Jews whose ancestors lived in the Polish and Lithuanian provinces surrounding Kaunas and Grodno. Jews of this period lived in settlements of fewer than 80 people and almost invariably intermarried, factors that would have promoted the transmittal of the gene. This ability of a mutant gene belonging to one individual to quickly attain a high frequency within a small community is known in genetics as the founder effect. The effect can operate even in the case of a "lethal" gene (one that kills its victims before they can propagate) if the gene confers some selective survival advantage on carriers (a possible immunity to TB in the case of Tay-Sachs).

Chromosomal aberrations are the other form of genetically transmitted birth defect. They tend to be more devastating than single-gene disorders because whole communities of genes are involved, rather than just one. An estimated 20,000 infants are born with abnormalities of the chromosomes each year in the United States. These aberrations result from accidents that cause the victim to end up with either too much or too little of a particular chromosome. The best-known of these disorders is Down's syndrome, in which the victim has an extra chromosome beyond the normal 46, a condition known as trisomy. Conversely, when someone is missing a chromosome, it is labeled monosomy. Since the Down's victim always has part or all of an extra 21st chromosome, the defect has been given the name trisomy 21. But one could just as easily have an extra 13th or an extra 18th chromosome, in which case the conditions would be called trisomy 13 and trisomy 18.

How do these accidents come about? The most common way is called nondisjunction, and it works like this: before fertilization and during the meiosis process—in which chromosomes split up so that the resulting sperm or ova will have 23 chromosomes apiece—the split goes awry and one sex cell gets both of a pair of chromosomes, giving it a total of 24, and another sex cell gets neither, giving it 22. Now imagine that an egg with 24 chromosomes gets fertilized by a sperm with 23. The resulting embryo will have 47 chromosomes, including 3 of a particular pair rather than the desired 2. This form of nondisjunction is believed to occur more often in women than in men because the incidence of Down's and other trisomies corresponds strongly with increasing maternal age but much less with the age of the father. The explanation could be the poor shelf life of the mother's ova. A woman is born with all the eggs she will ever have, and she draws on them, one at a time, for the whole of her reproductive life. It is possible that age may cause these ova to deteriorate, so that when the time comes for final meiotic division an error occurs.

But there is another form of nondisjunction, one that may occur immediately *after* fertilization, during the early cell division of the embryo. Suppose the zygote, as the embryo is called at this stage, has four cells that are about to divide into eight. Suppose also that something goes wrong and that one of those cells divides unevenly into one cell with 47 chromosomes and another with 45. Some of these abnormal cells will continue to reproduce, and the individual will thereafter possess both normal and abnormal cells, a condition known as mosaicism. The proportion of abnormal cells will determine how symptomatic the individual will be.

Two other things that can go wrong with chromosomes are deletion and translocation. These come about when a piece of a chromosome breaks off, perhaps as the result of exposure to X rays or ingestion of certain destructive chemicals. The segment can be lost forever, in which case there is a deletion. Or it can reattach itself to a healthy chromosome, in which case there is a translocation. Should the translocated piece of chromosome be a passenger aboard a sperm or ovum involved in fertilization, the embryo will acquire not only two of that particular chromosome, as it ordinarily would, but also the extra piece, resulting in a birth defect.

About 95 percent of all Down's syndrome results from nondisjunction before conception. The other 5 percent is due to translocation or mosaicism. No matter what the scenario, the overabundance of 21st chromosome wreaks havoc on fetal development, causing the classic features of Down's: the eyes that appear to slant; the flat profile with its pug nose; the small, rounded head; the sparse hair; the large, protruding tongue; the ruddy cheeks; the speckled irises; the small ears; the short, fleshy neck; the short, stubby hands with their characteristic transverse palm crease; and the rag doll limpness. It is a medical curiosity that people with Down's syndrome bear a striking resemblance to one another, no matter what their parents look like. This is the case with many other genetic disorders as well.

The extra 21st chromosome also causes a number of internal abnormalities. It may produce heart defects, and it blights the child's neurons, or nerve cells. Neurons have small, treelike branches, called dendrites, that receive communications from other neurons. Tiny projections along the dendrites, called dendritic spines, enhance these transmissions. Down's children have been shown to have fewer and narrower dendritic spines. This may slow down message reception, and it could be one reason why Down's victims have poor mental function. A biochemical cause is being investigated as well. It appears that certain chemical processes in the brain, including the metabolic consumption of sugar, occur faster in Down's people than in normal individuals. How this might affect cerebral function isn't clear.

Down's is responsible for between 5 and 10 percent of all severe mental retardation. In the vast majority of cases, the chromosomal damage is a chance occurrence, whose probability increases with maternal age. But recently it has been found that Down's sometimes occurs in clusters, inspiring theories that another component, perhaps a virus or background radiation, may play a role in the disease's causation. A study done in southern Illinois, for instance, showed that over a five-year period one county had five times the number of Down's cases as would be statistically likely. In one year alone, 1978, it had twice as many cases as in each of the other four years. The average age of the mothers was only 22.

It was in January of 1959 that Jérôme Lejeune, of the University of Paris, announced that he had found 47 chromosomes in the cells of three Down's children, demonstrating for the first time the link between chromosomes and birth defects. In the brief period since that historic discovery, a number of additional chromosomal disorders have been identified. Among them are several other trisomy conditions that, like Down's, affect the autosomes. The most notable of these are trisomy 8, trisomy 13, and trisomy 18—trisomy 8 being the least severe of the three. It is marked by the partial presence of an extra 8th chromosome, producing mental retardation, large ears, crossed eyes, prominent lower lip, and skeletal anomalies, particularly missing kneecaps. Trisomies 13 and 18 inflict extensive malformations, ranging from profound retardation, craniofacial deformities, heart defects, and growth deficiencies to hernias, urinary tract anomalies, and "rocker bottom" feet. They occur once in many thousands of births and are generally incompatible with life; the afflicted children die in early infancy 90 percent of the time.

As a rule, most other trisomies of the autosomes spontaneously abort before birth. As for monosomies—disorders in which the victim is lacking a chromosome—there is only one condition that is compatible with life. It is called Turner's syndrome, and it involves not the autosomes but the sex chromosomes. The disease, which is limited to women, is marked by a single X chromosome in each of the cells instead of the normal XX. No analogous disease exists in men, whose normal configuration is XY, because the human organism does not seem to be able to survive with a Y chromosome alone. Men may also suffer from disorders of the sex chromosomes, however. Among these are Klinefelter's syndrome, in which the victim has an extra sex chromosome, giving him an XXY configuration in his cells, and fragile X syndrome, in which the victim has a normal XY configuration but has a fragile site on his X chromosome. Women, on the other hand, may have a disorder called triple X syndrome, distinguished by an XXX configuration. The XXX female often remains asymptomatic, but may exhibit mild mental retardation, unusual height, and underdeveloped female sex characteristics.

In addition, there are a number of chromosomal abnormalities caused by the deletion of parts of chromosomes. Among these are cri du chat (cat's cry) syndrome, in which a deletion of a segment of the 5th chromosome causes severe retardation, failure to thrive, a moon-like face, and a peculiar mewling cry, like that of a kitten; partial deletion of the 4th chromosome, associated with severe mental retardation, eye defects, a beaked nose, genital defects, and underdevelopment of the jaw; and Prader-Willi syndrome, thought to be caused by a deletion of part of chromosome 15 and characterized by severe obesity, short stature, mental retardation, ravenous appetite, dwarfed genitalia in males, and childhood diabetes.

Science has made phenomenal progress in the past 20 years in identifying the presence of chromosomal disease. A geneticist will take a small sample of blood from an individual and put it in a culture, adding a chemical to stimulate cell division. Later, a second chemical halts the proceedings when the chromosomes are in their most visible phase. A blood cell is then put under the microscope, and after a stain is applied to make the chromosomes stand out sharply, a photograph is taken. The resulting print is enlarged and the geneticist then cuts out each pair of chromosomes and arranges them according to size and shape. This diagram, called a karyotype, enables him to image chromosomal abnormalities graphically. He can actually see the extra chromosome in Down's syndrome, for example, or the broken-off piece in cri du chat.

Geneticists are now working to identify where along the chromosomes the genes for particular traits lie. This process is called mapping. For example, on which chromosome do the genes for eye color reside? Or the genes that dictate development of the heart valves, the teeth, the kidneys, and so on? The answer to such questions would explain why a deletion of one part of the 18th chromosome produces a syndrome in which the victim has long, tapering fingers and a "carp-shaped" mouth, whereas a deletion of part of chromosome 13 results in tiny eyes and no thumbs.

Another 5 percent of all birth defects can be blamed on known environmental causes. Since X rays are a greatly diminished factor—physicians having long abandoned the practice of irradiating pregnant women—these external agents fall into basically two categories: maternal illness, which is responsible for an estimated 3.5 percent of all defects, and toxic substances, which generate the other 1.5 percent. (There may well be other environmental threats to the fetus, such as low-level radiation, but the hazards have yet to be proven.)

The role of maternal illness first came to light in 1941, when it was learned that rubella contracted during pregnancy could inflict grave harm on the unborn. This discovery prompted a long search for other such villains. Probably the most dangerous to be implicated are cytomegalovirus (CMV), a type of herpesvirus, and toxoplasmosis, a parasitic disease spread to expectant women by cat feces and inadequately cooked meat. Both of these diseases are relatively asymptomatic in the mother but can have disastrous consequences for the developing fetus. CMV affects thousands of babies every year, causing a dreadful congeries of damage that includes microcephaly, cardiac defects, seizures, deafness, blindness, learning disorders, and psychomotor disabilities. It is believed by some to be the primary cause of hearing loss in children in the United States. Toxoplasmosis, whose victims also number in the thousands, causes microcephaly, hydrocephaly, blindness, and convulsions. The probability of insult from these two diseases is so high that many doctors recommend therapeutic abortions to women who have been exposed during pregnancy. A less frequent menace, but one still capable of having dire effect on the central nervous systems of infants, is genital herpes, usually contracted as the baby passes through the birth canal. Recently, the incidence of herpes in newborns was reported to be rising sharply. Together, these four illnesses have been assigned the acronym TORCH complex, which stands for toxoplasmosis, rubella, cytomegalovirus, and herpes. The *O* stands for "other," representing an additional set of diseases known or asserted to cause birth defects, including syphilis, gonorrhea, Group B Coxsackie virus, chicken pox, and Venezuelan equine encephalitis.

A number of chronic maternal disorders can also produce congenital impairments. The most notable of these is diabetes mellitus, which by itself is said to cause malformations in more than 1,500 babies a year. Infants of diabetic mothers tend to be stillborn or premature and are frequently oversized for their gestational age. Among the anomalies generally found are cardiovascular, skeletal, and neural-tube defects. These children are also more likely to suffer from such potentially lethal neonatal conditions as respiratory distress syndrome, hyperbilirubinemia, and hypoglycemia.

Maternal high blood pressure, whether preexisting or pregnancy-induced, deserves mention as a cause of birth defect, primarily as a contributor to low birthweight and prematurity. Other illnesses that may affect the unborn are thyroid disease, which causes cretinism, a condition of mental deficiency and short stature that used to be a threat in the industrial world until iodine was found to prevent it (cretinism remains a problem in iodine-poor countries like Zaire, where 8 percent of the population is said to be affected); phenylketonuria, a formerly lethal inherited disorder that is now producing birth defects for the first time because of the survival of its victims to childbearing age; pregnancy jaundice, which is associated with fetal growth impairment; lupus; uncontrolled epilepsy; ovarian or adrenal tumors, which may cause masculinization of a female fetus; and high fever, which has been linked to an increased incidence of spina bifida, anencephaly, cleft lip and palate, and mental retardation. (In this last regard, there exist studies that implicate anything that elevates body temperature, including hot tubbing and sauna bathing.)

The list of environmental substances suspected of being teratogenic is much too long to reproduce here. Among the ones frequently mentioned are hair sprays, lead, cyclamates, nitrites and nitrates, sodium fluoride, marijuana, and vaginal spermicides. Most of them have been the subject of conflicting reports, and their teratogenicity has not been proven.

However, a number of agents are *known* to be damaging to the fetus. By far the most widely used of these contaminants are alcohol and tobacco. Alcohol, as in beer, wine, and whiskey, is reponsible for a condition known as fetal alcohol syndrome. The victim suffers from a constellation of defects, including growth retardation, mental deficiency, and such distinctive facial traits as an underdeveloped chin, low-set ears, abnormal eyelids, and a glassy-eyed expression. Some 2,000 infants acquire the syndrome annually in the United States, and an estimated 35,000 are affected less adversely by maternal alcohol consumption. Two thousand years ago, the Carthaginians forbade the drinking of wine by newlyweds for fear that a malformed child would result. But it wasn't until the last decade that our own civilization began recommending to pregnant women that they abstain from drinking. Tobacco smoking, meanwhile, has been positively associated with fetal growth retardation. Women who smoke tend to have babies up to six ounces smaller than normal.

The risks to the fetus of addictive narcotics like heroin are well established. In addition, certain recreational drugs, particularly barbiturates and LSD, have been accused of causing malformations. One study of 44 women who took LSD before and during pregnancy reported that 6 of them gave birth to deformed infants. Other studies are inconclusive.

Among medicinal drugs known or thought to be teratogens are certain anticonvulsants such as Dilantin (phenytoin); chemotherapy drugs, including aminopterin and chlorambucil; anticoagulants, such as warfarin; certain antibiotics, notably streptomycin and tetracycline; female sex hormones, particularly diethylstilbestrol (DES), which caused a wave of genital cancer in young women whose mothers took it during pregnancy; tranquilizers, such as Valium and Librium; anesthetics, which have been implicated in abnormal births among operating room nurses; and most recently the anti-morning-sickness drug Bendectin, whose link to reduction deformity and abdominal malformations has been postulated but never proven.

Then there is a whole class of environmental chemicals that are theoretically a threat if ingested accidentally. The only ones whose dangers have been confirmed are organic mercury and certain pesticides. Mercury's teratogenicity became evident two decades ago when an epidemic of cerebral palsy and other neurologic disorders occurred among children in Minamata, in southwest Japan. It turned out that expectant mothers were eating fish and shellfish contaminated by methylmercury, which had been dumped into Minamata Bay by nearby factories. Later, there was a similar outbreak in Iran caused by grain that had been treated with a fungicide containing methylmercury. The threat of pesticides to human reproduction was demonstrated several years ago when farm workers spraying fields with dibromochloropropane (DBCP) were found to have become infertile. Then, in April 1984, the U.S. Environmental Protection Agency restricted the amount of another pesticide that could be present in food products. The substance, ethylene dibromide (EDB), has produced genetic damage as well as cancer in laboratory animals. The EPA action followed the discovery of high levels of EDB in a variety of foods, including some well-known cake and pancake mixes, and citrus fruits. Recalls of the offending products were carried out in many states.

A controversy now rages over two other potential sources of malformation—chemical waste and Agent Orange. A variety of human ills have been attributed to toxic-waste sites around the United States, but conclusive proof of their guilt is lacking. In San Jose, California, where a chemical solvent called trichloroethylene leaked from an underground storage tank into the local water supply, neighborhood residents claimed 55 subsequent miscarriages, 7 stillbirths, and 16 babies born with cardiovascular defects. The county health department admitted that the neighborhood's rate of birth defects was twice that of the county at large, but it declared that the difference was not "statistically significant." Several years ago, in Niagara Falls, New York, more than 400 families were forced to evacuate their homes near a 16-acre landfill called Love Canal, where during the 1940s and 1950s more than 20,000 tons of polychlorinated biphenyls (PCBs), dioxin, and other long-lived poisons were dumped. The chemicals had seeped into the soil, creating a severe health hazard. In 1982 the government announced that a study showed it was safe to begin moving back into homes as close as a block and a half from the landfill. This assertion was exploded when new chemical leaks were detected. At the same time, some university researchers found that field mice living near the site were suffering from internal organ damage that was shortening their life span. In Times Beach, Missouri, and surrounding communities, residents were evacuated after the discovery that dioxin mixed with oil had been sprayed on the roadbeds as a dust control measure in the early 1970s. Dioxin, a byproduct of the manufacture of certain chemicals, is believed to be among the most toxic of all substances, causing cancer and birth defects in laboratory animals even in minute quantities. Yet, its teratogenicity in man has never been confirmed. In late 1983 the U.S. Center for Disease Control announced that after an extensive physical examination of Times Beach residents, it could find no "meaningful ill-health effects." The residents were not convinced and still fear that they will suffer long-range consequences in the years ahead.

No less fierce is the debate over Agent Orange, the defoliant used in Vietnam by American forces in an attempt to strip the jungles bare and flush the enemy out of hiding. More than 11 million gallons of the herbicide were sprayed over millions of acres of Vietnamese countryside in a nine-year program code-named Operation Ranch Hand. One of the by-products of the manufacture of Agent Orange is dioxin, whose danger was not understood by the thousands of U.S. servicemen who obediently sprayed the chemical, patrolled through fogs of it, drank water tainted by it, and, for laughs, doused each other with jets of it. Today, many veterans claim they are experiencing unusually high rates of birth defects, cancer, and other horrors, which they blame on their exposure to Agent Orange. The Veterans Administration has stubbornly rejected these claims, arguing that the disease rates in question are well within the norm. Several research studies have only intensified conjecture. In 1983 the Vietnamese government announced that a survey of some 40,000 families in northern Vietnam revealed that women whose husbands had fought in the south and had thus been exposed to the defoliant experienced more stillbirths and delivered more congenitally malformed babies than women whose husbands had remained in the north. The deformities included neural-tube defects, limb reduction, cleft lip, Siamese twinning, hydrocephaly, and cardiac defects. One of the Vietnamese researchers said that although statistically he should have found only 1 case of anencephaly in every 2,777 births, he instead encountered 1 in every 198 births. But an Australian study of men who had fathered children with birth defects in the years 1966–79 found no correlation between Vietnam service and genetic damage. Meanwhile, the Veterans Administration conducted medical examinations on 85,000 American veterans and reported finding no untoward health effects clearly related to Agent Orange. "There were a wide variety of health problems," said one VA official, "but they were of the sort that one sees in a population of males growing older." The veterans' organizations were not satisfied. Further studies have now been undertaken by the U.S. Air Force and the U.S. Center for Disease Control. The first results of the Air Force study support the VA's conclusions.

In May 1984 a class action lawsuit by 20,000 Vietnam veterans and their families against the seven chemical companies that manufactured Agent Orange was settled out of federal court. Without admitting any liability, the companies agreed to create a $180 million fund to help pay the medical expenses of those servicemen and their children who might have been damaged by the herbicide. But the settlement left unresolved the question of how dangerous Agent Orange really is, and it did not speak to the issue of whether the Veterans Administration owes disability compensation to the veterans.

The reasons why it is so difficult to determine what is causing birth defects—whether it is Agent Orange or anything else—are several-fold. First, scientists are generally working with small statistical populations. Birth abnormalities seldom occur in such large numbers that a clear deviation from the past is discernible. If the incidence of spina bifida goes from 1 per 1,000 to 3 per 1,000, is that because of a new teratogen, or is it merely part of the random ebb and flow pattern of nature? Second, there is the problem of the passage of time. Months may elapse between exposure to a toxin and the birth of a child, and it may be many months more before the birth defect is diagnosed. Can a woman recall everything she ate or drank well over a year ago? In the case of a gene that has mutated, whole decades might pass between the exposure of the father or mother to some environmental agent and the birth of the affected child. The likelihood of tracing things back becomes remote. Third, there is the sheer volume of potential teratogens to sort through. Every day a pregnant woman comes in contact with thousands of substances, each of which could conceivably cross the placenta and attack the fetus. How does the researcher single out which one it was? Fourth, laboratory testing is of little value. Administering a material like Agent Orange to animals will not reveal definitively whether it is harmful to people. Only tests on humans can prove that, and those are ethically untenable.

Compounding the problem for the investigator is the capriciousness of birth defects. Two individuals can be exposed to the same teratogen, and one of them will beget abnormal children and the other will not. This is why most teratologists and geneticists believe that at least 20 percent of all congenital anomalies are multifactorial in origin—that they are caused by the complex interplay of both heredity and environment. Many kinds of inheritance fall into this category. Intelligence is one example. Persons can be born with various "smart" genes; the more of them they have, the brighter they will potentially be. But to the extent they don't also receive proper education and nutrition as youngsters, their intelligence will be diminished. In the same way, a fetus's genes may make it susceptible to developing certain birth defects, but if there is no toxic environmental factor to push it over the critical threshhold, it will not manifest the abnormality. This explains why spina bifida, cleft palate, schizophrenia, and diabetes tend to run in families, yet their occurrence seems to follow no pattern. The same is true of pyloric stenosis, an abnormal narrowing of the stomach sphincter that blocks the flow of food to the small intestine. The defect seems to be inherited; however, for it to develop, it is thought that three conditions must be satisfied: the baby must generally be male, it must have a genetic predilection, and it must be subject to a maternal viral infection during gestation.

Believe it or not, there is some good news regarding birth defects. According to the Center for Disease Control, in Atlanta, which monitors congenital impairment in the United States, the incidence of both neural-tube defects and Down's syndrome has been declining dramatically in recent years. The downward trend for neural-tube disorders began 50 years ago, when what amounted to an epidemic of these illnesses was raging. At the epidemic's peak in 1932, hospitals in Boston and in Providence, Rhode Island, were reporting a phenomenal 6 cases of spina bifida and anencephaly per 1,000 live births. No one knows why the rate was so high then, much less why it began to drop. All that can be said, on the basis of a century and a half of British statistics, is that neural-tube defects have historically tended to wax and wane in frequency. The most significant improvement has come about in the last 10 years. In 1970 an estimated 10,000 children were born with spina bifida and anencephaly in the United States. Today the number has plummeted to 4,000 to 5,000, or about 1.3 cases per 1,000 births. Similar declines have been noted in Canada, Britain, and Northern Ireland.

In the same vein, the incidence of Down's syndrome has shrunk by about 33 percent during the last 25 years. In 1960 an estimated 5,700 Down's children were born each year in the United States. Today, the annual total stands at approximately 3,700. It is far easier to account for the decline of Down's syndrome than for that of neural-tube defects. The answer can be summed up in two words: fewer births. The introduction of the Pill and the trend toward having smaller families have played major roles in curbing Down's. So has the fact that women over 35 are having proportionately fewer babies. In the past 25 years, the number of children delivered by older women has dropped from 12 percent of all births to a mere 6 percent. Women over 35 used to deliver 50 percent of all Down's youngsters, but the percentage has fallen precipitously.

The reduction in family size, however, does not fully explain the neural-tube riddle. The downturn began long before the movement toward smaller families. Some have suggested that the decrease in both Down's and neural-tube disorders is due to new techniques of prenatal diagnosis. By the use of ultrasound and amniocentesis, these and other fetal abnormalities can be detected while the child is still inside the womb, enabling the parents to secure an abortion, if they so desire. But the truth is that diagnostic procedures (discussed more fully in the following chapter) have not made a large enough contribution to account for the lower figures. That is why Dr. Godfrey Oakley, of the Center for Disease Control, admits he is whistling in the dark when he boasts of progress on the neural-tube front. "Why am I concerned?" he says. "Because this is a disease which over a 150-year period has come and gone and come back again. Yes, things are better now, but it might just turn around and go in the other direction."

Meanwhile, Oakley reports that other birth impairments are on the rise. Ventricular septal defect, an abnormal opening between the heart ventricles, has trebled in incidence, from approximately 3,000 cases annually in 1970 to 9,000 cases today. The reason remains obscure. Inexplicable, too, are a twofold increase in renal agenesis, a lethal but rare condition in which the child is born without kidneys, and a threefold jump in congenital hip dislocation, a defect of the hip joint causing a limp and apparent shortening of a leg. Simpler to account for is a surge in the incidence of patent ductus arteriosus, a circulatory disorder that is common in prematurity. The explanation lies in the improved survival of low-birthweight infants. The recent revolution in salvaging premature babies is cause for another concern of Oak-ley's: he fears it may be accompanied by an escalation in the number of children acquiring cerebral palsy. The incidence of CP now ranges between 3.5 and 5.9 per 1,000 births.

Certain other isolated phenomena have been noted as well. In 1983 several medical centers—one in New York City, one in Rockland County, New York, and a third in Amarillo, Texas—reported a sud-den and precipitous increase in the number of cases of severe infant hearing loss. Dr. Jane Madell, director of audiology at one of the cen-ters, the New York League for the Hard of Hearing, said she had seen 24 children with profound hearing impairment in a six-month period, compared with only five in the preceding six months. A year later the grim findings continued. "We are currently seeing two-and-a-half to three times as many children as we did in any six-month period dating back to when we began to keep records in 1910," said Dr. Madell. She added that the trend, which began in the summer of 1982, has since been noted by a large number of centers in locations as widely scattered as Canada, Rhode Island and California. An inves-tigation has been opened by the Center for Disease Control. Among the possible explanations are an increase in the incidence of cytome-galovirus among pregnant women, the ongoing salvage of increasing numbers of low-birthweight infants (most of the victims seen at the New York League were born prematurely), and the use of ultrasound as a prenatal diagnostic tool. The last theory has been largely dis-counted because many victims did not undergo the procedure.

In 1981 an unprecedented number of cases of craniosynostosis, a rare skull deformity, were reported to have occurred in the Colorado mountain towns of Steamboat Springs and Idaho Springs. The nor-mal incidence of the defect, which involves a premature fusing of the child's skull sutures so that brain growth is inhibited, is 1 in 2,000 births; but in Steamboat Springs, which has a population of 5,098 and fewer than 100 births a year, 5 babies were born with the defect in little more than four months; and in Idaho Springs (pop. 2,077) 2 cases were seen in three days. Both communities take their drink-ing water from sources that have been polluted by hard-rock mining operations. As if to underscore the possible association with water quality, all of the stricken babies in Steamboat Springs were conceived during the spring runoff period, when water quality deteriorates. Alerted by the bizarre development, the state public health depart-ment reviewed all births in Colorado from 1978 to 1983 and found something even more alarming. Statewide there were 188 cases of craniosynostosis in those five years—which is two to three times the expected number. A major epidemiological study was begun in May of 1984.

Also in 1981 it was reported that birth defects in rural Dade County, Florida, were nearly twice as common as in nearby urban areas. The disclosure was linked to a finding that the rural residents had twice the amount of pesticide in their bodies as people living in northern states, a consequence of the spraying of citrus and other crops.

Some disturbing data of another kind were uncovered by the National Center for Health Statistics in its periodic survey of 42,000 American households. The center found that between 1957 and 1981 the number of children suffering from chronic "activity-limiting" illnesses like asthma and diabetes went from 1.7 percent to 3.8 percent of all children under 17. In other words, more than two million youngsters are today unable to participate in a normal range of school and play activities, compared with only one million children in the late 1950s. When this alarming statistic was announced, in early 1982, it prompted a University of California at San Francisco team led by Dr. Peter Budetti and Paul Newacheck to investigate further. Their inquiry was still under way as of this writing. The team first ascertained whether the increase was a "paper" one created by better survey methods, that is, whether the number of children with handicapping conditions had been heretofore underreported. Budetti and his associates found that this explanation accounted for only "a small part" of the trend. The team has now turned its attention to learning what environmental or other factors might be responsible for the change. A number of suspicions have been raised. One is that modern neonatal intensive care, by keeping alive more premature and handicapped newborns, is adding to the population of children who are more prone to chronic illness. Another is that the change in women's lifestyles over the last quarter of a century is responsible. More women are smoking, for one thing, and a larger number of them are working throughout pregnancy, possibly exposing their unborn children to hazards in the workplace. Yet another hypothesis is that people with genetic flaws are now living long enough to pass their faulty genes along to offspring.

"We are looking at a whole range of environmental variables," said Newacheck, "including air pollution, water pollution, and diet. We're going to get pretty specific. We'll even see if there are more heavy metals in the food people eat."

No one is more acutely aware of the difficulty in isolating what causes defects in children than the CDC's Oakley. "One might argue that occupational exposures, and pollution of the air and water are all potential causes," he says, "and my feeling is we ought to look very hard for them because they are eminently preventable. But I wonder if we have given enough attention to pre–Industrial Revolution environmental factors. It would be a mistake to assume that most kids who are born with birth defects today are the victims of chemicals manufactured by man in the last 25 years. Birth defects have been relatively constant over the last 100 years, with only a few exceptions. The rates have not, I repeat, not shot up because of some new danger. Something was causing defects in the past, and is causing them now. Maybe it's a contaminant in the food, a fungus perhaps. Who knows? I'm not saying we shouldn't look at new causes. I'm only saying we don't know what causes most birth defects and we ought to be looking further than just drugs or dioxin."

6

Suffer the Children

Arctic stillness had settled on the Waukegan night. It muffled the voices of the medical team double-timing its way through the snow, muffled even the sound of the waiting helicopter, whose blades whipped at the air with a strange, dull *clump*. Time itself seemed to be moving numbly, inching along as if walking on ice, granting a precious extension to little Jonathan Friend, who by now should have been dead.

Jonathan made a cumbersome cargo, that February night in 1982, as the medics bore him along. Only four hours old, he lay inside an incubator, gasping painfully for breath. The source of his respiratory trouble was a birth defect known as diaphragmatic hernia. This malformation begins very early in fetal life when the diaphragm, the sheet of muscle that separates the chest cavity from the abdomen, fails to close off and the stomach, spleen, bowel, and kidney push into the chest. The child's lungs are left with no room to grow.

Sometimes just one of the lungs is underdeveloped at birth. But in Jonathan's case both lungs were tiny and inadequate. Moreover, an air leak had developed in his right lung, and the acid content of his blood had risen to dangerous levels because of a lack of oxygen. Even at best, newborns with diaphragmatic hernia die 50 to 75 percent of the time. For a case as severe as Jonathan's, the mortality rate is around 90 percent.

His only hope lay in immediate surgery by the most skilled hands available. Unfortunately, he had chanced to be born in an unequipped community hospital. Chicago, a full 50 miles south, was the nearest place where such expertise existed. To compound matters, it was right in the middle of the coldest stretch of weather in northern Illinois history, hampering efforts to transport him.

Their breaths chasing behind them like a formation of white dragons, the medics rushed into the roiling swirl created by the helicopter rotors. Hurriedly, they loaded Jonathan aboard in his Plexiglas crib, and with the absolute ease of a seedling letting go, the helicopter separated from the earth and banked off into the darkness.

After a half-hour flight, the pilot put down in a Chicago park, and Jonathan was rushed by a waiting ambulance to the nearby Children's Memorial Hospital. There, a pediatric surgeon named Margaret Olson made an incision in his abdomen and pulled the bowel back down into its proper place. Then she repaired the hole in the diaphragm with nonabsorbable sutures. But the battle was only half over. Postoperative care is critically important with these youngsters. Their diminutive lungs must be pampered until they expand in size. Moreover, the high acid level of the infant's blood causes the pulmonary blood vessels to close off, threatening the body's oxygen supply still further. To allow the lungs to heal, the hospital put the boy on a revolutionary new high-speed ventilator, which was able to deliver him small volumes of air at very low pressure, doing so 150 times a minute, five times the normal rate. To cope with the circulatory problems, they gave him vasodilators, which counteract blood vessel constriction. Five weeks and $60,000 worth of treatment later, a healthy Jonathan Friend left the hospital in his mother's arms. He was the first baby with such advanced diaphragmatic hernia ever to survive at Children's Memorial. Although his lungs will always be underdeveloped, which will rule out participation in strenuous sports, he should otherwise lead a relatively normal life.

"Right after he was born, they told me they didn't think he'd even make it to Chicago," Carol Friend told me months afterward, as Jonathan, dressed in a sailor suit, romped happily around the family's living room. "It was up to God, and He sure did a good job."

Jonathan Friend represents one of medicine's triumphs. The profession has known many similar victories in its war on birth defects. One of the earliest followed the 1964 rubella epidemic in the United States, which inflicted blindness, hearing loss, heart defects, and retardation on 20,000 infants whose mothers were exposed during pregnancy. The appalling toll acted as a goad to intensive research. By 1969 these efforts had borne fruit in the form of a vaccine against the disease. A massive inoculation program was undertaken, the goal being to immunize all girls before they reached childbearing age. The incidence of rubella-induced birth defects has dramatically declined since then.

Another breakthrough occurred when doctors learned how to prevent a second cause of severe brain damage in babies, Rh incompatibility. This problem arises when a mother has Rh-negative blood and the father has Rh-positive. If the baby inherits the Rh-positive gene, then the mother's body may treat the baby's blood as a foreign substance and may muster antibodies into action to destroy the alien blood cells. The consequences for the baby may be severe, ranging from stillbirth to a toxic buildup of bilirubin in the brain that is associated with cerebral palsy and retardation. Rh incompatibility is generally not a threat during the first pregnancy. In order for the immune response to be triggered, the child's blood must mingle with the mother's, which usually happens only during birth or miscarriage. The firstborn is safely delivered before the antibodies form. But subsequent offspring with Rh-positive blood may not be so lucky. If sensitization has occurred, the antibodies, guarding the mother's body since the earlier pregnancy will cross the placenta and attack. In the early 1960s, doctors began treating Rh disease with blood transfusions, administered to the fetus via a long needle inserted into the uterus. This palliative approach gave way to a preventive one in 1968, when it was learned that gamma globulin from Rh-negative women, injected into an Rh-negative mother within 24 hours after each delivery or miscarriage, would destroy whatever Rh-positive blood cells it encountered. The mother's body would be tricked into not forming any antibodies of its own. RhoGAM and other brands of immunoglobulin have greatly reduced the need for prenatal transfusions.

Gains continue to be made in the detection of congenital defects prior to birth. Amniocentesis, which involves the withdrawal of a sample of amniotic fluid from the uterus, permits an analysis in the laboratory that can diagnose many abnormalities. Virtually all chromosomal disorders, for example, can be identified by studying fetal cells in the fluid. Also distinguishable through amniocentesis are nearly a hundred single-gene disorders, including Hurler's syndrome, maple syrup urine disease, and Tay-Sachs disease. For neural-tube defects, a complex screening process called alpha-fetoprotein testing has been devised, which draws on three separate technologies—blood chemistry, ultrasound, and amniocentesis. AFP testing is so reliable and inexpensive that in Britain and in parts of the United States it is used to screen large populations of pregnant women.

Ultrasound is a valuable tool in its own right for detecting fetal anomalies. In the second trimester, it is able to confirm the presence not only of anencephaly and spina bifida but also of hydrocephalus, microcephaly, and various defects of the limbs, heart, kidney, and bladder. In addition, there are two experimental techniques—fetoscopy and chorionic villi sampling—that have been developed in the last several years. Both, however, carry potential risk to the fetus. Fetoscopy involves the insertion of a thin needle into the womb, much as in amniocentesis. But the needle, which is called a fetoscope, is equipped with a viewing instrument that uses a fiberoptic light source. The perinatologist can actually look directly at fetal and placental surfaces. The doctor may also use the fetoscope to obtain biopsies of fetal skin and blood, through which he or she can detect the presence of hemophilia, sickle-cell anemia, and beta thalassemia. Chorionic villi testing is the newest wrinkle in prenatal diagnosis. It involves studying tissue samples taken directly from the embryonic membranes. The test can be performed much earlier in pregnancy than other exams can, and, if concerns about its safety are laid to rest, it may become the front line in the fight against birth defects. (A fuller discussion of these and other methods of prevention may be found in Chapter 13.)

Meanwhile, some of the most spectacular progress has come not in the realm of diagnosis and prevention but in the surgical repair of defects, as in the case of little Jonathan Friend. Since Jonathan's unprecedented survival, Children's Memorial Hospital has had four more survivors of diaphragmatic hernia who would have died just three and a half years ago.

An even more dramatic example of a surgical breakthrough is in the treatment of gastroschisis, a defect that occurs about once in every 2,000 births. The problem originates 10 weeks into a pregnancy when, owing to a structural weakness, the abdominal wall ruptures and the internal organs spill out of the fetus's body. Such infants are born with their intestines lying on their abdomens like a string of bright red sausages. Surgical treatment involves stretching the abdominal wall and delicately replacing the viscera into the abdominal cavity. But the key to success is postoperative care. The intestines have been severely traumatized by their exposure first to amniotic fluid, then to air. They will need some 6 weeks to heal, a time during which the child can take no food by mouth. Old-fashioned forms of intravenous feeding were not really up to the job of nourishing a human infant for so long. Consequently, as late as 1970, the mortality rate for gastroschisis was 80 percent. Here the development of hyperalimentation, the technique for infusing a total, balanced diet by means of a cardiac vein, has completely reversed the odds. Today, the mortality rate has dropped to a mere 5 percent.

A related defect is omphalocele, a rarer occurrence, in which the viscera bulge out of the abdomen through a membraneous sac. Omphaloceles come about for unknown reasons. Early in fetal life the midgut grows faster than the abdomen's ability to contain it; hence it projects partway into the umbilical cord. It is supposed to return to the body by the 11th week of gestation. When it doesn't, the result is an omphalocele. Generally, these cases are harder to manage surgically than gastroschisis. The opening in the abdomen is much larger and more difficult to close, more internal organs are involved, and the abdominal cavity itself is usually smaller than normal, making it necessary to put the gut back in stages. Replacing it all at once compresses the lungs and leads to respiratory failure. Then, too, omphaloceles are more often accompanied by other malformations, including those of the brain and heart. But despite these impediments, the success rate of surgery is improving steadily.

Vesicointestinal fissure is a syndrome that often is associated with omphalocele. There is no rectum, the bladder is open, and in boys the penis is abnormally formed. "As late as 10 years ago the medical journals said these babies shouldn't be salvaged," says the Chicago surgeon Susan Luck, who specializes in abdominal repairs. "Today, we try to reconstruct the bladder and perform a colostomy [creation of an artificial anal opening in the abdomen]. And we recommend they be reared as girls, even if they are genetically males. There have been suicides among adolescents reared as boys without normal penises."

Some of the most heartbreaking birth defects are the craniofacial malformations. Studies have shown that they are often the hardest handicaps for the victim to deal with psychologically: a head misshapen, its features grotesquely skewed, cloven, exaggerated, sunken, or absent; everything pulling the symmetry apart to create a gross distortion of a normal face. Master plastic surgeons such as Paul Tessier, of Paris, Joseph Murray, of the Boston Children's Hospital, and Linton Whitaker, of the University of Pennsylvania Hospital, are performing what can only be described as miracles. The dome skull, pop eyes, and beaked nose of Crouzon's disease are reconstructed to give the individual an almost normal appearance. So, too, are the missing cheekbones and eye deformities of a condition known as Treacher Collins syndrome. Cleft lips and palates are joined, ears are realigned, and jawlines are brought into harmony with the greatest finesse. Often the skin of the face is rolled down like a stocking while work proceeds directly on the bony surfaces of the skull. This not only allows the surgeon maximum access to the bones; it eliminates the problem of scars. Anyone who has ever *seen* a face pulled down in this way becomes everlastingly conscious of how transient and meaningless a face really is. It is nothing more than a rubber mask. While the face is removed, many things can be done. If a child's eyes are set too far apart, a piece of skull is excavated from the middle of the forehead and the orbits pushed closer together. The pieces of skull can then be utilized for other purposes, say, building up a missing nose. These deft procedures go on within a millimeter or two of the brain, the optic nerve, and the olfactory nerve. The tiniest slip could blind a child or leave it brain damaged. It is a truly incredible form of medicine.

Without question, however, the most impressive developments have come in the field of cardiac surgery. The heart is the fountainhead of all life; without a viable heart pumping in the chest, there is no point in repairing anything else.

Congenital heart disease is the most common cause of death in newborns, next to prematurity. Just under 1 percent of all children have a cardiac defect. Some 8 percent of them have a condition called transposition of the great vessels: the pulmonary artery and the aorta are reversed, arising from the wrong pumping chambers and drastically reducing the amount of oxygenated blood that gets to the body; 25 percent have a ventricular septal defect, or a hole between the two lower chambers; 11 percent have an atrial septal defect, or hole between the two upper chambers; 9 percent have a coarctation, or crimping, of the aorta; 10 percent have tetralogy of Fallot, a combination of four defects that causes chronic oxygen deprivation and growth retardation; 5 percent have an aortic-valve defect; and 2 percent have a tricuspid atresia, an absence of the valve between the two right-hand chambers of the heart. A variety of other abnormalities make up the remaining 30 percent.

With the advent of the heart-lung machine, in the 1960s, a new era of direct surgical repair of damaged hearts began. Twenty years ago nothing could be done for an infant with transposition of the great vessels, for example. The child just died. Today an ingenious procedure called Mustard's operation makes the best of the situation; instead of repositioning the two inverted blood vessels, it changes the function of the upper heart chambers to conform. The survival rate stands at 98 percent. In tetralogy of Fallot the strategy is to repair all of the defects at once, when the child is about four years old, with the survival rate now running better than 90 percent. Even when anatomy is missing, as in tricuspid atresia, there is generally some sort of solution—in this case, the creation of a direct route from the heart chamber to the pulmonary artery, bypassing the missing valve. Currently, cardiac medicine has reached the point where it has something to offer, even if it is only a temporary measure, to almost any baby born with an abnormal heart.

"Progress in heart surgery is being made so rapidly," says Chicago's Farouk Idriss, one of the nation's foremost pediatric heart surgeons, "that even if there is no procedure yet, you can do something to tide the child over 5 or 10 years until the new procedure is developed."

Unfortunately, the saving of a life by sophisticated means is sometimes only the beginning, not the end, of the misery for a child and its family. Years of suffering may follow. This is the part of the story that is seldom told.

On those occasions when parents have been forced to go to court for permission to let their stricken offspring die, their lawyers have emphasized how "burdensome" or "painful" continued existence would be for the infant. In a society where it is presumed that life is invariably a blessing, these claims have sounded hollow and false. The problem, however, is not with the sincerity of the claim. It is that words like *burdensome* are abstractions, unable to convey adequately the tormenting situations that a medical prolonging of life can sometimes impose. The three human tragedies that are recounted here illustrate the reality of the suffering.

Phillip Markham was born a few days before Christmas 1982, in a rural community west of Chicago. To every outward appearance, he was a fine, healthy baby—a little big, perhaps, at nine pounds, but certainly well put together.

Even when the hospital staff told Chuck and Lydia Markham that the boy had a heart murmur, some jaundice, and a case of hypoglycemia, it did nothing to dampen their joy. Phillip's birth was the fulfillment of a longstanding dream. Although, between them, they already had three children from previous marriages, they wanted to have one together. But there had been a major roadblock: Chuck's vasectomy. Doctors advised that, realistically speaking, a surgical reversal would have only a remote chance of working. Still, the couple decided, a slim hope was better than none. Chuck submitted to the procedure. A year passed, then another; Lydia did not conceive. The pair had just begun to accept the doctors' dubious forecast, when Lydia discovered she was pregnant.

Now, as they gazed at their infant son, squalling under the blue lights designed to heal his jaundice, they felt a keen satisfaction. In a few days Phillip would be out of intensive care and at home, where he belonged.

He was five days old when the call from the hospital caught Lydia as she was preparing dinner. Phillip was turning blue. Several times he had stopped breathing, and the nurses had had to revive him. "I don't want to alarm you," the doctor said, "but I think he's got something more complex than just a heart murmur. We want to send him over to Chicago to be looked at."

In the days that followed, Phillip was found to have enough medical woes for an entire children's ward. He had three cardiac abnormalities, including a hole between the heart chambers, a blocked tricuspid valve, and an extremely small set of pulmonary arteries, whose job it is to carry blood to the lungs for oxygenation. In a normal infant these arteries are supposed to be as thick as a pencil, but in Phillip they were no larger than pencil points. The net effect was that his body was getting almost no fresh blood. He also had a disease of the pancreas in which the cells that make insulin are overactive, pumping out so much of the sugar-metabolizing substance that the body is robbed of the blood sugar it needs to survive. No matter how much sugar the hospital put into Phillip's system, a few hours later his glucose level snapped back to zero again. The condition is the exact opposite of diabetes.

The heart abnormalities were identified shortly after New Year's Day by means of a procedure called cardiac catheterization. Surgeons inserted a slender tube into a blood vessel in Phillip's groin and threaded it all the way up to his heart. During the course of the procedure, they blew up a small balloon on the end of the catheter and pulled it through the defect between his upper heart chambers, intentionally creating a larger hole. The purpose was to allow oxygenated blood to mix with unoxygenated blood, and thereby lessen his "blueness." But this was only a palliative measure. On January 8 they went into Phillip's chest again, this time to execute what is known as a Waterston-Cooley shunt, which is the creation of an artificial canal between the aorta and the main shaft of the pulmonary artery to permit more blood to get to the lungs than can enter at the artery's constricted base. The surgeons warned the Markhams that there was just a 5 percent chance that Phillip would survive the procedure. But the child astonished everyone and pulled through. "It was phenomenal. There aren't words for it," says Lydia Markham.

Phillip's ordeal was only beginning, however. A week later he had his first pancreas surgery. It was necessary to remove most of his pancreas to slow down the wild production of insulin that was killing him as surely as the heart defects. In the meantime, he was put on a ventilator to relieve him of the great task of collecting enough oxygen in his lungs to aerate his trickle of blood.

After a few days it was discovered that even though his pancreas had been reduced to a tenth of its original size, Phillip was manufacturing insulin at a mad pace. Surgeons had to go back in and remove the rest of the organ, which left him with no insulin production at all.

Medical science had turned him into a diabetic, who for the rest of his life would need insulin shots to metabolize sugar. While they were probing through his abdomen, they also found he had a defective gallbladder. They removed that, too.

Now he developed a mystery virus that caused his temperature to shoot up to 105, followed by a severe bout of necrotizing enterocolitis. With part of his intestine dying, it was imperative to begin hyperalimentation feedings through a catheter surgically implanted in a heart vein. A few weeks later he required more minor surgery; his need for constant mechanical ventilation made it necessary to give him a tracheotomy to lessen the risk of bronchopulmonary dysplasia. But he developed BPD anyway. Then they had to cut him open again. A diuretic called Lasix, prescribed for him to prevent fluid from building up around his heart, had caused him to form kidney stones. When they went in to remove the stones, they made another dismaying discovery. He had only one functioning kidney.

Months went by, and, almost imperceptibly, Phillip somehow seemed to be getting better. His heart shunt had reduced his "blue" spells; they occurred only when he was angry or frightened. Daily injections of insulin were controlling his diabetes. And after six months doctors were finally able to wean him from the hyperalimentation line—not that he was able to take food by mouth yet. It still made him vomit 90 percent of the time. But he could be fed by a tube through his nose. More important, after eight months they were able to take him off the respirator. It appeared that he would be able to go home at last.

"Every day has been an eternity," an exhausted Mrs. Markham remarked one hot summer afternoon. She is a friendly woman of 35 who had been making the three-hour round trip between her house and the downtown hospital five times a week.

She was wearing a loose-fitting sun dress, and a pair of sunglasses rode the crest of her brown hair, which was damp from perspiration.

"Many times I've thought it would be better if he just died," she said of Phillip. "There was a point after his heart and pancreas surgery where my husband and I asked the doctors why the plug couldn't be pulled. I wanted to know why my son had to go through all this. As he gets older, he's going to be more and more aware of his discomfort. He is never going to lead a normal, productive life. He'll always have pin-sized heart arteries and won't be able to engage in any kind of activity. I don't know if they were trying to talk us out of the idea—obviously, they don't want to pull any plugs. But they told us if he could just give some happiness to his family, that would justify it. Even so, we got to a point, my husband and I, where we gave them 72 hours. We said, please, none of us can take it anymore. Let's just wait

72 hours and see what happens. And if he doesn't start to get better. . . .

"In that 72 hours I think I had a gut feeling that, yes, I wanted it to be over, because I didn't want my child to suffer anymore. He will need four or five more heart operations to enlarge his shunt as he grows. Then, at age 10, he might be a candidate for open-heart reconstructive surgery. I haven't been told whether he's a candidate or not. If he doesn't have it, he won't make it to adolescence. The heart's the bottom line. I can put up with his disabilities. So I won't have a long-distance runner for a son. So he'll always be a diabetic. What I'm frightened of is that he won't make it.

"My feeling as a mother was I didn't want to become attached to a child whom I was going to lose down the road. I'm scared to death of that. It would be so much harder to lose him now. When he was small and in an incubator, there was no interaction. I could hold him or pick him up, but there was very little bonding. Now he's developed a regular little personality. He recognizes me when I visit. Oh, God, it's harder, now that I'm coming to know this person."

Phillip was only a hundred feet away in a crib in the chronic-intensive-care unit. He is a husky baby, with alert, intelligent eyes and a quick grin that has charmed all the nurses. Mrs. Markham and I were sitting in a small room that is ordinarily used by the parents of dying children to comfort their youngsters. It is a perfectly normal room, consisting of a couch, two chairs, and a coffee table; nothing gives away the fact that so much sorrow has been expended there.

"That time we gave the doctors 72 hours," Mrs. Markham said, "I was quite convinced that Phillip was going to die. We brought clothes down to the hospital for him to be buried in. I even went so far as to arrange his funeral service. The undertaker still has the directions; I've never called to cancel. I guess I've never felt sure Phillip would live. Maybe it's better to leave the instructions standing, because if he dies I'll go to pieces."

The date for Phillip's discharge was tentatively scheduled for September 1. The Markhams had completely rearranged their lives to prepare for it. Told by the physicians that it was undesirable for Phillip to live so far from a major hospital, they had given up their rented house in the country and moved to the city, where they were only eight blocks from a giant medical center. Mrs. Markham was scheduled to take paramedic training so that she would be able to keep Phillip alive until the professionals came, should he suffer a setback. He was certain to have at least one "blue" spell a week, she was told, and he faced the continual threat of diabetic coma. "I've seen him go into insulin shock twice. It's very terrifying," she said. "Between his two problems, I'll have a candy bar in one hand and oxygen in the other. I'm really afraid I'm not going to have the expertise to deal with these emergency situations."

Their family life had been torn to shreds. Mrs. Markham's 10-year-old son was being cared for by a housekeeper, so that the couple could stay at the hospital for hours on end. Fortunately, the boy was taking it well and had even insisted on coming home early from summer camp to help take care of Phillip. But Mr. Markham's two children were another story. The 16-year-old boy had come to the hospital exactly twice and had become physically ill at the sight of Phillip with all the tubes in him. It had been necessary for him to leave. At home he never referred to Phillip by name, always calling him "the baby." The 20-year-old daughter was intensely jealous of the attention Phillip was receiving. "She has always been the apple of her father's eye," Mrs. Markham sighed. "She's a very self-centered girl who acts more like 12. When we told her we were moving into the city, she said, 'Well, maybe you'll pay more attention to your other children now.' "

Finances were the other crushing worry. They had used up their insurance in May, when Phillip's medical bills exceeded the $250,000 mark. Since then, the $50,000-a-month hospital charge for room and oxygen, as well as the staggering doctors' fees, had become the responsibility of Lydia and Chuck. Their personal bill now stood at $200,000, with another $50,000 expected to accrue before Phillip's discharge. The couple had applied to several public agencies for financial help. They were offered a cruel choice. As long as Phillip remained in a hospital setting, he could qualify as an independent public-aid child, and the state would pay all his bills. But if he went home, he would lose this status, and the Markhams would receive significantly reduced assistance. The doctors candidly predicted that Phillip's ultimate expenses might run somewhere in the neighborhood of another $100,000, assuming he underwent the full sequence of reconstructive surgery. The Markham's share of that would have to be repaid out of Chuck's $19-an-hour wage as a carpenter. Mrs. Markham said she and Chuck had figured out that they could afford to pay $500 a month to the hospital to cover any future debt. "At that rate, we would have to live to be 100 years old to get it all paid off," she joked. But though $500 a month would take a great bite out of their resources, she said they felt they had the moral duty to pay.

This would be in addition to the $170 a month the Markhams estimated it would cost to keep Phillip in diabetic equipment and on medications once he got home. "We're going to have to cut our lifestyles down severely," said Mrs. Markham. "We'll probably never be able to buy a house. It will definitely alter our ability to send our children to college. I'm sorry that we won't be able to do for this child what we've done for our others. There won't be trips or vacations. But it doesn't dampen our spirits. Since Phillip was born I've reevaluated. My small boy says that I don't yell at him anymore. He runs through the house with muddy feet, and all I want to do is hug him because he *can* run. With Phillip, where other kids might be given a bicycle, perhaps he'll have to settle for a walk in the woods with his parents. So, we'll discover nature instead of Saks Fifth Avenue. Maybe that's better for all of us."

Weeks later, I checked back with Mrs. Markham. She was near tears. Phillip had experienced three cardiac arrests in one day, and the doctors had had to put him back on the ventilator. Exploratory surgery had been scheduled for the following day to determine whether an obstruction in his airway might be causing the problem. Then, in two weeks, they would operate to see whether his Waterston-Cooley shunt had become clogged. They recommended he be put in a pediatric nursing home because he would require long-term ventilator therapy.

"The worst news," she said, "is that he evidently is not going to be a candidate for the ultimate heart operation. They've told us candidly that he won't make it to his 10th birthday. This one doctor told me confidentially to go ahead and maintain his diabetes, but his heart will get him first.

"This is such a bitter pill. I wish we had known this months ago. I don't know exactly what it would have changed, but I think we would have found it easier to say, 'Walk away from it.' I don't quite understand why this child is still alive. He's been trying diligently to die. But the doctors tell me they have a moral obligation to try to keep him alive. He's getting morphine now, and anytime you get that you know there's plenty of discomfort. But when I asked them what would happen if they just disconnected the ventilator, they said they had no guarantee he would die. They feel he would get enough air to keep alive but not enough to nourish his brain. He would most likely suffer severe brain damage. So we are between a rock and a hard place."

(Just before this book went to press, I learned that Phillip had suffered seizures and a series of silent strokes. He is now paralyzed on one side and has regressed dramatically in intellectual function. To add to his woes, he recently underwent stomach surgery to stop his incessant vomiting, and he has developed severe curvature of the spine, which may preclude his ever walking. These latest setbacks have pushed his medical bills well over the million-dollar mark.)

Susan West, of Santa Barbara, California, received the verdict about her son, Brian, only a short time after his birth in October 1980. She was still lying in bed in the maternity ward.

The doctor was wearing the look new mothers dread. The lips purse, the eyebrows knot, the fingers stroke the chin in keeping with the healer's ancient protocol for conveying bad news. "The baby has a number of problems," he began. And Susan West's heart sank.

One of Brian's problems was Down's syndrome. The other was esophageal atresia, a congenital defect observed once in every 3,000 births in which the esophagus does not link up with the stomach. The upper half of the tube ends in a blind pouch, and the lower half is a nubbin in the top of the stomach. "We can't do anything about the Down's, but we can about the esophagus," the hospital told Susan and her husband, John, a physicist. The medical staff proposed surgery to bridge the gap, using tissue derived from the child's own body.

The Wests spent some agonizing hours thinking it over. Their predicament closely resembled the one the Doe family would face more than a year later in Bloomington, Indiana. The Wests had been informed that the new esophagus wouldn't work as well as a normal one. Brian would always have trouble getting food down. Surgery would be a difficult procedure whose success rate falls significantly when, as in Brian's case, there is a chromosomal defect or mental retardation. Moreover, it would be necessary to teach Brian a special method of swallowing, something that would be hard enough to impart to a normal child, let alone a retarded one. Finally, repeated hospitalizations to dilate the new esophagus would probably be mandatory for several years. This would interrupt the program of early training the experts recommend for maximizing the potential of a Down's child.

"When we looked at the whole combination of things, we just had a gut feeling that Brian wasn't going to enjoy a very high quality of life," recalls Mrs. West. "He wouldn't have a very easy time of it. Oh, of course, you're thinking of yourself, too. You wonder how much you can handle, and once we brought him home, the rest of our lives would certainly revolve around this one person. But then, we also knew that if we couldn't manage it, there are many good group homes, church-run homes, where he could be placed. So the main consideration I don't think was us. We knew somehow it could be worked out.

"But we kept putting ourselves in Brian's position. Kind of like the old 'do unto others' idea. We asked ourselves how we would want to be treated if we were going to be severely retarded and have these awful physical problems, too, for who knows how many years. And both of us admitted that we wouldn't want to live like that."

So they told the hospital they thought it would be more humane to let Brian die. The hospital administration got upset. "We had meetings for about two weeks," says Mrs. West. "A social worker told us, 'Well, if he grows up and smiles and ties his shoelaces, that's quality of life of a kind,' and we said, 'Well, we don't see it that way.'

"All the way along we felt we were making this decision in love," she says. "We are Lutherans, good Christians. We're not fanatics, but we believe in God and heaven and certainly believed Brian would go there, and that it would be preferable to the kind of life he'd face on this earth."

When the Wests, who also have an older son, still would not consent to surgery, hospital attorneys obtained a judicial order authorizing the operation. Not wishing the notoriety or expense of a trial, the Wests decided not to dispute the action in court. A few days later they received notice that child neglect charges had been filed against them. To this day, they don't know who reported them to the child welfare authorities. The hospital denies responsibility. On the advice of an attorney, the couple pleaded no contest, and Brian was made a ward of the state.

"It was insulting," Mrs. West recalls. "Here we were being treated like criminals because we made a decision that we thought was a loving, merciful one."

Though it now had the clearance for surgery, the hospital decided to wait until Brian had gained some more weight—a matter of several weeks. During this interval, Brian suffered several bouts of pneumonia, because saliva kept overflowing into his windpipe from the blind upper pouch of his esophagus. On one occasion, his heart stopped, but it was possible to revive him. Food had to be funneled directly into his stomach through a hole that was opened into his abdomen.

By December the surgery could be put off no longer, even though Brian's weight was not optimal. The first phase of the procedure calls for doctors to perform an esophagostomy, in which a temporary fistula, or channel, is created between the blind pouch and the neck to allow saliva to drain outside the body. Phase two involves the actual joining of the pouch to the nubbinlike lower section of esophagus, a task complicated by the distance between the two—they may be as much as several inches apart. To close this gap, Brian's surgeon lengthened the lower segment by pushing up the stomach tissue at the base of the nubbin and molding it into a tube—incorporating some stomach into the esophagus. Having acquired enough slack to work with, the surgeon was then able to suture the two free ends together and create one continuous passage.

As Brian convalesced over the next month and a half, he experienced extreme agony. His stomach acid kept backing up through the makeshift esophagus, because the sphincter that normally holds gastric juices in check had been rendered useless by the surgery. The acid rose through the temporary fistula and started to drip down Brian's neck, causing excruciating burns. Mrs. West recalls watching the boy suddenly drop a toy he was playing with, arch his back, and scream as the acid bubbled onto his skin. The pain was so unbearable that for six weeks the nurses had to keep him bound hand and foot.

At length, the acid stopped flowing, and the hole in his neck healed. But when the moment of truth came and Brian was given something to eat by mouth, the food stalled part of the way down. Scar tissue was obstructing its path. Once again the surgeon tunneled her way into Brian's body. She found so dense a growth of scar tissue that she could barely insert the dilating instrument. In anticipation of future expeditions to widen the esophagus, she left a string inside the passageway, one end exiting Brian's nose and the other coming out of the hole in his abdomen. The string operated on the principle of a plumb line, guiding the dilator through the forests of scar tissue. However, in spite of periodic dilations and another major operation, nothing could prevent the return of scar tissue. The esophagus never once functioned.

In the meantime, Brian's life entered a kind of limbo. His new parents, the state of California, placed him in a pediatric nursing home that was a three-hour drive away from the Wests, who were now unable to visit him more than once a month. For the next year and a half, the child depended on nurses for affection as he battled one infection after another and dined on liquid meals that flowed directly into his belly. Then, in the autumn of 1982, he began his final descent into hell.

It started as a simple head cold, but it grew progressively worse. When Brian's lungs turned cloudy on the X rays and his breathing became labored, he was transferred to the hospital. There, on the Sunday before Thanksgiving, he went into respiratory failure and coma and had to be put on a ventilator. His infection, meanwhile, escalated into blood poisoning. When at last he came out of the coma, it was only a prelude to more crises—severe internal bleeding, followed by kidney failure. Brian's entire body seemed to be rebelling. The coup de grace came when a neurologist told the Wests that during the coma, the lack of oxygen had caused extensive brain damage. Even if Brian survived the onslaught of illness, he would be blind and essentially a vegetable.

On December 21, 1982, at the age of 26 months, Brian mercifully died.

The total bill for his life of futility was an estimated $200,000, much of it borne by California taxpayers. This caused Susan West to wonder bitterly whether the hospital would have pursued Brian's "welfare" so diligently "if they weren't going to make any money off this."

She said that the outcome of Brian's surgery had confirmed the couple's belief that they had been right to withhold consent. "When you have very serious defects like this, the decision should rest with the parents. If there are families who think they can handle this, more power to them. We'd never impose our views on others. But we don't want other people's views imposed on us, either. This is where the injustice is. These doctors who make these decisions for you, they don't stay around to find out what happened to you. They go home at night and never think of you again; and then who is it who has to live with their decision?

"I suppose there are parents who say, 'Oh, the child is ugly, let him die.' But most families aren't like that. Most parents love their children and are going to decide what's best for them based on that. It's not a good choice to let a baby die, but we saw it as being better than the alternative. The misery that child went through was hundreds of times worse than what it would have been if he hadn't had the surgery.

"Our doctor said to us recently, 'Well, I guess you guys are in a position to say, 'I told you so.' Maybe we are, but we're not exactly gloating."

Chubby and brown, her eyes darting like swallows, Taina Cabreja watched expectantly as Audrey Schlau, a nurse at Babies Hospital in New York City, detached the long plastic tube that was both Taina's lifeline and her shackle. Suddenly, Taina performed a jackrabbit leap and planted both of her sandaled feet together on the hard linoleum floor.

"I'm free," she said, with the wicked little grin of a bottle imp.

But only for the moment. Taina, who was two and a half years old, was less a bottle imp than a modern Rapunzel, held prisoner in the castle keep by technology. In her entire life she had never been beyond the lobby of the hospital.

When she was born at Babies, on January 5, 1981, she was six weeks premature and weighed only 1,700 grams. In her first few weeks of life, she developed severe necrotizing enterocolitis, which caused large segments of her digestive tract to degenerate. Surgeons had to remove part of her large intestine. Generally, one can live with such a deficit because the ileum, the bottom part of the small intestine, can take over the large intestine's function. But the surgeons had to take out all of her ileum, too. Rather than the normal 250 centimeters of intestine, she now possessed a mere 35 centimeters. To put it another way: if you stretch the average intestine out, its total digestive surface covers the area of a football field; but in Taina it was down to tennis-court size.

At this point the doctors had a choice. It was evident that the child had so little bowel left that she might never be capable of natural digestion. On the other hand, youngsters had been known to recover with less intestine than Taina. She was right on the line. The decision was therefore made to put her on hyperalimentation, or total paren-teral nutrition (TPN), as it is sometimes called, until such time as the intestine became functional. The technique is as extraordinary a life-saving measure as mechanical ventilation, and decisions to initiate or terminate its use are just as fraught with ethical cactus spines. If you gamble and win, the patient's bowel starts working and you can take her off the device. If you lose, her bowel never kicks in and she is chained to the IV forever.

Once they had resolved to go ahead, Taina's physicians implanted a permanent catheter in her superior vena cava, one of the great blood vessels of the heart. Through this catheter liquefied food was pumped into her all day long, every day of her life. The formula she was receiving was a complex blend of amino acids and other vital nutrients, as eminently nourishing as a steak, baked potato, and garden salad, but concentrated like astronaut's fare. Under its influence, she had grown into a normal-sized, even plump, little girl, without having eaten one normal meal by mouth since the day she was born. There were just two drawbacks. The first was that she had to remain fastened to the pump almost constantly, which all but confined her to her hospital room, with no more mobility than the six-foot tether of feeding tube would allow. The other problem was that hyperalimentation was slowly killing her.

No one knows why, but certain patients, exposed to the technique for long periods of time, develop cirrhosis of the liver. One theory has it that the liver needs food coming through the esophagus to stim-ulate it. But that's all it is—a theory. Whatever the scientific explana-tion, Taina's liver had begun to show alarming changes.

Unaware of her peril, Taina skipped around the toy-strewn hospi-tal ward, enjoying one of her rare hiatuses of freedom. For four hours a day she was given a respite from the tall, aluminum pole on wheels that held her IV bag and hyperalimentation pump.

Watching her play was her grandmother, Mrs. Ramona Gomez, a daily visitor. Mrs. Gomez, who is from the Dominican Republic, wore a sad expression. "I despair a lot," she confessed in Spanish. "I am afraid that someday soon Taina might die. But I am glad the doctors saved her. Where there's life, there's hope."

It was a hot July day, and Mrs. Gomez and Taina's teenage mother, Wanda Santos, were about to take the child for a walk in the hospital's garden, 11 floors below. Such truncated excursions were the extent of Taina's knowledge of the world.

"I guess she's happy," Wanda Santos said, as she and Mrs. Gomez got Taina ready for her garden walk. "She really doesn't know the difference. She probably thinks this is all there is to life."

Hyperalimentation is generally regarded as a benign therapeutic tool. First used on humans at the University of Pennsylvania in 1968, it has saved countless thousands of lives in the past 17 years. Only a small percentage of patients, perhaps 5 to 10 percent, develop the kind of complications Taina was experiencing. Nevertheless, the ethical questions persist. When the technique is used to prolong the life of someone who may never be able to survive without artificial feeding, it inescapably raises issues involving the quality of life. In these cases, typified by Taina, the life-support system can metamorphose into an object of tyranny. Theoretically, individuals can live for years enslaved by the TPN machine. In the end, what will inevitably destroy them, perhaps in adolescence—when their death will be far more difficult to bear—will not be their intestines at all, or even cirrhosis. It will be something far more ironic: there are a limited number of sites on the human body where an IV catheter can be implanted, and these access routes frequently wear out. When the doctors run out of IV sites, the child starves to death, a gruesome process that may take weeks.

"By postponing Taina's death, I wonder if we're not creating a monster," fretted Dr. Michael Katz, director of pediatrics at Presbyterian Hospital, which, like Babies, is part of the huge Columbia-Presbyterian complex. "If she had died as a tiny premie, it would have been sad but easier to cope with. But now she has developed into a person, who interacts with other human beings; so if she doesn't survive, the tragedy will be far worse. With that in mind, I still don't have a prescription for what is the right thing to do. I think everyone at this hospital would have done the same thing and put her on hyperalimentation. The rule of thumb says that the amount of gut she has could be enough. It's right on the edge. She may get well and she may not."

Katz lamented that medical insights are sometimes gained at the expense of someone's suffering. "Scientists are like toddlers," he said. "They put everything in their mouths and explore, and eventually make pragmatic discoveries. It is unfortunate that in this case the technology is there to sustain life but not to make life normal."

Nurse Schlau found the thought of not starting hyperalimentation on someone like Taina an abhorrent one. "I'm not really for using lifesaving measures on people there's no hope for, like those in a comatose state. But look at Taina. She's happy. She doesn't realize she's missing something. And if she is still alive five years from now, who knows, they may have found a cure."

Dr. William Heird, the hospital's specialist in hyperalimentation, said he would again start Taina on hyperalimentation if he had it to do all over. "With the amount of bowel she has, the chances were better than 50 percent that she'd be home by now eating selected foods. We're not quite sure why her bowel has never worked. But it's with children who have even less bowel than she does where the ethical question comes in. How far do you go with this therapy? We had another child here whose intestine was almost completely gone. There was no question but that the child would always need TPN. So it wasn't started in the first place. I feel that was the right decision. I wouldn't want to sentence my child to a life of TPN."

It was early afternoon when Taina returned from the garden. Her face glowed with pleasure.

"And did you see the birds in the garden?" Schlau asked her. Taina nodded gaily.

"And what else did you see?" Taina scowled in contemplation. "Did you see something that grew on the ground?" Schlau prompted. "Did you see f——"

"Flowers," shrieked the little girl.

For three more months, Taina survived on hyperalimentation as her liver became steadily more cirrhotic. As she grew weaker, her trips to the hospital garden grew more infrequent and finally stopped altogether. The hot summer turned into cool autumn without her ever knowing it. And then, on October 24, 1983, only two months shy of her third birthday, Taina Cabreja died. This time, she was truly free.

If this sad trilogy contains a lesson, it is that a dogmatic insistence on the treatment of all handicapped newborns is a short-sighted and potentially counterproductive policy. It refuses to look beyond certain immediate moral questions and consider the total future welfare of the infant. In so doing, it runs the risk of plunging the child, in the name of sparing it from evil, into a slough of perpetual torment. Just as fainting is often the individual's escape from short-term pain, so is death one's escape from long-range suffering. To deny a person such egress is a cruelty as abominable, in its own way, as any Gestapo device to keep the subject awake during his or her torture.

But always one returns to the same conundrum: How do we know at the moment of birth what suffering may await impaired babies down the road? Can we be confident enough of our diagnosis to say for sure that their lives will be intolerable? Unfortunately, no.

Acknowledging this fundamental limitation, one nevertheless cannot shrug one's shoulders and say, "Therefore I shall extend the life of every child because I can't be certain how any of them will turn out." This is an abdication guaranteed to cause a great deal of well-intentioned harm to some children and their families. Before making their treatment recommendations, most physicians will at least try to estimate the likely extent of an infant's handicaps, the misery that those handicaps will cause, and the odds that a therapeutic breakthrough might lead to a cure in the future. Ordinarily this is a subjective determination on the part of the doctor, based on his or her experience, clinical judgment, personal prejudices, and so on. It is not the sort of thing that lends itself to formal guidelines, defining which broad categories of children ought to be treated and which ones not. In fact, no one ever attempted to draw up such guidelines—until a few years ago when John Lorber came along.

Lorber, who practices medicine at the University of Sheffield, England, is to the treatment of myelomeningocele what Martin Luther was to the Roman church. Once a true believer, he later became a disillusioned apostate. His involvement with spina bifida goes back to the 1950s, when the overwhelming majority of children born with the disease died in infancy. This mortality rate wore heavily on doctors. It had been 300 years since the disease was first described by Nicolaas Tulp, who, coincidentally, was the lecturer in Rembrandt's famous painting *The Anatomy Lesson.* And yet, in all that time, practically no progress had been made in saving victims' lives. There had been some bizarre recommendations. A Dr. Newbigging proclaimed in 1834 that the sac containing the exposed spinal cord should be punctured. When children subsequently died from the procedure, he blamed it on bad nursing. A Dr. Morton suggested in 1877 that the sac be injected with iodine and glycerin, but his results were no better than Newbigging's. Even when a sound surgical procedure for closing up the lower back was introduced, in the 1890s, it failed to work because of a deadly complication, hydrocephalus. Hydrocephalus is a frequent companion of myelomeningocele. When the neural tube fails to close completely during gestation, blockages called Arnold-Chiari malformations tend to form in the brain stem and act as a dike on the cerebrospinal fluid, keeping it pent up in the brain. The resulting buildup in pressure causes serious damage to the cerebral tissues. Even when the condition is not manifest at birth, it is almost inevitably triggered by the lower-back surgery. In tucking the spinal cord into the vertebral column, the surgeon causes the fluid, which is crystal clear and very similar to seawater, to reverse flow back into the brain. Because of this perplexing circumstance, for the first half of the 20th century, doctors faced a Catch-22 situation. They could either let the infant's spine stay open, in which case infection would probably set in, causing the child to die or suffer terrible handicap, or they could operate and make the head swell like a pumpkin, in which case the child would again most likely die or suffer terrible handicap. But the horizon suddenly brightened when in 1958 a procedure was perfected known as the extracranial shunt. The shunt itself is nothing more than a thin Silastic tube, which is implanted in the center of the brain and run underneath the skin either to the right atrium of the heart or to the intestine, where the spinal fluid can safely drain. At last, the repair of myelomeningocele became feasible.

As the curtain rose on the 1960s, excitement began to ripple through the field of children's neurology. It looked as though this ancient enemy had at last been tamed. Nowhere was this heady feeling stronger than in Sheffield, where Lorber and his colleagues issued the clarion call for a vigorous surgical approach to all myelomeningocele victims. Backs were closed, heads were shunted, twisted skeletons were straightened, and bladders and bowels were subjected to various kinds of appliances and techniques to counteract incontinence. Optimism led to some exaggerated claims. One British doctor wrote in 1968 that he expected only 1 child in 10 would need a wheelchair, that 2 out of 3 children would go to normal school, and that 9 out of 10 would be educable.

By 1970, however the enthusiasm in England was dying down. Several long-term studies of these newly salvaged children revealed that though 60 percent of them were surviving, their lives were often of dubious quality. Fifty percent were almost totally paralyzed, only 25 percent could walk with leg braces, 83 percent had urinary incontinence, and over half were mentally retarded. No more than an estimated 10 percent would ever be gainfully employed. Taking note of this in 1971, Lorber issued his 95 theses, in the form of an article in a journal called *Developmental Medicine and Child Neurology*.

"The pendulum has now swung too far," Lorber wrote. "There are now many with dreadful handicaps who a short time ago would have died." Reporting the depressing results of his own treatment of 524 youngsters during the 1960s, Lorber set forth six criteria that were to be used to "select" children who would benefit most from therapy. These criteria were to exclude from treatment children with any one of the following conditions: gross paralysis of the legs, very hydrocephalic heads, spinal curvature, other severe congenital defects or birth injuries, and a myelomeningocele so high up the back as to affect a maximum amount of motor control. Those chosen for treatment, Lorber said, should receive prompt closure of the back to prevent infection and the full range of shunt, orthopedic, and urinary procedures. Those who do not meet the criteria should not have their backs closed, and should instead be made comfortable until they die, probably in six to nine months. To ensure that they expire, rather than survive with handicaps made worse by nontreatment, Lorber advocated withholding antibiotics, oxygen therapy, incubator care, and tube feeding, and further stressed that the children should be fed "on demand, no more." Since they were on morphine and asleep a large part of the time, they weren't likely to demand very much. If by some chance a nonselectee should survive past nine months, he could then be brought "back into the fold," as Lorber put it, and given surgery.

Justifying selection, Lorber said, "Patients who survive with severe handicaps and who require constant medical and surgical care for as long as they live have immense social, psychological, and financial difficulties, and so, too, do their families. The prospects for open employment, marriage, or anything approaching a normal life are poor, and the cost to the community is immense."

The net result of Lorber's policy was the death of approximately two-thirds of all children born with myelomeningocele and the survival of only one-third. Lorber admitted that selection was not a particularly good solution. "There is no 'good solution,'" he wrote, "to a desperate, insoluble problem, merely a 'least bad solution.' . . ."

Lorber's ideas were quickly accepted throughout Britain and even received the sanction of the Department of Health and Social Security. But selection has been less well received in the United States. Nevertheless, some American medical centers have practiced it. Back in 1974 Dr. David Shurtleff and his associates at the University of Washington School of Medicine described the system they used, which differed from Lorber's in that intellectual criteria, not physical ones, were paramount. To qualify for back surgery under the Shurtleff guidelines, a child had to have a brain mass that was at least 60 percent of the norm and no indication of conditions like Down's syndrome, central-nervous-system bleeding, or structural brain deformity that would interfere with good cognitive function. The location of the spinal-cord defect, whether high or low, was not a factor. Shurtleff and his colleagues added the proviso that the child not have a major malformation such as irreparable heart disease that would preclude self-care as an adult, and that it have either a family with sufficient economic and intellectual resources or a commitment by a social agency to see to its foster care and medical expenses.

"Our approach," wrote the Shurtleff group in the *New England*

Journal of Medicine, "has been based on the need to identify hopeless, burdensome cases before initiating expensive and, it is hoped, life-prolonging treatment. . . . We believe brain function to be the most important criterion for treatment. . . . Most of our families have been able to cope with physical and physiologic abnormalities but not with severe retardation."

The team went on to assert that "the cost of painful suffering by the patient must be judged against his future potential rewards. The emotional and physical pain that we cause child patients to suffer must be justifiable in terms of some reasonable hope for a future happy social adjustment."

(Dr. Shurtleff told me recently that improved medical management has reduced the number of spina bifida victims he sees who display poor intellectual potential. Moreover, the legal and social climate has changed so that alternative arrangements can be made when the family situation is undesirable. As a result, only rarely does the team fail to treat a child now.)

At the University of Oklahoma Health Sciences Center, in Oklahoma City, Dr. Richard Gross and his colleagues use yet another method. A decision is delayed while the child is evaluated by a team consisting of an orthopedist, a pediatrician, a neurosurgeon, a urologist, a nurse clinician, a social worker, physical and occupational therapists, and a psychologist. No specific criteria are used, but the factors stressed by Lorber and Shurtleff are considered. If the team thinks that surgery is appropriate or if it can reach no consensus, a recommendation in favor of treatment is made to the parents. If the team's assessment is pessimistic, nonintervention is advised. The ultimate decision then rests with the parents.

From 1977 to 1982 the team evaluated 69 babies, suggesting surgery for 36 of them and nontreatment for 33. No parents refused consent for recommended surgery, and five couples insisted on surgery over the advice of the team. This would seem to challenge what is an article of faith in the right-to-life movement—that given half a chance, parents will selfishly sentence their impaired children to death.

The Oklahoma authors made very clear their feeling that the future of a handicapped child must not be considered in a vacuum, but must be looked at within the context of the family's wishes and society's willingness to help. "There is no evading the fact," they wrote, "that external circumstances are crucially important in the outlook for the newborn with myelomeningocele. Thus, the treatment for babies with identical 'selection criteria' could be quite different, depending on the contribution from home and society."

Complicating the acceptance of selection in the United States is the fear of prosecution. All it takes for a doctor to be subject to legal action is one dissenting nurse who turns him or her in. When the University Hospital in Stony Brook, New York, determined not to operate on Baby Jane Doe, both the parents and the hospital found themselves entangled in a nightmarish legal skein. To many hospitals, it isn't worth it.

But selection also remains moral anathema to a number of American practitioners. The ethics of allowing large numbers of children to die disturbs them on its face. Of equal concern is the fact that a percentage of the children chosen for nontreatment manage to survive anyway, often in a worse state than if they had been treated initially. Estimates as to the size of this group vary. In some studies no children have lived longer than nine months; in other studies survivors have numbered as high as 10 percent. Dr. John Freeman, of Johns Hopkins University, cited a dreadful case some years ago of a boy with a very severe myelomeningocele who received no treatment at birth, on the assumption he would die. Placed in an institution, he surprised everyone by remaining alive and was belatedly operated upon. But the early failure to perform a hydrocephalus shunt on him caused his head to swell greatly, leading to blindness and mental retardation. And inattention to his orthopedic and urinary problems brought about severe spinal curvature, hip dislocation, and kidney disease. At the age of eight he was in a school for the blind, had an IQ of 80, could barely sit because of his skeletal problems, and had little rapport with his parents, who, having expected him to die, never formed the parent-infant bond during the critical period following birth.

Freeman deplored the ambivalent treatment attitudes that led to such a tragedy, and he wrote, "If the goal of the original nontreatment was the death of the child, the child should be considered a nontreatment failure. If the goal of the original physician had been total care, the child would still have been paraplegic, but possibly with a normal IQ, with vision, without hydronephrosis, and quite possibly with a family which could have developed an emotional relationship to him. . . . The long-term result of the treatment this child received, or did not receive, is that he is a failure for either goal."

Notable among the opponents to selection is Dr. David McLone, of Chicago's Children's Memorial Hospital, who is the leader of a crusade to treat all babies born with myelomeningocele. "Our attitude is to be aggressive with these kids," says McLone, who reports a survival rate of 80 to 90 percent. He boasts that 70 percent of the children he has operated on later display normal intelligence. Half of them can walk with leg braces. A new self-catheterization technique that the child can be taught, called "clean" intermittent catheterization, can mitigate the urine incontinence, and a dietary program can manage the bowel problem.

"If you have normal intelligence and can walk in the community, then you can live alone and compete for jobs," insists McLone.

"There are definitely times down the road," he concedes, "when, even though the operation was a success, it becomes clear that a problem has arisen. A shunt malfunctions two years later, or an infection sets in, and the result is catastrophic. Or perhaps the child is profoundly retarded or not moving, and needs a kidney operation. In such circumstances, after consultation with the parents, we may elect not to be too aggressive. But these instances are rare. In spina bifida, there may be times to allow the child to die. But it's certainly not at birth."

The long-range implications of McLone's approach remain to be seen. The children in his program are still very young. The hardships they will face as adults are many, ranging from the simpler concerns of getting about in a society built for ambulatory people to the more complex issues of obtaining a job and forming romantic attachments. It is one of the more unfortunate aspects of myelomeningocele that while the victim's sex hormones work properly, causing the usual changes at puberty and giving the individual all the normal sexual urges, the nerves to the genitals are very often damaged. This results in loss of sensation to the reproductive organs, and in men, an inability to develop an erection or to ejaculate sperm. Prosthetic implants are available to empower a man to have intercourse. But what effect it will have on the human mind if one has to insert a catheter into the urethra every time one wants to urinate and to squeeze a pump every time one wants to have sex will be known only as these children get older.

7

The Law and
Handicapped
Newborns

Watching a legal trend develop is like looking over the shoulder of a photographer as he prints up a picture. The paper starts out as a blank sheet, but after a few moments in the chemicals, faint outlines begin to appear. At this point, it remains impossible to distinguish what the final outcome will be. We can even be thrown off the track if one corner of the print reveals itself before the others. Eventually, however, the hidden image is coaxed into sharp and recognizable focus. Ah, but wait. Sometimes, the photographer is not satisfied with the print. He returns to the enlarger and by blocking light with judicious hand movements, "burns in" or "dodges out" parts of the scene that please or displease him. Only when the entire procedure is over can we appreciate the result.

Where matters of law are concerned, a similar process of resolution occurs, with lower courts providing the faint and often conflicting outlines and the higher courts giving the final definition. This tedious sequence can consume many years, as the judiciary is evolving a point of view. It is therefore frustrating, but not surprising, that the courts have been slow in arriving at a position on the care of defective newborns. Even now, only the broader outlines of judicial sentiment are visible. The full picture remains unclear.

Few areas of the law are as shrouded in gray as the question of allowing handicapped babies to die. Theoretically, for a mother and father, in collaboration with a physician or hospital, to deny a child lifesaving medical treatment, or sustenance, would seem prima facie to be a crime. Certain legal experts have flatly argued that they are criminally liable for homicide—not homicide by commission, where an overt act upon another's person results in death, but homicide by omission, where something one *doesn't* do brings about death. Parents have the obligation to feed, clothe, and provide medical care to their children. If they don't do these things and if an offspring dies as a consequence, they have committed murder as surely as if they had held the child underwater until it drowned. The same may be said of a doctor, who has the contractual obligation to provide essential treatment to a newborn patient. Failure to carry out this duty is also murder, at least on paper. But if this seems too strong a charge, there are other criminal complaints that might be lodged against parents and doctors. These include manslaughter, conspiracy, and child abuse or neglect.

Yet prosecutors have been notably reluctant to file such charges. Parents who would be put in the prisoner's dock posthaste for battering their sons or daughters or keeping them chained in the attic are routinely given dispensation when they engineered or attempted to engineer their defective infant's death. Only part of the absence of prosecution can be accounted for by failure of district attorneys to learn of newborn nontreatment. When Drs. Raymond Duff and Alexander Campbell, of the Yale–New Haven Hospital, publicly announced in 1973 that 43 infant deaths at the hospital in the preceding two years had been the result of withdrawal of care, no DA leaped forward to announce a grand jury investigation. No gumshoes began hanging around the hospital's neonatal ward trying to get the goods on the staff. This makes for a peculiar paradox. According to the Constitution and every custom of the United States, all human beings are entitled to certain basic rights, the most fundamental of these being the right to life itself. At the time of birth, a child, whether congenitally impaired or not, becomes a citizen of this country and is presumably clothed in the same rights as any other citizen. Yet it would appear that, by more or less common consent, severely defective babies have become a group unto themselves, a small segment of society whose lives others may extinguish without fear of serious punishment.

Allowing handicapped newborns to die falls under the broad legal heading of euthanasia, a once-taboo practice that has been gaining some respectability in recent years. A 1950 Gallup poll asked people whether they thought doctors should be permitted to end a patient's

life by painless means if the patient and the family request it. Nearly
two-thirds said no. But when the same question was put to Americans
in 1973, 53 percent answered yes. *Euthanasia* literally means "good
death," and it can take several different forms. It can, for example,
be voluntary—that is, performed at the patient's request. Or it can be
involuntary—that is, undertaken without his or her consent. Where
babies are concerned, it is always involuntary because the child obviously
cannot grant permission. Euthanasia may also be of an active or passive kind. It is said to be active (direct) when the cause of death is
some positive action. Conversely, it is described as passive (indirect)
when death results from a failure to act, as in the omission or withdrawal of life-preserving treatment. Active euthanasia remains as illegal as it ever was; one cannot, for instance, inject a child with a lethal
dose of tranquilizer to bring about its death. Passive euthanasia, on
the other hand, lies in the gray area of the law. The simple fact is that
most people, the courts included, consider allowing someone to die to
be less objectionable than directly causing someone to die. (It is interesting, however, that active euthanasia may sometimes be the more
compassionate choice. In the case of Baby Doe in Indiana, it would
have been more humane from the child's point of view to die quickly
and painlessly by injection than to linger for many days hemorrhag-
ing and without food.)

To date, there has been only one criminal action in the United States
for failure to treat a handicapped newborn. The case occurred in
Danville, Illinois, where Dr. Robert Mueller and his wife, Pamela, along
with their attending physician, Dr. Petra Warren, were accused of
conspiring to murder the couple's Siamese twins. The twins, named
Scott and Jeff, were born on May 5, 1981, joined at the hip and shar-
ing a leg, bladder, and lower bowel. It appeared that a surgical separation was impossible and that they would spend the rest of their lives
fused together. Within hours of their birth in Danville's Lakeview
Medical Center, the order "Do not feed in accordance with parents
wishes" was written on their medical chart. However, some guilt-rid-
den nurses disobeyed the order and gave the children Similac, while
an unknown informant notified the state child welfare authorities.

What followed was a brutal experience for the Muellers, who by
every account were decent, caring people. First the children were taken
away from them on a neglect petition. In granting custody to the welfare department, Judge John Meyer, of Vermilion County, declared,
"The juvenile court must follow the Constitutions of Illinois and the
United States, each of which contains a bill of rights. These bills of
rights give even to newborn Siamese twins with severe abnormalities
the inalienable right to life. Has our society retrograded to the stage

where we mortals can say to a newborn abnormal child, 'You have no right to try to live with a little help from us?' . . . Anyone that has sat through this trial, unless they have a brick in place of a heart, must have compassion for all involved, but when we put ourselves above the law and our Constitutions, we get in trouble. . . ."

Then the Vermilion County prosecutor, Edward Litak, filed attempted-murder charges. In doing so, he rather theatrically told the press, "One could easily imagine the pain of the parents. . . . But you also have to feel sorry for the children, hearing the nurses' statements: how they cried in pain because they were hungry; how the cries dwindled down to whimpers as they were starved to death; how the skin started to wrinkle. . . . These were two infant human beings, that feel things just like any other human being does."

The law took the position that as burdensome as life might be for people permanently joined at the pelvis, it did not give their parents the right to decide on their behalf that such a life was not worth living. Since the parents had apparently tried to claim that right anyway, they had to pay the price.

A preliminary hearing ensued in which nurses from the maternity floor were put on the witness stand. None of them was willing or able to link the parents or the attending physician directly to the "Do not feed" order. A key witness could not remember details of a critical telephone conversation she had supposedly had with Dr. Warren. Circuit Court Judge Richard Scott had little choice but to dismiss the criminal charges, finding no probable cause. However, Litak was not finished. The following March, he tried to obtain a grand jury indictment. The jurors refused to hand one down.

In the meantime, the Muellers were reawarded custody of Scott and Jeff. Noting that the couple had regularly visited the twins at Chicago's Children's Memorial Hospital, the boys' new home, Judge Meyer remarked on how the Muellers "have bathed, changed, clothed the twins, performed physical therapy routines, played with them and have actually participated in their care, treatment, and discharge planning." His words, though necessary to establish that the Muellers were not neglectful, conjured up a pathetic image of a mother and father forced to prove to a world of condescending strangers that they were indeed loving parents after all.

When Jeff and Scott were a year old, doctors at Children's Memorial determined that surgical separation of the twins might not be as impossible as was originally thought. In fact, it might be wiser to attempt it. Scott, the weaker of the two, had developed a heart condition. If the boys remained joined and Scott should happen to die, Jeff would probably be doomed as well, because of their common bloodstreams.

In addition, separation would enable surgeons to do cardiac surgery on Scott without endangering Jeff. But a separation posed some curious legal issues of its own. Which twin, for example, should get the leg they both shared? These and other questions had to be settled by the two guardians ad litem who had been appointed by the courts to represent each child's interests. Fortunately, everything was expeditiously resolved, and on July 15, 1982, a surgical team led by Dr. John Raffensperger successfully parted the boys in a harrowing operation that lasted nine hours.

Raffensperger is a brilliant, though haughty, pediatric surgeon who affects an air of irascibility. He growls. He is likely to turn on his heel and walk off in midconversation. However, he also has a compassionate streak, and society's treatment of the Muellers has infuriated him. "The judge and the district attorney should both be shot," he fumes. "Bringing the courts into these cases is a tragedy of the highest order. It's none of their damned business."

Instead, Raffensperger asserts, life-and-death decisions regarding damaged offspring should be the province of parents, in consultation with their doctors, relatives, and clergymen. "These decisions," he contends, "are never made lightly by the family, and to publicize it in any way only adds to their tragedy."

Litak, by way of reply, says he had no choice but to bring charges. "Illinois law says you cannot take human life without justification. Justification means a necessity, such as self-defense, which did not apply in this case. Here were two human beings capable of life. If you deprive them of life, you are committing murder. The law says nothing about the quality of that life." Litak claims he was not interested in putting the Muellers in prison. "I only wanted to establish that they had done wrong. Anyone can see there were extenuating circumstances."

The twins, at last report, were faring moderately well. Scott had been placed in a pediatric nursing home in Chicago, his cardiac problems in abeyance. Jeff was still struggling to learn to walk, hampered by bone deformities of the leg he once shared with Scott. The Muellers, meanwhile, have suffered serious marital problems because of the episode, according to family sources.

A prosecution of a similar nature occurred in Leicester, England, in the fall of 1981. Dr. Leonard Arthur, a highly respected pediatrician, was tried in connection with the death of an infant suffering from Down's syndrome. The parents had reportedly rejected the child because of its handicap. Shortly after the birth, Dr. Arthur wrote the following treatment order: "Parents do not wish it to survive. Nursing care only." Then he prescribed dihydrocodeine, a morphine derivative, to be given every 4 hours. The baby died 69 hours later, allegedly without having been fed. The cause of death was listed as pneumonia induced by dihydrocodeine poisoning. To the embarrassment of the prosecution, the initial charge of murder was reduced during the trial to attempted murder when a pathologist's testimony showed the boy could have died from causes unrelated to Dr. Arthur's actions. The child had calcification of the brain, fibroelastosis of the heart, and congenital lung defects, overlooked in the original autopsy report. Consequently, the issue before the court became not whether Dr. Arthur had actually killed the child but whether he had intended by his actions to do so. The jury took just two hours to deliver its verdict: not guilty.

The experience of these two cases goes a long way toward explaining the dearth of prosecutions for failure to treat handicapped babies. In the Danville affair, little was accomplished except the humiliation and harassment of two people who had already suffered one of life's worst tragedies, the birth of defective offspring. In the Leicester matter, the crown's prosecutors came off looking foolish for having put on a poor case. Thus, compassion probably stays the hand of some district attorneys, while others fear losing in court and inciting a backlash of sympathy for the parents or doctor in the process.

But the reasons for prosecutorial paralysis would appear to go deeper than that. And any explanation should be made to account for the relative infrequency with which civil action is initiated to compel treatment of handicapped children. This lack of activity has been noteworthy, given the large number of impaired babies born each day and the strong likelihood that some of them are subjected to a withdrawal of treatment. The answer to the puzzle would seem to reside within the law itself.

Much of the difficulty can be traced to the conflict between two distinct legal traditions, each one deeply rooted in British and American case law and each one incompatible with the other. Tradition A confers great autonomy on parents in making decisions about their own lives and those of their children. Tradition B seeks to protect children from injurious parental decisions. The origins of Tradition A are lost in antiquity, but certainly its bloodlines are very British and are homologous with those that produced the system we call democracy. The notion that the government is the servant, not the master, of the people goes hand in hand with the idea that the individual and the family are not subject to state control. There are few nobler sentiments than the declaration that men and women are kings and queens in their own castle. What is less noble is that the sovereignty of the rulers of the family was frequently won at the expense of the common people of the family, its children. The harshest expression of this state of affairs was found in the prevalence of infanticide.

Since earliest medieval times, British society has harbored mixed feelings toward infanticide. Though prohibitions against the practice were on the books, they were erratically enforced, such mitigating circumstances as parental poverty and the illegitimacy of the child being taken into account. A substantial part of this ambivalence was pragmatic necessity in an era before birth control, but it was also rooted in a cultural attitude, prevalent in many parts of the world, that held youngsters to be of lower status than their elders. This ethic found expression in the workplace, where children were made to labor inordinately long hours, and in the home, where they were bullied with impunity—cruelties that fill the pages of many a Charles Dickens classic. Most particularly, it lent itself to the idea that the slaying of a newborn was somehow not as heinous as the slaying of an older person and that it could be understood, if not justified, within certain family planning contexts. One can detect in this thinking an echo of the old Roman doctrine of *jus vitae necisque,* the power of life and death that fathers in ancient times wielded over their children. This ambivalence toward the killing of newborns is reflected even in modern-day Britain, where there are two discrete laws dealing with murder—a homicide act covering the death of persons over the age of one year, and an infanticide act pertaining to babies. British juries have been notoriously loath to convict mothers of criminal homicide for taking the lives of their small children. The infanticide act was drafted to meet the need for a somewhat lesser offense, one compatible with the British notion that infanticide, almost by its very commission, is evidence of insanity. The law, which went into effect in 1922 and has been amended on several occasions over the years, provides that women who slay their infants while mentally unbalanced from the effects of childbirth, shall be punished as if they had committed manslaughter, not murder. In practice, the law takes an exceedingly generous view of what constitutes mental unbalance. Nearly any woman who kills her infant would so qualify. Interestingly enough, prescribed punishments are rarely meted out. According to the legal historian Catherine Damme, of the University of Texas, only 49 percent of all mothers convicted under the act in 1923 were imprisoned. Today, that number has dwindled to 1.3 percent. A full 68 percent of mothers who kill their infants are granted probation!

Much of U.S. law and custom derives from British roots. That the United States inherited a depreciatory attitude toward children, which was long ingrained in the national consciousness, was evidenced by

the enormous difficulty reformers had in passing child labor legislation. Infanticide was not uncommon in America. But there never arose
in the United States a legal distinction between homicide and infanticide. Parents who slay their children are tried under unitary state
homicide statutes, and in most situations are dealt with severely.
Nevertheless, the British tradition that parents possess great power
over their families has continued to flourish in American law. A number of cases have, for instance, established people's right to educate
their children in whatever schools they please. In the past two decades,
a significant series of Supreme Court decisions has institutionalized
this concept by defining a constitutional right of personal and family
privacy. Although not explicitly stated in the Constitution or its
amendments, this right is held to be implied in the spirit of that doc-
ument. The cornerstone of the principle was set down in a 1965 ruling in the case of *Griswold* v. *Connecticut*. In *Griswold* the U.S. Supreme
Court struck down a state law prohibiting the use of contraceptives
and in so doing forbade the states from invading the "intimate relation" of husband and wife. Justice William O. Douglas argued, "Would
we allow the police to search the sacred precincts of marital bedrooms
for telltale signs of the use of contraceptives? The very idea is repul-
sive to the notions of privacy surrounding the marriage relationship.
We deal with a right of privacy older than the Bill of Rights."

In 1972, in the case of *Eisenstadt* v. *Baird,* the *Griswold* decision was
extended to permit contraceptive purchases by single people, and the
right of privacy was amplified. The Supreme Court asserted a "right
of the individual, married or single, to be free from unwarranted governmental intrusion into matters so fundamentally affecting a person
as the decision whether to bear or beget a child." The culmination of
this string of cases was the Supreme Court's 1973 decision legalizing
abortion. The *Roe* v. *Wade* ruling did essentially three things: it put a
woman's desire to terminate her pregnancy under the umbrella of
her right of privacy; it extended this zone of privacy to include her
relationship with her doctor; and by conferring the right to an abortion in the third trimester for reasons of maternal health, it declared
flatly that the mother's well-being was more important to the state
than the life of a viable fetus. This is certainly not the same as saying
the mother's rights are more important than those of a *born* child, for
the fetus is not yet a person, under law, while the born child is; however, it is traveling down the same philosophical road.

Over the past few years there has also emerged a new species of
lawsuit that has come to be known as "wrongful birth" and "wrongful
life" litigation. Wrongful birth is an action filed by parents contending
that a doctor's failure to diagnose handicaps during prenatal testing

resulted in the birth of a defective child who would otherwise have
been aborted. When such an action is filed on behalf of the handicapped child, it is called wrongful life. Implicit in both of these kinds
of cases is the belief that a child should not have been born, that its
life is of negative value. Quite a large number of parents have been
awarded damages under wrongful-birth claims. (The action is recognized in a number of states, including New York, Texas, Minnesota,
New Jersey, California, and Michigan.) But fewer wrongful-*life* suits
have been successful, not because the courts aren't sympathetic but
because judges have a very difficult time assessing damages. How does
one compute the value of nonexistence compared with the hardships
and / or enjoyments of a handicapped existence? It is impossible to
calculate. Even so, California courts have approved two wrongful-life
suits. In 1980 Shauna Temar Curlender was granted damages by an
appeals court, which agreed with her attorney's claim that "she had a
right never to be brought into existence." Shauna suffered from the
dreaded genetic killer Tay-Sachs disease. The suit alleged that two
genetic testing laboratories had mistakenly told Shauna's parents that
they were not Tay-Sachs carriers, causing the couple to go ahead and
have a child. Then, in 1982, the California Supreme Court approved
special damages to pay for the treatment and education of Joy Turpin, a Fresno youngster who was born totally deaf. A few years before
her birth, her parents had taken their first daughter, Hope, to a community hospital for evaluation of a possible hearing defect. The hospital assured them the child's hearing was normal. On the basis of that
report, the couple conceived a second daughter, Joy. Both children
turned out to have a hereditary hearing ailment. It was the parents'
contention that they would not have had another baby had the hospital not erred.

There is a common thread running through every one of the above
cases, from *Griswold* to *Turpin*. It is the idea that parents may make
reproductive and family decisions free from state intervention, that
children are not invariably a blessing, and that parents have rights not
to have them, especially defective children. One can see vestiges of
medieval British pragmatism in this doctrine. And it does not take a
tremendous leap of the intellect to see at least a shadow of it in the
failure to prosecute parents and doctors who have withheld care from
handicapped babies.

Now, in contrast, let us examine Tradition B, which might fairly be
called the *parens patriae* doctrine. *Parens patriae,* literally translated,
means "parent of the country." It refers to the state's power to act as
guardian of the welfare of minors, in addition to that of insane and
incompetent people. The theory is that the state's interest in protect-

ing the lives and health of its citizens takes precedence over the parents' interest in control over their children. Therefore, the courts have generally ruled that a couple does not have the right to refuse customary medical care for their offspring. An early case in this regard (1899) was that of *Regina* v. *Senior,* in which a father was convicted of manslaughter under an English statute making it a crime to willfully neglect a child in a manner "likely to cause such child unnecessary suffering or injury to its health." The man, described as a "good and kind father" in all other respects, had denied his small infant medical attention for diarrhea and pneumonia. He did so because he belonged to a religious sect called the Peculiar People, whose adherents believed that illness should be cured with prayer. His conviction was upheld on appeal. Half a century later, in an Illinois case called *People ex rel. Wallace* v. *Labrenz,* the court approved a blood transfusion for eight-day-old Cheryl Linn Labrenz, who was suffering from Rh blood disease and who, without treatment, was facing death or severe brain damage. Her parents, devout Jehovah's Witnesses, had refused to permit the transfusion on the grounds that Scripture says, "Ye shall eat the blood of no manner of flesh," and that their sect interpreted this to mean transfusions were a sin. The mother told the court she feared that breaking God's commandment would destroy her daughter's chance of an afterlife. The judges rejected the argument that the transfusion violated the Labrenzes' religious and parental rights, noting that "neither rights of religion or rights of parenthood are beyond limitation." In 1983, Tennessee courts ordered chemotherapy for the 12-year-old Pamela Irene Hamilton, who was suffering from Ewing's sarcoma, a bone cancer that had caused a football-sized tumor to grow on her thigh. Her father, an ordained minister of the Church of God of the Union Assembly, objected. He said that his denomination eschews medicine, believing "only God can heal," and that the order infringed on his freedom of religion. The courts mandated traatment of Pamela even though the girl herself was opposed to it, an act her lawyers equated with "rape."

Parens patriae power has also been exercised to overrule a couple's choice of a particular medical treatment for their youngster, where no religious issue was involved. In 1978 the Massachusetts Supreme Judicial Court ordered the parents of the two-year-old Chad Green, a leukemia victim, to continue the boy's chemotherapy treatments, which they had opposed. The court later rejected the parents' petition that they be allowed to supplement the chemotherapy with "metabolic therapy," a daily regimen that included laetrile, enzyme enemas, and megavitamins, including 80 milligrams of beef pancreas, 40 milligrams of calf thymus, 45,000 units of vitamin A, and 3,500 to 4,000 milligrams of vitamin C. The court found this treatment to be harmful to the child, by causing cyanide, a component of laetrile, to accumulate in his body and by threatening him with vitamin A poisoning. Said the court, "The judgment of the parents has been consistently poor, from the child's standpoint, and his well-being seriously threatened as a result. . . . . This case well illustrates that parents do not and must not have absolute authority over the life and death of their children." Unfortunately, during the appeals process the Greens left the country for Mexico, where Chad died on October 12, 1979.

The essence of the *parens patriae* doctrine, that a child's right to life and health justifies state intercession, puts it on a collision course with the first tradition, that of family autonomy. The net effect, then, is to create a triad of competing rights: those of the child, those of the parents, and those of the state on behalf of the child. It is a mix that is kept in delicate balance a good deal of the time. The desired goal is that the child's best interests will coincide with the parents' wishes. Should these interests be significantly jeopardized, however, by parental whim, the state is empowered to step in.

Determining someone's best interests in the medical sense requires asking whether a specific treatment is of benefit to the person. This can be a multifaceted issue, taking many factors into account, but basically it boils down to this: Does the treatment improve the length and quality of the person's life sufficiently to justify its use, especially in light of any harm it may inflict, and does it outweigh the alternatives? If you apply this test to children like Pamela Hamilton or Chad Green, for example, it is clearly in their best interests to receive chemotherapy. The treatment, though obnoxious, has a demonstrated ability to shrink cancers and therefore holds out the reasonable promise of restoring such children to normal lives. With a nostrum like metabolic therapy, or with no treatment at all, they are almost sure to die. A parent may argue their child's best interests must be viewed in a theological perspective, that the value system of God transcends that of man, but as the Supreme Court once ruled, "Parents may be free to become martyrs themselves. But it does not follow they are free . . . to make martyrs of their children before they have reached the age of full and legal discretion when they can make that choice for themselves."

Where the best-interests formula dissolves into confusion is in the case of severely handicapped newborns. The reason for this is not that impaired children have any fewer rights than the rest of society (although some commentators have tried to make that claim; the Nobel laureate Francis Crick, for example, who won the prize for DNA research, was once quoted as saying, "No newborn infant should be

declared human until it has passed certain tests regarding its genetic
endowment and . . . if it fails these tests, it forfeits the right to live").
It is that it is often hard to discern exactly what a defective child's best
interests are.

Can anyone, for example, be sure of what is in the interest of an
infant with severe spina bifida and brain malformations associated
with profound mental retardation? Or of a child with trisomy 13 who
needs a lifesaving cardiac procedure? Performing surgery on such
youngsters would *not* be like giving chemotherapy to Chad Green.
There is no hope of producing anything remotely resembling a normal life. The children will lack mobility, will relate to the environment
in only rudimentary ways, and may even be in pain. Are there enough
benefits in such lives to warrant their extension, or do the babies'
interests lie in an early death? Reasonable people may form an opinion on either side of the question. In view of the ambiguity, authorities are understandably reluctant to institute legal proceedings.

This is not to imply that the issue of withholding care from impaired
newborns never comes to court. It has received sporadic airings. Generally, these have taken the form of emergency hearings at the lower-
court level to ensure some sort of treatment for a malformed child.
The customary vehicle is either a hospital request that the court order
treatment over parental objection, a neglect petition seeking to remove
a child from its parents' custody, or both. More and more of these
cases have been forced upon a reluctant judiciary as hospitals have
become frightened that they might conceivably be prosecuted for
withholding treatment, and as more nurses and other hospital personnel, with the encouragement of the prolife movement, have started
informing on doctors. I say reluctant judiciary because most judges
fear and dislike such cases. Possessing no medical background, lacking a body of past law to use as a reference point, and frequently not
having the stomach to make hard choices where small children and
heartsick parents are concerned, many jurists will try to shun these
issues if they can. When a hearing of the matter is unavoidable, lower-
court judges have usually fallen back on sanctimonious interpreta-
tions of the law, preferring to wax platitudinous about the wonder
and inviolability of life rather than to wade into the marshy ground
of making newer, but more perceptive, law.

Thus, the tone for a number of court decisions to come was set by
Judge David G. Roberts, of Maine, in one of the earliest of these hearings —the 1974 case of "Baby Boy Houle." The child, who was the
son of a U.S. Air Force sergeant and his wife, was born at Maine
Medical Center in Portland on February 9 of that year. He suffered

from brain damage, a seizure disorder, unfused vertebrae, and a tracheoesophageal fistula. In addition, the entire left side of his body was seriously deformed, leaving him with, among other things, a misshapen left hand, no left eye, and virtually no left ear. Believing that his prospects of having a reasonable quality of life were practically nil, his parents refused consent for a correction of the tracheoesophageal fistula. Several doctors disagreed and took the case to court. In his ruling, Judge Roberts did not for a minute concede that a child's future should play any role whatsoever in medical decision making.

"Though recent decisions may have cast doubt upon the legal rights of an unborn child, at the moment of live birth there does exist a human being entitled to the fullest protection of the law. The most basic right enjoyed by every human being is the right to life itself. . . . . The issue before the court is not the prospective quality of the life to be preserved, but the medical feasibility of the proposed treatment compared with the almost certain risk of death should treatment be withheld. Being satisfied that corrective surgery is medically necessary and medically feasible, the court finds that the defendants herein have no right to withhold such treatment and that to do so constitutes neglect in the legal sense."

In a similar vein was the 1978 ruling of a Massachusetts judge ordering surgery for a month-old infant named Kerri Ann McNulty. She had been diagnosed as having congenital rubella, cataracts in both eyes, congestive heart failure, respiratory difficulty, deafness, and probably severe mental retardation. The father wanted the ventilator stopped and would not consent to cardiac catheterization and surgery. Once again the court slammed the door on quality-of-life considerations, declaring, "I am persuaded that the proposed cardiac surgery is not merely a life prolonging measure, but indeed is for the purpose of saving the life of this child, regardless of the quality of that life."

The thinking embodied in these and similar decisions seems patently simplistic, reducing matters to a question of whether it is medically possible to extend a life, and ignoring the question of whether it is emotionally possible to enjoy that life. But this stance has the strong appeal of making the judge look ostensibly like a defender of human values, a keeper of the flame, resisting the high-handed actions of filicidal parents. It presupposes that longer life is universally preferable to death, enshrining existence as a kind of religion. And it rests on the assumption that because it is morally offensive to proclaim one person's life more or less meaningful than another's, one may never attempt to render judgment on any infant's quality of life. The catch in that assumption is that it merely masquerades as kindness. The real beneficiaries are the individuals washing their hands of the treatment decision—the judge and, perhaps, the medical staff as well, all of whom have assured themselves of a clear conscience. But what of the severely handicapped newborn who, because of this judicial stance, must actually live minute by minute the nonverbal, nonambulatory, half-conscious existence that he or she has been guaranteed, with its pressure sores, full diapers, and feeding tubes? For the child such a ruling might amount to cruelty.

Despite this doctrinaire logic from the bench, however, change was in the wind. A sustained sequence of scientific and social events had begun to come to a head in the 1970s, presenting the American legal system with an unprecedented challenge. New life-support technologies were making human beings the masters of death; the growing secularization of society was undermining old prohibitions; an increasing emphasis on individual autonomy was bestowing on people more power over their own fates; and a breakdown of the extended family was dictating alternative arrangements for the elderly and infirm. All of these forces conspired to create thorny ethical dilemmas that would be settled only in the courts. A string of cases now forced the judiciary to think more profoundly not just about the right to live but about the right to die. And these cases, although they almost invariably involved adult patients, would ultimately influence the care of defective newborns.

Probably the most far-reaching, and without question the best-publicized, of these legal imbroglios was the one concerning Karen Ann Quinlan, an attractive 22-year-old woman who suddenly ceased breathing for at least two 15-minute intervals on the night of April 15, 1975. Given mouth-to-mouth resuscitation and rushed to the hospital, she was placed on a ventilator in a comatose condition. In days to come, her doctors determined that she had suffered irreversible brain damage. Though she retained some minimal brain function— she moved, reacted to light, blinked, and uttered small cries—and thus was still legally alive, she could not control her own respiration and was in a "chronic, persistent vegetative state," with no awareness of her surroundings and no hope, the doctors said, of recovery.

It soon became apparent, however, that she could live indefinitely on the life-support machine. After months of watching their emaciated daughter curl into an insensible, fetal ball, Miss Quinlan's anguished parents felt she should be allowed to die in peace. They asked the doctors to discontinue the ventilator treatment. The physicians refused, contending that as long as Miss Quinlan was alive, it was their duty to treat her. Her father, Joseph, then petitioned the court to appoint him her guardian with the authority to refuse further extraordinary medical procedures on her behalf. The lower court refused, and Mr. Quinlan took the matter to the New Jersey Supreme Court.

In a landmark decision, the court decreed that the machine could be turned off on a patient who, like Miss Quinlan, had not yet suffered brain death. The justices observed that if Miss Quinlan were mentally competent, she would have the right to refuse continuation of her life, since the same right of personal privacy and bodily integrity that permits someone to have an abortion also allows a patient to decline medical treatment. They reasoned that this right to decline care "should not be discarded solely on the basis that her condition prevents her conscious exercise of the choice."

To a counterargument by the New Jersey attorney general that the state has a compelling interest in prolonging all life, the court replied, "We think that the State's interest . . . weakens and the individual's right to privacy grows as the degree of bodily invasion increases and the prognosis dims. Ultimately there comes a point at which the individual's rights overcome the State interest."

Because Miss Quinlan was unable to assert her right to privacy, the court said, the only way to prevent the destruction of that right was to permit the guardian and family of Karen to "render their best judgment . . . as to whether she would exercise it in these circumstances." Such a standard is known as the substituted-judgment test, one of two methods used to determine whether medical treatment should be provided for an incompetent patient—that is, one unable to speak for oneself. The other test is the so-called best-interests test alluded to earlier in this chapter. The substituted-judgment test calls on the patient's guardian or the court to decide what the patient would choose if he or she were fully cognizant and able to communicate. Its drawback is that unless the patient made it clear before becoming incompetent how he or she would want to be treated under a given set of circumstances, it is a purely subjective inference on the part of the guardian. The best-interests test is broader, in that it allows a consideration of the patient's objective needs, as well as his or her probable desires. The New Jersey high court did not give Miss Quinlan's parents complete authority to make this substituted judgment. It required that they also obtain the agreement of her doctors and the ethics committee of the hospital where she was being treated.

In weeks that followed there was much discussion between the Quinlans and doctors, which culminated in Miss Quinlan's being removed from the ventilator. But instead of dying, as expected, she amazed everyone and began breathing on her own. She remains alive today, at the age of 30, as comatose and insensible as ever. She is fed through a nasogastric tube. Her mother, who visits her almost daily, recently explained that though the feeding tube itself could be construed as an extraordinary measure for someone like Karen, removing it "was simply something we did not want to do."

Despite the bizarre outcome of the Quinlan case, the New Jersey decision has had great influence. For the first time, a court recognized the fallacy of what the University of Washington law professor Arval Morris has called "the law's defective premise," to wit, "that life, whatever its form, nature, or content, is necessarily and always a good, and that death, or any event that hastens death, is always and necessarily an evil and should be illegal."

Several years later a similar theory was applied in the case of Brother Joseph Fox. Brother Fox was an 83-year-old member of the Society of Mary, a Catholic religious order that operates a high school on Long Island. In the summer of 1979 he sustained a hernia while moving flower tubs on a roof garden at the school. His doctor advised an operation, and the elderly teacher agreed.

During the operation, Brother Fox suffered cardiac arrest and an interruption of oxygen to his brain and wound up on a ventilator in a chronic vegetative coma. His chances for recovery were next to none. On being advised of this, his religious superior, Father Philip Eichner, informed the hospital that Brother Fox had often declared that he would not want to be kept alive by any of this "extraordinary business," should he ever be in Karen Ann Quinlan's predicament. The hospital replied that it could not, in good conscience, shut off the ventilator and let the old man die. Father Eichner then had himself appointed Brother Fox's guardian and pursued the case through the courts. In the middle of the legal fight, Brother Fox died, but not before he had run up $87,000 in medical bills and $20,000 in legal fees. The New York Court of Appeals ruled on the mooted case anyway, affirming a lower-court decision that the ventilator be disconnected.

Somewhat different issues were at stake in the 1976 case of *Superintendent of Belchertown State School* v. *Saikewicz*. Joseph Saikewicz was a profoundly retarded man of 67 who had lived in Massachusetts state institutions the major part of his life. He had been at the Belchertown State School since 1928. Possessing an IQ of only 10 and a mental age of approximately two years and eight months, he was unable to speak and communicated solely through gestures and grunts. On April 19, 1976, he was diagnosed as suffering from a severe form of leukemia, and William E. Jones, the superintendent of the state facility, sought the appointment of a guardian ad litem to determine whether chemo-therapy treatments should begin. Saikewicz had no known relatives beyond two sisters who declined to become involved.

After an investigation, the guardian ad litem decided to recom-mend against chemotherapy. He did so because the potential benefits of the treatment were outweighed by the burdens it would impose. At Saikewicz's age, chemotherapy had no more than a 30 to 40 percent chance of inducing remission of the disease, and such remission would last only 2 to 13 months before the leukemia would return with a vengeance. The disease itself was inevitably fatal. Meanwhile, the chemotherapy would have toxic side effects, including severe nausea, bladder irritation, numbness of the extremities, and hair loss. Most important, Saikewicz's retardation would prevent him from compre-hending what was being done to him. He would undoubtedly react with fear and would need to be restrained. The Massachusetts courts agreed that chemotherapy should be withheld, noting that the bene-fits to Saikewicz of a few extra months of painful life did not warrant the suffering it would entail. Saikewicz died on September 4, 1976.

In a written decision issued a year after Saikewicz's death, the Mas-sachusetts Supreme Judicial Court declared, as the New Jersey court had earlier in the Karen Quinlan case, that a mentally incompetent person has the same right to refuse medical treatment as a normal person. The court said, "[T]he state must recognize the dignity and worth of such a person and afford to that person the same panoply of rights and choices it recognizes in competent persons. If a compe-tent person faced with death may choose to decline treatment which not only will not cure the person but which substantially may increase suffering in exchange for a possible yet brief prolongation of life, then it cannot be said that it is always in the 'best interests' of the ward to require submission to such treatment."

The court, quoting in part the guardian ad litem, observed that while many normal people would elect to undergo chemotherapy, the barriers erected by Saikewicz's mental retardation made his situation unique. " 'If he is treated with toxic drugs he will be involuntarily immersed in a state of painful suffering, the reason for which he will never understand. Patients who request treatment know the risks involved and can appreciate the painful side-effects when they arrive. They know the reason for the pain and their hope makes it tolerable.' To make a worthwhile comparison, one would have to ask whether a majority of people would choose chemotherapy if they were told merely that something outside of their previous experience was going to be done to them, that this something would cause them pain and discom-fort, that they would be removed to strange surroundings and possibly restrained for extended periods of time, and that the advantages of this course of action were measured by concepts of time and mortality beyond their ability to comprehend."

A substituted-judgment standard comparable to the one used in the Quinlan case was invoked. The court noted that although Saikewicz's situation wasn't directly analogous to Miss Quinlan's—since he had some cognition—his lack of mental competency nevertheless made it necessary for a proxy to exercise his right to privacy for him. The court determined that were Saikewicz miraculously able to stand outside himself for one moment and decide what should be done to him under the circumstances, he would opt not to have chemotherapy.

One of the things that shone through the Massachusetts decision very clearly was the court's discomfort with "quality of life" considerations. While the justices obviously thought the subject relevant to the case, they treated it gingerly. Nobody wanted to say that the reason one should not make a Joseph Saikewicz undergo extremely unpleasant treatment was that a retarded existence was so abysmal as to be not worth the candle. Accordingly, the court took pains to point out that the *quality* of someone's life should never be used to judge the *value* of that life. It emphasized that in the *Saikewicz* context, quality of life should be construed to refer only to "the continuing state of pain and disorientation precipitated by the chemotherapy treatment," and that Saikewicz's inability "to appreciate or experience life" had no place in the decision. American courts are wary of recognizing, at least in so many words, anything beyond physical suffering and vegetative coma as constituting a poor quality of life.

Despite the finding in *Saikewicz* that treatment may be withheld on behalf of an incompetent individual, a New York court in 1981 took a different view in the case of John Storar. Storar was a profoundly retarded man who had been in a state institution since 1933. At the age of 52 he was suffering from advanced bladder cancer, which had spread to his lungs in spite of the radiation treatments he'd been receiving. It was doubtful he would survive more than three to six months. Regular doses of narcotics were required to ease the severe pain associated with his illness. The immediate problem was that he was losing huge amounts of blood through his cancer sites and needed transfusions of two units of blood every week or so. These procedures were disagreeable and somewhat painful, and, with a mental age of about 18 months, Storar did not understand the reasons for them. Thus, it was necessary to restrain him physically and to keep him sedated while they were administered. Moreover, they were not lifesaving, but only life prolonging, since the cancer was incurable. In light of these facts, his mother, a 77-year-old widow who visited him

almost daily, requested that the transfusions be halted. A lower court
agreed that this would be in Storar's best interests, but the New York
Court of Appeals reversed the decision on the grounds that the transfusions were "analogous to food—they would not cure the cancer, but
they could eliminate the risk of death from another treatable cause."
The justices held that "a court should not in the circumstances of this
case allow an incompetent patient to bleed to death because someone,
even someone as close as a parent or sibling, feels that this is best for
one with an incurable disease." Therefore, although a mentally competent cancer victim has the unequivocal right to refuse any treatment
he or she desires, and thereby to cheat the disease of its final tor-
ments, a John Storar, because of his feeblemindedness, must evidently be made to experience each painful moment of his cancer right
up to the end. Without intending to be cruel, the New York court had
taken someone who had drawn a short straw the very day he was
born, and visited a parting injustice upon him as he lay dying.

A crucial distinction is made over and over again in these kinds of
cases, and it would be useful at this juncture to examine it further.
The distinction is between "ordinary" care and "extraordinary" or
"heroic" care. A dispute arose during the Storar case, for example,
over whether the blood transfusions constituted extraordinary or
ordinary therapy. The difference is important, for the courts will often
give their blessing to the withdrawal of extraordinary treatment, but
not to what they consider ordinary. Strangely, however, nobody quite
agrees on what the terms mean.

In everyday usage, the distinction is generally interchangeable with
the idea of usual versus unusual care, or simple versus complex care.
Hence, extraordinary medicine might be all those treatments that are
seldom applied or experimental, such as artificial-heart transplants;
and ordinary medicine might be all those that are routine, such as the
administration of antibiotics. Or, extraordinary medicine might be taken
to mean all those treatments that are highly sophisticated and elaborate, requiring enormous technology and expense; and ordinary
medicine might be those that are basic, time-honored, and relatively
inexpensive. Both of these definitions consider the therapy itself to be
the sole determinant of extraordinariness. There are a number of
weaknesses in this view. To begin with, medical progress makes everything relative. Today's breakthrough is tomorrow's commonplace. Two
generations ago insulin and electroencephalography would have been
deemed extraordinary, but today they are old hat. Second, the definition is crippled by its reliance on subjective judgments. How sophisticated is sophisticated? How routine is routine? These are matters
that can vary from observer to observer.

The President's Commission for the Study of Ethical Problems in Medicine and Biomedical and Behavioral Research encountered this problem when it interviewed a doctor and a judge who had figured in the final death agony of one Abe Perlmutter. Perlmutter, a former cabdriver and athlete, was living in Florida when, at age 73, he was stricken with amyotrophic lateral sclerosis, or Lou Gehrig's disease. The progressive neuromuscular disorder, which is always fatal, robbed him of almost all voluntary movement, made speech an extreme effort, caused his respiration to fail, and required his being put on a mechanical ventilator. Perlmutter rebelled at living in this condition; with great difficulty, he maneuvered the breathing tube out of his throat. His doctors, afraid they would be legally liable if he died, reinserted it. "I'm miserable, take it out," Perlmutter kept telling his family. A lawyer finally brought his case before a judge, who conducted a bedside hearing. At the hearing, Perlmutter said that whatever was in store for him if the ventilator was removed "can't be worse than what I'm going through now." The judge, John Ferris, then ruled that no one may force Perlmutter to undergo an artificial prolongation of his own life if he does not wish it. The 1978 case is a centerpiece of the body of case law establishing the right of critically ill people to refuse treatment.

Let us now examine how the same form of care, ventilator therapy, can be seen as extraordinary or ordinary, depending on who the observer is. Both Judge Ferris and Dr. Marshall J. Brumer, Perlmutter's attending physician, testified before the President's Commission. Both were asked their feelings about ventilators (or respirators, as they are often called). Brumer said, "I deal with respirators every day of my life. To me, this is not heroic. This is standard procedure. . . . I have other patients who have run large corporations who have been on portable respirators."

But Ferris countered, "Certainly there is no question legally that putting a hole in a man's trachea and inserting a mechanical respirator is extraordinary life-preserving means. I do not think that the doctor would in candor allow that this is not an extraordinary means of preserving life. I understand that he deals with them every day, but in the sense of ordinary as against extraordinary, I believe it to be extraordinary."

A better definition of extraordinary-ordinary makes the patient's condition and welfare integral parts of the equation. The notion of a therapy's burdens versus its benefits is introduced to the discussion. Something becomes extraordinary when it is immoderately burdensome to the patient or when the prognosis is so dim that, whatever one may do, the chance that the patient will survive or live a good life afterward is remote. Thus, the same treatment may be ordinary in one set of circumstances and extraordinary in another. For example, intravenous feedings might be ordinary treatment when one is speaking of a person recovering from stomach surgery. But they might constitute extraordinary treatment when applied to a child with a hopelessly terminal brain defect. Similarly, giving something as prosaic as a penicillin shot to Karen Ann Quinlan might be considered extraordinary because her life is going to be inexpressibly bleak whether you cure her infection or not. This view has its roots in theology. It was first promulgated in 1582 by the writer Soto, who declared that abbots can, under the terms of religious obedience, require their subjects to use medicine that can be taken without much hardship but that they cannot force them to undergo excruciating treatments, because God does not demand that man preserve his life by such means. In a more modern context, Pope Pius XII told a group of anesthesiologists in 1957 that a physician has the duty to use "ordinary means" to heal patients. But he is not obligated to provide treatments "which cannot be obtained or used without excessive expense, pain, or other inconvenience, or which, if used, would not offer a reasonable hope of benefit." Unfortunately, although this definition of extraordinariness is better, it is far from perfect, since it, too, requires that subjective judgments be made as to what is or is not burdensome.

Given the relativity of the terms, and the fact that no one can agree on common definitions, the distinction between extraordinary and ordinary treatment is not very helpful in a legal sense. Imagine if a legislature wrote a law saying that hospitals need not use extraordinary means to keep people alive. One hospital might turn off all the ventilators and another might not. One hospital might think it extraordinary to use blood transfusions to keep a mentally retarded cancer victim alive, and another one might not. No law could conceivably cover all contingencies and shades of meaning. For this reason, an increasing number of people associated with bioethical issues are abandoning the old distinction between extraordinary and ordinary care.

The questions raised in *Quinlan,* in *Saikewicz,* and in similar cases have inspired judges to reflect more deeply on the issues surrounding handicapped children. The first sign of a deviation came in 1979 in the case of Phillip Becker, the 12-year-old Down's syndrome victim whose parents refused to allow surgeons to correct his heart defect. A doctor testified in court that the cardiac anomaly would cause lung deterioration, making Phillip, who was a cheerful boy with an IQ of 36, progressively short of breath and reducing him eventually to a bed-to-chair existence. Death would occur by age 32, whereas the potential life expectancy of a Down's individual is somewhere in the forties or early fifties. The Beckers, who had placed Phillip in a group home soon after his birth but who visited him regularly, argued that the surgery itself has a 5 to 10 percent mortality rate and that Down's syndrome victims faced a higher-than-average risk of postoperative complications. Both the trial court and an appellate court upheld the Beckers' choice. The California and U.S. supreme courts refused to hear the matter on appeal.

The case set off a furor. The legal scholar John Robertson, of the University of Texas, wrote, "The Becker decision does not withstand critical scrutiny, and for that reason is unlikely to be a precedent followed by other courts that carefully consider the issue. . . . It is very difficult to argue that the operation is not in Phillip's interest. Without it he is certain to die a slow, painful death in the next five to ten years, with the last years full of agony and suffering. With it he is assured a long life of ordinary health."

In an interview with the *New York Times*, Phillip's father insisted in retrospect that the surgery was not in Phillip's interest. "It was risky," he was quoted as saying. "It might extend his life for a few years, but for what purpose? He's almost 17 and he's still carrying a teddy bear."

The effect of the Becker decision was blunted several years later when the Beckers lost a fight to keep another couple from gaining custody of Phillip. This time the California Supreme Court became involved, ruling against the Beckers. In 1983 Phillip finally underwent surgery.

But if Robertson believed that the initial Becker ruling would remain an isolated one, he was wrong. In 1982 Judge John Baker, of Bloomington, Indiana, approved the decision of Baby Doe's parents that their infant be allowed to die. The Indiana Supreme Court indicated its satisfaction with the verdict by refusing to hear an appeal. Less than two years later, New York's highest court, followed by a U.S. district judge and a U.S. appellate court, refused to interfere with the family's wishes in the case of Long Island's Baby Jane Doe. At one point the U.S. Supreme Court itself declined to enter the case and order surgical repair of the child's myelomeningocele. Thus, by the spring of 1984 the high courts of two states and a string of federal courts, including the nation's chief tribunal, had all given their imprimatur to a parent's right to let a defective baby die. None of these courts had gone so far as to enunciate an actual doctrine, based on legal principles, that could be applied to future cases. But they had at least opened the door of precedent. And where involuntary euthanasia is concerned, to permit one instance of it is to sanction the legitimacy of the entire concept. As of this writing, the question no longer seems to be, *Can* one let impaired babies die? It appears to be, *When* can one let them die?

This apparent trend has made many people uneasy. Even those without an ideological ax to grind are dismayed by the abuses that might arise when parents are allowed to choose death for their children. There is the fear that permitting these decisions to be made by parents alone, or in concert with their doctor, would deprive a child of due process of law, in effect turning the nursery into a courtroom where the parents and doctor act as judge and jury. A related fear is that parents would be motivated not by a concern for the child's welfare but by their own self-interest—that is to say, by their desire to be free of the child, whom they might see as an albatross, a potential source of lifelong anxiety and financial and social embarrassment. Even parents who do not knowingly harbor such thoughts might fall prey to unconsciously selfish impulses, critics say. According to John Robertson, "[T]he parents in such a threatening situation may have a strong need to deny the existence of the child as an independent being with needs and interests. [They] may sincerely believe that they have the child's best interests at heart, but they may not be in a position to assess or voice that interest without bias. Allowing the parents rather than an independent advocate to speak for the voiceless child may deny the basic fairness usually accorded persons when fundamental rights are at stake."

Various solutions have been proposed, some of them ill-considered, others thoughtful. In the wake of the Bloomington case, a number of states passed laws designed to curb euthanasia of handicapped children. Similar federal bills were pending in Congress at the time of this writing. The Reagan administration's position was that there were already enough laws on the books, that it was less a problem of legislation than of enforcement: a curtain of hospital secrecy was keeping authorities from learning about imperiled youngsters in time to help them. The Baby Doe regulations sought to correct this evil. To still others, these were heavy-handed approaches that took the discretion for treating a newborn away from those closest to the child and put it in the hands of politicians and bureaucrats. It seemed odd to assume that a legislator or a G-13 paper pusher in Washington should have more medical judgment and compassion than a doctor and a baby's parents.

How then to guard against the occasional abuse? One potentially helpful solution was advanced by the President's Commission for the Study of Ethical Problems in Medicine and Biomedical and Behavioral Research. It suggested that hospitals establish an internal review procedure to monitor parent-physician decisions to terminate life-sustaining treatment. In some cases, the commission said, this might simply require a second physician's opinion as to whether a child has a terminal condition. In other cases, the full-scale services of a hospital "ethics" committee might be called into play. The American Academy of Pediatrics then put forth the specific form such an ethics committee might take. It should have a minimum of 10 members, including a pediatrician, a hospital administrator, an ethicist, a clergyman, a lawyer, a representative of a disability rights organization or the parent of a disabled child, a member of the community, and a nurse. The committee would have essentially two duties: drafting institutional guidelines on when life-sustaining treatment might be withdrawn, and reviewing any specific proposals to withdraw such treatment. The academy was careful not to propose making the committee the final arbiter. Instead, it expressed the opinion that the "collaborative atmosphere" of the review process "will usually remedy any deficiencies in the decision-making process so that the committee and all those concerned with the case can agree on an appropriate course of action." Where the committee continues to disagree strongly with a parental decision to forgo treatment, it should take steps to report the case to "the appropriate court and/or child protective agency," the academy said.

Advocates of ethics committees believe they offer a number of advantages. They might provide at least some measure of due process for a child without exposing the family to the chilling prospect of a court hearing. Equally important, they would put a nontreatment question before a group of disinterested parties, reducing the likelihood of bias, whether conscious or unconscious. Finally, they would bring together a number of individuals with diverse points of view, which might be a drawback in circumstances requiring unity of purpose but which is an additional safeguard when a life is at stake. "An institutional ethics committee will not be a panacea for making ethically correct decisions," the academy's committee on bioethics has written, "but it should increase the probability that such decisions are informed and consistent with the broadest moral values of our society."

Following many months of wrangling over its original Baby Doe regulations, the Reagan administration eventually accepted the idea of establishing ethics committees. In releasing its revised regulations in January of 1984, the administration granted hospitals the option of creating these committees, which would then assume primary responsibility for advising doctors who were considering the withdrawal of care from sick babies. Though the regulations were struck down, the idea continues to gain strength.

For all their apparent good points, ethics committees are not favored by right-to-life groups. One organization, the American Life Lobby, instantly announced opposition to the new Doe rules, claiming that the White House had "caved in to the medical/hospital industry." The feeling is that utilizing an ethics committee's help in deciding a child's fate is evidence on its face that subjective quality-of-life judgments are going to be made. This violates the conviction of prolife groups that the potential quality of a child's life has no place in medical decisions and that treatment should be governed by objective standards mandating "equal treatment regardless of handicap." These groups also fear that ethics committees could easily become dominated by a strong-willed doctor with an antihandicap leaning.

It is very difficult to determine which road society is ultimately going to take on these issues. Since the courts are our final arbiter of what is legal, if not moral, what bears most watching is the direction in which the judiciary proceeds. Recent lower-court actions suggest that it is taking a position that offers parents and physicians wide latitude in involuntary euthanasia choices. Whether this will become the law of the land awaits a definitive declaration from the U.S. Supreme Court, which has yet to rule on any of the substantive issues surrounding the alleged right to die. The broad outlines of the picture have come into focus. It remains to be seen what "burning in" or "dodging out" may yet be done.

8

Sanctity of Life vs. Quality of Life
The Ethics of Neonatal Care

Quality of life is an expression that has crept into our collective vocabulary over the last several decades. It is one of a family of phrases from the humanist tradition; as such, it has acquired a broad set of applications, connoting a concern with everything from clean air and better schools to wildlife conservation. But it has a more visceral meaning in the medical sense, having come into vogue concurrently with the unprecedented explosion in health care technology. The need for such a concept arose when natural death became a thing of the past, and the moment of dying ceased to be outside of our control. No longer is it Shakespeare's fell sergeant, "so strict in his arrest." Its timing has become elective. As a result, the old question of whether we can save the patient's life has given way to a newer one: How desirable is the kind of life that we can grant? What will its quality be?

Although the phrase *quality of life* is seemingly of recent vintage, it is really quite old. The Roman dramatist Seneca, a philosopher of the Stoic school, wrote, "Mere living is not a good, but living well. Accordingly, the wise man will live as long as he ought; not as long as he can. He will mark in what place, with whom, and how he is to conduct his existence, and what he is about to do. He always reflects concerning the quality, and not the quantity, of his life. As soon as there are many events in his life that give him trouble and disturb his peace of mind, he sets himself free. And this privilege is his, not only when the crisis is upon him, but as soon as Fortune seems to be playing him false."

Ideas of self-discipline and detachment motivated Seneca. His was an attempt to neutralize the implacable forces of the cosmos by stressing only what was within one's power, that is, the inner self and how one lives. We of today are anything but Stoics, so it is understandable that our concern with the quality of life must be seen in different terms. Yet it springs from a similar need to free the individual from slavery to outside forces. We find it no longer incumbent on people to accept things as they are or always have been, simply because the community, law, religion, big business, or any other external voice demands it. This view appears to be the true legacy of the 1960s, and though the experimentation it unleashed is easily parodied—legions of self-actualizers on a quest for personal fulfillment—and though it is fading a bit with time, it has undoubtedly changed forever the relationship of the individual to society. As more people have refused to live what Socrates called the "unexamined life" and are routinely reassessing previous assumptions about role, status, sexual morality, and duty to the state and to God, it seems natural that the value of existence itself should under certain circumstances be a fitting subject for examination.

Is, for example, a life of severe retardation, perhaps accompanied by great physical discomfort, worth living? Such a question seems legitimate enough, in light of the current climate of inquiry, but its corollary—Can the life be terminated if the answer is no?—is at odds with the hallowed dictum that all human life, whatever its limitations, is sacrosanct.

It is this conflict—between the *quality* of life on the one hand and the *sanctity* of life on the other—that lies at the heart of the debate over the withholding of treatment from impaired babies. It is evident that some children's lives are going to be abysmal, no matter what is done for them medically. Should this fact be allowed to determine whether they receive care? Quality of life says yes. Sanctity of life says no.

"I don't think you can say that biological existence is an absolute value," observes the Reverend James Bresnahan, professor of medical ethics at Northwestern University Medical School. "Merely to say, 'I've done my job keeping the child alive,' isn't enough."

Bresnahan is one of a new breed of moral philosophers who have breathed fresh life into the field of ethics over the past few years.

Before the late 1950s, ethics was a dying discipline. Its brain was hardening from too much theory and not enough practical application, and its heart was weakening from an overdose of ethical "relativism," the immobilizing notion that there is no right and wrong. This last was a reaction to three developments, all of which undermined previous faith in an absolute morality. The first of these was the work of Freud, who reduced "good" to the actions of a fail-safe personality device called superego. The second was the unsettling finding by anthropologists that what was moral to an Eskimo or a Fiji Islander was not necessarily moral to an Englishman or an American. The third was the conclusion of Albert Einstein that such comforting old standbys as space, time, and mass were not fixed but were relative and subject to change. The onslaught of these determinations had left philosophers groaning by the side of the road. Then, fortuitously, help came from an unexpected quarter—medicine. By turning their attention to the practical and concrete problems posed by advanced medical technology, philosophers were able to revive the lost art of applied ethics and make their profession relevant to the real world again. In the words of the ethicist Stephen Toulmin, of the University of Chicago, medicine "saved the life of ethics."

Bresnahan believes that when considering whether to treat a handicapped child, one ought to give weight to the future suffering that the child will endure. This suffering is not exclusively physical, he says, but also mental. "Suffering isn't only pain. Suffering is the loss of ability to do certain things. And it isn't just the child's suffering we should be concerned about, but that of the parents as well. They suffer out of empathy with the child. As far as I'm concerned, quality of life has to be a factor."

But disagreement quickly arises on this basic point. Attorney Lee Dunn, one of the nation's premier specialists in health law, complained in an interview recently, "I don't know what *quality of life* means. It's a catch-all term which people can hide behind. They can say, 'We'll withhold care, it's better for the baby,' when in fact it's really better for themselves."

The idea that parents might wash their hands of a child simply because it is defective or will inconvenience their lives troubles Dunn. "I think if you go around conceiving children you take a responsibility on yourself," he said. "The law is consistent. You have an obligation to provide care and sustenance to that child. It's a horrible situation to be faced with, but you can't just throw up your hands."

This is not to say there aren't times when a child should be denied *extraordinary care,* Dunn conceded. He cited the case of anencephalic babies who, born with fragmentary brains or none whatsoever, have a natural life expectancy of mere days. "If it's clear that extraordinary care will not be curative, the courts will authorize its withdrawal. But not ordinary care. This is where some hospitals run into problems. They figure, 'Let's withdraw *all* treatment.' "

Dunn is representative of those who reject quality of life as a criterion in treatment decisions. These advocates argue that such decisions should be based solely on medical criteria, that is, on whether therapy will relieve the child of a life-threatening or debilitating condition. Therapy ought not to be curtailed, except in instances when the infant is "born dying," as it were, or is in the end stages of terminal illness— where no remission is possible and the life support is just prolonging the moment of death, perhaps painfully. At no time should physicians entertain the question of whether life as a severely handicapped individual is so meaningless or onerous as to justify the discontinuation of treatment.

"That means," writes Paul Ramsey, a leading proponent of this viewpoint, "that the standard for letting die must be the same for the normal child as for the defective child. If an operation to remove a bowel obstruction is indicated to save the life of a normal infant, it is also the indicated treatment of a mongoloid infant. The latter is certainly not dying because of Down's syndrome." Ramsey, a religion professor at Princeton University, contends that such a "medical indications policy," as he calls it, "is the only way to take a middle path between relentless treatment of the voiceless dying, which refuses to let them die even when disease or injury has won, and killing . . . or neglecting to sustain those who simply are voiceless incurables. . . . Morally, it is never right to turn against the good of human life. In the case of one's own life, public policy could go so far as to place that in an area of liberties. But to allow private individuals to turn against the good of another's life would be to promote injustice."

It is worth noting that, as in Lee Dunn's example, anencephalic children are frequently used by supporters of the medical indications policy to illustrate when treatment may be justifiably withheld. For instance, the final version of the Baby Doe regulations declared, "Withholding of medical treatment for an infant born with anencephaly, who will inevitably die within a short period of time, would not constitute a discriminatory act because the treatment would be futile and do no more than temporarily prolong the act of dying." But with modern resuscitation techniques it is feasible to keep even hopelessly ill children such as anencephalics alive for extended lengths of time. This prompted the Australian ethicist Peter Singer to observe, "The judgment that someone whose life could be indefinitely prolonged by available medical means is 'terminally ill' and therefore should not have his or her life prolonged is not a *medical* judgment; it is an ethical judgment about the desirability of prolonging that particular life." In other words, argues Singer, even those who believe themselves opposed to quality-of-life measurements inevitably find themselves making them.

Be that as it may, the "medical indications" faction regards quality-of-life decisions warily, for they require a verdict to be rendered upon the merit of an individual's continued existence, which could lead to valuing one person more highly than another. Hence, in this view the quality-of-life outlook is a sort of cancer that will spread beyond sick newborns to various other vulnerable segments of the population, who will be judged according to their social utility and eliminated. "The importance of maintaining the highest regard for the sanctity of life can only really be appreciated in the context of the kind of society in which we live," writes Dr. Eugene Diamond, professor of pediatrics at Loyola University. "With a birthrate below replacement and with the mean age of the population constantly increasing, the next focus will unquestionably be upon the 'quality of life' of the aged. . . . The sanctity-of-life ethic which now spreads its tattered mantle of protection over newborn defective infants must be upheld. It is really protecting all of us."

Still, a number of people with excellent humanitarian credentials are quite willing to assert that quality-of-life judgments are appropriate in certain situations. The Reverend Richard McCormick, a Jesuit and professor of Christian ethics at the Kennedy Institute, Georgetown University, does not believe that it diminishes the value of human beings to say that life for its own sake is not an unqualified blessing. Writing in the *Hastings Center Report,* he asserted, "One can and, I believe, should say that the *person* is always an incalculable value, but that at some point continuance in physical life offers the person no benefit. Indeed, to keep 'life' going can easily be an assault on the person and his or her dignity. Therefore, phrases such as 'the good of life in itself' are misleading in these discussions."

McCormick sees no contradiction between sanctity and quality of life. "Actually the two approaches ought not to be set against each other in this way. Quality-of-life assessments ought to be made within an overall reverence for life, as an extension of one's respect for the sanctity of life. However, there are times when preserving the life of one with no capacity for those aspects of life that we regard as *human,* is a violation of the sanctity of life itself." In reply to the accusation that quality-of-life language implies that not all lives are equally deserving of protection, and that it thus encourages discrimination, McCormick says, "Every *person* is of 'equal value.' But not every *life* . . . is of equal value if we are careful to unpack the terms 'life', 'equal,' and 'value.' If 'life' means the continuation of vital processes but in a persistent vegetative state; if 'value' means 'a good to the individual concerned'; if 'equal' means 'identical' or the 'same', especially of treatment; then I believe it is simply false to say that 'every life is of equal value.' "

Joseph Fletcher, a well-known Episcopal theologian from the University of Virginia, believes it is a kindness to children, at times, to let them die. "To contend," he says, "that there are cases in which it is good, and therefore right, to induce the end of a person's life obviously assigns the first-order value to human well-being, either by maximizing happiness or minimizing suffering; it assigns value to human life rather than to merely being alive. [In] this view it is better to be dead than to suffer too much or to endure too many deficits of human function."

Suppose, for the sake of argument, that is is proper to include a child's potential quality of life in reaching a decision on whether to treat him or her. What then? How does one define the point at which quality becomes so poor as to be unacceptable?

Surely one of the essential considerations, as both Fletcher and Bresnahan suggest, is the extent of a child's suffering. We must be more explicit, though, and distinguish between the suffering of infants while they are undergoing the pain of treatment and the suffering of more mature individuals leading the handicapped life we have enabled them to experience. In regard to the newborn's anguish, it may seem appropriate at the outset to ask whether it is even correct to speak of "suffering" in the context of an infant. Suffering can be a complex, rather sophisticated human experience. Can a baby suffer?

"Newborns react to pain," writes Thomas Murray, an associate with the Hastings Center, a New York institute for the study of ethics and social policy. "They flinch, their face contorts, they cry." While one could argue, Murray says, that suffering requires something in addition—"a history which has known the absence of pain, a language for comprehending and expressing the fact that I have pain and that it might be otherwise"—Murray is himself satisfied that newborns do suffer. "After all, it is the pain which is not understood, which seems random and for which no end can be envisioned that produces the greatest suffering. It is, in other words, pain as an infant experiences it."

Problematic as the question may be, there is one feature of a baby's medical ordeal that is unique: it will not be remembered by the child when he or she gets older. I recall a pediatrician once expressing precisely that rationale for performing painful surgeries on handicapped infants. "If it gives them a good life later on, and they'll never know what they've been through, what's the matter with that?" he asked. This is, perhaps, a high-handed way of looking at things, but I wouldn't say it's wrong. The operative phrase, however, must be "a good life." The treatment should genuinely result in a more satisfying existence, or else the physician could justify inflicting any pain, provided the patient did not recall it.

A credible case can therefore be made for imposing a certain amount of suffering on the newborn in the furtherance of worthy medical goals. But turning to the severely disabled as they grow older, we confront a much more complicated issue. We find ourselves having to define that elusive phrase *a good life*. How much suffering is compatible with a life of acceptable quality? Any attempt to answer this question faces formidable obstacles. For one thing, people have different capacities for tolerating misery. What is so unendurable to one person as to inspire thoughts of suicide, is to another person a price gladly paid for the privilege of being alive. There is also a lack of agreement as to what constitutes true distress. Is an otherwise healthy and comfortable person with an IQ of 10 "suffering" by the textbook definition? Very likely not, since such individuals are not in any pain and have no idea how much of life they are mssing. They are concerned only with their next meal or act of elimination. But are they suffering in another sense by enjoying little meaningful human communication and activity?

It is interesting that to some people only great discomfort and crippling physical handicap constitute suffering. These persons might accept euthanasia for the child in bodily agony, yet balk at discontinuing treatment of the profoundly retarded but pain-free infant. Others contend that the loss of cognitive function alone is the dividing line between a good quality of life and a poor one. By this reasoning, individuals with extensive and painful physical handicaps would be considered to have an acceptable quality of life so long as they had sufficient intellectual power to appreciate living. It might illuminate matters if we stopped trying to fit retardation into the neat category of suffering and substituted instead the notion of deprivation. As a counterpart to physical suffering, deprivation would allow one to express the negative aspects of the intellectually impaired person's life in a meaningful way. The extreme desolation of the person without cognition would then be seen to represent a burdensome existence, analogous, perhaps, to quadriplegia. The concept of deprivation would also provide a hook for the very real anguish of the moderately retarded, who are often quite aware of their own shortcomings and bitterly resent them.

There is another issue to consider, and that is the alleged nobility of suffering. As Emily Dickinson wrote:

> To fight aloud is very brave,
> But gallanter, I know,
> Who charge within the bosom,
> The cavalry of woe.
>
> Who win, and nations do not see,
> Who fall, and none observe,
> Whose dying eyes no country
> Regards with patriot love.

History is full of great sufferers, from Ulysses and Saint Jerome to Toulouse-Lautrec and F. Scott Fitzgerald. The view that it is admirable to persevere Job-like in the face of extreme adversity has a long and venerable past. Says Dr. Eric Cassel, "In some theologies, suffering has been seen as bringing one closer to God. This 'function' of suffering is at once its glorification and its relief. If, through great pain or deprivation, someone is brought closer to a cherished goal, that person may have no sense of having suffered but may instead feel enormous triumph."

John Donnelly, a professor of philosophy at the University of San Diego, has gone so far as to find a bright side to birth defects. "For example," he writes, "the infant suffering from some currently incurable physiological ailment (e.g. cystic fibrosis, sickle cell anemia, etc.), and his guardians, could be thankful for his/her affliction, which enables them to develop traits of character and mental sets not so readily fostered in a healthy body or nontragic situation."

Most people would not take quite so sanguine a position. Among them is Albert Jonsen, of the University of California at San Francisco, who favors the use, in certain circumstances, of quality-of-life criteria to make treatment decisions regarding handicapped newborns.

Jonsen was one of the participants at an explosive 1974 medical conference in California's Sonoma Valley. The purpose of the conference, which brought together 20 prominent persons from such diverse fields as medicine, nursing, law, ethics, economics, anthropology, social work, and journalism, was to consider the ethical problems raised by neonatal intensive care. It was sponsored by UCSF and was supported by funds from the Robert Wood Johnson Foundation and the Henry

J. Kaiser Family Foundation. The panelists included Drs. William Tooley, Roderic Phibbs, Robert Creasy, and Robert Jaffe, all of UCSF, and the revered Dr. Clement Smith, of Harvard Medical School.

The Sonoma Conference on Ethical Issues, as it was called, received considerable subsequent publicity, owing to the startling consensus that emerged from it. Seventeen of the 20 experts indicated they would intervene directly to "kill" a defective infant whose prognosis was a lingering, painful death. (Two answered no, and another was "uncertain.") This amounted to a ringing endorsement of active euthanasia by a panel that included some of the most esteemed baby doctors in the United States. The participants also expressed *unanimous* approval for two lesser but still controversial propositions, the withdrawal of life support from a severely defective infant and the failure to resuscitate such an infant at birth.

In a follow-up paper, Jonsen, Tooley, Phibbs, and a fourth UCSF colleague, Michael Garland, collaborated on a nine-point "moral policy for neonatal intensive care." One of the points read, "Life preserving intervention should be understood as doing harm to an infant who cannot survive infancy, or will live in intractable pain, or cannot participate even minimally in human experience."

Elaborating, the authors wrote, "The first condition recognizes the possibility that some infants may be born with irreparable lesions incompatible with life. They are already in the dying state and, while care should never be neglected, efforts aimed at prolongation of life are best viewed as harming rather than helping such an infant. The second condition envisions the case of an infant who is in constant severe pain which cannot be alleviated either by immediate treatment or as the result of a long course of treatment. The third condition is perhaps the most controversial. Participation in human experience means the assessed expectation that the infant has some inherent capability to respond affectively and cognitively to human attention and to develop toward initiation of communication with others. . . . While we are reluctant to quantify or describe in detail the levels of affective and cognitive activity, we would prefer to err on the side which favors the life of the child. A baby with Down's syndrome would fulfill the criteria, whereas one with trisomy 18 would not."

Ten years after the publication of the paper, Jonsen remains leery of identifying the precise point at which a prognosis becomes so dismal that to prolong life is to "do harm." But he recently left no doubt that, in his view, the quality of life would have to be very low indeed to warrant the withholding of care. "Retardation, alone, would not be enough," he told me. "There would also have to be additional factors: spasticity, pain, the absence of communication. I'm speaking of severe spina bifida, for instance, where there is loss of motor control, bowel and bladder function, plus severe retardation, so that you have physical pain as well as the absence of cognition."

The California ethicist's thinking is reflected in the report of the President's Commission for the Study of Ethical Problems in Medicine and Biochemical and Behavioral Research. (Jonsen was among those who served on the 11-member commission, which spent three years studying bioethical issues ranging from genetic engineering to human experimentation.) Its report on forgoing treatment for defective newborns was released in March of 1983 and summed up its findings this way:

"Many therapies undertaken to save the lives of seriously ill newborns will leave the survivors with permanent handicaps, either from the underlying defect (such as heart surgery not affecting the retardation of a Down syndrome infant) or from the therapy itself (as when mechanical ventilation for a premature baby results in blindness or a scarred trachea). One of the most troubling and persistent issues in this entire area is whether, or to what extent, the expectation of such handicaps should be considered in deciding to treat or not to treat a seriously ill newborn. The Commission has concluded that a very restrictive standard is appropriate: such permanent handicaps justify a decision not to provide life-sustaining treatment only when they are so severe that *continued existence would not be a net benefit to the infant*" (italics mine). The commissioners added that "net benefit is absent only if the burdens imposed on the patient by the disability or its treatment would lead a competent decisionmaker to choose to forgo the treatment."

This is useful up to a point. But the report did not give specific examples of handicaps where there would be no net benefit in prolonging life. In fact, it found it easier to say what defects did not merit withholding treatment than which ones did: "The Commission believes that the handicaps of Down's syndrome . . . are not in themselves of this magnitude and do not justify failing to provide medically proven treatment, such as surgical correction of a blocked intestinal tract." With no further guidelines, *net benefit* remains a nebulous term. Are there net benefits in being a wheelchair-bound myelomeningocele victim? Several college professors and lawyers with the disease would testify that there are. Then what if a person is not only paraplegic but blind and deaf as well; are there net benefits in that? Perhaps, if one has loving and indefatigable parents and friends who can render even so limited an existence pleasant and intellectually stimulating. But what if the person has no measurable IQ? Again, net benefits might still be found, in the sense of one's being warm and fed and caressed. Yet, it is difficult to imagine a competent decision maker accepting the prospect of such a life. Because of its vague language, the commission report gives us little to go on.

In a thoughtful disquisition on the subject, the Reverend McCormick argues that life has meaning only insofar as it is capable of human interaction, and he uses a quaint example to illustrate his belief. He cites peasants forced to move to another climate or country to preserve their health. For people whose native village is "as dear as life itself," such a prescription would be cruel, even extraordinary. Why? Because it would, among other things, remove them from home and friends—from intimate relationships. "Life, the condition of other values and achievements, would usurp the place of these and become itself the ultimate value. When that happens, the value of human life has been distorted out of context.

"If these reflections are valid," McCormick continues, "they point in the direction of a guideline that may help in decisions about sustaining the lives of grossly deformed and deprived infants. That guideline is the potential for human relationships associated with the infant's condition. If that potential is simply nonexistent or would be utterly submerged and undeveloped in the mere struggle to survive, that life has achieved its potential."

What McCormick appears to be telling us is that the child who is so retarded or so distracted by medical problems that he or she cannot relate to other people in any meaningful way is living a purposeless life. Death would be a merciful option, an option that McCormick doesn't shrink from advocating. Nor does it dismay him that parents would have to exercise this option on behalf of their baby. "Parents must make many crucial decisions for children," he says. "The only concern is that the decision not be shaped out of the utilitarian perspectives so deeply sunk into the consciousness of the contemporary world. . . . It remains, then, only to emphasize that these decisions must be made in terms of the child's good, this alone."

This perspective is not at all inconsistent with Christian philosophy, as has been affirmed by the Reverend John Paris, of the College of the Holy Cross. If one truly believes there is a hereafter, says the Reverend Paris, then the death of a child, or of anyone else for that matter, is not an evil but a part of the natural order of things. "Life is not only a gift and a task," he says; "it is also a journey. We are on a journey from God back to God and death is a part of that journey. Death is not the victor, it is the transition state, not a final state. . . . Thus, it is eternal life and not life itself which is the ultimate."

He continues, "If you doubt that this is an age of nonbelief, ask yourself what is the response of all those believing Christians who enter hospitals when the death process begins. When was the last time you heard anyone say: 'This patient had a wonderful life; he fought the good fight . . . Now it is time for him to go to his Maker.' . . . For the individual whose journey has indeed come to its conclusion, for example, the individual with end-stage liver disease whose heart stops, we do not say: 'At last he is at peace.' Instead we shout: 'Code Blue.' That is the problem."

We now have two criteria to use in calculating an infant's future quality of life: the intensity of the child's suffering and his or her potential for forming human relationships. Is there a third?

A number of authors have suggested that the family situation is of critical importance. Defective newborns require a great deal of attention not only in the short run but in the long run as well. It would be pathetic, for example, for incompetent individuals to be in the care of negligent parents who did not regularly bathe, feed, and exercise them in a humane manner. Physical solicitude is only half the need, however. Of equal importance is emotional support. Handicapped people have the same need for love and affection that normal people do. In fact, their needs may be greater, particularly when the individuals are sentient enough to be aware of their own deficiencies. Thus, a major part of their treatment is having a strong, caring family unit. To perform medical miracles on impaired children only to send them home with bitter, resentful parents—or, arguably worse, to condemn them to life in an institution—seems a waste.

The pediatric surgeon Anthony Shaw considered the family milieu important enough to include it in a quality-of-life formula he devised several years ago. The formula goes like this: $QL = NE \times (H + S)$, where QL represents quality of life, NE is the child's natural endowment, and H and S stand for contributions from home and society. Thus, an anencephalic baby, whose life is destined to last but a few days, would be judged to have a natural endowment of zero and a QL that would likewise be zero. A child with lesser impairments, for example, Down's syndrome, multiple limb deformities, or myelomeningocele, would have a higher NE, so his or her QL would correspondingly rise. But it could also fall if H or E drags the formula down. As Shaw wrote in the essay collection *Infanticide and the Value of Life:* "Clearly if the family of a baby with Down's syndrome refused to care for it, and society's sole contribution is a crowded, filthy, understaffed warehouse, that infant's quality of life equals zero ($NE \times (0 + 0) = 0$) just as surely as if it had been born an anencephalic."

Shaw continued, "It is not surprising then that the degree of effort made by many physicians on behalf of some defective newborns is directly related to the willingness of families and/or communities to provide sufficient resources and support to compensate for these infants' deficient *NE*. If, as Robert Louis Stevenson wrote, 'Life is not a matter of holding good cards, but of playing a poor hand well,' the impaired individual needs that help from *H* and *S* if he is to play his hand at all."

There have been other attempts, interestingly enough, to state the problem of quality of life in mathematical terms. In the same collection of essays, Richard Brandt, of the University of Michigan, wrote, "But what criterion are we using if we say that such a life is bad? One criterion might be called a 'happiness' criterion. If a person *likes* a moment of experience while he is having it, his life is so far good; if a person *dislikes* a moment of experience while he is having it, his life is so far bad. Based on such reactions, we might construct a 'happiness curve' for a person, going up the indifference axis when a moment of experience is liked . . . and dipping down below the line when a moment is disliked. Then this criterion would say that a life is worth living if there is a net balance of positive area under the curve over a lifetime, and that it is bad if there is a net balance of negative area."

Applying his curve to the seriously defective newborn, Brandt puts the pain and constant lack of interesting stimuli a child may experience on the negative side and the pleasures of eating, drinking, and being fondled on the positive side. He concludes that "the brief enjoyments can hardly balance the long stretches of boredom, discomfort or pain. . . . It may fairly be said, I think, that the lives of some defective newborns are destined to be bad on the whole, and it would be a favor to them if their lives were terminated. Contrariwise, the prospective lives of many defective newborns are modestly pleasant, and it would be some injury to them to be terminated, albeit the lives they will live are ones some of us would prefer not to live at all."

Having tried to lay down some quality-of-life criteria, we must now address the propriety of using them. It is not possible to have heart-to-heart talks with impaired infants to learn whether they would prefer death to a painful or circumscribed existence; hence, others must decide the matter for them. On what basis does one human being make a life-and-death judgment for another? Some authorities have attempted to make the discussion hinge on the notion of personhood, that is, the status or elusive quality of being a person. Consider the case of a 40-year-old man who, as the result of a stroke, is facing a life of diminished mental capacity and the loss of the use of his limbs. We would not draw back from treating him; rather, we would almost certainly attempt, with our full resources, to rehabilitate him. One compelling reason for our doing so is that we regard him as a person, a unique individual with a claim on our attention. Is there some qualitative difference between a newborn infant and an adult that makes it more acceptable to contemplate not treating the child? Does the infant become more of a person as he or she ages?

Personhood and the concept of human rights are intimately related. Under the legal definition, a *person* is someone who has both rights and duties, and to whom, as a consequence of his or her rights, corresponding duties are owed. If impaired infants are somehow not persons in the same sense as older people, then perhaps they have fewer rights and are owed fewer duties. Perhaps they have less of a claim to a right to life.

This is not so exotic a proposition as it sounds. Certainly, ethicists have spent thousands of hours pondering it. The question of when the human organism becomes a person has direct bearing on the issue of abortion, for example, and a heated moral debate continues to rage as to whether the fetus qualifies as one. Under our current laws, however, the fetus is not a person and the born infant is, owing to a peculiar transformation of status that occurs as the child travels a few inches down the birth canal. The distinction has caused some notable legal wrangles for physicians who have performed second-trimester abortions, only to have the unwanted fetus unexpectedly survive. The law requires the doctor in such situations to go instantly from the abortion mode to the lifesaving mode. "It's like landing a jet plane," says Dr. Thomas Kerenyi, one of the nation's preeminent authorities on abor-. tion. "You're supposed to throw everything in reverse." Among the best-publicized cases in this regard are those of Drs. William Waddill and Kenneth Edelin. Waddill, of Orange County, California, administered an abortion by saline injection to the 18-year-old daughter of a high school principal. Saline is used to poison the fetus and cause it to be expelled from the uterus. The girl's baby emerged alive, however. What happened next remains unclear. Waddill maintains he did not try to save the child's life, because in his clinical judgment it stood no chance of survival. A second physician accused Waddill of choking the infant and threatening to inject it with a lethal dose of potassium chloride, charges that Waddill vehemently denied. He admitted placing his hands on the child's neck but said he was only testing the carotid arteries to see whether there was blood flow to the brain. Two murder trials ended in hung juries.

Dr. Edelin, of Boston, was convicted of not resuscitating a fetus following a surgical abortion. After cutting into the mother's uterus, he detached the placenta from the uterine wall and spent the next three minutes trying to peel away the amniotic sac. Only then did he remove the by-now-lifeless fetus. The district attorney decided that those three minutes in which Edelin ignored the life of the infant constituted criminal negligence, reasoning that the child became a separate "person" the instant the placenta was detached. Edelin's conviction was later overturned on appeal.

While the prolife movement lobbies for a new definition of when a child becomes a person (or at least when it acquires the rights of a person), hoping to push the timing back to encompass the period before birth, others have suggested a change in the other direction, so that the euthanasia of born infants might be sanctioned as a kind of "postnatal abortion." These advocates have tried to identify those aspects of personhood that are lacking in fetuses and newborns and whose absence might justify our withdrawing their right to life. Some have argued, for example, that no infant is a full person until it is a year old, at which time it acquires language and begins to interact verbally with people in a manner that sets humans apart from other species. Using that rule of thumb, we could say that newborns with grievous birth defects are not persons and therefore have no rights; consequently, they could ethically be allowed to die. The problem is, the same could be said of healthy children as well.

Michael Tooley, professor of philosophy at the University of Western Australia, has argued that to have a right to something, one must be capable of desiring that thing. He cites the example of a houseplant, which has an interest in being watered but, lacking the capacity for desires, cannot be said to have a *right* to water. Carrying his reasoning further, Tooley says, "[S]omething cannot have a right to continued existence unless it is capable of having a desire to continue to exist." This, in turn, presupposes "self-consciousness," that is, a concept of itself as a continuing subject of experiences. By this definition, defective newborns, unable to conceive of themselves as existing in the present, and therefore incapable of desiring a continued existence in the future, would not possess what Tooley calls "a serious right to life" and could be eliminated. Again, however, this could be a justification for killing anyone who lacked self-consciousness and abstract reasoning, including not only normal infants but, seemingly, adult retarded people and coma victims—and even, as Tooley himself has noted, people who are asleep. Tooley attempts to deal with these loose ends but not very convincingly.

Still another theoretician, H. Tristram Engelhardt, Jr., of Georgetown University's Kennedy Institute of Bioethics, has written that even if newborns aren't persons in a strict sense, they may satisfy less stringent requirements entitling them to certain rights. Specifically, they are capable of assuming a role in human relationships—the role of "child"—and are consequently treated by their elders as if they were persons. This concept would give some protection to normal infants, but it would seem to leave open the question of whether it is proper to withhold treatment from defective children, since they may not be accepted by their parents in the social role of "child."

Some authors have pointed out that defective infants are at times so grossly misshapen that they lack many of the physical attributes we would associate with human form, and they may be so profoundly retarded as to have no chance of ever relating to the world in human ways. They may never develop even the most minimal personality, and they may spend their entire life in a vegetative state, unaware of themselves or their surroundings. These writers suggest that it is absurd to speak of such individuals as being "persons" with rights and duties.

The trouble with many of these arguments is that they either rely on belabored logic or else are so insensitive as to send a chill up one's spine. A case in point is what Peter Singer had to say in a commentary in *Pediatrics:*

"Whatever the future holds, it is likely to prove impossible to restore in full the sanctity-of-life view. The philosophical foundations of this view have been knocked asunder. We can no longer base our ethics on the idea that human beings are a special form of creation, made in the image of God. . . . Once the religious mumbo-jumbo surrounding the term 'human' has been stripped away, we may continue to see normal members of our species as possessing greater capacities of rationality, self-consciousness, communication, and so on, than members of any other species; but we will not regard as sacrosanct the life of each and every member of our species, no matter how limited its capacity for intelligent or even conscious life may be. If we compare a severely defective human infant with a nonhuman animal, a dog or a pig, for example, we will often find the nonhuman to have superior capacities, both actual and potential, for rationality, self-consciousness, communication, and anything else that can plausibly be considered morally significant. Only the fact that the defective infant is a member of the species *Homo sapiens* leads it to be treated differently from the dog or pig. Species membership alone, however, is not morally relevant. . . . A dog or a pig, dying slowly and painfully, will be mercifully released from its misery. A human being with inferior mental capacities in similar painful circumstances will have to endure its hopeless condition until the end—and may even have that end postponed by the latest advances in medicine."

It is a pity that Singer, a well-known animal liberationist, ruined a basically sound argument with some tasteless metaphors. His invidious comparison of defective newborns to dogs and pigs was so heavy-handed that it is not likely he won any converts to the euthanasia cause; meanwhile, it predictably outraged the right-to-life faction.

Rather than go through these ethical gymnastics in regard to the notion of personhood, it seems more sensible to frame the proposition not on the child's right to live or on the lack thereof but on his or her simple right to die without extensive suffering.

One moral philosopher who has done just that is Joseph Fletcher, who has outspokenly stated his opinion that infanticide is a justifiable and honorable practice. Fletcher does not abandon the idea of personhood. In fact, he has drafted his own list of traits that he believes are prerequisites for it, although he prefers to call it humanhood. His list includes the following:

(1) A minimum IQ of 20 (*"Homo* is indeed *sapiens* in order to be *Homo,"* he says.)
(2) Self-awareness
(3) Self-control
(4) A sense of time
(5) A sense of futurity
(6) A sense of the past
(7) The capability to relate to others

And so on through about 10 more qualifications. But Fletcher does not utilize his list as a justification for letting defective newborns die. He relies instead on a principle of "loving concern" to develop his thesis.

"Some writers have argued," notes Fletcher, "that a fetus is a person as truly as an infant is, and that therefore both abortion and infanticide are unjust killing. . . . I would support the opposite position, i.e., that both abortion and infanticide can be justified if and when the good to be gained outweighs the evil—that neither abortion nor infanticide is as such immoral."

In his book *Humanhood: Essays in Biomedical Ethics,* Fletcher goes on to say, "Careful and candid analysis will show that deciding whether and when an infant is a person is not the determinative question. The right one is, 'Can a person's life ever be ended ethically?' It all turns on the issue of whether the value of a human life is absolute or relative. . . . In this mode of ethical reasoning the criterion of obligation is caring or kindness or loving concern. . . . Its basic value stance is that we ought to do whatever promotes well-being and reduces suffering, and therefore if ending a life is judged to do so, so be it."

Fletcher is widely recognized as the father of "situation ethics," the theory that the correct solution of any moral problem depends more upon the situation itself than on any a priori rule and that the key to the solution is always love and what will bring the greatest benefit. Ethics is rather like the island of Cyprus, in that it is divided into two somewhat hostile camps. There are the consequentialists, who believe that the morality of an action lies not so much in the action itself as in the rightness of the end result, and the deontologists, who believe that morality is to be found in the rightness of the action regardless of the end result. Deontology holds that there are certain eternal moral principles and obligations, such as the duty to respect life and the duty to tell the truth. Consequentialism recognizes no such demands.

Consequentialism's most famous form of expression is utilitarianism, the doctrine of the philosopher Jeremy Bentham and of his disciple John Stuart Mill. The central doctrine of utilitarianism, that "good" lies in what promotes the greatest happiness of the greatest number, has often been criticized as being a justification for slavery, genocide, and other examples of the tyranny of the majority. Yet its tradition is basically altruistic. While "situation ethics" is very much a form of utilitarianism, in that it claims that there is no absolute code of conduct that applies 100 percent of the time, Fletcher is careful to stress his adherence to basic human values. He writes that "it is wiser to be guided by moral principles than by moral rules. . . .

A consequentialist, faced with a child with severe defects, might decide that the child would be better off dead and authorize the discontinuation of treatment. His approach would be pragmatic and flexible, and he would be unencumbered by moral imperatives. A deontologist, on the other hand, would wrestle with conflicting moral obligations. He might decide that the duty not to cause pain and suffering outweighed the duty not to cause death, but he would be much less likely to come to that conclusion. According to Fletcher, it is situation ethics that seems best suited to the needs of medicine. "By training and practice," he writes, "[doctors] appreciate the need of diagnosis and treatment case by case. They are accustomed to judge what is best, not so much according to general rules as according to general principles."

Indeed, it is probable that more physicians embrace situation ethics than practice deontology. But at least one prominent pediatrician expresses a great deal of scorn for Fletcher's philosophy. He is Dr. William Bartholome, who was one of the physicians involved in the Johns Hopkins case of some years ago in which an infant with Downs syndrome and an easily correctible duodenal atresia was allowed to starve to death over a 15-day period. Bartholome was so horrified by what he had been party to that he has since then spent his professional career in the study and refinement of medical ethics.

"Fletcher's out to lunch," he commented to me bluntly during a recent medical seminar. "There's just no way to apply his ideas to actual cases."

The relativism of Fletcher's philosophy disturbs many people. It relies heavily on vague language and hinges entirely on subjective judgments by the infant's proxies as to what constitutes "kindness" and "well-being." By setting such a loose standard, it would seem, at least in the eyes of critics, to encourage wholesale, and inconsistently applied, nontreatment.

By contrast, Robert Weir, a professor of religious studies at Oklahoma State University, proposes what he believes is a more stringent guideline, one that emphasizes the burden of continued existence, rather than its projected lack of quality. The question to be asked, Weir says, is not whether life with certain handicaps is meaningful, as quality-of-life advocates suggest, but whether death might be more in the child's interest than remaining alive. Such a stark standard, he says, would work to reduce, rather than increase, the number of children subjected to nontreatment. Weir contends that there is such a thing as "a fate worse than death." This he bases on his assumption that most people, if asked to compile a list of the worst things that could befall them—including, say, intractable pain, paralysis, severe mental deficiency, involuntary imprisonment, irremediable damage to personal reputation, and death of spouse and children—would rate one or more items as more terrible than their own death. Thus, by extension, he believes it appropriate to apply a test to children that asks whether life with their specific congenital defects represents "a fate worse than death." If so, he would consider it morally permissible to induce a painless demise.

This standard sounds as vague as Fletcher's on the face of it, except that Weir does something that few other ethicists have dared to do. He plunges in and identifies a number of congenital conditions that are "worse than death" and that hence justify the withholding of life-saving medical treatment. For example, he names trisomy 18, trisomy 13, Lesch-Nyhan syndrome, Tay-Sachs disease, and cri du chat syndrome. These conditions, although they are in most cases life shortening, differ from such rapidly terminal conditions as anencephaly and renal agenesis in that the victims are not necessarily "born dying." Lesch-Nyhan children may live a number of years, during which time they will be severely retarded, subject to painful, involuntary writhing movements, and given to compulsive self-mutilation, sometimes biting off their own fingers. Children with cri du chat syndrome may survive to adulthood, though they will be profoundly retarded and subject to heart disease and curvature of the spine. In short, to allow these youngsters to die is essentially a discretionary matter because their lives could, if one wished, be prolonged for quite some time. Yet, Weir's proposal is not all that radical. His "fate worse than death" list comprises some of the most terrible disorders known to medicine, and most doctors and ethicists, if pressed, would agree that children suffering from them should not be subjected to heroic medical treatment. Even the conservative Paul Ramsey makes an exception to his prolife philosophy in the case of Lesch-Nyhan syndrome. (Weir, incidentally, does not support nontreatment in the far more controversial area of Down's syndrome, myelomeningocele, and severe intraventricular hemorrhage.) However, he becomes radical indeed when he goes on to openly advocate the intentional killing of infants who, upon having treatment withheld, lapse into a lingering and painful death. He suggests as a possible method of dispatching them the injection of intravenous potassium. "[T]he intentional killing of birth-defective newborns," he writes, "is necessary in rare circumstances as a moral option of last resort in neonatal medicine. Nonvoluntary euthanasia in NICUs is justifiable under three necessary and jointly sufficient conditions. First, the withholding of treatment shall have been done . . . with the proxies determining that *life-prolonging treatment is not in the best interests of the child.* Second, having made the decision to allow the child to die, it becomes clear to the decision makers that the child is not going to die quickly and is going to *endure prolonged suffering* in the absence of treatment. Third, the decision to cause the child's death is carried out in a manner that will *quickly and painlessly* end the child's life." Weir concludes by suggesting that such killing be undertaken not only out of mercy but "as an act of conscientious objection to laws that proscribe intentionally killing neonates even for humane reasons."

Thus, Weir has raised a question that goes well beyond the issues involved in the Baby Doe affair: he has introduced the issue of *killing* versus *letting die,* transforming the subject into something more than a matter of whether we employ lifesaving technology or not. Granted, Weir would place a strict limit on the circumstances under which direct action might be taken to terminate life. But his ideas spawn other possibilities, such as that of our actually initiating the dying process in children who have not presented us with the opportunity on their own. For given Weir's description of Lesch-Nyhan syndrome as a "fate worse than death," and his subsequent support for end-stage mercy killing, one wonders why he doesn't go a step or two further and propose a simple lethal injection for *all* Lesch-Nyhan children at the outset, regardless of whether they need lifesaving treatment. The restriction of matters to children who need life support is, after all, rather arbitrary. Seen from one perspective, this sort of blatant euthanasia may be justified morally for the same reason as the with-holding of medical care: it prevents a life of suffering. But viewed in another light, it presents a bewildering new set of problems. The actual instigation of death may well be a threshold our culture may never wish to cross. The British philosopher Philippa Foot has observed that "it is active euthanasia which is the most liable to abuse. Hitler would not have been able to kill 275,000 people in his 'euthanasia' program if he had had to wait for them to need life-saving treatment."

The potential abuse of involuntary euthanasia is a matter that preoccupies Foot in her writings. She is deeply troubled by the fear that a child's proxies will make decisions that are inimical to the youngster's interests. "The fact is, of course," she writes, "that the doctors who recommend against life-saving procedures for handi-capped infants are usually thinking not of them but rather of their parents and of other children in the family or of the 'burden on soci-ety' if the children survive. So it is not for their sake but to avoid trouble to others that they are allowed to die. When brought out into the open this seems unacceptable: at least we do not easily accept the principle that adults who need special care should be counted too burdensome to be kept alive."

This also worries Dr. Norman Fost, of the University of Wisconsin Medical School, who frequently writes and lectures on the subject of medical ethics. "This is an extraordinary amount of power to give one person over another," he complained not long ago in an address before a medical conference. "Where else but in the parent-child relation-ship can one person bring about another's death simply by expressing the desire?"

Fost argued that parents make poor spokespersons for the child's interests and that disinterested third parties, such as ethics commit-tees, make better proxies. "Parents don't know all the medical facts," he says. "They may have an exaggerated notion of what a handicap entails; for example, they may know less than anyone else on the scene what it means to be a Down's victim. But even more, they may look on the child as a threat to their quality of life. They may not want to raise a handicapped child. If I need a lifesaving operation, the last person I'd want to decide whether I should have it or not is the guy who just said, 'If Fost lives, my life will be ruined.' "

However, Dr. Marcia Angell, deputy editor of the *New England Journal of Medicine*, strongly disagrees. "In the case of handicapped newborns, it is difficult to imagine people who are *less* malicious or indifferent than parents. . . . Probably most parents would give their lives for their children; the circumstances in which parents would prefer death to survival for their child must be extraordinary indeed."

Despite what Angell says, many parents undoubtedly *do* think of themselves when confronted with the question of treating their handicapped newborn. The child's survival, assuming it is in a severely impaired state, is going to distort their lives in cataclysmic ways. Among the things that will be affected are their psychological well-being, their other children, their daily mobility, their job opportunities, their finances, and where and how they live. To meet this vast disruption in their lifestyle, they will receive only limited help from society. Thus, while parents undoubtedly consider their own interests in making a decision, *selfishness* is perhaps the wrong word to describe their impulse. One might more accurately call it a form of self-defense.

Underlying the ethical dilemma posed by impaired newborns is the confusion that surrounds the proper goals of medicine. Are physicians commanded to prolong lives, or are they commanded to prevent suffering? Is their primary mission to fight disease or to promote the patient's welfare? The conflict is an ancient one, and it is expressed succinctly in the Hippocratic oath, which states, "I will follow that system of regimen which, according to my ability and judgment, I consider for the benefit of my patients, and abstain from whatever is deleterious and mischievous." Here, in one seemingly straightforward sentence, are contained the seeds of imbroglio. For while the oath seems to counsel doctors to do what is good and to avoid what is harmful, it ignores the fact that the two admonitions sometimes pull in opposing directions. Doing good, in the medical sense, is customarily interpreted to mean preserving life, ameliorating illness, making the patient *feel* better, and in general doing what is seen to be in the patient's best interests. This ethic, which bids doctors to concentrate on achieving good outcomes, is commonly referred to as the principle of beneficence. Doing harm, in the medical sense, has been variously interpreted as causing death, causing pain, inflicting suffering, and in general doing what is not in the patient's interest. The ethic that binds doctors to avoid such behavior is known as the principle of nonmaleficence. Obviously, a possibility of conflict arises. For example, under the principle of beneficence one might feel obliged to preserve a life, say that of a child with only a few inches of functioning bowel. But under the principle of nonmaleficence one would be reluctant to place the child on permanent hyperalimentation, condemning it to years of hospital confinement.

Contributing to the confusion is the oft-quoted maxim *Primum non nocere* ("First of all, do no harm"), which is taken by many physicians to epitomize their professional duty. The origins of the maxim are shrouded in mystery. Nowhere in the medical essays attributed to Hippocrates, or in the oath itself, is there an indication that the obligation to do no harm was intended to take precedence over the obligation to preserve life and ameliorate disease. Exhaustive searches through post-Hellenic medical history have yielded no clues to the maxim's source either. One author has speculated that it is of quite recent vintage and that it was converted into Latin by some nineteenth- or twentieth-century physician to give it a special cachet. In any event, a literal reading of "First of all, do no harm" would seem to direct physicians to put the avoidance of pain and suffering above the preservation of life. Perhaps this is as it should be. The concept of extraordinary versus ordinary means was originally devised by Roman Catholic theologians in the preanesthesia era to absolve patients who declined lifesaving surgery from the charge that they were committing the sin of suicide. There is thus a historical precedent for the idea that the prevention of suffering has priority over the prolongation of someone's life.

On the other hand, as is pointed out by Robert Veatch, professor of medical ethics at Georgetown University's Kennedy Institute of Bioethics, to apply *Primum non nocere* as an absolute—Do *no* harm—would mean that no physician could ever treat anyone. "Surgery and chemotherapy would always be immoral. If failing to benefit is morally different from, and less onerous than, actually harming, one could always avoid doing harm simply by doing nothing." It is clear, then, that some harm attendant to the practice of medicine is thus permissible as a matter of rationality, so long as there is a net benefit to the patient.

But these are loaded terms. What is *harm?* How does one compute *net benefit?* In the case of an impaired infant, how are the terms to be applied? Suppose we are presented with a child who has congenital heart disease, glaucoma, and enlargement of the liver as a result of clinically diagnosed Hurler's syndrome. We know that because of an incurable inability to metabolize certain carbohydrates called mucopolysaccharides the child is going to be severely retarded, growth stunted, and probably blind, and that it will develop grotesque facial features and a humped back prior to dying an early death. If we perform cardiac surgery, we might prolong the child's life, but all we may be doing is forcing it to experience a few years of terrible misery. Are we satisfying the principle of beneficence by treating the youngster, or are we violating the principle of nonmaleficence? Has there been a net benefit in removing the life-threatening ailment without curing the life-stultifying disorders? To put it bluntly, have we harmed the child by saving its life?

In the traditional medical view, death is the ultimate harm, not life. It would seem to turn conventional logic on its head to say that saving a life is a treatment failure and that nontreatment is a treatment success—or that there are net benefits in being dead, since the individual will not exist to knowingly reap them.

On the other hand, in an analysis of *Primum non nocere,* Albert Jonsen has written, "If 'do no harm' means having always the motive to care for the other, termination of painful or seriously debilitated existence might be considered a 'caring act.' . . . Due care consists of assessing medical actions in relation to certain goals. It might be argued that sustaining life of low quality is not a goal of medical actions since medicine is concerned only with restoration of health in some functional sense. At this early stage of this difficult discussion, I would suggest that it is legitimate to invoke the 'do no harm' maxim as a justification for termination of life."

H. Tristram Engelhardt has attempted to apply the legal concept of "wrongful life" to the question of nontreatment of defective newborns. This theory, asserted in court on behalf of abnormal children whose births could have been prevented but were not, argues that death is preferable to a severely handicapped existence. It views the gift of life as a tort, an actionable injury. Engelhardt writes, "In some cases, on balance, where the quality of life may total out in the negative, the concept of wrongful life suggests that social canons should be developed to allow a decent death for children for whom the only possibility is protracted painful dying. One needs a concept of tort for wrongful continuance of existence." He adds that there may be a *duty* not to prolong life. "[T]he maxim *primum non nocere* . . . may not always require sustaining life. At times the maxim may even require the contrary."

In the eyes of the Reverend James Bresnahan, medicine has cultivated a dangerous obsession with stamping out death. The result is that the patient is sometimes subjected to arduous therapies and an unwarranted extension of life simply because the physician is unable to admit defeat. "The war on death and disease," he says, "at times takes on similarities to war between nations, in that both seek the total destruction of a hated enemy. Anything goes, any kind of firepower, so long as that end—destruction of the enemy—is achieved. The folly of such a military policy was seen in Vietnam, where we burned down villages to save them. And it can be seen in the war on disease when we inflict further suffering on a patient in the name of saving his life."

9

Families in Distress

THE MENDENHALLS

To a motorist roaring past on the lonely highway, it looks like any of a thousand farms, with its drafty clapboard house, its 40-odd acres of land, and some angus cattle, black and dour, grazing in the fields. No one would suspect that such an unremarkable homestead is more like a prison where, for the past 18 years, Alice Mendenhall has been quietly doing time. Having just passed her 40th birthday, Alice sometimes wonders where the old saying about the punishment fitting the crime ever got started. As far as she can tell, the only thing she ever did wrong was to bring a baby into the world.

Lori, her daughter, was born in 1966. She is severely microcephalic, with an IQ of no more than 20. She also has emotional problems and throws screaming fits that occupy entire days and nights. Physically, she is confined to a wheelchair because of severe curvature of the spine. From the moment the sun begins to brighten the eastern sky until well into the evening, Alice tends to Lori's every need. Often she must stay up with her throughout the night as well. In Alice's words, her daughter has "made an old woman out of me."

The Mendenhalls, who also have a normal, 16-year-old son, named Dwayne, live within a few miles of the Ohio-Indiana border. Alice's husband, Jack, squeezes a small income out of his tiny spread raising steers, hogs, and soybeans, but he must supplement the family finances by working full-time as a machinist. He is a good and gentle man, with an appetite for work, but he doesn't have much time or patience to help his wife with Lori. Any decisions about the child's care, he leaves entirely to Alice.

Lori was a handful for her family right from the start. "She came home from the hospital demanding attention," her mother recalls. "She was a miserable little person, crying all the time as though she was in pain. And she would abuse herself. She'd lay in her crib at night and bang her head. It was all we could do to keep her from cracking her skull."

Because of a malfunctioning stomach valve, Lori suffered from projectile vomiting as an infant. She had to be fed almost hourly in order to get enough food in her stomach to keep her alive. Between the head banging and the round-the-clock feedings, Alice says she did not get more than three hours' sleep a night for the first four years of Lori's life. In desperation the Mendenhalls placed the child in a state institution because Alice was close to having a breakdown from taking care of both Lori and Dwayne and helping with the farm chores.

But after a year the couple was so distressed by the inhumane conditions at the institution that they brought Lori home. Since then she has never lived anywhere else. Her care has become virtually the total occupation of her mother's life.

It is an exceedingly difficult job. Lori's tantrums and head banging have grown worse with age, and Alice must frequently wrestle her into submission. "She's 65 pounds and she's strong," sighs Alice. When Lori wants something, she will repeat it over and over "until you give it to her or lose your mind," her mother confides. Lori is not toilet trained and must wear special diapers; moreover, the digestive problems of her infancy have taken the adult form of extreme constipation. Alice must manage the girl's bowels with enemas and by manual stimulation. "It's no fun for either of us," she says.

The only respite Alice gets is the five hours a day Lori spends in a class for profoundly retarded children. Still, Alice must work for her few moments of freedom. She has to drive Lori a distance of 16 miles daily. That leaves her approximately four hours to herself. In the past 12 years, the Mendenhalls have had but one vacation—5 years ago when Alice's parents agreed to babysit with the children for a week so that Alice and Jack could go to Florida. "We knew it would be the last vacation we would ever take," says Alice. "My folks are both in their late seventies now. They could never handle Lori again."

Lori developed her curvature of the spine when she was 13. Doctors gave the Mendenhalls a choice of performing corrective surgery or not. They said the operation was exceedingly risky and would require Lori to remain motionless on her back for months afterwards, a degree of cooperation that would be almost impossible to get from Lori unless she was strapped down. Without the surgery, they predicted, she would die in her early twenties.

The Mendenhalls looked at each other in puzzlement. Die? How could anyone die from curvature of the spine? Compression of the heart, the doctors explained.

Alice recalls how she and Jack walked around in the rain for an hour, trying to make up their minds what to do. Both of them were crying. At last they decided against the surgery. "We told each other that we'd given her 13 years of a good life. If she lived to be 21 and was content with her existence, that would be better than a lot of people have."

Now, as Lori approaches the age of 19, it appears the doctors were wrong. Her heart is in perfect condition. "As far as I know, she could live forever," Alice says. However, something is about to befall Lori that Alice believes is worse than death. The state has decreed that retarded people can continue in special education classes only through the age of 18. In a few months Lori will be cast adrift. Alice fears that the child, who greatly enjoys school, will become depressed, the way she does in the summer months when there are no classes. "By this time next year," says Alice, "it will be just Lori and I sitting here on the farm all day long. I'm terrified of it. It's a jail. We'll both sit here and get nuttier by the day."

Nonetheless, there are no alternatives that Alice can foresee. Lori is far too retarded to participate in a sheltered workshop. The Mendenhalls cannot afford the monthly cost of a private instititution, and even if they could—perhaps by selling their farm—there aren't many facilities in their part of the state for adult retarded people. As for the state institutions, the mere thought causes Alice to shudder. "The institutions in this state are awful places," she says. "I have a friend who heads a watchdog group that brings suit against them for things like attendants hosing patients down with scalding water. I know of a case where a retarded child was thought to have dental problems because his mouth was swollen. When the dentist got there he found that a mouse had made a nest in the boy's mouth."

Alice describes what she feels for her daughter as ambivalence. "It's ambivalence in its extreme form. You want relief from bondage, and yet you don't want to part with the child, either. I had a night recently when I got very little sleep. She kept getting me up hour after hour. Then, in the morning, I didn't hear from her for ever so long, and I found myself thinking it would be nice if one morning she just slipped away. Just died. And then, of course, my next thought was how would I cope with that? I probably love Lori in a way that isn't healthy. When a person is this dependent on you, you don't know where they begin and you leave off.

"I feel like I've wasted my life, though. I can't help it. I feel like I've been waiting for life to happen. I'm going to be a mommy to a little kid forever. After 18 years, I am tired and bitter, and my back hurts from lifting her 65 pounds all day and all night."

It galls Alice that she has seldom received help from family or friends, not even so that she and Jack could have a night out. People, she explains resentfully, generally say three things to her. "They tell me, first, 'You must be very special to have been given such a child'; and then, 'I don't know how you do it—I know I couldn't'; and finally, 'Bye now.' "

Alice has come to believe that it would have been better if Lori had died at birth, and she wonders what she and Jack would have done if there had been any life-or-death decisions to make when Lori was an infant. Alice likes to think she would have been "brave enough" to let her daughter die. As for those parents who do face this choice, Alice believes they should be able to exercise it. "I feel very strongly about that," she confides. "I think the judge who says, 'This child will be taken away from these parents and treated,' I think that judge should have to change the diapers when the child is a teenager, and the judge ought to have to walk the kid all night long while she's screaming. I hear some people with a retarded child say that everybody should have one of these kids, that it's the best thing that ever happened to them. That's cuckoo. How can anyone think the best thing that could happen is to have a child less than whole?"

To contemplate the future disturbs Alice immensely. She does not want her son to be burdened with Lori's care, if she and Jack should die, nor can she stand the idea of her daughter's fate being adjudicated by a court. "That's probably the biggest fear I have, that she will be put in some place untended and unloved and maybe abused. She cannot do anything for herself, cannot protect herself. I'll say one thing. If I ever find out I've got cancer or anything, I plan to take Lori in the car with me and let the gas run. I won't leave her care to be decided by some judge, and I will not have this imposed on my son's life. It's a very primitive thing, sort of like the mother pig that kills her piglets if she thinks they're in danger. But that's what I'd do."

If there were laws of thermodynamics that applied to families, one of the laws would certainly state that a handicapped child tends to absorb every available ounce of a family's energy. The degree to which the child comes to dominate its parents' existence is, of course, directly proportional to the severity of its defects. But even a mildly disabled youngster is a source of concern and despair.

It is difficult to fully appreciate the all-encompassing effects these offspring can have on a family. The combination of physical and emotional demands imposed on a parent often exceeds the individual's ability to cope. Perhaps one can begin to understand the extent of these demands by first considering how much effort it takes to care for normal children, particularly in their first several years. There are feedings to administer, diapers to change, baths to give, and infections to treat. Toddlers must be dressed, undressed, soothed, and entertained, and every move must be monitored lest they endanger themselves or others. Most parents are glad when their youngsters reach an age when they can do some of these things for themselves. Now, imagine children who will never be able to achieve this self-reliance. Suppose they have physical handicaps that require certain caretaker functions to be performed for them forever. Perhaps they must be bathed or dressed, or need help to get around. Or suppose they are mentally retarded, so that for years they remain locked in the infant stage of development. One must give them the kind of attention ordinarily reserved for children under two. Of course, even if they should master certain aspects of taking care of themselves, they will require lifelong supervision, maybe of such a stringent nature that the parents do not dare leave them alone in the house. The feeling that one is inexorably trapped is hard to fend off.

Imagine also that a parent feels regret for all the things that the child will never become. Seeing the neighbor's children attain various milestones can be a desolating experience. Girl Scouts, Little League, first dates, high school proms, college degrees, jobs, and marriage—many, if not all, of these will be permanently out of reach of the disabled child. Few mothers and fathers can escape a sharp twinge of sadness for what might have been. Parents may also feel torn between meeting the time-consuming needs of the disabled younster and the normal needs of the other children in the family. The choice may involve either overworking oneself or feeling guilty about short-changing somebody. Finally, imagine a couple's sense of helplessness in knowing that should the child outlive them, he or she may be utterly at the mercy of strangers. Suppose parents make provision with legal trustees for their child to be placed in a reputable institution after their deaths. The institution may close. Trustees die; law firms dissolve. Even if these catastrophes don't occur, who is going to visit the institution to make sure that the standard of care hasn't declined? It is a dilemma that has no real counterpart in nature, for the usual method that animals have for dealing with defective offspring is, as Alice Mendenhall points out, to bring about their deaths in early infancy.

The impact that a child with birth defects has on a family is by no means limited to the above concerns. There are very practical consid-

erations as well. The child will inevitably place some degree of financial burden on the parents. Public and private agencies may be able
to help defray some or most of the medical expenses, although this
depends on a variety of factors, including the nature of the child's
disease or defect, his or her age, the family's economic means, the
availability of programs in a given geographical region, and the generosity of a state legislature at any given time. But even if 100 percent
of the doctor and hospital bills are picked up, which is not likely, there
remain such things as special foods, eyeglasses, corrective shoes, leg
braces, wheelchairs, and walkers. The Mendenhalls estimate that they
spend some $700 a year on Lori above what they would if she were
normal. If, on the other hand, she were in a private institution, that
amount might rise substantially. Meanwhile, a family's ability to earn
more income is sorely inhibited. Jobs or promotions that require a
move to other cities must be passed up because the child has to remain
close to a particular hospital. Wives must sacrifice their careers to stay
home and provide care, which not only creates an unhappy woman
but also cheats the family purse of the second paycheck it desperately
needs. As a result, the family's lifestyle undergoes a general decline.
Dream houses go unpurchased, second cars are forgone, and the child's
brothers and sisters are forced to make sacrifices that they should not
have to make. It is sad to have to explain to one's teenager that he or
she won't be able to go to college because the money is needed for the
care of a sibling with a much lower IQ.

Society's contribution to easing these burdens is piecemeal and
insufficient. Families like the Mendenhalls are left almost entirely alone
to cope with their lifelong heartache. No one steps in to help dispel
the steamcooker effect of 20, 30, perhaps 50, years of being responsible for a completely dependent person. We no longer even have the
luxury of an extended-family tradition, which was once our way of
dealing with weakness and infirmity in the group. Farouk Idriss, a
cardiac surgeon in Chicago, recalls how in his native Lebanon there
are always willing family members around to share the travail of constant care. And should parents die, these relatives will see to the child's
needs for the rest of its life. "In Lebanon, our family structure is such
that the firstborn male takes care of the entire family when the father
is dead. You don't have nursing homes; you don't need them. You
raise children, and they take care of you when you are old."

This failure of society to help shoulder the burden angers the Reverend James Bresnahan. He contends, "If you and your wife have to
take home, say, this severely retarded child and handle it alone, financially and temperamentally, imagine how it wears you out. You can't
stand to look at that child, and all the talk in the world about the

infinite value of life and the beauty of a handicapped child means nothing if we can't help the parents who have the burden of raising it.

"If it's immoral to let a child die, then it's also immoral to leave two people alone to bear the lifelong cost of what we've insisted on."

Few things in life are more psychologically crushing than to learn that one's newborn baby has congenital defects. Elemental passions can quite easily erupt. How elemental was illustrated in July of 1983 when a veterinarian from Harvey, Illinois, was charged with the murder of his son, who had been born with a cleft palate and deformed hands. According to police and hospital authorities, the father went berserk in the delivery room within moments after the birth, seizing the infant and hammering its head on the floor. (As of this writing, the case had not yet come to trial.)

Obviously, most people's reaction to the birth of a damaged newborn is less barbarous, but often scarcely less destructive. The entire personality is suddenly placed inside a crucible and made to undergo alterations and stresses that may distort it temporarily or even permanently. If these distortions are of a significantly negative nature, they can rend the family structure and cause long-range physical and psychic harm to the defective child. In a sense, the experience of having a defective baby might be compared to drinking a magic potion with the power to magnify every existing characteristic in a person, be it a good trait or a bad. Hence, one's strong points are often accentuated, as when the mildly altruistic person becomes a self-sacrificing martyr. And weak points may grow disproportionately large, as when the moderately self-centered person, who would not be considered cruel under other circumstances, becomes capable of the most reprehensible indifference and callousness toward his or her abnormal offspring. But all parents, no matter how admirable their ultimate adjustment, go through certain readily identifiable stages while coming to grips with their handicapped newborn.

As long ago as 1961 a pair of groundbreaking researchers named A. J. Solnit and M. H. Stark discovered that these parents undergo a process that is surprisingly similar to grief. At first glance this seems odd because the child is still alive. But it turns out that what parents are grieving for is the loss not of a real child but of the idealized "perfect" child they have carried around in their minds throughout the months of pregnancy. The mourning process they go through may take a very long time, but it cannot be short-circuited. It must be experienced before the parents can become fully attached to the living, impaired infant.

Other researchers later refined Solnit and Stark's work. Marshall Klaus, of Michigan State Uiversity, and his colleague, John Kennell, of Case Western Reserve University, have identified five distinct stages through which one passes in learning to cope with a malformed child. They are as follows:

(1) *Shock:* Parents describe their initial reaction as a feeling that the world has "come to an end." It is a time of irrational behavior, feelings of helplessness, and an urge to flee.

(2) *Denial:* The parent feels that it cannot really be happening. This stage is associated with primitive superstitious feelings and impulses to "barter" with God, for example, the idea that giving to charity might cause the birth defect to disappear.

(3) *Sadness, anger, and anxiety:* A period of tears and emotional turmoil. Some people feel angry—toward the baby, toward the doctors, toward themselves or their spouse.

(4) *Equilibrium:* A gradual lessening of emotional intensity, which often takes months. The parent finally begins to believe he or she can manage caring for the baby. The authors note, however, "Even at best, this adaptation continues to be incomplete. One parent reported, 'Tears come even yet, years after the baby's birth.' "

(5) *Reorganization:* Many parents feel guilt. They blame themselves for the birth defect, for having smoked or drunk too much during pregnancy or having donated a bad gene. In some instances, each parent blames the other, which can be very deleterious. It is during this stage that one comes to recognize that the baby's problems are not one's fault.

Siblings go through stages, too. Small children may feel they caused their brother or sister's birth defect by having harbored negative feelings about the new baby's arrival. They may be frightened that the defect will happen to them. They are almost sure to feel neglected because the parents' time is monopolized. Older children may become a "third parent" to the child, feeling strong protective urges. This role can cause problems if neighborhood children should taunt the handicapped child or exclude him or her from play. The siblings may be torn between a desire to defend their brother or sister and a desire to be accepted by their peers.

Among the things that often make it harder for parents to deal with a defective newborn is the behavior of those around them. As Klaus and Kennell write, "With their ability to produce a normal child called into question and their emotional reserves at a low, they must face grandparents, friends, and neighbors. In this case society has few of

the built-in supports that are available in other crises such as the death
of a relative or a community disaster. For example, friends and relatives send gifts and cards to the hospital after the birth of a normal
baby, but, confused about the proper procedure when the baby is
abnormal, they may find it easiest to forget to call or send anything.
Parents are often reluctant to send out announcements of the birth
or even to name the baby. As a result, they are likely to experience
intense loneliness during the period immediately following the birth."

The "grieving" process that a couple goes through with a handicapped child is in one major respect different from, and arguably
worse than, experiencing an actual bereavement. In the case of death
the child is gone, and once mourning is over, life goes on. But the
handicapped youngster is always present as a constant reminder of
the lost "perfect" child. Some parents never get over this grief. Particularly where they have a retarded child, who is going to be perpetually dependent on them, they are apt to remain in a state of what is
called "chronic sorrow."

Nevertheless, most parents eventually reach a point where they are
able to accept their child's disabilities. In fact, some are able to make
truly inspiring adjustments.

THE SULLIVANS

Terrence and Monica Sullivan, of suburban Chicago, are the parents of a 17-year-old boy named John. He has brought an extraordinary light into their lives, although he has never uttered a single word
and never will.

When John was born, doctors were puzzled by his various abnormalities. They did not fit any known pattern or syndrome. He had
brain and motor damage, webbed fingers and toes, and the series of
four interrelated heart defects called tetralogy of Fallot. One of his
eyelids was locked shut, and he had a hernia and an undescended
testicle. In spite of these defects, however, he was in no immediate
danger of dying, unlike many other multiply handicapped newborns.
"We didn't have to make any life-or-death decisions for him at that
point," Monica Sullivan says.

After studying the boy's reflexes and general neurologic situation,
physicians at the hospital told the Sullivans that they didn't expect
John ever to sit up, walk, or talk or even to recognize anyone on sight.
They advised that he be institutionalized. "But we just couldn't do it,"
Terrence recalls.

The doctors also told the couple that their son might not live to see his first birthday, adding rather tactlessly that they would not be too surprised if the Sullivans should walk into his bedroom one morning and find him dead. "I wish they hadn't told us that," says Monica, "because then every morning you look."

Instead of dying, John survived. Today he is a happy but severely limited adolescent who functions at the level of a child 18 to 24 months of age. His IQ is too low to measure, although for a long time it was thought to be about 20. Recently, the doctors at the testing clinic raised it a few points after John displayed a fit of anger. Rage is considered a sign of intelligence. John stands just three feet tall and weighs only 50 pounds. He can walk, although with a precarious flatfooted gait that Monica says elicits stares on the street. He is not toilet trained, nor can he speak, but he has mastered several fundamental hand signals. For example, he claps his hands to indicate he wants a cookie. He touches his head for something to drink, and his lips for something to eat. He can hold a spoon and lift food to his mouth. "He can do very simple puzzles, put things into a container, and can roll a ball back to you," says Monica. "How much is up there; who knows?" she adds, tapping her forehead.

When John turned nine, the Sullivans were faced with their first true moral crisis. His cardiac malformations had to be repaired or he would die. One heart surgeon told them baldly that he didn't operate on children like John. There was a waiting list, he said, and he felt the surgery should be reserved for youngsters with some promise. "We decided to get John the operation anyway, just as if he was a normal kid," says his father.

So another doctor was found, and John underwent the rigors and dangers of open-heart surgery. In due course, additional procedures were performed to correct his eyelid and his hernia. Why did the Sullivans pursue so diligently the survival of a profoundly retarded child who was leading what some people would judge to be a pointless life?

"I just couldn't let him die," says Monica. "Despite all of his handicaps, I have learned a great deal from him. Having a child like John has matured me emotionally, made me more of a fighter, more of my own person." A slim, contemplative woman in her late thirties, she recalls that when she was pregnant with John, she nurtured ingenuous fantasies of how he would one day achieve greatness and reflect her brilliance as a mother. "And then he didn't turn out like other people's babies, and I found I couldn't live my life through my child. I had to find other ways to be fulfilled, something besides my son getting A's in school and being on the baseball team."

Terrence is an administrator at a local college. An articulate, engaging man, he has that elusive quality of personality that people refer to as solid. He opines that John has had more of a positive effect on them than a normal child would have. "John teaches you the simple pleasures, the things that are fundamentally important. He doesn't know or care what car payments are. And he is forgiving of everything. You get nothing but hugs and smiles from John."

Monica says that, despite his condition, John has seldom been a real burden to them. "In retrospect, he causes us no more inconvenience than a normal child. He's so small you can move him easily. For a long time, if you put him somewhere, he'd stay put, just like an infant. Yes, inconvenience in the sense of having all these years of diapers. It's not pleasant to change a diaper on a 17 year old. And it is tough getting him to walk up and down stairs. He has to do it a certain way or not at all. But not an inconvenience in any real sense. We've always been able to get babysitters who get to know John and understand what his signs mean. He's no trouble. The sitter puts him in bed, and he stays there without crying. So we get to go out whenever we want."

Does she have any regrets about John? "Well, you regret it when you wonder what he might have been. But I don't regret it in the sense that I wouldn't have had him all over again the way he is. Neither of us say, gee, I wish he'd never been born. But if I had one wish in the world, I wish that he'd be healthy. You hate to see someone you love suffer."

Monica confesses that occasionally, when visiting women friends who were pregnant when she was, it occurs to her that their children are in high school now. And then it hits her with a jolt that that is where John would be, if he had been normal. "John's kind of ageless, I guess," she remarks wistfully. "He's Peter Pan."

The Sullivans' second son, who is now four, is adopted. They chose not to have another biological child, because even though two chromosome tests on John showed no abnormalities, the doctors told the couple there was still a 50 percent chance they could have a second baby with problems. "And it might not be caught by amniocentesis, since it didn't show up in the chromosome test," explains Monica.

Recently, the Sullivans took the big step of putting John in a live-in facility. They chose a school for the severely retarded in a community north of Chicago. "We always figured to place John somewhere," says his father, "but both of us felt that if John is to leave home, it would be at the age when kids normally go to college. I know it doesn't make sense, but we wanted to have the same good feelings other parents have."

The school is licensed to take care of students only until they are 21, however. The Sullivans will have to find another home for John after that, a more difficult task because there are fewer facilities for the adult retarded than there are for children.

Unlike many people in similar straits, they do not worry about what will happen to John after they die. "We'll ultimately make provision for his care through trusts and wills," Monica says. "And we are fortunate to have family that would take John into their homes."

Nor have they been plagued by financial worries. John's considerable school expenses are paid for by government agencies.

Terrence admits that his son costs the taxpayers a great deal of money. But he points out that anybody could have a child like John happen to them. "It's a kind of group insurance that you buy," he observes.

There is no doubt that for the Sullivans the tragedy of having a child with birth defects has provided an opportunity for emotional growth. Raising a handicapped youngster can bring significant rewards—opportunities not only for giving joy to the less fortunate but also for discovering new reserves of strength and compassion in oneself. However, it is also clear that for many others the experience will be a source of lasting pain and sadness, a seismic shock from which one never entirely recovers.

One of the major dangers is that the caldron of inner rage, guilt, and longing for escape may boil over, poisoning the atmosphere between husband and wife. People adjust to trauma in different ways. If these adaptations clash, it may cause domestic rupture. The rate of divorce in families with defective offspring is very high. Financial worries, the inordinate claim on parents' time and energy, and the presence of the child as a constant reminder of the parents' reproductive failure—all take their toll. As a woman remarked bitterly in a study by the Michigan researcher Michael Trout of 500 families with sick or handicapped babies; "This defective baby is supposed to be the best product of the love between me and my husband?" Sometimes, too, one or both of the marital partners may need to break free from the intolerable stress, perhaps by having an affair or just running away. In the end some marriages simply cannot withstand the weight.

THE BLAKES

Peter Blake fainted the first time he saw his daughter. He barely made it from the delivery room to the smoking lounge before collapsing to the floor.

Terri agrees that her husband's way of dealing with Michelle was in stark contrast to her own. She says it caused her to reassess the kind of person he was. "I couldn't understand why he couldn't at least come out of his cave and muster sympathy for this person who was going to die. There was so little he had to do. Once he told me to go up and rest and he'd burp her. But after a while I heard her crying like mad and went downstairs. He said, 'I'm tired of trying to burp her.' I said, 'Then why did you tell me to go and rest?' "

Sometimes, she recalls, her husband would come right out and say he wanted the baby to die. "He'd ask, 'When is it going to die? I want it to die.' " She says that when her friends would come over, Peter would insist that Michelle be hidden upstairs, "like she was a freak."

Peter is quick to defend himself. He says he didn't do anything he is ashamed of. "I could have behaved a lot worse. Yes, there were times when I was completely distraught, when I was at the end of my rope, and I'd explode internally. I'd get upset and have these hostile feelings that were never turned into actions. I was kind of thinking out loud and resenting the fact that I didn't have a normal child. I didn't really want Michelle to die, but I felt if it was inevitable, then for everyone's well-being let it be sooner.

"Sure, at times I insisted the child be put upstairs when friends came. But there were times I didn't, too. It was for the sake of the person visiting us and for our personal comfort as well. I mean, with anybody who has a child there are times you put it upstairs when there are people over. But looking back on it, these were all feelings I should have kept to myself, because my wife resents me now. She remains a martyr, and our marriage is shot to hell."

Both of them agree that Michelle was the cause of their eventual divorce. "His values are different," Terri says. "I think that would have eventually split us up, but Michelle accelerated it." Peter recalls, "Towards the end, it just came between us. We weren't communicating well. Everything we talked about was life and death. Will Michelle wake up tomorrow? Will she make it to Christmas? The simple, day-to-day things in life just disappeared."

Michelle died on February 15, 1982. She was seven months old. Long afterward, her mother still cries remembering the morning she died, and how the funeral director came to their house with a tiny casket, and how they dressed Michelle in her green pajamas with a pretty hair ribbon and kissed her good-bye.

"Yes, I cry," confides Terri Blake. "I cry for what a sad little person she was. Every parent has dreams for her child, and here all she could hope for was to have a gentle death."

The Blakes asked the local hospital whether they could donate Michelle's body to science. The hospital administrators said they couldn't use it.

Are there alternatives for families that cannot cope with a severely impaired child? Two are generally proposed: adoption and institutionalization.

Those who abhor the practice of withholding treatment from defective newborns commonly contend that there are large numbers of willing couples who are eager to adopt such youngsters, if the natural parents do not want them.

This is not a viable argument for two reasons. First, it is based on a questionable premise—that the parents' motivation is to be rid of the child. On the contrary, many of these mothers and fathers are loving people who have proven their parenting skills with other children and who sincerely wish to spare their infant further suffering. It is wrong to confuse their compassionate instinct with rejection of the child.

A second and more fundamental objection to the argument is that there are simply not enough adoptive parents to accommodate all the handicapped children available. It is true that certain kinds of children, such as those with Down's syndrome and spina bifida, are not especially difficult to place, thanks to the assiduous efforts of the Down's Syndrome Congress and the Spina Bifida Association of America, each of which maintains an adoption network. But youngsters with less well represented afflictions have a far harder time finding homes.

Child welfare agencies report that a large number of people already do give up their defective children at birth. It happens more often than is commonly thought. Disabled youngsters represent some 10 to 20 percent of all children in public guardianship, a percentage somewhat higher than the 7 to 8 percent incidence of handicap among the general juvenile population. The typical profile of parents who waive their custody rights would surprise many people. It is not the lower-class couple with six other children; it is the young, upwardly mobile middle-class couple that does not wish to disrupt its lifestyle with a handicapped child.

The ethicist Albert Jonsen recalls the time when he and his family lived in Quebec:

"We used to buy vegetables from a French Canadian farm family who had 15 kids, including two of them with Down's syndrome; very low-level Down's syndrome, at that. But the two children fit right into the family. They each had their jobs to do. However, it's a completely different thing if you have a striving young couple in a small apartment in Manhattan, both of them working, and all of a sudden they have a Down's baby to take care of. They're not going to be so ready to accept it."

Adoption officials in several states report that only 50 percent of all handicapped children who are put up for adoption find permanent homes. The rest remain wards of the state, normally in foster or institutional care. One state, for example, reported that it has 23,000 wards and that approximately 12 percent of them are handicapped. An estimated 1,400 of these children, then, will never get adopted.

As a rule, agencies have more success in placing physically handicapped children than in placing retarded children. According to one agency, the average length of time it takes to locate a home for a physically disabled child is approximately five months, but for a retarded youngster it is eight months or longer. "We have people who call in asking to adopt blind children or deaf children," says an adoption director, "but I can't think of when we ever got a call for a mentally retarded child. People just don't want retarded kids. I think they have a fear that they won't know how to handle them or that they won't be able to relate to the parents enough."

Many states use a variety of incentives to induce people to adopt disabled children. It is the usual practice to defray the hospital and doctor bills for any preexisting medical condition until the child is 18 or 21. States will also pay the legal fees for the adoption itself, and sometimes provide a monthly room and board stipend as well. This stipend may be as high as $250-a-month for a child in his teens.

It sometimes happens that when an impaired youngster is adopted, it is by a couple that already has a disabled son or daughter. People whose households are oriented toward the care of one such child often find it easier to handle another. Even so, it is rare to find couples willing to take severely disabled children into their homes. One must seriously question an argument against letting disabled babies die that relies so heavily on a resource that is unreliable. The Chicago pediatric surgeon John Raffensperger also thinks that with so many normal children needing homes in our society, it would be wrong to add to the surplus with an influx of impaired babies. "It's tragic," he says, "to talk about adopting a child like this who has no potential when there are children battered and abused for whom no adoptive parents can be found."

Institutionalization is the other option that is frequently mentioned as an alternative. Institutions perform an essential function in society. They are a solution, albeit an imperfect one, to unmanageable domestic situations involving a disabled son or daughter. Various scenarios may necessitate the placement of these children in a residential facil-

ity. They may be too ill to be cared for at home. Their presence may
be unduly disruptive to the rest of the family. They may have become
intractable, or simply too large to be lifted and set down a dozen times
a day. The mother and father may have decided that after years of
being dedicated parents it is time for them to find a little peace. Or
they may wish to see their child provided for before they die. I recall
a touching statement made at a New York state legislative hearing by
a 69-year-old Brooklyn woman who wished to find a place for her 42-
year-old deaf and retarded daughter. The daughter had lived at home
for years, spending the day in her father's barbershop, because of
New York's severe shortage of community-based residences for disabled adults. "My husband and I sacrificed our lives for her," the woman
said. "Before I shut my eyes, I want to make sure she's cared for." It
is apparent that institutions of one sort or another will always be essential
parts of the landscape.

Yet, I wonder whether those who propose them as an answer to
infant euthanasia have really thought about what it means to spend
one's life in an institution. For all our progressive talk, there are still
hundreds of institutions in this country in which the living conditions,
by any standard, remain subpar. This is not to deny the existence of
many fine residential facilities where the staff makes every effort to
bring some happiness and purpose into disabled children's lives, and
very often succeeds. Unfortunately, even the best of these homes are
unable to replace a parent; loneliness is the permanent condition of
the institutionalized child. One is forced to the conclusion that, no
matter how devoted the staff may be, institutions cannot help being
warehouses of endless sorrow.

But aside from these emotional concerns, our current institutional
system has other shortcomings. Mainly, there is a shortage of facilities. One private children's home in Illinois has a waiting list of 15
years! Another turns away 100 applicants a year. A Massachusetts
Department of Public Health survey of the four pediatric nursing
homes in that state reported some more distressing news. Published
in the *New England Journal of Medicine* in 1983, the study found that
the homes had a very low turnover rate because of the long-range
nature of their patients' illnesses. New admissions had consequently
declined from a total of 95 per year, when the nursing homes were
first opened a decade ago, to 25 in 1980. And this is occurring at a
time when improved neonatal intensive care is prolonging additional
lives and thereby increasing the number of severely disabled children
requiring placement. More than 100 children who were certified for
admission to the homes over a period of eight years were never actually
admitted, because there weren't enough beds. On the other hand, the

homes were not discharging patients whose conditions had improved, because of a shortage of intermediate-care facilities where they could send them. Inadequate state reimbursement ate into the nursing homes' profit margin, giving them little incentive to upgrade the standard of care. The study team wrote, "Consumer satisfaction has minimal influence on the quality of services provided, because families have few alternatives available to them."

A corollary problem is the deplorable lack of residential settings for the *adult* mentally disabled. In years past there was a rush to build facilities for children, but almost no accommodation was made for the adult population. This was irrational, since most children's homes are licensed to care for patients only up to the age of 21. Where do you put them after that? The presumption that the retarded die young is no longer justified. More and more of them are living longer because of better medical management.

There are many reasons why private health care providers don't wish to get into the adult retarded market. It costs more to take care of older people; they are less likely to have active, interested parents willing to make annual contributions; and they don't look or act as cute. But the myopic failure of society to plan for the disabled once they "age out" of children's facilities has created a national dilemma. Accordingly, patients who have reached their majority face uncertain futures. They may be lucky enough to find placement in one of the facilities that do exist. They may be sent back home to their family. Or, as is the current practice in some states, they may be put into a geriatric nursing home, to spend their days among people waiting to die.

Still, there are places that offer parents the comfort of knowing that their impaired child is in good hands. Misericordia Home in Chicago is one of them. Misericordia represents residential care at its best. It is actually two programs in one. There is a pediatric nursing facility on the city's South Side, which cares for the nonambulatory patient with severe mental and physical handicaps, and there is a residential school / vocational program for the ambulatory retarded on the city's North Side. Recently, Misericordia opened a splendid complex of group homes at the North Side center, called Heart of Mercy Village. Gleaming new houses built in the Williamsburg style, and furnished as smartly as any suburban dwelling, will be home to dozens of moderately retarded adolescents, primarily those with Down's syndrome. The supervisors are all young married couples who have volunteered for two-year stints as "core families." Their charges attend school by day and enjoy a program of activities in the evening. All have a set of chores, from washing dishes to emptying garbage, and they are made to feel as productive and useful as possible. By night they sleep in carpeted, curtained bedrooms that are indistinguishable from those of a private home.

Yet, even at Misericordia one cannot escape a feeling of repressed despair. Not every child at the North Side center is the higher level Down's youngster destined for Heart of Mercy Village. Many of them are like Tommie and Danny. Tommie is a 9-year-old Down's child with an IQ below 30. It is a peculiarity of Down's syndrome that within its narrow context it allows as much variation in ability as exists in the normal world. Tommie is incapable of speech or concentration. He spends his days in a class where they learn to put forks and knives in a silverware tray and put cubes and circles into the correctly shaped slots. Yet as elementary as these exercises are, Tommie ignores them and spends much of the time pounding his head on the desk, a practice known to psychologists as self-stimulation, or self-stimming. His teacher calms him down and teaches him body awareness by rubbing his bare back with cocoa butter or by squeezing his hands gently. Such nerve stimulation is thought to awaken the brain and make the child conscious of external sensory information. The teacher thinks someday, perhaps when he is 20, Tommie might be able to manage simple tasks, such as putting laundry into a washing machine. "I have to believe these kids will improve, or I wouldn't be teaching them," he says.

Danny is 18 years old, but he looks 11. He has known how to walk for only the past six years. He has an unknown form of retardation, and his IQ is so low as to be unmeasurable. The aim with a child like Danny is just to keep him busy. He learns useful skills, such as a two-step handwashing technique, but he doesn't know that one must turn on the water faucet. Out of a group of seven youngsters in his class, only two know how to pick up a bar of soap. They cannot dress themselves, and they never will. Bobby has a pensive countenance, and if it weren't for the fact that he drools continually, one would swear there was great intelligence within him. "It's the total absence of thought," says his teacher. "It mimics keen concentration."

At the South Side center the hopelessness one feels is even more pronounced. You meet children like Chris and Mark. Chris is eight. Like all of the patients at South Side Misericordia she is dressed in clean, stylish clothes and lives in immaculate, cheerful surroundings, a tribute to the dedication of the staff. Chris is profoundly retarded and has no motor coordination whatsoever. She cannot even work the muscles of her mouth, so she must be fed through a tube in her nose. Other children at South Side Misericordia are fed through a catheter that goes directly into their stomach. They dine on meat and vegetables that have been liquefied in a blender. Some of the children have enough body control to sit on a special beanbag chair, staring at television, but Chris does not. She must sit in a wheelchair, held in by straps, her limbs and her head hanging down at odd angles, like a rag doll. She often cries because she doesn't like the wheelchair. She finds it uncomfortable.

Mark suffers from a severe form of cerebral palsy that has paralyzed him almost completely but has left his mind untouched. His body is a ruin. He breathes with a pathetic rale, the result of severe respiratory illness, and his limbs are as skinny as broomsticks from atrophy. Though 10, he does not weigh more than 30 pounds. In the mornings he is bused to a school, but the rest of the time he must lie in a special crib, being moved from his stomach to his back and to his stomach again, to avoid pressure sores. He wears rubber pants because he is incontinent, and his face must lie on a napkin because he drools. Yet, incongruously, he has an active thought life. Though he cannot speak, he can answer questions by rolling his eyes up for yes and shaking his head for no. He can do arithmetic and is able to communicate certain basic ideas by means of an electric board whose buttons light up at the slightest pressure. The buttons allow him to express such thoughts as "happy," "sad," "hungry," "thirsty," "home," "lotion," "breakfast," and "I am sorry." You cannot be with Mark for very long. He breaks your heart.

Misericordia is run by a shrewd, devout woman named Sister Rosemary Connelly. Sister Rosemary must bestride two worlds, the materialistic and the idealistic, to keep Misericordia afloat. One moment she is plotting how to make up Misericordia's $350,000 operating deficit, which represents the difference between the $54 a day per child that the state pays the institution and the $3.2 million it actually costs to run the facility each year. The next minute she is dreaming up ways to improve the life of a child who cannot lift a fork to its mouth.

"Our overall aim," she says, "is based on our belief that the glory of God is in every living person and that everyone in our care has the right to live life to its fullest, whatever that might be."

It upsets her deeply that society has not provided enough facilities like hers. "Especially for the severely disabled adult, there's nothing out there that's appropriate or good, compared to the number who need care. I don't think anyone knows how many adult disabled there are, because so many live at home with aging parents who are terrified they are going to die before their child. You can't imagine how these parents cope. They lead truly sacrificial lives, and they don't even have the freedom to die."

This concern has caused Sister Rosemary to apply for special licensing so that when the 200 children in her care reach 21, they can continue to live at Misericordia. "It would really be hard on our parents if we had to send their children home to them. I don't think they could manage."

Sister Rosemary does not go in for the oversentimentalizing of the retarded that some people indulge in. A hardheaded realist, she knows too well the difficulties inherent in caring for people with low IQs. "Our staff is a miracle of God's grace," she says. "Changing diapers for a 20-year-old is not pleasant, but they do it gladly. And when you listen to them talk about the progress some of the kids are making, it sounds like they are talking about people who are going to be bank presidents. And all it is is that after five years someone has finally learned to make eye contact or to pull up a sock."

Nor does Sister Rosemary have any illusions about the suffering some of the patients in her nursing home endure. "We believe the children in our South Side home have a right to love and respect and dignity, but we don't believe in keeping them alive at any price. We think they're going on to something better. Some of those poor children, when I hear that God has taken them, I rejoice."

10

Shortchanging
the Disabled

In 1981 Ronald Reagan did a peculiar thing, given his commitment
to saving the lives of defective newborns. He ordered his staff to trim
the federal budget for special education by nearly 30 percent. This
would have significantly harmed a program that is vital to four million
disabled American youngsters. Fortunately, the cuts were narrowly
averted when Congress refused to agree to them.

The same year, Reagan directed the Department of Health and
Human Services to accelerate a review process involving more than
one million people receiving federal disability payments. The
assumption both in Congress and in the White House was that many
of them were cheating. First, the administration rather ruthlessly
tightened the eligiblity requirements, and then it threw onto the
recipients the burden of proving that they were too disabled to work.
Since the judgments were, for the most part, based on the submission
of forms, without a single personal interview, it was difficult for these
individuals to demonstrate the severity of their handicaps. Then, too,
there were people so mentally or physically impaired that they could
not manage the paperwork. The result was that 500,000 handicapped
individuals were purged from the rolls, losing not only their monthly
income check but their Medicaid eligibility as well. Some 60 percent
of those who appealed in court had their payments restored, but the
government refused to keep the money coming while the appellate
process was going on, a period typically lasting six months. Mean-

while, 50 percent never appealed at all, frequently because they didn't understand how the system worked; this means that an unknown number of genuinely disabled people were permanently thrown to the wolves before the reviews were finally stopped in 1984.

This was Reaganthink at its most puzzling—insisting that defective infants be treated with justice and equality, while at the same time letting disabled schoolchildren and adults suffer social and economic deprivation. The policy seemed to ignore the welfare of babies once they left the special-care nursery. It was a strange paradox and called into question the administration's moral leadership with respect to impaired newborns.

Still, when the White House shortchanged the handicapped it was merely carrying on an ignoble American tradition. The fact is that the United States has historically ignored the needs of disabled people and their families, and it is doing so even now.

Nevertheless, it would be wrong to say that no progress has been made. One has only to look at what life was like for seriously disabled people in the mid-1950s to appreciate how far we have come. The warehousing of the retarded in huge, barnlike state institutions was at its high-water mark in those years. The profoundly feebleminded were left to vegetate, often in their own filth, while the more moderately retarded were kept idle until their mental abilities irrevocably deteriorated. It was not unknown for patients to be the subject of sterilization or unauthorized medical experiments. For those who were not institutionalized, life was nearly as barren. It was an endless routine of sitting around the house and staring out a window. Special education was conducted on a small scale, its programs rigid and archaic. Sheltered workshops for adults barely existed. Physically impaired people who might have entered the community were inhibited by the lack of ramps, graded curbstones, special buses, and other public accommodations. Financial assistance to the families of the handicapped was meager or nonexistent. The disabled population was, in every sense, a neglected minority.

With the 1960s, however, came a new perception, inspired by the civil rights struggle and the coming-of-age of American democratic principles as well as by the palpable example of tragedy—thalidomide babies and the homecoming of thousands of maimed Vietnam War veterans. A growing awareness of the plight of the handicapped began to bring pressure for reform. Class action lawsuits were filed seeking to depopulate overcrowded institutions and to expand special education on the grounds that disabled children deserved free public schooling like anyone else. Other suits sought to make city streets and public buildings accessible by wheelchair. In 1973 a major milestone

was reached when Congress passed legislation that effectively outlawed discrimination against handicapped individuals in any program
supported by federal funds. Disabled people consider this law their
bill of rights. Less than a year later the federal government assumed
responsibility for the financial support of the nation's aged, blind, and
disabled population, a function formerly handled by each of the 50
states. The federal action created a national standard of payments,
eliminating large geographical disparities. Finally, in 1974, another
piece of federal legislation, Public Law 94-142, guaranteed a free public
education to all handicapped children, regardless of the extent of their
disabilities. This encouraging ferment seemed to herald a new era, in
which the disabled would be free to grow and develop to the limits of
their potential.

Without question, there have been tangible improvements. For
example, the United States currently spends approximately $10 bil-
lion a year to educate handicapped children, ranging from those with
mild learning disabilities to the most cognitively impaired. There is
scarcely a handicapped youngster in any of the nation's 16,000 school
systems who is not receiving some form of educational training, whereas
10 years ago more than one million disabled children were completely
locked out of the schools. The aims of this education are multifarious.
In regard to the severely retarded, the goal is simply to occupy the
youngsters and perhaps improve their basic communications skills.
But with more educable children the emphasis is on vocational training and the acquisition of knowledge, with an eye toward creating
productive wage earners who would otherwise have been condemned
to lead fallow lives.

In addition, many states have forged ahead with deinstitutionalization, discharging thousands of residents from dismal, overflowing state
hospitals and placing them back into the community. In a few model
states, this has been accomplished with skill and creativity. Rhode Island,
for instance, has mainstreamed much of its retarded population into
group homes, which are small independent residential units of no
more than 15 people who are supervised by live-in house parents.

In the meantime, the daily lives of millions of physically handicapped Americans have been improved by the redesign of public
facilities, which allows them greater mobility.

But the tide of progress has halted and now seems headed in the
other direction. The U.S. Commission on Civil Rights reported in 1983
that in spite of every attempt to protect the rights of the handicapped,
"historical patterns of exclusion, segregation, and isolation" continue
today. The commission declared, "Discrimination against handicapped people persists in such critical areas as education, employ-

ment, institutionalization, medical treatment, involuntary sterilization, architectural barriers, and transportation."

One of the most ominous signs of a waning of public interest in disability came in 1981, the same year in which the White House tried to gut special education. Congress, reacting to a Reagan initiative, slashed by 25 percent the funds available to the states for what are known as maternal and child health services. The appropriation for MCH services was reduced from $496 million, woefully inadequate to begin with, to $373 million. These outlays, authorized under Title V of the Social Security Act of 1935, go to subsidize crippled children's programs in all 50 states—programs that represent the backbone of the nation's effort to treat birth defects and chronic childhood illnesses. In addition, MCH services include programs concerned with good prenatal care for low-income women, genetic screening and counseling, the prevention of sudden infant death syndrome, and the treatment of hemophilia. The budget ax also lopped 30 percent off the subsidy for another important item, community health centers, which provide free neighborhood medical treatment to indigent mothers and their children. This amounted to another expression of indifference to the issue of congenital abnormality, because the offspring of the poor are more likely to be premature and birth impaired.

In the same session, once more at Reagan's behest, Congress cut Medicaid allocations by $866 million, forcing state public-aid agencies to impose severe restrictions on how much they would reimburse hospitals for poor people's medical claims. This action came on the heels of Reagan-dictated alterations in the Aid to Families with Dependent Children cash assistance program. The changes compelled states to tighten eligibility standards for public aid, which in turn caused hundreds of thousands of people to lose their Medicaid benefits. Because the majority of AFDC recipients are children, they have naturally felt the greatest impact. According to one estimate, nearly 700,000 children nationwide have lost their Medicaid coverage because of AFDC revisions. Virtually all of these children are from families well below the poverty line, and many of them are chronically ill.

Since then Congress has continued its Spartan regimen. In fiscal year 1984, Title V programs received an appropriation of only $399 million, still 20 percent below their 1981 level. Meanwhile, funds for the federal developmental-disabilities program have been frozen at a $60 million level for the past five years. In fact, the $62.1 million appropriation in 1984 was actually less than the 1980 appropriation of $62.4 million. The federal budget office has estimated that when inflation is factored in, the developmental-disabilities program has suffered a 43 percent cut in actual buying power in those five years. The program is crucial to the welfare of retarded children and adults, providing funding for vocational education, employment services, community-living projects, and the training of developmental therapists. It also supports a protection and advocacy system whose mission is to safeguard the rights of the mentally disabled, particularly against abuses in large institutions. The advocacy system has recently been granted authority to obtain the records of clients who are housed in institutions and who are without legal guardians; yet, without money to pay for investigators, the prerogative is useless. The developmental-disabilities program also provides counseling and guidance to the parents of the disabled, helping them find appropriate facilities for their offspring. In mid-1984 Sen. Lowell Weicker, a Connecticut Republican, himself the father of a Down's syndrome child, proposed legislation to raise the funding level for developmental disabilities to $82.1 million in 1985. Much of the increase would go for a new emphasis on adult services and non-sheltered employment. But as of this writing the bill's chances of success in a year of giant budget deficits were unknown.

Every one of these cuts affects the treatment or prevention of handicaps. Considering that most, if not all, of the reductions were orchestrated by Ronald Reagan, one must again ask how such an administration can legitimately claim to be the defender of disabled infants. To insist that life be extended medically and then to withdraw the necessary social services to nurture that life seems patently hypocritical.

It is instructive to take a closer look at this belt-tightening. Among the major casualties have been the state-run cripped children's programs, which minister to youngsters who suffer from a wide variety of congenital defects, including cardiac malformations, central-nervous-system disorders, single-gene defects, and orthopedic ailments. These agencies serve a triple purpose. Their first function is to provide diagnostic and referral services, advising parents on what is wrong with their child and where to obtain the best medical care. Their second function is to provide family counseling when the child is causing domestic strain. Third, they sometimes defray the cost of treatment if the client is of modest income and has no Medicaid card or private insurance. Demand for the agencies' services has been multiplying during these recessionary times, as more people become unemployed and lose their health insurance and as harsher eligibility requirements throw the poor off of Medicaid. One state program reported an 8 percent increase in the number of clients who had lost private health insurance in 1983. But, ironically, at the same time their caseload is rising, crippled children's programs are staggering from severe cutbacks.

Each agency has met the crisis in a different way. Montana was forced to eliminate the treatment of all gastrointestinal defects, limit the treatment of cleft palate and cystic fibrosis, and cut out all follow-up care for neurological problems and hydrocephalus. In addition, physical, occupational, and speech therapies were curtailed. South Carolina tightened its income test for eligibility and reduced the qualifying age from 21 to 18, excluding from further services 1,585 children who had been on the rolls. Alabama reduced its age of eligibility from 21 to 19, excluding some 1,200 disabled young people from assistance. Illinois put a $15,000 ceiling on what it will pay for a child in any one year, and it no longer will take any children whose defects can be corrected with one surgery. Idaho instituted a 10-day limit on the length of hospital stay it would cover (there was formerly no limit), then had to retrench after a newborn with serious cardiac defects ran up a $37,000 hospital bill in the first 10 days of its life (it died five days later). The new limit became 10 days or $10,000, whichever came first. Finally, in 1983, when Congress made emergency Title V funding available to the states on a one-time basis through the jobs bill, Idaho was able to raise its ceiling to 15 days or $15,000. Colorado was especially hard hit. In March of 1983 it ran out of crippled children's money completely and for at least four months, until the jobs bill money became available, it had to refuse to fund all surgeries and hospitalizations for disabled children. Dozens of low-income families were forced either to find alternate sources of funding, to pay for the treatment themselves, or, most likely, to postpone the procedures until money became available. Colorado also ran out of funding for its special newborn-care program, which focuses on cardiac problems, gastrointestinal problems, and respiratory distress syndrome. From October 1982 until June 1983, the state could not assist parents of newborns financially. Since neonates need immediate care, parents could not postpone procedures and were forced to bear the immense cost of hospitalization themselves.

Other Title V cuts have caused extensive dislocations of their own. Particularly hurt have been programs that provide free prenatal care and nutritional advice to low-income women. Good medical treatment during pregnancy is, of course, a prerequisite for the prevention of prematurity and low birthweight, two primary contributors to birth defects. Yet, 44 states have been forced to drastically scale back these services. In 1982–83, Michigan was forced to close three large maternity, child, and infant care clinics in Detroit. This adversely affected 6,000 pregnant women and robbed 11,000 young children of their primary medical care. The state also phased out its Improved Pregnancy Outcome project. Arizona was forced to eliminate free prenatal services in all but one county, depriving some 800 pregnant women of care. These women are responsible for 2 percent of Arizona's 50,000 annual births, and because they are poor, they will add disproportionately to the 3,500 low-birthweight babies born in the state each year. Alabama was compelled to close six maternity, child, and infant care clinics, a move that affected 10,000 women. The state also dropped its Improved Pregnancy Care project. And Chicago, with one of the highest infant mortality rates among American cities, closed its only hospital for low-income teenage unwed mothers and shut a maternity and infant care clinic that served 16,000 pregnant women.

In a move that drew national attention, a U.S. Department of Health and Human Services review commission decided in 1983 not to renew the funding of three juvenile-amputee clinics, including the renowned Area Child Amputee Center in Grand Rapids, Michigan, and facilities at UCLA and New York University. The Grand Rapids center, which was founded in 1955, pioneered in the care and management of the juvenile amputee. It receives referrals from throughout the nation and handles a caseload of 300 children annually. When the Associated Press learned of the closings and circulated the story over its news wires, the issue landed on President Reagan's desk. The administration, red-faced, quickly reversed itself and restored funding. It is interesting that the Grand Rapids center received federal funding of $245,000 when it opened thirty years ago. Today it scrapes by on only $225,000.

The episode prompted Jeffrey Taylor, Michigan's chief of the division of maternal and child health, to remark, "It makes me wonder if they want to put the kids back on skateboards, selling pencils. I can't believe it."

But the Medicaid restrictions are by far the most disturbing, for it is Medicaid that is the primary source of financing for the health care of poor women and their children. If one is unable to qualify for assistance, and yet is too destitute to personally afford the cost of treatment or medicine, one is in a position fraught with danger. Many people in these circumstances end up not seeing a doctor until it is too late.

Thousands of impoverished people have been dismissed from the Medicaid rolls by the states. New Jersey, for example, eliminated 35,000 recipients in 1981 as a result of AFDC eligibility changes. Sixty percent of these were children. Oklahoma disqualifed 17,000 children, and New York disqualified 11,000. A number of states, including Alabama and Florida, will no longer qualify two-parent households for Medicaid, no matter how low the family income, unless one of the parents is incapacitated. It is an undocumented, but unquestioned, fact that able-bodied fathers are forced to leave home so that a sick child can qualify for assistance. Other states have medically needy, unemployed-parent, or under-21 programs that may extend Medicaid coverage to two-parent homes, but the income ceiling for eligibility is unrealistically low. For example, Arkansas has an under-21 program, which is designed to provide free medical care to children but not to adults in an intact household. In order to qualify, however, a family of three has to earn less than $225 a month, which is $2,700, a year. A couple that earns $3,000 a year could not get medical care for its youngster no matter how sick the child might be. Arizona has a medically needy program, but the parents must earn less than $4,300 for a family of three. The Children's Defense Fund, a Washington-based child advocacy organization, reports that in some states 50 percent of the families making less than $6,000 a year (the U.S. poverty line in 1982 was $7,690) are ineligible for coverage because both parents live in the home. The lack of access to Medicaid can be best brought home by this: as the 1983 recession brought an estimated 18 percent more children under the definition of poverty, the number of children qualifying for Medicaid coverage actually *dropped* an estimated 12 percent.

Sara Rosenbaum and Judith Weitz, of the Children's Defense Fund, have tried to calculate the human cost of these budget cuts. They found that in parts of Detroit, where unemployment is rampant and where Medicaid coverage has been seriously curtailed, the infant mortality rate stands at 33 per 1,000 births, almost equal to that of Nicaragua. By contrast, the overall U.S. infant mortality rate is 11.2. Presumably, mothers and children in these neighborhoods, owing to their financial plight, have diminished access to medical care and good nutrition in the months before and after birth. As a result, many babies die. To illustrate the connection between prenatal care and infant death, the Children's Defense Fund reports that one percent of all Detroit mothers who gave birth in 1979 did not see a doctor until the day of their delivery. Among these woman the infant mortality rate was 88 percent. Meanwhile, in Jersey City, New Jersey, where economic conditions are similar to those in Detroit and where Medicaid availability has also been substantially reduced, the infant death rate rose from 12.8 percent in 1981 to 24.3 in 1982, a 90 percent increase in one year. Rosenbaum and Weitz allege that since 1978 there has been a steady shift among the poor away from early prenatal care and toward late (third-trimester) care or no care whatsoever. The rate of late or no care among minority women has risen by 63 percent in Florida, 29 percent in South Carolina, and 34 percent in New York State. The situation has become so bad in New York, says the Children's Defense Fund, that one minority woman in five received late or no prenatal care in 1982.

It seems, then, that we have created a self-defeating scenario. Poor women are being discouraged from seeking prenatal care by its unavailability and by their inability to pay for it. Consequently, they will have more low-birthweight and disabled babies. If we then make it harder for these infants to get proper medical attention after birth, we are assuring that any motor deficits and retardation they have will get worse. At least some of them will survive to become a long-range burden to society. With estimates for a lifetime of institutional care now running in excess of $1 million, it does not seem very cost-effective to economize on maternal and child health care. One hundred retarded babies would obliterate all the savings.

"This country sees the trees, but not the forest," complains Rosenbaum. "We have developed amazing lifesaving operations to save premature and sick babies. But we've not been energetic in investing in preventive services to avoid some of these tragedies. Prenatal care costs $1,500, counting routine medical visits and delivery. A complete food package for pregnant women costs $30 a month. But it costs $1,000 a day to grow a baby in an incubator. Would you rather grow a baby in his mother's stomach or an incubator?"

America's equivocation in applying its full resources to treating and preventing birth defects, and to bettering the lives of the handicapped, has had concrete and disturbing results.

In New York State, for instance, the deinstitutionalization program has come a cropper. More than a decade ago a federal class action suit was filed against New York officials demanding they reduce the resident population at a Staten Island state hospital called Willowbrook. Conditions were incredible. Retarded people were lying naked on the floors, feces were smeared on the walls, and more than 5,000 patients were crammed into a facility that should not have housed more than 1,200. In 1975 New York signed a consent decree under which it agreed to reduce the size of the institution to 250 inmates by 1981 and to move the rest of the patient population into community-based living facilities. These residences—which would utilize apartment buildings and small, converted nursing homes—were to contain no more than 6 to 10 patients per unit, in line with the prevailing expert opinion that the handicapped do better, and often blossom, when they live in as close to a normal environment as possible. A special review panel of distinguished psychologists that was established to oversee the deinstitutionalization effort believed that even smaller units, consisting of just 3 patients, were the optimal living arrangement.

New York was so committed to the project that it decided to make the consent decree apply to all the institutions in the state. In the past nine years, thousands of inmates have been discharged from New York's 20 state hospitals for the retarded, lowering the total patient census from 20,000 to 11,500. But the state has not planned for this exodus properly. In order to keep the inmate count in constant decline, it has forbidden new admissions to the state hospitals. Unfortunately, there are not enough beds available in community facilities to handle both the discharged patients and the new applicants. Hence, thousands of New York parents have had to keep their severely handicapped children at home, even though the children's conditions desperately warrant institutional care. According to Arthur Webb, commissioner of the New York Office of Mental Retardation, the state will need 9,000 new community beds by 1995 to handle the demand for services. At the moment, there is a waiting list of approximately 1,000 families.

Acquiring more community living arrangements, however, is going to be a difficult task. The New York City housing market is the tightest in the nation. Rents in the nicer areas of town have been pushed up to prohibitive levels. The state has thus been constrained to lease buildings in the city's seamiest sections, which has posed considerable security problems and dampened the enthusiasm of the staff who must work there. Another source of worry surrounds those living units containing only three residents. The Office of Retardation has found them too expensive to run, in that it is impossible to effect economies of scale. Webb had begun to phase them out in favor of 8- to 10-bed units when the independent review panel obtained a restraining order to stop him. The psychologists like the 3-bed arrangement. The final indignity is that the state has long since failed to meet the 1981 deadline for scaling Willowbrook down to 250 patients. One thousand inmates are still domiciled there.

"It is terrible how we deal with social problems in this country," says Leslie Park, executive director of United Cerebral Palsy of New York City. "If the Defense Department wants to buy a new tank, they first try it out before they place an order for 500. But we almost never do that in social welfare situations. We jump right in without any studies. State institutions are too big? Well, we'll throw [the patients] into the community then. But nobody stopped to realize that you don't know what you're getting in a community program. They've had to put facilities into places where people are afraid to even go out at night,

where they can't get good staff. The result is it can be a worse situation for a retarded person than any state institution."

In Illinois the drying-up of funds has had a dire effect on a number
of programs. One of these is the Illinois Institute for Developmental
Disabilities, a large service, training, and research facility for the
retarded, located on Chicago's near West Side. The Institute has
undergone a gradual erosion of its mandate over the last few years.
Eight years ago it had a residential wing, but this was discontinued
for economic reasons. Within the past year alone the facility has had
to cope with funding cuts of 10 to 20 percent. It is now limping along,
with barely enough money to pay its heating bills, and there is talk of
having to close it down. The hardest hit of its programs is its diagnostic center, which is the only state-run project of its kind in Chicago
and surrounding counties, a region that is home to almost 7 million
people. The diagnostic center offers parents complete medical eval-
uations of their retarded children, calling on the services of neurologists, psychologists, hearing specialists, bone specialists, dentists, and
eye doctors. The staff determines the child's level of retardation and
then recommends a program of special education, vocational training, and physical therapy that is tailored to the youngster's needs. It
is all done free of charge. The center performs an important function, and its director, Dr. Edward Page-El, is justly proud. Imagine,
then, his dismay when in the 1983 budget he found his allocation for
salaries cut in half, from $500,000 to $250,000. It was a near disaster.
In the next few months, Page-El was forced to cut his staff from 26
employees to 13, losing, among others, a full-time physician, an
audiologist, and a number of social workers. "Whenever there's a fiscal crisis in the state, it's always programs for the mentally disabled
that get hurt first," laments Page-El.

Special education, which is the jewel of America's commitment to
the handicapped, is also facing an uncertain future. It is suffering
from the same problem that education in general is experiencing,
namely, a lack of funds. Fortunately, its fundamental provisions are
written into the law requiring school districts to provide free education to the disabled. Such costly procedures as the expert evaluation
of each handicapped pupil and the drafting of instructional programs
tailored to individual needs are inviolable items and may not be trimmed
from the budget. Another advantage distinguishes special education
from more endangered programs for the disabled—it has a large
upper-middle-class constituency. A substantial number of children
enrolled in special-ed classes are the sons and daughters of affluence.
This inevitably gives it more clout in Washington and in state capitals
than programs like Medicaid and crippled children's, which are spe-

cifically aimed at the poor. Nonetheless, there is a burgeoning backlash in several state legislatures, where it is felt that enough money
has been spent on educating the handicapped and that it is time to
pay more attention to normal children.

Working with budgets that have been frozen for up to four years,
special-education districts are employing various stratagems for saving money, most of which are detrimental to the students. For example, some states are using a tougher definition of who is eligible for
special education. By stipulating that there must be a medically
acceptable diagnosis of disability, a great many learning-disabled children—so-called slow-learners—may be excluded. In addition, though
expert evaluation of a child's disability is required by statute, nothing
in the law dictates how many experts must participate. Consequently,
districts are cutting back on the number of specialists they use. Teaching professionals are mandated, too, but nothing says they have to
have master's degrees in special education. Districts are thus opting
for teachers with lesser credentials. The most widely used strategy,
however, is simply to hire fewer teachers and increase the teacher-
student ratio. For obvious reasons, this is not in the child's interest,
because any youngster, particularly one who suffers from intellectual
or physical deficits, learns better in smaller classes.

"Where special ed is concerned, you can either do a Cadillac or a
Volkswagen version," says John Butler, a developmental psychologist
at Harvard Children's Hospital in Boston, who is conducting a study
of special-education students in five cities. "Many states are going the
VW route," he says.

In California, special-education funds have been frozen for nearly
three years, although new residents continue to pour into the state at
the rate of 1,000 a day. Fifteen to 20 of these newcomers are disabled
children requiring special education. To accommodate this swelling
enrollment, districts have had to increase class sizes significantly, from
an average of 10 handicapped students per teacher to as many as 20.
Revised eligibility standards have been invoked to disqualify slow
learners and give priority to the medically disabled. Meanwhile, districts have had to cut payrolls to meet their rising costs. Los Angeles
County was forced to lay off more than 300 special-education administrators and Santa Clara County approximately 70—this in a state
that expends more money on special education than any other in the
nation. In 1983 California spent $1.4 billion to educate 365,000 spe-
cial-education students, 40,000 of them severely disabled. Other states,
with less money and perhaps less commitment, are making even more
revisions.

"Everything's relative," says California's special-education director,

Lou Barber. "Given what we could be doing, it's not utopia. But we're doing better than some."

Of all the ways in which the United States neglects handicapped children and their families, none is as grotesque as the failure to protect parents against catastrophic medical expenses. Impaired children will often require a huge amount of medical attention. As we have seen, some of them have abnormalities that call for a series of corrective surgeries, or they are subject to periodic acute episodes necessitating frequent short-term hospitalizations. Other children have chronic incapacitating conditions that demand continuous and elaborate care. These children generally must remain in long-term facilities, either hospitals, state institutions, or private skilled-nursing homes, although some are treated at home by their parents. Whichever mode of treatment applies to a child, it is exorbitantly expensive. A string of surgeries for myelomeningocele, for example, can easily top $200,000. Hospital charges for pediatric intensive care are currently in the range of $800 to $1,500 a day, depending on the degree of service rendered. And the cost of maintaining a child in a residential institution is currently running between $22,000 and $37,000 a year.

Society has evolved an incoherent and completely inadequate system of helping parents cope with these enormous expenditures. The financial supports that do exist either were devised to suit an earlier era, when medical and living costs were far below what they are now, or were intended as a safety net for the very poor, with scarcely a thought given to people of higher incomes. Furthermore, these supports make up a bewildering patchwork that varies from state to state. Within each state, programs exist inside a vacuum; there is little attempt to make them interlock, which leaves whole categories of conditions and entire economic classes to fall between the cracks. Scant effort is made to inform the general public as to what kinds of financial aid are available, so that parents seeking assistance are forced to stumble through a bureaucratic maze.

In general, state governments are more supportive in defraying the costs of long-term residential care than in assisting with hospital bills, which tend to be more volatile. Most states will pick up all or the lion's share of the annual cost of institutionalizing a child, in private as well as in state facilites. But there is a severe shortage of such residences, and waiting lists are usually quite long.

As far as hospital expenses are concerned, there is a potpourri of state programs for parents who lack adequate health insurance, but these programs reimburse the hospitals only to a limited extent, and they are very choosy about which families qualify. Many states have what are called perinatal programs, which will pay neonatal intensive-care charges for the first 30 days of life. But they require a financial-means test, and parents over a certain income limit are not eligible for full aid, even if they have no health insurance. And 30 days means 30 days. If parents wait until their child is 10 days old to apply, the perinatal program will pay only for the next 20 days. After the 30th day other arrangements must be made. The next step might be to contact the state crippled children's program. These programs, though, are selective as to which diagnoses they will underwrite, and they are excluding more and more conditions as money grows scarcer. One state, for instance, will not care for children with asthma, diabetes, chronic lung disorders, liver and other abdominal conditions, and kidney or bladder disorders. Crippled children's agencies are grossly underfinanced, with annual budgets of generally less than $13 million, budgets that in some larger states must be stretched to service as many as 40,000 children. Thus, these agencies, too, exercise a stringent means test and will try to exhaust alternative avenues of financial help before stepping in with cash. The usual place they send parents to is Medicaid. But Medicaid has the stiffest financial-eligibility requirements of all. Couples may still receive aid if their incomes exceed certain limits, but it will necessitate using up most of their own resources first. They will have to drain their savings account, sell off any stocks or bonds, sell any income property they may own, and consign a confiscatory portion of their incomes over to the state. If they are still too affluent for Medicaid, they will have to work out a debt payment schedule with the hospital, which will require them, just as Medicaid does, to liquidate a major portion of their personal assets. Some hospitals insist on a large deposit before they will continue to treat a child.

Parents are put in similar straits when they try to obtain costly rehabilitation items for their children, such as wheelchairs or leg braces. A good wheelchair may cost up to $600. If the parents lack adequate insurance, or if the insurance has run out, as often happens, they have essentially three options. They can try to get their state crippled children's program to pay for the chair, if their income is low enough. Or they may turn to one of the voluntary charitable agencies, such as Easter Seals or United Cerebral Palsy, which will sometimes help. More than likely, however, they will have to pay for it themselves.

In a curious way, a person in extreme poverty is more insulated from the devastating expense of raising a handicapped child than are the working poor and the middle class. Society is geared up, however insufficiently, to help the poor meet these exigencies. Various instruments are in place, including Medicaid, Social Security disability payments, and crippled children's programs. Alarmingly, however, even these props are becoming undependable, as the safety net for the poor is systematically dismantled by current governmental policy. In any case, none of these programs are structured with the higher-income family in mind. This amounts to a national scandal.

The fact is that middle-class families in the United States face economic disaster if they have a severely disabled child requiring extensive medical treatment. America's method of assisting them is to gut their households and divest them of nearly every asset they have worked years to acquire, the avowed and inexplicable purpose being to reduce them to poverty. And this is done with a zeal approaching the punitive, as if it were somehow a family's fault that it conceived an impaired child, or as if having a few luxuries were a sin. The following case history illustrates the point.

Chuck Frame is a victim of the American dream in reverse. Five years ago he was an up-and-coming entrepreneur with a pleasant middle-income way of life. He owned his own business, a typesetting and graphic-arts firm that he had built up from scratch over the course of eight years. He had seen it grow from a part-time scheme that he operated out of his bedroom to a full-fledged enterprise based in downtown Chicago. The salary he paid himself was $24,000 a year, with the promise of a lot more.

Then, almost overnight, Frame found his world turned upside down. He was forced to give up his typesetting firm and, with his wife and three children, was obliged to begin living at the poverty level. Was this the result of a business miscalculation on Frame's part, or some regrettable caprice of the marketplace? Incredibly enough, it was the result of an intentional governmental policy.

One of Frame's children, Melissa, aged eight, is partially paralyzed, because of a birth injury to one of her neck vertebrae. She has the use of her arms but no control over her body from the chest down. Among the anatomical functions affected is her breathing. Her ability to sustain her own respiration has slowly deteriorated since infancy, so that when she turned five, it became necessary to place her permanently on a mechanical ventilator.

So refined have these machines become that it is now possible for ventilator-dependent children to be cared for at home and thus live a semblance of a normal life. This is the option the Frames chose, rather than leave Melissa in a hospital intensive-care ward. But it involved turning their apartment into a miniature intensive-care unit. To do so there must be adequate space for the ventilator and backup equipment, and a private nurse must be on duty at all times to adjust the settings, suction out the child's windpipe, and apply resuscitation in emergencies. The cost of this home care is steep—on the average, it runs approximately $8,000 a month.

The Frames were in a bind: They were obviously unable to afford such a sum on their own, and their health coverage on Melissa had long since run out. There was no alternative but to apply to the state for Medicaid. But the public-aid department told the Frames that since the family was over the poverty line, they would be subject to a concept called a spend-down. Under the spend-down system, which is employed in many states, a family is allowed to keep a certain meager amount of its income for food, rent, clothing, and other essentials. The rest, no matter how much or how little, must be surrendered to the public-aid department or spent directly on medical bills. On top of that, the family is required to empty out its savings account and convert most of its assets to cash, all of which must similarly be applied to medical expenses. In other words, the state isn't satisfied until applicants have been practically picked clean.

In the Frames' case, as a family of five, they were entitled to hold out $436 a month on which to live. On the basis of Chuck's monthly take-home pay of approximately $1,800, from which he was permitted to deduct another small amount for transportation to and from work, the Frames were compelled to reimburse the public-aid department at a rate of $1,200 each month. This amounted to 60 percent of Frame's *pretax* earnings! It was to be turned over as a lump sum every six months. If these requirements were met, the remainder of Melissa's medical bills would then be defrayed by public aid.

Two thoughts occurred to Frame. First, $436 was just not enough for five people to live on at current prices. It comes to $2.90 per family member a day, or about enough to buy lunch. Yet out of that would somehow have to come everything, from rent and shoes to the gas and electric bills. Second, why work day in and day out to produce money you are going to give away, when you can spend the time better doing things like growing food, making clothes, and doing your own carpentry, the better to survive on such a pittance? After some agonizing thought, Frame came to the conclusion that there was only one thing for him to do—he had to dissolve his printing business and stay at home. Meanwhile, his wife, Doreen, went to work to earn the $436 a month they were allowed.

"It is very strange," says Frame. "Why should we have to become low-income people to fit under the state's guidelines, all because Melissa happened to be born into our family? I can't understand it. It isn't very cost-effective from the state's point of view, making me quit my business. We were paying more in taxes when I was able to work than they get out of us in the spend-down."

For two years, the Frames lived at a subsistence level. They were able to keep their apartment only because the landlord was a personal friend and gave it to them at a rock-bottom price. Much of the food they ate came from their garden. Frame had to sell his $4,000 Volvo in favor of a $600 van, which he says was held together by his own sweat. They lost their own health insurance because they could not manage the premiums. When their two-year-old daughter caught the croup, they couldn't afford a doctor and had to rely on free medical advice. They rode bikes almost everywhere they went to save on gasoline; they bought no clothes and never had a night out. It is the kind of sudden loss of status that 19th-century novelists were forever writing about. One does not expect to encounter it in 20th-century American life.

Finally, when things looked the bleakest for the Frames, a path out of purgatory appeared. Under a new congressional ruling, states have the option to waive the income test for Medicaid eligibility. The option is restricted, however, to certain narrowly defined situations. The child must be so chronically disabled as to need constant hospital-like care; it must be possible to treat the youngster as well and more cheaply at home; and the family must have no insurance. If all three provisos are met, Medicaid will pick up the entire cost of home care without a spend-down. The ruling came about in a serendipitous way. During a November 1981 tour of Iowa, Vice-President George Bush encountered the case of a chronically ill Cedar Rapids girl named Katie Beckett, who had been confined to a hospital since she was four months old. Her parents, a lumber salesman and his wife, wanted to take the three-year-old child home, but Medicaid, which was perfectly content to pay her $12,000-a-month hospital bill, said it would not pick up her $2,000-a-month bill for home care. The upshot was that the Becketts couldn't afford their daughter's upkeep and that she had to remain in the hospital. Flying in the face of logic, the state was studiously rejecting a way to save the taxpayers $10,000 a month. Troubled by this bureaucratic inflexibility, Bush passed his concern along to President Reagan, who, reacting angrily, ordered an exception to be made in the Medicaid regulations so that Katie could go home. In late 1982 Congress voted to allow state Medicaid agencies to pay for home care in similar cases if they wished, ruling that the aid need not be contingent on the parents' income. This "waiver" of the means test for Medicaid eligibility has become known as the Katie Beckett rule. For the Frames, it was a godsend. The family was recently approved for 100 percent Medicaid coverage without a spend-down.

But the new waiver has not been adopted by all states. Moreover, it pertains to only a small class of families. As of this writing, fewer than 50 families have been helped under its provisions in even the largest states. The circumstances must almost exactly parallel the case of Katie Beckett for a family to qualify. This smacks of concretist thinking, and it does little to offset the financial agonies of thousands upon thousands of Americans whose impaired youngsters do not quite meet the criteria.

The rationale for not providing a safety net for people in higher income brackets is that they have more money and that they are more apt to have private health insurance. The fallacy in this line of reasoning is that no amount of income is a sufficient hedge against medical expenses that can easily top $100,000 and sometimes go over $1 million. Where these crushing bills are concerned, everyone short of a Rockefeller must be considered poor. As for the assumption that middle-class people invariably have insurance, it is erroneous on several counts. To begin with, not everybody signs up for coverage, and not everybody always purchases the right kind. Chuck Frame had Blue Cross, but he had injudiciously elected not to carry major-medical coverage. Other people take out policies that will pay expenses up to a certain limit, say $100,000. Beyond the limit the bill becomes the family's obligation. Finally, it is folly to think that anybody's insurance benefits are permanent. With people constantly being laid off during periods of economic crisis and losing their company-paid coverage, and with businesses winning concessions from their unions that involve a loss of health benefits, anyone could be left insurance-naked at any time. It strikes me as unjust, then, to predicate policy toward middle-income people based on some mythical immunity to economic shock that they supposedly enjoy. And it seems reprehensible to say that they cannot get government assistance unless they are first transformed into paupers.

"The middle class gets it in the neck," says Gene Bilotti, who is administrator of disabled children's programs in Illinois. "If a family making $40,000 a year has a child with a severe disability, we first bring them to their knees financially, and then, when they are bankrupt and without money, that's when we finally say, 'Now, we'll help you.' "

In 1984 a bill went before Congress that offered some hope of erasing these injustices. Sponsored by Sen. John Chafee, a Rhode Island Republican, the bill would allow states to qualify people for Medicaid, regardless of their financial level, if they spend more than 5 percent of their gross annual income on services for their handicapped child. It must be pointed out, however, that states would not be compelled to do this; they would merely have the option, which they lack now. Money for this expansion of Medicaid services would presumably come from the bill's other primary provision, which directs states to relocate their retarded or severely disabled population into small community group homes whose size would be no more than three times the average family size in a particular neighborhood. The bill would encourage this relocation by earmarking federal funds so that they must be used for group homes instead of to support large state institutions. It is common wisdom that group homes are not only better psychologically for the disabled person, but significantly less expensive to operate than big institutions. Hence, whatever savings were realized by the switchover could then be applied to help parents with their medical expenses. As the Chafee bill reached the hearing stage, intense opposition was building up against it from parents' groups, who feel their children would be better served by being left in the institutions. They fear the impermanency of the community living arrangements and the lack of structure. This opposition may defeat the bill, in which case the Medicaid provision will die along with the deinstitutionalization plan.

Americans would do well to emulate the paradigm of several societies that are far more supportive of the disabled and their families. In Great Britain, for example, a handicapped child's medical costs are the obligation of the state, as might be expected under a socialized system of medicine. But there is also a considerable array of supplementary services that the government provides free of charge to Britain's five million disabled people. Wheelchairs, artificial limbs, sip-and-puff devices, and other special equipment fall into this category, as do some prescription drugs. There are, in addition, several major allowances for which families with handicapped offspring are eligible, regardless of their income. One of these, called the attendance allowance, is for children and adults who require constant supervision. Another, called the invalid-care allowance, is intended to compensate families for the lost earnings involved in raising the child, as well as for certain hidden expenses, which were well outlined by E. C. Gilchrist, of Britain:

"[T]here may be considerable wear and tear on clothes (particularly shoes) from deviant walking patterns or from [leg braces]; expense of many pounds per week may be incurred in visiting a child in hospital or in frequent outpatient attendances; . . . there may be need for washing and drying machines where a child is incontinent, and a family may have urgent need of a car (or a second car for the mother's use) because of the limitations on the whole family of the handicap of one member."

A third available grant is called the mobility allowance and is for all people aged five years and up who are unable or virtually unable to walk. Paid weekly, it is designed to assist them with transportation costs. An independent organization named Motability helps disabled people who want to use their mobility allowance to buy a vehicle. There is also a government family fund that was established to provide these families with assistance they cannot get under other programs; for instance, a grant might be applied toward a car purchase, an alteration to the home, laundry equipment, special furniture or bedding, and vacation expenses.

The state's concern is not limited to financial assistance. Social workers are on call to help a family work through the intense emotional distress of raising an impaired youngster, or with more practical problems, such as how to adapt the home to the child's requirements. Free domestic help is available in times of special need, as when the other children in a household have fallen ill or during a woman's subsequent pregnancies. The British government also provides a free system of day care, transporting the children each morning to a center, where they receive education, physical therapy, and psychological counseling individually designed for each child's specific needs. Furthermore, there is a flourishing system of "respite" care, which permits parents to domicile their severely disabled children by the day or week and gain time for personal activities or a vacation. As of 1979 there were 2,050 beds designated for respite care in Britain's 86 facilities for disabled children and adolescents. The goal is 8,000. (Some parts of the United States are now experimenting with respite care too.)

Services are similarly progressive in Sweden. Everything from medical treatment, surgery, and drugs to day care, special equipment, transportation, and housing is supplied free of charge by the state. Home care is considered the ideal, and strong community support of the family is mustered to promote this end. Parents are paid a generous annual stipend to keep their children at home. And a network of small, comfortable group homes is also in place, should institutionalization be necessary. Among Sweden's most dramatic programs is one that grants parents up to 60 days of paid work leave to allow them to be at the bedside of their hospitalized child. If the youngster happens to die, burial is at state expense. To encourage hiring of the handicapped, the state provides incentives to employers in the form of economic subsidies. In addition, the state and local governments have instituted a bold plan in which the disabled are provided with personal assistants who help them get to work, go to school, and handle various tasks in the home. There are up to 70,000 of these attendants in Sweden, serving 350,000 disabled people. The program does have its critics: some contend that it encourages the handicapped to do less for themselves. But, by and large, it seems to have been a success. Meanwhile, the government provides housing for the disabled in apartment buildings called *koncentrat* or *Fokus* housing. Typically, a *koncentrat* consists of 6 to 15 specially designed units scattered throughout an apartment complex of 100 to 200 units. The government leases the apartments to disabled people and their families. Home samaritans, as attendants are known, are on call 24 hours a day, working out of a staff office on the premises.

In Australia an admirable system of vocational and rehabilitation training has evolved. Large, modern rehabilitation centers help physically and mentally impaired people improve their physical, social, and occupational functioning. Besides providing medical services—including speech therapy, physiotherapy, and psychological counseling—these centers teach basic work habits, tool usage, and independent-living skills. There are also work adjustment centers, which provide a transitional setting to prepare more advanced individuals for the labor market. Contract work is performed, involving the manufacture of items like leather belts, luggage racks, and tents. And the Australians have cleverly improved upon the sheltered-workshop concept. Instead of taking the familiar form of an unproductive assembly line made up exclusively of retarded people, the Australian plan mixes the disabled in with normal workers to create a thriving business. One firm reportedly has 1,200 employees, of whom 200 are severely disabled. The dual goal of helping the handicapped and making enough money to support their care is thus achieved.

As these examples show, it is possible to treat the disabled and their loved ones more humanely than is the current practice in the United States. Isn't it time Americans learned that lesson? It exposes the bombast behind our sanctity-of-life pretensions when we cannot provide better existences for the congenitally impaired babies whose lives we insist be saved.

11

The High Cost of Saving Babies

In the end, the issue of whether to let defective babies die may be solved, not by the elegant arguments of ethicists or by rhetoric in a court of law, but by the grim realities of the marketplace. The rising cost of medical treatment is placing a tremendous burden on society's resources. Americans spent $322 billion on health care in 1982, or 10.5 percent of the gross national product, up from 5.3 percent in 1960. These expenditures continue to mount at a rate of nearly 13 percent a year, far above the pace of inflation. Canada does slightly better, spending just 8 percent of its GNP on health, but only a tough stance on the part of the government has been able to hold the line. Given all of the other commitments society professes to have, from housing to education and national defense, and given the size of federal deficits, one wonders how long we can go on this way. It is possible that we are near a day of reckoning, when it will be necessary to decide how much money we want to spend on what kinds of medical care and for whom.

Since treating birth defects is a particularly expensive form of medicine, it is almost certain to come under scrutiny in the years ahead. The hospital bill for a very low birthweight infant or a child with severe anomalies often exceeds $100,000 in the first few weeks of life alone, a sum that is well beyond most parents' means. The intercession of insurance carriers and governmental agencies is thus assured. A number of authorities have already begun to question the wisdom of spending so much of the public's money on so few patients when the success rate is rather low. One of these critics, Dr. William H. Kirkley, of Fort Lauderdale, Florida, made the issue the subject of his presidential address at the 1980 conference of the South Atlantic Association of Obstetricians and Gynecologists.

"When one goes into an Intensive Care Nursery," said Kirkley, "he will almost always find a group of dedicated people who have as their goal survival of the neonate. . . . Their every effort is toward that accomplishment. Whether or not the infant has a congenital anomaly is secondary. No thought is given to the fact that it will probably die and the parents will have spent thousands of dollars for naught or, worse still, will have spent thousands of dollars and countless hours in anxiety only to have a less than normal child survive. Somewhere this latter possibility must be taken into consideration.

"We are all finally reaching the point of realizing that this country does not have unlimited funds for medical purposes and certainly our patients do not. Thus priorities must be set, and some thought must be given to economics, even though economics is a very emotional factor when priorities are being set on human life."

Terrance Swanson, professor of law at Indiana University, has urged that instead of bending all medical efforts to save children with Down's syndrome, the United States should adopt a mass screening and abortion program to reduce the incidence of the disorder. He hypothesized that it could save the country as much as $100 billion in custodial-care costs over 20 years. Swanson said, "If we allow our genetic problems to get out of hand by not acting promptly to ameliorate the situation, we as a society run the risk of over-committing ourselves to the care and maintenance of a large population of mentally deficient patients at the expense of other urgent social programs."

Although many might consider it unseemly to speak in the same breath of saving money and of saving human life, the issue appears likely to gain momentum as the cost of sustaining birth-impaired people accelerates. Before we get into the specifics of what society spends on congenital disability each year, however, it would be useful to take a moment to examine the total picture with respect to health care costs.

Approximately one out of six Americans was admitted to a hospital in 1979, an average of 100,000 people a day, or 37 million admissions. That was a 26 percent increase over 1969. Thus, the utilization of hospital services grew more than twice as fast as the population, which increased by only 11 percent in the same period. Americans also made more than 1 billion visits to physicians' offices in 1979, averaging 4.7 visits per person. The United States is a very well doctored society, which is as it should be. But it must not be forgotten that each office visit, each hospital procedure, has to be paid for.

Since 70 percent of all medical fees are picked up by third-party payers, none of those directly involved in treatment have had much to lose from making the most prodigal use of health resources. Bills are mailed off to some impersonal patron who, until recently, has approved them with only moderate complaint. Hence, doctors and hospitals have felt little pressure to keep costs down. They have effected few economies, and many have pursued the latest technologies with abandon, buying each piece of state-of-the-art equipment that comes along. Likewise, there has been scant incentive for consumers not to run to the doctor every time they have a head cold. Ultimately, of course, it is all of us who pay for these extravagances, not third parties. We pay for them in the form of higher corporate and personal insurance premiums and escalating taxes. The recognition that there must be limits has begun to force changes.

In the past several years federal and local governments have taken some dramatic steps to try and contain medical costs. Federal Medicaid grants to the states were cut 3 percent in 1982, 4 percent in 1983, and 4.5 percent in 1984, with the result that the states have slashed reimbursements to hospitals and doctors. In late 1983 Washington imposed major changes in Medicare, going for the first time to a system of "prospective" payments. Rates governing the treatment of the nation's 26 million elderly and 3 million disabled are now predetermined for each of 467 categories of illness called diagnostic groups. A fixed amount, and no more, is to be paid for patients who fall within each category, with no distinction made between severe or mild cases. This replaces a system of near-rote reimbursement of claims that had seen Medicare's spending for hospital care rise from $3 billion in 1967 to $39 billion in 1983.

Unfortunately, no matter what cost-containment schemes government adopts, it seems doubtful that runaway health care rates can be controlled without a fundamental change in consumer attitudes. It is, after all, people's own desire to banish death that lies at the heart of soaring costs. Most of us have come to regard top-of-the-line medical treatment as a fundamental right. We crave new discoveries that will extend our life span or improve our flawed bodies, and we will brook no interference with that goal. But breakthrough treatments and revolutionary technologies come very dear. A Jarvik artificial-heart transplant costs upwards of $250,000. A bone marrow transplant to cleanse the body of leukemia comes to $75,000. Nuclear magnetic resonance machines, soon to go into general use, hold out the hope of early detection of cancerous tumors, but the projected cost of a scan is $1,000, and the machine itself costs $1 million. In vitro fertilization may bring the joys of parenthood to childless couples, but it carries a price tag of $35,000. The bill for these immensely expensive items, which the public has commissioned so insouciantly, is directly reflected in the national outlay for health.

Advanced technology adds to the cost of health care in another way as well, for, ironically, though we can postpone the death of those who were formerly doomed, we seldom can cure their underlying ills. It becomes necessary to maintain their precarious health by means of periodic and costly therapies. Kidney dialysis patients, for example, require three treatments a week for the balance of their lives, at a current rate of $30,000 a year. The federal government agreed to subsidize these expenses in 1972, in response to an appalling situation spawned by a shortage of dialysis machines. Mindful of a need to ration the use of the machines, some communities had designated committees to choose candidates for treatment. These committees, which came pejoratively to be known as God committees, were taking it upon themselves to use social-worth criteria as a basis for judgment and were weighting their allocations toward the well-to-do, the intelligent, and the white-collar. Public revulsion prompted Congress to enter the picture, but its well-intentioned deed has saddled it with a crushing obligation. The caseload of the free dialysis program has mushroomed from 11,000 patients costing $242 million in 1972 to 60,000 patients costing $2.6 billion a year today.

The treatment of hydrocephalus is another case of a partial victory over disease that contains the seeds of future expense. A brain shunt shortly after birth can endow afflicted children with years of life, but as they grow, they will require a series of additional surgeries to revise the shunt, each at considerable cost. One child needed 23 separate shunt revisions. Cystic fibrosis is yet another example. Its victims are surviving well into their thirties, where just a few years ago they tended to die in their teens. This improvement has been made possible by the development of adroit techniques to drain the lungs of excess secretions and by the use of antibiotics to fight dangerous respiratory infections. But patients still suffer frequent pulmonary complications and will require hospitalizations throughout their lives on a regular basis. It is not the practice at present to cut off treatment of the patient with kidney disease, hydrocephalus, or cystic fibrosis merely because these individuals are placing a strain on the health care system. Nor has anybody indicated a desire that research into these or any other diseases be curtailed because it is too costly. One may reasonably assume, then, that expensive, new technologies will continue to be developed and brought on line until such time as society issues different standing orders to the medical establishment.

But are we far from the day when we will have to change those orders? Even with the shift to a prospective-payment plan, Medicare is slated to go broke by 1990, at which time it will be paying out $86 billion for hospital care. States, meanwhile, will continue to be overwhelmed by Medicaid costs, there being a limit on the savings that can be achieved. Raising taxes might be one solution. But it seems possible that at some point society will have to whittle down its consumption of health services. One place where it may decide to begin is in the treatment of birth defects.

People with congenital defects make heavy use of the health care system. According to the March of Dimes, 1.2 million infants, children, and adults are hospitalized annually for treatment of birth impairments. Many of them have more than one admission a year, and they represent a sizable fraction of the 40 percent of all hospital patients who require surgery. A sad fact of life about birth defects is reflected in the hospital admissions data. With most human ills, be they heart ailments, nervous-system disorders, cancers, or strokes, the rate of hospitalization tends to grow with the increasing age of the population; but it is the other way around for people with birth defects. The National Center for Health Statistics reports that 332,000 people with congenital anomalies were admitted to hospitals on a short-term basis in 1979 (this figure excludes infants and residents of long-term institutions). Of those, 160,000 were under the age of 15; another 99,000 were between the ages of 15 and 44; 53,000 were between 45 and 64; and only 21,000 were over 65. This declining curve reflects the strong tendency of the birth impaired to die young. In actual numbers, more than 60,000 Americans die annually from birth defects, which, as a category, are the fifth-leading cause of death, ahead of motor vehicle accidents, pneumonia, hardening of the arteries, and high blood pressure.

The congenitally impaired also make up a significant percentage of the institutionalized population in the United States. This population accounts for 43 percent of the nation's total expenditures for catastrophic illness. While the 3 million people who were institutionalized in 1974 composed just 1.3 percent of the population, the $9.5 billion it cost to treat their catastrophic illnesses constituted 8 percent of the money expended on all Americans for health care that year.

A feel for how costly it is to treat birth defects may be gained from the following samples of hospital fees. In Boston a 960-gram premie was in the hospital for 36 days at a cost of $84,198. In Los Angeles a child with congenital heart disease was hospitalized one month *without surgery,* and the bill came to $40,598. In New York a child with an omphalocele had a three-month hospitalization, for which the charge was $134,851. In Chicago a premie who developed necrotizing enterocolitis required repeated surgeries and fifteen months of hyperalimentation at a total cost of $353,748 (she finally died). A Boston youngster with myelomeningocele had eight hospital admissions in an eight-month period, running up a bill of $108,123. A girl with the same disease in Chicago required eighteen months of care at a cost of $598,430. Another Chicago child was born without an anus and with an incomplete esophagus; the bill for treating her for six months was $140,254.

How much is this in aggregate terms? In all, the United States spends $2.65 billion annually on neonatal intensive care for 220,000 premature and malformed infants, or about $12,000 a child. Another $2.35 billion is spent on the hospitalization of birth-impaired older children and adults. Some $350 million more is expended on visits to doctors' offices.

But these figures don't begin to tell the story of what impaired youngsters cost society, because so many of them will require custodial care and other social services for as long as they live. If a Down's child is institutionalized starting today, the bill to the taxpayer will be $1.5 million over the course of his or her lifetime. This estimate is based on today's average institutional cost of $30,000 a year, without consideration of future inflation. It also assumes a life span of 50 years. It has been conjectured that 20,000 chromosomally abnormal infants are born in the United States each year. If only a fourth of them are ever placed in institutions, the care of just one year's cohort will cost Americans $7.5 billion. Every year, as more chromosomally impaired children are born, a new commitment of $7.5 billion is created. In 10 years the burden will have grown to $75 billion. According to an estimate by the Spina Bifida Association of America, the lifetime expense of raising a child with myelomeningocele will be $270,000. Assuming, conservatively, that 3,000 American youngsters are born with the defect each year, the cost of lifetime care for all of them will be $800 million. And these figures cover merely the more well known birth defects. There are hundreds more that will require attention throughout life. The March of Dimes estimates, for instance, that it will cost $2 billion to give continuing care to the 20,000 youngsters who were damaged by the rubella epidemic of 1964–65.

None of these figures appear to make note of the loss to society of the child's productivity as a potential wage earner. Nor do they tabu-

late the associated costs that the government must bear, including the
provision of special education, disability payments, and public accommodations for the handicapped. The closest thing I have seen to any
such accounting is one published by the Health Resources Administration of the U.S. Department of Health and Human Services, which
projects that by the year 2000 the nation will be spending $67 billion
to cover the direct and indirect economic costs of birth defects. On its
face, the estimate is too low, if only because it does not count as defects
certain metabolic disorders like diabetes that, while congenital in origin, may not manifest themselves at birth. And though it does try to
quantify lost worker productivity, it does not factor in the cost of special education or residential care. If these elements are taken into
account, it is clear, birth defects will by the 21st century be costing
society well over $100 billion a year.

Even now, if one simply counts the documentable expenses of medical care, residential care, and special education, one finds that the
United States is spending upwards of $20 billion a year to minister to
the victims of birth defects. That is equivalent to almost 3 percent of
the national budget, and it is more than the federal government spends
on transportation, the space program, housing and urban development, education, agriculture, or natural resources and environment.
It is more than the state budgets of Pennsylvania, Ohio, Texas, or
Illinois, and it is more than the budgets of Tennessee, Idaho, Arizona,
South Carolina, Iowa, New Hampshire, and Kansas combined.

Many consider it distasteful, however, to allow financial considerations to influence the controversy over the treating of defective newborns. Economics, they say, should never be allowed to decide moral
issues. Yet, as the Harvard geneticist Aubrey Milunsky declares, "With
burgeoning costs on all sides and no end in sight, it is inevitable that
pressure will be brought by society to bear on this monetary aspect of
the problem."

Suddenly, we find the tool of cost-benefit analysis being applied to
neonatal intensive care. Medicine has lagged well behind business and
government in the use of this approach, owing to a natural reluctance
on the part of doctors and health policy planners to reduce lifesaving
matters to dollars and cents. But financial exigencies are causing an
abandonment of such fastidious devotion to principle.

Perhaps the first attempt to make intensive care justify itself in terms
of net gain per dollar invested was a study carried out by the French
Ministry of Health in the early 1970s. The government was disturbed
by France's perinatal mortality rate of 26 per 1,000 births, which was
very high compared with that of the other countries of Western Europe.

Among 850,000 French babies born in 1970, there were 22,000 perinatal deaths and 40,000 cases of congenital handicap. This state of
affairs was estimated to be costing French society 15 billion francs
(approximately $3 billion) a year in social welfare for the disabled and
in lost job productivity. Consequently, the Ministry of Health was
seeking the most effective crash program to get the mortality rate
down to 18 per 1,000 births by 1980, a rate that would match that of
the Netherlands. Seven possible measures were evaluated with respect
to how much each would cost the government over a 15-year period
and how many death and handicap cases each would avert in that
time. The most cost-effective item on the list was found to be equip-
ping all delivery rooms with resuscitation apparatus and retraining
doctors, nurses, and midwives in the fundamentals of resuscitating a
dying newborn. The cost of saving a life in this way without subsequent handicap was assessed at only $40. Much farther down the list
was the creation of 25 neonatal intensive-care centers throughout
France. It was found that the cost of saving a life in an NICU was
$1,100. Even more disconcerting, observed one of the architects of
the study, "these centers, while saving many lives, tend also to increase
the number of handicap cases." For both of these reasons, NICUs
were deemed not very cost-effective. (The Ministry of Health did not
adhere strictly to the results of its cost-benefit study but instead adopted
a mix of approaches. In fact, a sizable number of intensive-care units
are now operating in France. Once implemented, the ministry's plan
succeeded beyond all expectations, pushing the mortality rate down
to the target level by 1975, instead of 1980.)

More recently, two similar studies were performed in North America. The first, published in 1981, was conducted by Dr. Peter Budetti,
of the University of California at San Francisco, for the U.S. Office of
Technology Assessment. Budetti concluded that intensive care of
infants weighing 1,500 grams or less was only "marginally" cost effective. And he discovered that, for the subgroup of babies below 1,000
grams, it was possible for the enormous custodial expenses of the few
severely abnormal survivors to outweigh the economic benefits gained
from producing a great number of normal survivors. Budetti concluded, though, that ethical considerations would keep the government from ever abandoning intensive care simply to avoid the
exceptional costs generated by abnormal infants. "Because the lives
of many healthy babies would be lost without intensive care," he wrote,
"such a decision would never be made on cost-effectiveness grounds
alone."

In 1983 a Canadian team from McMaster University reported that
neonatal intensive care was cost-ineffective for infants weighing less

than 1,000 grams and that it was cost-effective only in certain narrow circumstances for babies between 1,000 and 1,500 grams. The McMaster team noted, "A program that does not meet the cost-benefit criterion . . . represents a net drain on society's resources—that is, the program consumes more resources than it saves or creates."

The significance of these various studies lies not in what they say about neonatal intensive care, because their findings were, by their authors' own admission, tentative. Rather, it lies in the fact that the studies were carried out at all, for they seem to portend a new approach toward health care—an approach marked by a dispassionate attempt to parcel out society's scarce medical resources in the most advantageous manner. It is not difficult to imagine a time in the near future when even the richest, most developed countries will be forced to make trade-offs, dropping certain programs in favor of others, or riding coach instead of first class en route to the same therapeutic end. Ultimately, they may have to go to an outright system of health rationing. Then the truly wrenching questions will have to be confronted. Will we write off the poor and treat only the well-to-do? Will we cast the elderly adrift and favor the young? Will the nonproductive people— the retarded, the mentally ill, the physically disabled—be given short shrift because treating them provides little return on investment?

Rationing is already an instrument of policy in Great Britain, where treatment is withheld from two out of every three myelomeningocele victims, where kidney dialysis, in the main, is reserved for people under 55 years of age, and where intensive care is generally denied infants weighing less than 750 grams. The operative discriminating mechanism in Britain is the attending physician's "clinical judgment," which tends to reduce treatment choices to a rather cold appraisal of the probability of therapeutic success. Such thrifty pragmatism is one reason why the British have been able to hold their health spending down to only 5.5 percent of the domestic national product.

Yet, health rationing is not unknown in the United States, although its existence is seldom acknowledged. The most glaring example is that of organ transplants. They are so expensive—a heart transplant can, by the time the final bills are in, run in excess of $200,000—that few people's insurance will cover the entire cost. And most public-aid departments will, as a rule, not pay for them, contending that such surgeries are still too experimental and marked by a poor long-range success rate. Consequently, only the very rich or the overinsured can be sure of obtaining such an operation if they need it.

It reflects how we allocate all other scarce resources in our free-market society that we distribute extraordinary surgery just to those who can afford it. This kind of triage is certainly regrettable, but it may be merely the beginning. As ever-more arcane treatments are being developed at staggering cost and as society's commitment to pay for them is declining, it seems conceivable that something will have to give.

"I see a lot of nastiness coming," says Earl Frederick, president of Chicago's Children's Memorial Hospital, one of the nation's largest pediatric institutions. "What direction it will take, I'm not sure. What do you do? Stop the free dialysis program? Or do we shrink the neonatal program in half? Society is going to have to set priorities."

The dilemma posed by Frederick is not so farfetched. Kidney dialysis and intensive care for premature babies cost an identical sum every year: $2.6 billion. It is not beyond the realm of possibility that someone will propose that a choice be made between keeping each of the nation's 60,000 kidney patients alive or treating each of the 220,000 babies who require intensive care each year.

For now, however, a more subtle form of pressure is being exerted on health care providers to keep costs down. A closer look at Frederick's hospital is instructive because many institutions around the country share its plight. Children's Memorial is a major provider of services to the poor. Sixty-six percent of its neonatal population and 30 percent of its older patients are on Medicaid. The state of Illinois used to pay the hospital a per diem allowance for Medicaid patients; then, at the end of the year, the difference between the per diem and the hospital's actual costs was subject to "reconciliation," a negotiating process by which the hospital would recoup more of its costs. But under the U.S. Omnibus Budget Reconciliations Act of 1981—a piece of legislation that also cut state Medicaid grants and, by changing the requirements for eligibility, disqualified 750,000 needy beneficiaries nationwise—the states were permitted to draft their own Medicaid rules. Illinois has used the opportunity to do away with the reconciliation process. The per diem is all that hospitals get. Since the per diem has a ceiling of $435 a day and since it costs a hospital like Children's Memorial $875 a day to care for a patient, the hospital is forced to absorb more than half its costs. But the state did not stop there. It has also told Children's Memorial it will pay for no more than 16,000 Medicaid patient days a year. Children's ordinarily accumulates 23,000 Medicaid days annually. The choice for the hospital then becomes either to discharge more poor children sooner, perhaps before they are fully well, or to try to underwrite the extra 7,000 patient days itself. To this last end, it was able to persuade the state to give it an advance from its next year's allocation to meet the pinch. "We're borrowing against the future," says Frederick sadly. A large Medicaid provider like Children's is thus forced into a corner. It can make up some of its losses by "cost-shifting," that is, laying off some of its costs on more affluent parents in the form of higher fees, but there is a limit to how much of this it can do.

"Very soon now we will have no choice but to reassess the way we are spending our resources," says Frederick. "We're right on the cutting edge; all hospitals are going to have to go through this soon. I don't know whether reassessment means we'll stop doing certain procedures on all kids, or only on those who can't pay. Or whether it's going to come out of the neonatal program or what. But if small neonates don't get taken care of, it will have to be a societal decision. You can't ask a doctor or a hospital to make that kind of choice.

"I think ultimately society is going to have to rethink all the advances we've made, and their high costs; all the wonderful things we can do, like transplant kidneys, hearts, and so on. It'll still go on, maybe, but not at the same rate as in the 1960s and '70s."

Frederick concedes that a great deal of money is spent on treating sick and defective children. But he says it pales before the amount spent on other age groups. "Look at the way Medicare money is spent. Half the Medicare dollars go for treating people in the last year of their lives. Money spent on neonates is peanuts compared to the Medicare budget. Oh, it may be large in terms of the individual infant, but there aren't that many of them compared to the vast numbers of elderly. And why is so much money spent on the last year of life when we're all going to end up in the grave anyway? Who are we kidding? Maybe we need to revise priorities and spend less at the other end of life. Of course, I'm biased because I take care of kids."

In Fort Worth, Texas, Stanley Hupfeld heads the All Saints Episcopal Hospital. He believes the money expended on low-birthweight infants and malformed children is worth it because the public says it is. "One does wonder what genetic difficulties we are thereby passing on to future generations that would otherwise have been selected out. And next to the cost of their initial care, the cost of their lifelong care may be spectacular. I don't think we as a society have really dealt with that effectively. But I don't think it's for hospitals and physicians to make those decisions. Our responsibility is to do what we are doing, that is, if something is technologically available, we should do it. It is up to society to make the ultimate decision."

The funding squeeze has been felt very strongly by the Children's Hospital in Denver. The state of Colorado pays only 28 cents on the Medicaid dollar, leaving the hospital to eat 70 percent of its costs to treat the indigent. As a result, the hospital's losses went from $2.7 million in 1976 to $6.4 million in 1980. According to Dr. L. Joseph Butterfield, the hospital's director of regional program development, the institution is forced to make up for its losses through donations; last year, for example, it took in $800,000 in a Memorial Day telethon.

Butterfield is a staunch proponent of more, rather than less, spending on children's medicine, although he acknowledges that individually, sick newborns make the biggest dent in the system. Their parents, he says, are often less financially secure and need more state help. "They are generally young, and they have put off buying health insurance to buy a TV set. And then they have a premie, and they become medically indigent. It's a double tragedy."

To Butterfield, the solution lies not in cutting off funding for services like neonatal intensive care but in using existing resources more efficiently. He says that level III intensive-care nurseries should have a "step down" arrangement with level II nurseries, so that when a child's condition improves, he or she may be transferred back into a more economical kind of care, opening the bed up for a new child. However, he does not believe that society will sit still for cutting back on the caliber of treatment. "The public doesn't want cheap, bad care. Health isn't like ballpoint pens. As health technology gets more sophisticated, it gets more expensive too."

But has our ability to afford the expense really declined? David Rothman, director of the Center for the Study of Society and Medicine at Columbia University's College of Physicians and Surgeons, thinks not. He is troubled by what he calls "the incredible waste of dollars one sees every moment of one's life in this country." Rothman asserts, "Americans generally do a bad job of thinking about the allocation of resources. For playing in a Superbowl, each winning player will get $72,000 and each loser $52,000. Think of it, $72,000 for one man's work on a Sunday afternoon. I'd much rather see that money spent to save two children in an intensive-care unit."

There is, of course, no guarantee, as Rothman admits, that if the Superbowl were canceled the money would go instead into infant medicine. Still, it starts one thinking about social priorities. As Kenneth Vaux, professor of ethics at the University of Illinois, says, "We are a frightfully wealthy society. We don't live on a lifeboat, we live on a luxury liner."

Frightfully wealthy is accurate. As a crude measure, our annual gross national product is equivalent to $13,360 for every man, woman, and child in the United States. Compare that with Haiti's $220, or Egypt's $590. The problem, perhaps, is not that we lack money but that we lack a sense of proportion in how to spend it. A peek into our skewed system of priorities is provided by a recent study released by the Children's Defense Fund of Washington, D.C. The organization has done some intensive research into how the U.S. Department of Defense, one of the largest spenders of federal dollars, uses its money. It found the following:

- The DOD owns a hotel at Fort De Russy on Waikiki Beach. A military resort, it is a popular vacation spot for military officials and retirees. Its current fair-market value is $100 million, according to the Children's Defense Fund.
- Military bands are costing the nation $100 million a year. The Fund believes that volunteer high school bands could be used to play at patriotic events, thus saving the nation money.
- Each nuclear-powered aircraft carrier costs the taxpayers $3 billion. Each of the 100 B-1 bombers we are planning to build costs $250 million. Tne 240 MX missiles we are going to construct will run $110 million apiece, and the 35 TR-1 spy planes under development will cost $40 million apiece.

If we built 90 B-1 bombers instead of 100, we would have enough money to fund all the neonatal units in the country for a full year. Unlike babies, the bombers will be obsolete inside a very short time, so it might be a shrewd trade-off. One does have to raise questions about a world in which it is necessary to spend $26 billion on MX missiles that we intend never to use, when that same $26 billion could alleviate so many domestic human tragedies.

Nevertheless, it is unrealistic to expect sudden changes from American policymakers. Any substantial reductions in defense spending seem unlikely in the foreseeable future. Besides, there is no assurance that such reductions, if adopted, would be translated into more health care spending. The long and the short of it is that if Americans are going to continue demanding more sophisticated and expensive health care for all who need it, they are going to have to ante up. And if they don't want to pay for it, they face some hard choices.

The conflict between heart and pocketbook has already begun. In March of 1984 the Missouri General Assembly, considering a $79 million emergency-spending measure, voted to earmark $200,000 of it to finance a liver transplant for a dying 16-year-old girl. The child's family had no other way to pay for the lifesaving operation, a predicament that an increasing number of families are finding themselves in, as surgery grows ever more spectacular and costly. When news of the legislature's generosity spread, six desperate families immediately called the state capitol asking for similar help. Panicked that they had opened a Pandora's box that would obligate the state to pay for all children's organ transplants, the legislators had shamefacedly to retract their offer.

One can sympathize with the Missouri lawmakers. There are, for example, 400 American youngsters who are born each year with a defect called biliary atresia. Without a liver transplant they will die in early childhood. Yet, to pay for transplants for all of them would cost the government $80 million, not to mention another $2 million a year to cover the immunosuppressant drugs the children will need for the rest of their lives. Furthermore, one can hardly stop with children. Justice demands that government also pay for the 5,000 older people who need liver transplants annually, and the 15,000 who might benefit from a heart transplant. The total bill for all this perpetuation of life would approach $4 billion a year, a truly staggering sum to spend on 20,000 people.

But one also grieves for that Missouri child and her family. To know that the technical means are there to save a life but that the economic means are not must be crushing beyond all ken. "They've slammed the door on us," the girl's mother said.

Was this tragedy unique or a prelude of things to come? Will the sound that echoes down our hospital corridors be the sound of a slamming door?

12

The Handicapped Speak

About suffering they were never wrong,
The Old Masters: how well they understood
Its human position; how it takes place
While someone else is eating or opening a window or just
walking dully along. . . .
—W. H. Auden, "Musée des Beaux Arts"

So pale, her hands. They rest shyly in her lap, a permanent lap defined by legs that never move. "Sometimes," she says, "I wish I could be like everybody else." At this, the young woman's voice rises wistfully and for a moment seems to leave the room and waft outside.

"I tell my dad," she says in a dreamy way, "that when the day ever comes that I can walk, I hope it's snowing outside. And I'll go down to the lake and put my foot in the water so I can see how that feels."

Any discussion of euthanasia for severely impaired babies must eventually take up a central question: How do the congenitally handicapped themselves feel about having survived? Susan Brown is 26, an attractive, bright woman who entered this world with a severe case of myelomeningocele. She has spent her life in a wheelchair, paralyzed from the waist down.

When Susan was born, her parents and the surgeon had to make a momentous decision. In those days, 1958, most myelomeningocele victims fared poorly. Up to 80 percent of them died or suffered severe mental retardation, no matter what treatment was offered. Medical control of spina bifida was still in the experimental stage. The surgeon's choice was this: he could close up Susan's back and grant her a heavily clouded future, or he could do nothing, in which case she would probably die from a meningitis infection. He elected to gamble on life.

Susan has beaten the odds, but it has been a long and difficult road for her, with more than its share of suffering, surgery, and monotony. She has had a plastic shunt implanted in the depths of her brain to alleviate her hydrocephalus. She has had operations on her heel tendons to correct a splaying of her feet. Because she possesses no control over her bladder function, she has had to undergo an ileal conduit procedure, which involved the creation of a new urinary opening in her abdomen. Urine is now collected in a bag outside her body. Prior to the ileal conduit, she was plagued by kidney infections, which would drive her temperature up to 105 degrees. She has also had to have operations to relieve agonizing pressure sores, which come from sitting for extended periods in the same position.

One of nine children, Susan lives with her mother and father in a cloistered setting that is slowly undermining her native good spirits. She is largely homebound, has no job, few activities, and spends her days watching soap operas, listening to records, and tending to her four-year-old nephew. "I get bored," she complains. "Especially when it snows and I can't go outside."

One of the ironies of Susan's life is that it was more interesting several years ago. For six months she worked in a fast-food restaurant, operating the pop machine. Unfortunately, she had to quit because sitting on a telephone book in order to reach the machine's levers was giving her pressure sores. After an operation to alleviate the sores, she returned to the restaurant and asked for her old job back. "But the new manager had the place all rearranged and congested, so there was no room for my wheelchair anymore," she recalls. "He gave me an interview, and he was trying to be nice, but he said it wouldn't work out. 'My workers have to be fast,' he said, 'and I don't think you're fast enough.' I said, 'I did it before, and I can do it again.' He said he'd call me back, but he never did. I was slightly mad about that. I told everyone not to go to that restaurant, that it had lice."

For a time, she was a volunteer at the same pediatric hospital where her surgeries were performed. She functioned as a sort of big sister to younger children with spina bifida, as well as an informal consultant to their parents. "I would tell them how it feels to have spina bifida. Then they'd ask me how they should treat their kids, and I'd say, 'Well, you'll have bad times and good times, but you've got to treat them like other people.' "

But the volunteer work fell through when she turned 18 and grew too old to be treated at the pediatric hospital. Now she is seeking another paying job. One problem she shares with many disabled people is that she didn't finish high school. The realities of special education are such that many students start their education later and finish it earlier than their normal peers. Lack of mobility and frequent absences are usually the reasons for this. Susan is contemplating getting her high-school-equivalency certificate to silence prospective employers who keep asking for a diploma. Her career goals are a trifle fanciful, reflecting a grandiosity and a general naïveté about life that are not uncommon in the handicapped. One of her desires is to be a news photographer. Another is to be a rock singer. She rejects her mother's more down-to-earth suggestion that she become a secretary. "I like to be on the go too much," she says. "I wouldn't want to be chained to a desk."

She has frequent arguments with her family over another matter. She would like to move out of her parents' house and live on her own. "My mom and dad are overprotective with me, and I don't like that much," she says. "I tell them I'd like to get an apartment. They say, 'We don't think you can handle it.' And I say, 'All I'm asking for is a chance, and if I don't make it, at least I can say I tried.' Sometimes I feel like a prisoner. There's very little privacy, and I have all these restrictions. Like my brothers and sisters can stay out till midnight, but if I go out I have to be in by 10. There are bad things that happen in our neighborhood, and they are afraid I'll get hurt. I can't blame them for that, but if I'm with friends, I can't see what the problem is."

Susan tries to stay socially active. She has a circle of cronies whom she sees in good weather. She bowls and occasionally goes to a movie, and she shot a pretty good game of pool before the local pool hall closed down. Most of her friends are from the immediate neighborhood, where she is known affectionately as Wheels.

Life has its mortifying social moments, however. "Sometimes the ileal-conduit bag leaks when I'm with friends," she says. "Not everybody is understanding. Sometimes they tell me about it in front of a lot of people. I have no bowel control, either, and that's the most embarrassing thing. I can't really tell that I'm doing it; I just go. People know I can't help it, and I know I can't help it, but it still gets me upset."

Her other physical worry is her hydrocephalus shunt. "I've never had it revised," she says. "I don't think it's working anymore. But then I'm not draining spinal fluid anymore, either. Since I've never had seizures from it, the doctors don't want to fool with it. I see them about once a month, and they check the shunt and my kidneys."

She conceives of the shunt as a foreign intruder. "I can't feel it, but I know it's there. Somtimes, I wish they'd take it out, but then I remember I might get water on the brain again and I might not be as lucky as I was when they caught it the first time."

Until recently, Susan had a steady boyfriend, but they broke up. "He was very nice. A lot of guys look at my handicap first without looking at me. But he didn't seem to be that way. I'm a very nervous person. I shake a lot. But every time I was around him, I felt secure; I was just myself. But then all of a sudden, without giving me any reason why, he just said we shouldn't see each other anymore."

Susan says she would like to get married someday. "I'd prefer to marry somebody who isn't handicapped. I used to date this handicapped guy in school, and I don't know why, I just got a bad feeling going with another person who was handicapped."

She says she likes to feel that she isn't much different from anybody else. "The only thing I can't do is walk. I hate it when people use the word *crippled*. I looked it up in the dictionary, and it referred to a person who can't do things for herself, and I'm not that. I'm definitely not that. Oh, I do get depressed sometimes. I even get the feeling that I wish I hadn't been born. That maybe I'd be better off dead, because my parents have been through a lot. The doctors told them I'd never make it to 21. But on the other hand, I'm really glad I'm alive. I know there are people out there who are worse off than me."

Susan Brown belongs to the large, anonymous mass of congenitally disabled individuals who do not fit any of society's common stereotypes about the handicapped. She is not the dynamic, overachieving supercripple we often encounter in inspirational media tales; nor is she a pitiful, helpless creature who must be waited on hand and foot, an image fostered by the annual muscular dystrophy telethon, with its maudlin parade of "Jerry's kids." People like Susan are spread across America, in every city, in every hamlet. One doesn't sense their presence, for they are invisible, thanks in part to their own shyness and lack of mobility but even more to society's unwillingness to let them participate in the drama of life. One is reminded of the actress Zsa Zsa Gabor's alleged refusal two years ago to perform onstage unless thirteen handicapped people in wheelchairs were moved out of their front-row seats. It suits our culture well to have the handicapped out of sight, for then we do not have to deal with them, talk to them, hire them, or look at them. They sit in their homes or in institutions, leading lives of surpassing tedium. This is certainly not true of everyone. A significant percentage of the disabled have made excellent strides despite their handicaps. The Spina Bifida Association of America, for example, has among its members a number of successful myelomeningocele victims, including a Georgia attorney who works for a public employees union, a New York psychotherapist, a teacher, a medical counselor, and an Illinois woman who is married and the mother of two children. But there are only 300 people with spina bifida in the association. There are more than 70,000 spina bifida victims in the United States overall. It is probable that more of them lead stagnant lives like Susan Brown's than do not. The same is true of the estimated 350,000 cerebral palsy victims in the United States. And of the 6 million mentally retarded. And of the hundreds of thousands of victims of crippling hereditary disorders and other anomalies.

One can only surmise the state of mind of so many people. Part of the reason for the uncertainty is that relatively few scientific data have been amassed on the later psychological outcome of birth impairment. There are understandable reasons for this. Since most birth-defective children did not survive 20 years ago, there have not been large cohorts of adolescents and adults to study until recently. Also, follow-ups on those who have survived have not been notably successful. The few studies that have been published tend to emphasize individual cases derived from psychotherapeutic practice. This presents an inherent difficulty: individuals for whom help is sought are usually the ones who are doing poorly. Extrapolations from these case histories may tend to give a false picture of the disabled population at large. Even now, when good national statistics regarding the psychological status of the handicapped would be eminently useful, not enough researchers are pursuing them. Cost is the main deterrent. Population-based surveys would have to be enormous in scope, since disability rates tend to be low. A questionnaire submitted to 20,000 families might yield only 20 cases of myelomeningocele, hardly a number to base firm findings on. To get a barely adequate sample of 200 individuals with spina bifida, the study population might have to be as big as a quarter of a million people, creating a prohibitively expensive enterprise. Easier to mount are studies of concentrated populations of the disabled, conducted through hospital clinics, for instance. But again, the samples tend to be small.

Possibly the most thoroughgoing research project ever to explore adaptation to handicap was carried out on Britain's Isle of Wight, where the entire population of 11,865 schoolchildren was studied. The investigators found that whereas the rate of psychiatric disorders among all children aged 10 and 11 was 6.8 percent, among youngsters with a chronic physical disability it was 11.5 percent, almost twice as high. And among those with neurological and epileptic conditions, the rate was 34.3 percent, five times that found in the general population. However, when one looks for other studies that might confirm or dispute the Isle of Wight survey, one finds an annoying paucity of literature.

But though it has rarely been quantified precisely, there is little doubt that congenital disability has a profound and frequently negative effect on personality adjustment. Current theory ascribes this to an early failure of the handicapped child to pass through the normal stages of infantile ego development on his or her way to a sense of identity. These normal phases of "separation and individuation" have been described by the child development expert Margaret S. Mahler as follows: There is the "differentiation" phase (5 to 10 months), when the infant, stimulated chiefly by visual perceptions, distinguishes more sharply between the self and the mother. This period is followed by the "practicing" phase (10 to 16 months), when the child, now gifted with independent locomotion, experiments with separating himself physically from the mother. He will make brief forays to other parts of the house but after a few moments away from her will look around for her to reassure himself of her presence. It is during this period of increased motor control that the child experiences what the researcher Phyllis Greenacre describes as "a love affair with the world." The child seems exhilarated by his own faculties, particularly his newfound ability to walk upright, which Mahler considers an enormously important step in emotional development. Without any help, he is free to explore and test the world to his heart's content. At the same time, he is making new and delightful discoveries about his own body, developing a positive "body image." Next, comes the "rapprochement" phase (16 to 24 months), during which time the child returns to closer ties with the mother, having seemingly become frightened by his own desire to separate. Yet, the individuation process continues unabated, as the youngster becomes aware that he can no longer amalgamate his own self with his mother's. Finally, comes the phase of "consolidation of individuality" (24 to 36 months), when the maternal image becomes internalized and permanently available to the child. Possession of this constant image of the love object permits the youngster to separate physically with diminished tension. This period is also distinguished by the child's achievement of an internalized image of himself, paving the way for the development of a healthy sense of identity.

For certain readily apparent reasons, the disabled child cannot always proceed through these phases in a timely fashion. The child with motor disorders, for instance, is delayed in developing locomotion. He will have decreased opportunity to explore his environment and to distance himself from his mother both physically and psychologically. He may never experience the pleasure that comes from walking upright, nor will he receive the early intellectual stimulation that comes from investigating the myriad objects he encounters. Hence, the separation and individuation process is hindered. In a similar vein, a blind child will have no visual image of the mother, thus delaying the onset of the differentiation phase. He will be late in developing such crucial concepts as object permanence (the idea that objects can exist independently of one's perception of them) and cause-and-effect relations. He will be further inhibited in the separation-individuation process because his independent locomotion is restricted and because he cannot see his mother to reassure himself of her presence while making explorations. For these and other reasons, disabled children may stay locked into more primitive forms of ego development.

When the youngster finally does begin to form a sense of identity, it is liable to be tainted by his perception of himself as defective. "From the child's point of view," writes Dr. Robert Prall, professor of child psychiatry at the Medical College of Pennsylvania in Philadelphia, "the defect may interfere with his achieving the gratification of ego-building experiences which independent functioning, mastery of locomotion, hand-eye coordination, and bodily processes provide. Defects in the body image, self-image, and self-esteem result and the child develops a concept of himself as different, inadequate, clumsy, stupid, deformed, inferior, or unwanted and unloved."

Even more injurious to the handicapped child can be the attitude his mother displays toward him. She may be overcome with shame, self-blame, and depression, all of which interfere with her ability to become emotionally attached to the child. If maternal warmth is sufficiently absent, the child may regress or remain fixated in the most primitive stages, writes Prall.

Additional factors may exacerbate the child's difficulty in forming normal relationships with his mother. Repeated separations because of hospitalization and surgery are substantially disruptive. And the inability to feed naturally, which is experienced by certain youngsters—for example, those with cleft palate or esophageal atresia—can leave the child marooned in a stage of oral fixation.

Most authorities stress the overriding importance of both parents in the healthy ego formation of the handicapped child. The noted child psychiatrist Bruno Bettelheim has stated, "Children can learn to live with a disability. But they cannot live well without the conviction that their parents find them utterly loveable . . . if the parents, knowing about [a child's] defect, love him now, he can believe that others will love him in the future."

According to the child psychiatrist Jerome Schulman, of Chicago, "The determinant in 98 percent of the cases is the parents' attitude toward the child. If they are comfortable with the child's handicap. then the child is comfortable with himself. This is because a person's opinion of himself relates mostly to his parents' opinion of him."

But if the ideal is a healthy parental attitude toward disabled off-spring, the reality often falls short. One researcher after another has found that parents frequently react in ways that are destructive to their handicapped progeny. Philip Pinkerton, of the University of Liverpool, has listed the most common of these as denial, where the mother and father refuse to face up to the fact of the child's disability; overprotection, where the youngster is emotionally smothered; and anger, which may precipitate outright rejection of the child.

Denial, writes Pinkerton, can interfere with sound medical manage-ment of the youngster's condition. Parents may indulge in "doctor-shopping," he says, rejecting the diagnosis and "trundling the unfor-tunate child from one specialist to another in the hope of securing more palatable, or less unequivocal pronouncements, and thereby fostering false aspirations." He cites the case of a mother who refused to accept the mental disability of her 13-year-old son, a victim of Down's syndrome with an IQ of 53. She told Pinkerton, "I mean, he doesn't *appear* to be intellectually handicapped. . . . I mean there are so many brilliant people who are brilliant at their subject but absolutely hope-less with just common every-day things."

Overprotection has multiple roots. It can spring from pity, or it can be a sublimation of deeper feelings. The parent may unconsciously resent the child, and compensates for it by making a grand show of excessive solicitude. Or the same parent may feel at once responsible for the child's defect and compelled to "make it up" to the child by doing everything for him. In either case, the child suffers by not learning independence. Dr. Elva Poznanski, of the University of Illi-nois, believes the consequences may be profound: "The problems bred by overprotection are many and varied. For example, in our hospital physicians and physical therapists sometimes find that a new level of motor functioning cannot be reached without hospitalizing the child and in effect doing a 'parentectomy.' The frequent description of the handicapped child as being excessively passive and immature seems to correlate with parental overprotection."

An equally pernicious form of overprotection, Poznanski says, is the tendency for parents to create an island of social isolation for themselves and their handicapped young. "Parents of chronically ill children tend to retreat from relationships with their neighbors, sel-dom take their handicapped children on vacations or outings, and tend to discourage any socializing by the handicapped son or daugh-ter."

Anger and guilt seldom are far from the surface, Poznanski writes. "All parents, whether of normal or of handicapped children, face the occasional wish that their child did not exist. Such feelings can be

dealt with when they are fleeting. But where the wish occurs frequently and with intensity, the parents are apt to suffer intense guilt.
Handicapped children, because they make more demands on their
parents and offer fewer rewards, can at times produce even angrier
feelings than parents would normally feel. The parental feelings of
anger at all the extra burdens, their irritation with the child's relentless demands, the subsequent guilt they feel at their own anger and
hostility toward the helpless child—all these can be devastating for
family life."

It seems abundantly clear that it is crucial to the child's future mental health that his parents actively want him to be part of the family
circle. In the loud and frequently acrimonious debate over whether
couples should be allowed to decline livesaving treatment for their
disabled infants, the failure to consider this fundamental fact is
inexplicable. By forcing parents to take to their hearts a severely
impaired infant that they obviously have grave qualms about raising,
we are doing the youngster no favor, and we may be causing it a great
deal of permanent emotional harm.

Many authorities have found that among the hardest disabilities for
both parents and victims to accept are the more visible deformities,
particularly those that affect the face. It seems to be a universal human
tendency to shun those whose looks do not conform to some ideal,
even if the object of avoidance is one's own child. Natasha Josefowitz,
of the University of New Hampshire, has written, "Recent studies have
shown that even in nursery school, children tend to select as their
friends their better looking peers. . . . The homely or malformed child
will have to compensate for his unattractiveness by an unusual personality."

The sociologist Frances Cooke Macgregor, who once undertook a
massive study of 115 facially deformed patients, has written that a
conspicuous defect "may well be as severe a social and economic
handicap as complete physical incapacity. This is due in large measure to the profound social significance of the face and the attitudes
and prejudices of society toward one whose appearance is atypical."

Macgregor found that her subjects suffered from psychological disturbances that were often more serious than their physical impairments. These disturbances ranged from inferiority feelings, self-
consciousness, and withdrawal to paranoid complaints, hostility, and
outright antisocial and psychotic states. Frequently, the seeds of these
emotional problems are sown very early in life by an adverse parental
reaction to the deformity. This may lead to frank rejection of the
youngster; parents have been known to place a son or daughter in an

institution simply because they cannot stand the sight of it. Something of this sort has been seen with victims of a grotesque disorder called Apert's syndrome, which is characterized by a peaked and elongated head, wide, bulging eyes, underdeveloped jaws, and lobster-claw hands and feet. These children have on many occasions ended up in institutions for the retarded, but doctors now suspect that Apert's syndrome inflicts no organic retardation and that these children come to function this way because of profound rejection during the formative period.

Fortunately, with advanced methods of plastic surgery, many facial deformities can be repaired, resulting in greater acceptance and improved mental adjustment for the child. One hospital in Israel is offering surgical correction of some of the more obvious stigmata of Down's syndrome, in the belief that it will prove of social benefit to the youngster.

Dr. Linton Whitaker, a Philadelphia plastic surgeon, recently surveyed 47 people whose craniofacial deformities had been repaired at his hospital to discover whether surgery had made any difference in their lives. Some 55 percent of adolescents and 91 percent of adults reported feeling better about their appearance and more confident. Parents reported satisfaction with the surgery, even when it did not meet all their expectations. "Since the family relationship is so significant for the young child," wrote Whitaker, "one cannot ignore the importance of parents' feeling relaxed with their child."

Another group of disabilities that are especially hard for patients and their families to cope with are anomalies of the genitourinary system. Extrophy of the bladder, for example, is a condition in which the bladder lies outside the abdomen and is turned inside out, so that urine delivered from the kidneys drips constantly onto the surface of the body. The defect, which results from a failure of the abdominal wall to fuse during embryonic development, is frequently associated with severe malformations of the sex organs. Males may have diminutive penises and females may lack vaginas. Moreover, the pubic bones are often separated, inflicting a waddling gait on the victim. Extrophy of the bladder is a notably repugnant deformity. The organ appears bright red through the abdominal opening, and because there is a continuous seepage of urine, bad odor and infection are commonplace. The defect can be surgically managed up to a point, by means of an abdominal closure and an ileal conduit, but repair of the defective genitals is much more difficult, particularly in males. The social and sexual ramifications of having a tiny or nonfunctional penis are a source of great distress to both the victim and his family, causing psychological maladjustment and even suicide.

Dr. Abraham Fineman, of the Children's Medical Center in Boston, once conducted a psychiatric study of 10 victims of bladder extrophy and their families. The patients ranged in age from 3 to 26 years. Fineman wrote in the *American Journal of Orthopsychiatry*, "The attitudes of the mothers varied from direct abandonment to extreme overprotection involving refusal to bear more children and slavish devotion to the damaged child. The anomaly, involving the sexual organs, apparently stimulated a good deal of superstitious and magical thinking. Parents expressed the feeling that the genital anomaly in the child was related to a weakness or deficiency of their own reproductive systems, and where the child was a boy, the father invariably was stigmatized as lacking in virility."

The treatment of choice in 1957, when Fineman published his study, was to redirect the ureters away from the bladder to the lower bowel. Urine and feces were then excreted simultaneously through the anus, as through the cloaca of a frog. This caused children in the study to develop a concept of themselves as "a receptacle filled with dirty fluid," wrote Fineman. "One 5-year-old boy spoke of an imaginary playmate named Danny Sewer."

Adult males in the study were deeply affected by having a poorly formed sexual apparatus. One of them, wrote Fineman, developed a highly active fantasy life bordering on the manic. "He experienced gross perceptual distortions of body parts following a plastic procedure to his penis, feeling that the added length and weight . . . would be so great that he would be literally thrown off balance if he turned around a corner." A second man became a quiet, withdrawn, schizoid person who lived in virtual isolation. All of the men "were characterized by a feeling of unreality, as if not really belonging to this world," reported Fineman.

Ambiguous genitalia are another kind of malformation with potential for intense mental disturbance. There exist a number of conditions that cause a masculinization of the female organs or an incomplete masculinization of the male organs. These can have genetic origins, or they can result from an embryonic hormone dysfunction or a maternal ingestion of steroids during pregnancy. It is often impossible to tell from external appearance alone whether the child is a boy or a girl. A genetic female may have a penis-sized clitoris, and a genetic male may have labia or a blind vaginal pouch. Sometimes the child will have both sets of external genitals. The only sure method of determining the underlying sex is through chromosomal studies. There is also a much rarer condition called true hermaphroditism, in which the child has both ovaries and testes as well as ambiguous external genitalia. The birth of these unfortunate children amounts to an emotional catastrophe. Parents are overwhelmed with shame and anxiety about the child's future, and their turmoil is heightened by a need to make a gender assignment within a very short time. Current medical wisdom is to go by anatomy rather than by chromosomes. Thus, where children are genetically male but have poorly developed masculine sex characteristics, parents are frequently advised to raise them as girls in order to spare them anguish later in life.

It is a tribute to the human spirit that even with the most extreme or embarrassing disabilities, admirable psychological adjustments are possible. The best example of this is the inspiring way in which a number of the thalidomide babies of the 1960s have coped with their afflictions as they have reached young adulthood. Terry Wiles, of Britain, was born without arms and legs. All he had were two rudimentary feet attached to his pelvis. He also had one eye hanging halfway down his cheek, which had to be removed surgically. To compound matters, Terry was the product of an interracial union and was abandoned by his mother shortly after birth. For the first five years of his life, he lived in a large institution for severely handicapped children in Sussex, having virtually no contact with the outer world. He became a bitter little boy. Then a remarkable thing happened. A 60-year-old delivery truck driver named Leonard Wiles and his wife, Hazel, met him, became attached to him, and eventually adopted him. A more unlikely adoptive home it is hard to imagine. The Wiles were chronically in debt, scraping by on $30 a week, and they lived in a dilapidated cottage that was often without heat. Mrs. Wiles found herself initially averse to taking care of Terry, but some mysterious alchemy was at work, and Terry flourished. He went on to go to college, learned to type with his feet, took up short-story writing, and began playing the electric organ. In addition, he took singing lessons, learned to swim, and has even ridden a pony.

In their book *Suffer the Children: The Story of Thalidomide*, the Insight Team of the *Sunday Times* of London reported on the heartening adaptation of several other thalidomide victims. They told of an armless girl who was entering law school, a second child who had learned to drive a specially modified car, a third who became a swimming champion, and a fourth who married and was expecting a baby. According to the Insight Team, some 20 British victims of thalidomide had gone to college, and 30 more held full-time jobs.

Rolfe Schroeder is another person who has learned to live with a difficult handicap. Rolfe, 18, is a midwestern youth who was born with multiple bowel and bladder anomalies. Doctors diagnosed his imperforate anus immediately; there was only a dimple where the rectal orifice should be, and the bowel itself was an inch and a half short. Such malformations occur once in every 5,000 births. When he was 24 hours old, Rolfe had his first surgery, a procedure designed to bring the bowel down to its correct anatomical position and create an anal opening. But subsequent tests showed he had a further problem, which was diagnosed as a fistula, or abnormal passage, between his urethra and his colon. A second operation was performed when he was five months old, and three inches of tissue were removed. Neither operation was successful in giving Rolfe normal bowel and urinary function. For reasons doctors could not explain, he lacked any sphincter control. Until he was 13, he was subject to constant, involuntary bowel movements and an incessant dribble of urine. "He was teased unmercifully in school," his mother recalls.

Rolfe spent 15 years of his life undergoing $250,000 worth of reconstructive surgery in three cities. When he was 10, surgeons attempted to tighten his urinary sphincter, but something went wrong and the bladder necrosed, or died. Temporary tubes had to be placed in each kidney and connected to an external bag, to drain off urine. It was at this point that a pediatric urologist in Detroit, whom the Schroeders consulted out of desperation, discovered the cause of Rolfe's woes. Rolfe was missing the vertebra at the very base of his spinal column, the one that contains the nerves that oversee bowel and bladder function. It was impossible to correct this deficiency. And the only other hope, a rebuilding of the bladder, was ruled out during an extensive operation at Boston's Massachusetts General Hospital. Surgeons instead performed an ileal conduit procedure, in which they created a new bladder from a short segment of the upper bowel, disconnected the ureters from Rolfe's kidneys, hooked them up to the makeshift bladder, and then created a permanent opening in his abdomen through which urine could empty.

A few months later the doctors tackled Rolfe's bowel incontinence. An Australian doctor in the United States on a visiting fellowship suggested performing sartorius sling surgery, in which the sartorius muscle, the long structure that runs from the pelvis down to the calf, is looped around the bowel opening, thereby creating an artificial sphincter that could control the bowels. But two days after the sling procedure, the blood supply to Rolfe's bowel ceased and the tissue started to die, imperiling the boy's life. An emergency colostomy was performed, and a large segment of colon had to be removed. Now Rolfe was wearing a colostomy bag on one side to collect feces, and a second bag on the other side to collect urine. Both bags leaked, so that his flesh, from the chest to the pubic area, was constantly raw and bleeding. He underwent two skin graft surgeries to remove the irritated tissue.

Finally, when Rolfe was 15, another surgeon contrived the idea of looping a piece of the gracilis, one of the muscles of the thigh, around the teenager's anal opening. This time the surgery was successful. Today, at 18, Rolfe faces a lifetime of wearing the urinary bag. But he does have a measure of bowel control, and no longer needs the colostomy bag. So much of his colon is gone, however, that little moisture is absorbed by his body as waste passes through. The result is his bowel movements are excessively watery, diminishing the amount of control he might otherwise have. He still must go to the bathroom every few hours.

Despite his many tribulations, Rolfe is, to all appearances, a happy-go-lucky young man. He has an innately sunny disposition, which seems to have helped him adjust. He is in college, plays baseball and hockey to the extent that he can, is planning a career in either sports broadcasting or law, and holds down a part-time job as an usher. He refuses to let his disability hold him back.

"It used to interfere with my life a great deal," he says. "It was a nightmare. But since the gracilis operation it doesn't get in my way that much anymore."

Last year he met a young woman at a high school dance, and the two of them hit if off immediately. They dated for nearly four months, even working a summer job together at a school for the mentally handicapped, before splitting up because she was going away to school. "I told her about my problems," Rolfe says. "Her reaction was wonderful. I think the fact she's going into special education helped. She's especially understanding. I was real surprised to find it didn't bother her. For quite a while I was afraid girls wouldn't understand, but then I figured the only way I'd ever find out is to start dating. I don't see it as a barrier with women anymore. I really don't think I'll have any problem getting married or anything like that. It's not much more than finding the right person."

His experience in this regard is quite interesting, in light of the fact that studies indicate that a urinary appliance can be a distinct impediment to sexual adjustment.

Rolfe's parents are not convinced his seeming equilibrium isn't bravado. They fear he may be denying his true feelings to himself and others. "He seems adjusted," his mother confides, "but I don't know if we're not sitting on top of a volcano." As an example of his failure to be realistic, they cite an attempt he made to join the Marines last year. Rolfe "forgot" to tell the recruiting sergeant about his urine bag, a fact that embarrassingly emerged when the man came out to the house to interview the Schroeders. Rolfe also refuses to discuss his ailments with his family, acting as if they didn't exist. "He's like the dark side of the moon," says his mother.

Yet, in an interview, Rolfe seemed realistic enough about his handicaps. As he says, he doesn't get much opportunity to forget them. "It's hard not to face up to the thing. It's there all the time. But it's not that inhibitive. To me, it's a sleeping dog, and I'm going to let it lie."

Even though excellent adjustments can be made, a substantial number of birth defect victims share a less pleasant fate. Studies of adolescents with spina bifida, for example, show that social isolation is a major part of their lives. In 1981 Drs. J. H. Walker and Barbara Castree, of the University of Newcastle in England, reported that 38 percent of young adults with myelomeningocele saw a friend less than once a week. Only 22 percent of them had a romantic relationship. Half of the teenagers in another study had no social companions outside of the school setting, and in still another survey 25 percent "had not been visited, gone to visit, or otherwise been out with a friend in the twelve months preceding the interview."

The University of Newcastle team also found that none of the 43 subjects of their study were living an independent life. All of them, save for one who was in an institution, resided with their parents or grandparents. Some 40 percent of them required help with bathing, dressing, and other personal chores, which their relatives provided, "often with increasing difficulty." Only 20 percent of them had real jobs, while 13 percent had make-work posts, 27 percent were in adult day care, and 9 percent were pursuing education. A full 31 percent were unemployed. Walker and Castree wrote, "If the outcome of managing disabling disease in childhood is measured by the achievement of an independent and fulfilling life as an adult, success with sufferers from myelomeningocele . . . must be regarded as strictly limited."

Cardiac anomalies form another class of birth defect with a strong potential for causing long-term psychological damage. A team of researchers at Duke University Medical Center undertook a follow-up study of 37 young adults who had been treated at the institution for tetralogy of Fallot, the form of congenital heart disease that consists of four related defects and that causes respiratory difficulty and cyanosis. Although it is potentially fatal and requires multiple hospitalizations, it is completely correctable surgically. Each of the subjects in the 1974 study had undergone total repair, and 85 percent of them had been asymptomatic for a number of years. On the basis of a standard personality evaluation, 22 of the 37 test subjects were found to be neurotic. By contrast, only 7 neurotics would statistically be expected in any group of 37 people. Specifically, the subjects were revealed to have weak superegos and to be dependent, self-indulgent, overprotected, less well informed, lacking in ambition, and operating more on the basis of feelings than thought. Since the subjects who proved to be neurotic in the study had experienced significantly more hospitalizations as youngsters than the other subjects had, the researchers hypothesized that the negative effects of hospitalization had played a role in their poor psychological development.

It is one of the more mysterious aspects of the effect of birth defects on the human personality that people often fail to succeed even when there is no objective reason for the failure. The congenitally disabled are more apt not to hold jobs, although their handicaps would not preclude it. They are more apt not to marry, even when there is nothing that should stand in their way. As Dr. Elva Poznanski says, "The physical aspects of disease are more successfully dealt with than are the emotional side effects. The majority of handicapped children do not become Helen Kellers."

Obviously, emotional distress is highly correlated with birth impairment. That being so, one might suppose it to be reflected in a high suicide rate. Strangely, however, that does not seem to be the case. Although there are no conclusive studies on the subject, the rate of suicide appears to be no higher among the birth impaired than among the general population. But as a New York researcher of chronic illness points out, not all suicide gets recorded as such. "Suicide isn't the only form of self-destruction," she says. "Suppose you have a patient with end-stage renal failure on kidney dialysis, and he doesn't take care of himself. He doesn't follow his diet, and he dies. It doesn't get signed out as suicide; it gets put down as a medical death. Yet it may have been a self-destructive act. And many physical accidents and overdoses are suicide but aren't so listed. People with birth defects and other medical problems have greater opportunity to have masked suicides."

Nonetheless, people with birth defects do take their own lives in overt fashion. One poignant example occurred in 1978 in a suburb of Schenectady, New York. A 12-year-old March of Dimes poster child named Karl Huszar hanged himself with a nylon noose looped over the hinge of a door. Karl had been born with gastroschisis, a defect in which the intestines lie exposed on the outside of the body. It took five years to correct it surgically, and, according to reports, it left him with an unsteady gait and a hunchbacked posture. Yet, until the day he killed himself, Karl gave few outward signs of deep emotional distress.

And one cannot overlook the celebrated case of Elizabeth Bouvia. Mrs. Bouvia, 26, suffers from a form of cerebral palsy called spastic quadriplegia, which has left her almost completely paralyzed since birth. She possesses control only of her facial muscles and some minimal movement of her right hand. Moreover, she is wracked by involuntary spasms and painful, degenerative arthritis. In spite of her disabilities, she has led a relatively full life, earning a degree in social work from San Diego State University, becoming pregnant (though the pregnancy ended in miscarriage), and getting married (though the marriage collapsed after a year). But in late 1983 she grew disillusioned with life and resolved to terminate it. Unable to do so without the help of others, she checked into a Riverside, California, hospital and asked to be given only painkillers and hygienic care until she starved to death. The hospital refused to cooperate in a suicide and threatened to discharge her. Mrs. Bouvia then obtained an American Civil Liberties Union attorney and went to court, asserting her right to die. Her lawyer argued that her constitutional right of privacy gave her the same prerogative to refuse treatment that critically ill kidney or cancer patients have in rejecting dialysis or chemotherapy. Even though her afflictions themselves are not life threatening, he contended, the fact that she is unable to feed herself means that she would die without the assistance of others and that she therefore has the right to refuse that assistance.

After a widely publicized, nine-day hearing in December 1983, Judge John H. Hews, of the California Superior Court, ruled against Mrs. Bouvia. He agreed that she did have the fundamental right to take her own life, "but not with the assistance of society." Her right of privacy, he said, was outweighed by the interest of society in preserving human life. Mrs. Bouvia's reaction was to refuse further nourishment, whereupon the hospital, with court permission, introduced force-feeding. Although she struggled against it with what little might she possessed, a nasogastric feeding tube was inserted in her body, where it remained while the appeals process began. In January 1984 the California Supreme Court joined Judge Hews in denying her petition. As of this writing, Mrs. Bouvia has left the hospital. After a brief trip to Mexico, where again hospital authorities refused to help her die, a newspaper reported she had changed her mind and now wanted to live. Mrs. Bouvia denied the story on her return to the United States.

The affair raises some novel points of law, which need not concern us here. One might ask only how a society that values life too highly to assist a woman who wants to die can suspend its reverence long enough to electrocute a convicted murderer. More central to our discussion, though, is the question of why Mrs. Bouvia wants to die. During the hearing the hospital's attorney argued that it was because she was depressed about the miscarriage and the failure of her marriage. Mrs. Bouvia staunchly denied, however, that she was depressed or that her marital problems were in any way connected with her choice. It had more to do, she said, with her inability to partake of life, her intractable pain, and the endless indignities her existence subjected her to. "I suffer from severe spasticity and arthritis," she declared to reporters, "and from the humiliation of having all my meals fed to me and all of my elimination functions attended to by others." It also bothered her, she said, that after years of effort, during which time she had earned a college degree and tried to meet certain goals, she still was unable to live independently. "I had high ideals," she said. "I thought I could succeed. But little by little I realized that supporting myself and living an independent life is an impossibility. Now I know what it will take. I'm more realistic.

"I'm trapped in a useless body," she said. "Unfortunately, I have a brain. It makes it all the worse. If I were retarded or senile, I wouldn't know the difference or care. It's not that I don't have the will to live. . . . In reality, my disability is going to keep me from doing the living I want to do. You can only fight for so long. It's a struggle for a person like me to live and a struggle to die. It is more of a struggle to live than die."

If one takes Elizabeth Bouvia's stated wish for death at face value—and some skeptical minds may question her resolve—then her situation seems to exemplify, at its most extreme, the futility of life with a crippling birth defect. She has intelligence and self-discipline, and a desire to achieve. She has followed, word for word, society's prescription for success, and yet it has proven to be an empty dream. The human spirit can stand many frustrations. What it cannot stand is the destruction of the grand illusions. For Elizabeth Bouvia the grinding knowledge that this is all there is and all there ever will be has apparently been too much to bear.

Yet, it would be wrong to generalize from one woman's experience. The reactions of the congenitally impaired to their handicaps are far too diverse for that. In fact, the disabled community was appalled by the media attention Mrs. Bouvia's struggle received, and it angrily assailed her for betraying the cause. To these critics the aim of presenting a positive image of disability to able-bodied society, an image of active, aspiring people seeking greater opportunity, was jeopardized by her graphic embodiment of hopelessness. These are understandable sentiments. It is important to recognize, however, that just as Mrs. Bouvia does not stand for all disabled people, neither is she an isolated example of unhappiness. It is beyond dispute that there are an unknown number of handicapped individuals who lead lives of quiet desperation, deterred from final solutions like suicide only by their innate survival instinct or by the providential human ability to adapt to nearly all seemingly untenable situations.

In the final analysis, however, assessing the mental state of the congenitally impaired is an impossible enterprise. The information is conflicting, what little of it there is. And the biggest category of impaired people, namely, the mentally retarded, are largely inaccessible to us for study. Can any of us say for certain how a bedridden person with an IQ of 20 feels about life? John Robertson, of the University of Texas School of Law, once asked, "But in what sense can [anyone] validly conclude that a 'person' with different wants, needs, and interests, if able to speak, would agree that such a life were worse than death? . . . One who has never known the pleasures of mental operation, ambulation, and social interaction surely does not suffer from their loss as much as one who has. . . . Life, and life alone, whatever its limitations, might be of sufficient worth to him." On the other hand, it just as easily might not. It is an enigma that shall eternally mock us.

13

⤜⤛⤚

What the Future
Holds

Genetic Engineering and the
Prevention of Birth Defects

Only in this century have we been able to join in serious battle against
birth defects. And now, thanks to a development with profound consequences, we are about to gain the upper hand. Findings about the
gene and about cellular mechanics have brought us to the threshhold
of a new era, one in which many congenital defects, not to mention
many diseases we don't normally think of as birth related, will be treated
and cured with gene therapy. These same principles of molecular
biology promise to expand the ability of genetic counselors to identify
the carriers of most genetic disorders. Similarly, these principles,
combined with refinements in diagnostic technique, have vastly
broadened the scope of prenatal diagnosis. It has become theoretically possible to detect nearly all abnormal fetuses prior to birth. Finally,
doctors are also learning, although with some trepidation, how to repair
dangerous fetal maladies while the child is still inside its mother's womb.

Medicine is experiencing a heady feeling as it pushes back these
frontiers, for it is probing at the very heart of life itself. One cannot
convey how dry and technical the papers are that announce new discoveries in genetic research. And yet one reads them like prophecy,

for they portend events that will change forever the way we relate to the world.

The theater for this bold and sometimes frenzied research activity is the Lilliputian milieu of the gene, a level of existence so minute that its ratio to the visible world is as that of a 50-cent piece to the United States. It is here where all life, be it plankton or brontosaurus, is defined. The key to everything is the long, sinuous molecule we call deoxyribonucleic acid, or DNA, which lies coiled up inside the chromosomes of all living things. These DNA molecules are composed of chains of chemical subunits called nucleotides, thousands of which strung together constitute a single gene. These nucleotides come in four varieties, depending on whether they contain adenine (A), guanine (G), thymine (T), or cytosine (C). It is the exact sequence of the nucleotides that carries the instructions for the manufacture of specific proteins, the substances necessary for the growth and maintenance of a living organism. Scientists use the A, G, T, C alphabet to express this sequence, or, as it is commonly known, the genetic code. For example, the recipe for human insulin starts out "CCA CCG CCT CCC TAA TAG TAT" and continues on for hundreds of recurrences of A, G, T, and C. Horse insulin would have a slightly different sequence of nucleotides, as would Kodiak bear insulin, the same being true of every conceivable protein required for the functioning of every conceivable organism. Because there are so many potential permutations of the four letters of the code, it is easy to account for the vast complexity and variety of life.

The genetic code works roughly like this. The DNA molecule is actually two long strands that wind around each other in a kind of spiral called a double helix. Along this twin spiral, each nucleotide bonds with a complementary one on the opposite strand; as it happens, A pairs only with T, and G pairs only with C. When the body needs a particular protein, the gene responsible for producing it "unzips," that is, the two strands pull apart and lie exposed. An imprint of the code is then made and relayed to the cell's protein factory. There, the message is "read," and amino acids, the building blocks of protein, are requisitioned and fitted onto a growing chain according to the exact sequence dictated by the code. The finished protein may then be used by the body in the formation of blood and tissue or, if it is an enzyme, in one of the countless chemical reactions necessary to life.

This, then, is the process that governs organic existence. DNA may be visualized as the hereditary archive, the library of genetic information that has been handed down from one's ancestors. What sort of eyes, nose, arms, heart, and feet we have is largely dictated by the blueprints stored in that library. If there is a misprint in any of the designs—if the order of nucleotide bases in a gene is incorrect—then the cell factory will be instructed to supply the wrong amino acids, and the ensuing protein will be faulty. The end result may be a birth defect. For example, in sickle-cell anemia there is a T in the DNA code for hemoglobin where there ought to be an A. Thus, when the cell goes to make hemoglobin, it is always going to snap an inappropriate amino acid onto the protein chain. This one small "mutation," as such errors in the DNA code are known, is enough to wreak havoc on a victim's life.

One of the exciting ways this new understanding of DNA is being applied is in the prenatal diagnosis of congenital defects. The number of defects that can be detected before birth has been steadily growing over the past fifteen years. At first this ability was limited to detecting Down's syndrome and other chromosomal disorders by examining fetal cells shed in the amniotic fluid. Then it was discovered that open-neural-tube defects, such as anencephaly and myelomeningocele, could be identified by the presence of certain fetal proteins in the fluid. With the perfection of ultrasound, medicine became proficient at visualizing a wide variety of other malformations. Concurrently, tests were created for the diagnosis of some 75 inborn errors of metabolism—single-gene disorders, such as maple syrup urine disease, which are caused by a nonfunctioning enzyme. The tests involved chemical analysis of fetal cells for the presence or absence of specific enzymes. Yet, despite the progress medical science was making, it was only scratching the surface. There remained three thousand single-gene disorders that could not be diagnosed. And certain other illnesses, such as hemophilia and sickle-cell anemia, could be detected only by drawing fetal blood directly from the placenta, using an instrument called a fetoscope. The procedure carries a 6 percent risk of fetal mortality.

Then genetic engineers entered the picture, with techniques that go right to the source of inherited disorders—the faulty DNA itself. There are essentially two processes available to them. In the first method, the researchers make use of bacterially derived enzymes known as restriction endonucleases, which have the ability to go up and down a chain of fetal DNA and cut into it wherever they spot a specific nucleotide sequence. If the gene is normal, the endonuclease will cut the DNA into fragments of regular length. But if a sequence contains the wrong nucleotide, the restriction enzyme will ignore it and pass on to the next cutting site. The longer-than-normal DNA fragment thus indicates the presence of an abnormal gene. Let's use the exam-

ple of sickle-cell anemia again. At one point in the normal gene for
human hemoglobin, the nucleotide sequence is CCT GAG. In the
flawed gene of sickle-cell victims, it reads CCT GTG. It happens that
a certain restriction enzyme known to scientists as Mst II recognizes
the normal CCT GAG sequence. Whenever it sees that sequence in a
strand of DNA, it will make a cut. Imagine the enzyme clicking along
a hemoglobin gene, like Pac-Man, busily snipping it into fragments.
Suddenly it comes to CCT GTG. It doesn't know what to do, so it
simply moves along to the next occurrence of CCT GAG. When the
entire cutting process is complete, one of the resulting fragments will
be substantially longer than the others, telling the researcher that the
fetus has the sickle-cell gene. The technique was first demonstrated
in 1978 by Dr. Y. W. Kan, of the University of California at San Francisco.

The second method is to make a probe that will zero in on the
improper nucleotide sequence. Using a DNA synthesizer, a segment
of biologically active DNA is prepared according to specifications. These
call for positioning the nucleotides in the probe so that they comple-
ment the defective sequence in the abnormal gene. For example, if
the flawed gene has a T where it should have a G, as is true with the
Mediterranean blood disease beta thalassemia, then the synthetic piece
of DNA will have an A where it should have a C. This is to encourage
the synthetic piece to bond to any beta thalassemia gene that it
encounters. A radioactive tag is then attached to the probe to enable
geneticists to follow its travels. As in the endonuclease method, a sample of fetal cells is acquired by amniocentesis and the cell nuclei are
cracked open to expose the child's DNA. Enzymes are used to split
the DNA into fragments, and then the probe is mixed in with the
fragments. The researchers watch the radioactive tag to see whether
the probe has bonded to the DNA. If it has, the gene must be faulty.
A probe may similarly be prepared to bond to a normal hemoglobin
gene, which, if present, would indicate that the fetus will not suffer
from beta thalassemia.

The two techniques have had their principal clinical application thus
far in the diagnosis of hemoglobin disorders. But a team at Baylor
University's Howard Hughes Medical Institute, led by Dr. Savio Woo,
announced in the fall of 1983 that it had used a probe to test for the
presence of alpha 1-antitrypsin deficiency, a severe autosomal recessive disease that strikes one in 2,000 Caucasian children. Its chief
manifestation is the development of chronic emphysema in early
adulthood, but 14 percent of all stricken individuals will die of cirrhosis of the liver in early infancy. Its cause is a shortage of a particular
enzyme inhibitor, stemming from the substitution of glutamic acid for

lysine in the protein chain, which in turn results from the presence of an A in the genetic code where there should be a G. The team prepared probes for both the normal and the abnormal alpha 1-antitrypsin gene, and in so doing it was able to tell which fetuses had two of the recessive genes, and would thus develop the disease; which had a normal and an abnormal gene, and would therefore be genetic carriers; and which ones would be free of the illness altogether.

Woo also announced in late 1983 that he and his colleagues had succeeded in identifying the nucleotide sequence of the gene that codes for phenylalanine hydroxylase, the enzyme that is missing in phenylketonuria (PKU). It appears likely that a DNA probe will soon be prepared that will test for PKU prenatally. PKU is one of the best-known inborn errors of metabolism, having been first described in 1934 by Folling in ten severely retarded children. It has heretofore evaded prenatal diagnosis because the missing enzyme is a product of the liver and is not secreted by the fetus into the amniotic fluid and because it is not present in fetal blood. Hence, the sole method for screening PKU currently is to test the baby's blood shortly after birth. If the test is positive, the child can be put on a special diet that will avert retardation.

Theoretically, DNA analysis ought to enable doctors to diagnose all birth defects that have a genetic basis, and most scientists do indeed believe that this will someday be true. But reaching this goal requires an intimate knowledge of where specific genes lie along the chromosomes. Ten years ago geneticists had little idea of the location of any of our estimated 100,000 genes. Genes look pretty much alike under the microscope, and no road sign declares that this one is for eye color, this one for adrenalin, and this one for human growth hormone. Still, scientists have determined the chromosomal addresses of more than 1,700 genes, and they are "mapping" new ones all the time. Some authorities believe we will have charted the human gene map in virtually its entirety by the turn of the century. In a curious sense the exploration calls to mind the voyages of Magellan and Columbus, and yet everything is happening inside a petri dish.

The direct analysis of DNA also demands a precise knowledge of the nucleotide sequence of defective genes. Only several dozen human genes have been sequenced thus far. To get around this stumbling block, researchers have created another method of detecting genetic error in families with a known history of a hereditary ailment. It works like this. Everybody has what are known as variants or polymorphisms within their DNA structure. These are mutational bits of genetic material, and they are more common in the "spacer" DNA, the long stretches of DNA between the genes that do not code for proteins.

Sometimes these variants are physically close to a gene of interest, and the closer they are to that gene, the more likely it is that the two will be transmitted as a unit to the next generation during meiosis. If a variant occurs frequently within a family that also has a history of a genetic disease, and if that variant is generally inherited with the disease, then its presence in a fetus suggests that the defective gene is also present nearby. Scientists believe they can test for these "markers" without actually understanding the structure of the flawed gene. In this manner, they say, such dreaded hereditary illnesses as Duchenne's muscular dystrophy, cystic fibrosis, and hemophilia may be diagnosed prenatally. As of now, there exists no sure method of anticipating Duchenne's, a fatal degenerative disease that is possibly caused by an inborn error of metabolism (its victims have an abnormally high blood level of creatine phosphokinase). As is true of all sex-linked recessive disorders, it affects males almost exclusively, and the only way for carriers of the gene to avoid any chance of giving birth to affected children is a cruel one: they must undergo amniocentesis to determine a fetus's sex, and then abort it if it is a boy. The problem is, the disease strikes only 50 percent of a carrier's male children; half of a couple's sons would thus be aborted needlessly. By the same token, there is no technique for diagnosing cystic fibrosis in utero. Parents with one afflicted child suffer great anxiety during subsequent pregnancies before learning whether their other children will be affected. The disease, incidentally, which chiefly affects Caucasians and has an incidence of once in 2,000 births, is certain to become more prevalent as better medical management enables more of its victims to survive to childbearing age. Any diagnostic technique that can discover either of these two killers prenatally would be a boon.

All of the techniques of DNA analysis we have outlined lend themselves equally well to the screening, prior to conception, of couples who fear they are carriers of genetic disease. A sample of parental blood cells can be obtained painlessly and the DNA therein tested in the same manner as in fetal cells. This will undoubtedly become the preferred tool of genetic counseling within a few years. Unfortunately, it does not appear to have mass screening potential. The incidence of hereditary diseases is relatively low among the general population, and the cost of DNA testing is relatively high, running into many hundreds of dollars. It would therefore not be cost-effective to screen everyone of childbearing age for, say, cystic fibrosis or PKU. Instead, a target population would be screened, most probably an ethnic group at high risk for the disease.

Reliable tests exist already, however, for identifying carriers of certain diseases. Notable among these is the test for Tay-Sachs disease, the deadly autosomal recessive disorder that is most common among Jews of East European origin. One Jewish couple in 900 is at risk of having children with Tay-Sachs because both husband and wife carry the gene. The screening test measures each spouse's blood level of an enzyme called hexosaminidase A. The absence of this enzyme in an infant causes a fatty chemical called GM_2-ganglioside to accumulate in the brain, leading to the progressive degeneration of nerve cells. Carriers of Tay-Sachs will have just half the normal amount of hexosaminidase A in their bloodstream. In the event that both parents are carriers, a test of fetal cells can be conducted during pregnancy to determine whether the child is lacking in hexosaminidase A. If so, the parents are offered the option of abortion.

Meanwhile, late in 1983, the doctors at Massachusetts General Hospital in Boston reported that they had developed the first genetic test for detecting Huntington's chorea, the fatal neurological disorder that took the life of the folksinger Woody Guthrie in 1967. The disease, which afflicts 20,000 people in the United States, does not make its presence known until about the age of 40, when a slight clumsiness is noticed. Even then it is difficult to diagnose until several years later when a frank dementia and loss of motor control set in. Unaware of their fate, the majority of its victims will long since have married and had children, 50 percent of whom will themselves inherit the autosomal dominant disorder. Through this insidious camouflage Huntington's chorea ensures its perpetuation.

Using genetic probes, the Massachusetts research team, led by James Gusella, studied 570 skin and blood samples from a tribe of Venezuelan villagers that has one of the highest incidences of the disease in the world. From these studies, the team was able to locate a genetic marker, a distinctive stretch of 17,000 nucleotides on the fourth chromosome that appeared only in Huntington's victims. Presumably, the Huntington's gene is also on chromosome 4, in proximity to the marker. The test, which is expected to be available within two years, will end, for those who wish to find out, the terrifying suspense experienced by an estimated 100,000 Americans who, while knowing they are at risk for the disease, have been unable to tell early in life whether they will someday develop it. Moreover, the test can be used equally well for prenatal diagnosis, which should dramatically reduce the number of Huntington's chorea victims in the years ahead.

It would ultimately be a disappointment, however, if all that genetic research could provide was a better diagnosis of hereditary disease, without the ability to do anything about it. But most authorities believe that it will one day be possible actually to correct genetic flaws. Although it is commonly agreed that this will take many years, we have already had a glimpse of the future.

In 1983 a pair of West Coast researchers "cured" a severe brain disorder in the laboratory by inserting a healthy gene into a batch of defective cells. Dr. Inder Verma, of the Salk Institute in San Diego, and Dr. Theodore Friedmann, of the University of California at San Diego, utilized cells responsible for the hereditary disease, Lesch-Nyhan syndrome. Researchers have discovered that Lesch-Nyhan is signified by a defect in the gene that controls the production of an enzyme known as hypoxanthine-guanine phosphoribosyltransferase (HPRT). The enzyme is needed to metabolize purines, nitrogen compounds that are the end product of the digestion of proteins. Unconverted, the purines may build up in the nerve tissue and destroy its function.

Verma and Friedmann employed a novel approach to correct the Lesch-Nyhan gene. They first used a gene-splicing technique to put a healthy HPRT gene into a mouse leukemia virus (the virus was modified so that it would not cause cancer). Then human cells containing the Lesch-Nyhan gene were exposed to the virus, and the virus entered the cells. As Verma and Friedmann had hoped, the cells began to manufacture HPRT. The technique has been hailed as a method of treating a wide variety of human genetic illnesses, but its initial application will probably be limited to blood disorders and immune-deficiency diseases. It will be at least five years before the procedure moves out of the laboratory and into human trials.

Also on the West Coast, the biologist Leroy Hood and colleagues at the California Institute of Technology and the University of California at San Francisco announced in November of 1983 that they had isolated the gene in rats that controls the production of myelin, the substance that sheathes the nerve fibers. Because the rat's biochemistry is similar to ours, it is now believed possible to isolate the human gene responsible for myelin. This would have profound implications for the treatment of diseases like multiple sclerosis, which is characterized by a degeneration of myelin. The nucleotide structure of the normal gene could be determined and compared with that of afflicted individuals. A cure could then be envisioned in which abnormal genes are replaced with healthy ones. The realization of that cure, however, will have to await a means of delivering healthy genes to enough of a victim's cells to do the patient some good. Altering a few cells would not help, because many normal cells are necessary for the synthesis of myelin sheaths. To test one delivery system, the Caltech-UCSF researchers have injected normal myelin genes into mice embryos. The mice are afflicted with a twitching disease that results from myelin deficiency. Working with the embryo is ideal for gene therapy, because if one corrects cells sufficiently early in an organism's life, the majority of its adult cells will contain healthy genes as a result of simple cellular division.

Gene modification in human test subjects has been practiced only on a limited basis. Two years ago, however, a team at the National Institutes of Health tried out a new concept of treating blood diseases using humans as guinea pigs. The five volunteers suffered from either beta thalassemia or sickle-cell anemia. The research team was fascinated by the fact that the human body contains two genes for the production of hemoglobin—a fetal gene that handles the job prenatally and an adult gene that takes over after birth. The researchers reasoned that if a victim's adult gene is functioning inadequately, perhaps the fetal gene, which has remained latent since birth, can be reactivated. The tool they used was a drug called 5-azacytidine, which has the peculiar property of neutralizing chemicals that prevent gene expression. Team members had a hunch the drug could switch the fetal gene back on. And so it did. Within a week the blood of all the patients showed remarkable improvement. Unfortunately, long-term therapy was ruled out, for fear that 5-azacytidine might have cancer-causing potential.

These various forms of genetic engineering have raised difficult ethical questions. The most compelling fear is that gene modification techniques will one day be used to tamper with our basic genetic nature. A group of religious leaders headed by the author Jeremy Rifkin has petitioned Congress to impose a moratorium on research that might promote this result. Advocates of continued research contend that the introduction of genes into patients' somatic, or body, cells is essentially no different from any other kind of medical treatment that seeks to cure disease. They argue that it becomes unethical only if a patient's sperm or egg cells are altered, which would pass the new trait on to succeeding generations.

These are extremely vexing issues to sort out. On the one hand, the benefits of learning to cure hereditary disease seem to warrant pursuing genetic engineering to its logical ends. On the other hand, given the human propensity to make destructive use of every technology we master, it seems likely that abuses will occur. Can we afford to take that risk? It might have tragic consequences for unborn generations if a genetic mistake was unwittingly unleashed—or, worse, if a totalitarian regime began altering human beings to suit their grand plan. One shudders to think of what uncomplaining automatons could be created through some tinkering with the genes. Yet, would altering our DNA necessarily be inimical to our welfare? What, in principle, is wrong with building stronger, more disease-resistant people? Maybe nothing, but one can reasonably ask whether these creatures would still be people. Or would they, by definition, constitute some new and alien species?

So insoluble and disturbing are these questions that partisans on both sides seem to take a curious comfort from the fact that we remain very far from being able to reconstruct humankind. It is as if our present ignorance were an amulet against disaster.

In the summer of 1983 several medical centers in the United States announced that they were about to offer an advanced fetal diagnostic technique on an experimental basis. The technique is called chorionic villi sampling, and it displays great promise. It is a delicate but painless procedure. The obstetrician inserts a thin plastic catheter into the uterus through the vagina and the cervix, while a second doctor, following the procedure on a high-resolution ultrasound monitor, directs the placement of the catheter between the lining of the uterus and the chorion, a layer of tissue that surrounds the embryo and eventually develops into the placenta. The objective is to obtain a sample of villi, tiny, fingerlike projections along the chorion that transfer oxygen, nutrients, and waste between a mother and her embryo. Because both the chorion and the embryo cells are derived from the same fertilized egg, and thus contain identical genes, any genetic defects in the unborn child may be detected by a study of villi tissue.

Chorionic villi sampling was first developed in China in the early 1970s and has undergone trials in England, Italy, Czechoslovakia, and the United States. It possesses one important advantage over the older diagnostic technique of amniocentesis—it gives results much earlier. Amniocentesis, which involves extracting a small amount of amniotic fluid through a needle inserted in the mother's abdomen, cannot be attempted until the 16th week of pregnancy or later. Before that time, there is not enough amniotic fluid in the womb for the test to be administered safely. In addition, the procedure yields such a limited sample of fetal material that the cells must be cultured for up to four weeks before the laboratory has an amount it can analyze. Results are thus delayed until the 20th or 21st week, a delay that has serious psychological and medical consequences for a woman whose test comes back positive. The fetus will have "quickened"—that is, it will be making perceptible movements—and many mothers in these circumstances feel strong misgivings about abortion. Moreover, second-trimester abortions are significantly more hazardous than those performed in the first trimester. They cannot be done on an outpatient basis and involve procedures that are quite distasteful. By contrast, chorionic villi testing can be done early in pregnancy, generally between the 8th and 12th weeks, but sometimes as soon as the 5th week. Equally important, it produces a much larger sample of fetal tissue, often dispensing with the need for a culture. Test results may be returned within a day, facilitating a quick termination of abnormal pregnancy. Abortions in the 9th or 10th week, when the fetus is less than two inches long, are far simpler and less traumatic.

Enthusiastic proponents have predicted that chorionic villi sampling will replace amniocentesis as the primary prenatal diagnostic technique by the end of the 1980s. For now, however, it remains experimental, as doctors evaluate its safety. Fears have been expressed that the procedure, by disturbing the cervix and uterus, could induce miscarriages. A study published in Prague reported that of 107 patients who had undergone the test, 13 had suffered miscarriages, and a study in Milan reported a pregnancy loss in 5 out of 62 cases. The problem with interpreting these data is that first-trimester miscarriages are rather common anyway, whether an examination is performed or not. It is hard to say whether a pregnancy was interrupted by the villi procedure or whether it would have terminated on its own. In the Milan study, for example, one of the five lost fetuses had trisomy 14, a chromosomal condition incompatible with life. More research must be carried out, but current opinion in the obstetrical community is that the procedure carries little more risk than amniocentesis and is well suited, moreover, to recombinant DNA methods of fetal diagnosis.

If chorionic villi sampling lives up to its billing, it will have tremendous value in the detection of many hereditary diseases, but it is unlikely to replace amniocentesis as the means of diagnosing one category of birth defect—neural-tube disorders. Within the scope of our present knowledge, the only reliable way to identify a fetus with spina bifida or anencephaly is to analyze amniotic fluid for the presence of either of two chemicals, alpha-fetoprotein or acetylcholinesterase.

Alpha-fetoprotein, or AFP, is a substance that is manufactured in the liver of the fetus and normally excreted through urination. The level of AFP in the amniotic fluid increases steadily until the 15th week of pregnancy, at which point it suddenly drops off. When a fetus has a neural-tube disorder, excessive AFP is leaked into the amniotic environment through the open spinal column. Thus, the AFP level remains high, both in the amniotic fluid and in the mother's bloodstream, until the 20th week. This connection between AFP and neural-tube defects was discovered in 1972 by a pair of British scientists, Roger Sutcliffe and David Brock, of Western General Hospital in Edinburgh. The information quickly became the basis of a four-part screening procedure.

Under this procedure, a woman first undergoes a simple blood test. If the level of AFP in her bloodstream is high, the test is run a second time, to weed out false positives. If a second high reading is obtained, the next step is to administer an ultrasound examination. Ultrasound, which uses high-frequency sound waves to create a "picture" of the fetus, is able to detect almost every case of anencephaly. It can also reveal other circumstances that might account for an elevated AFP reading, such as the presence of twins or an error in dating the pregnancy. If none of these factors is present, the final step is to perform amniocentesis to see whether an open spina bifida exists. Some 90 percent of all anencephalies and 80 percent of all myelomeningoceles may be detected in this manner, in time for the mother to undergo a second-trimester abortion if she so desires. In addition, AFP testing can be used to identify fetuses with abdominal-wall defects, including omphalocele and gastroschisis.

The acetylcholinesterase test, which is newer, is similar in nature. Acetylcholinesterase is an enzyme that, in the case of neural-tube defect, leaks from the exposed membrane surface of the spine. This test has an advantage over AFP screening, in that it is more sensitive and eliminates false positives. However, AFP testing is currently far more prevalent, because it is significantly cheaper.

Alpha-fetoprotein screening was initially reserved for women at known risk of having an infant with anencephaly or spina bifida— namely, women who have already given birth to one affected child or who have a family history of the disease. It was clear, though, that 95 percent of all children with neural-tube defects were born to women who did not fit into this high-risk category. For that reason, in the late 1970s a number of cost-benefit studies were performed to determine whether it would be economically advantageous to screen all pregnant women for neural-tube defects even though the disorders occur at a rate of only 1 to 4 per 1,000 live births, meaning that the number of actual cases averted would be small. In 1979 Drs. Peter Layde and Godfrey Oakley, of the U.S. Center for Disease Control, reported in the *American Journal of Public Health* that the total cost of testing a hypothetical cohort of 100,000 pregnant women would be $2,047,780. The total benefits society would reap, however, by not having to care for the 59 spina bifida victims that would otherwise be born, came to more than $4 million. The conclusion: mass screening *is* cost-effective.

In Britain, where the incidence of neural-tube defects is higher than in the United States, mass AFP screening has been conducted by the National Health Service for at least six years. Some 50 percent of all British pregnancies are screened. In places like Glasgow, where the program is particularly centralized, up to 80 percent of the pregnant population undergoes testing. The concept has been implemented more slowly in the United States, primarily because of nagging ethical questions that surround the procedure. False positives yielded by the initial blood serum test can create powerful anxiety among mothers, who will have to wait for ultrasound and amniocentesis results before they will know for sure whether they are carrying an affected child. Approximately 50 women out of every 1,000 tested will show up positive in the first blood exam, but only one or two of them will actually be carrying a defective infant. Many people believe it borders on the criminal to send a woman home with a positive serum test result and let her agonize for several days without counseling. They are also afraid it might induce women to seek abortions without further corroborative evidence.

Equally disturbing is the fact that the final amniocentesis examination itself yields an occasional false positive. A research team at London's Queen Charlotte's Maternity Hospital reported in *Lancet* that of 6,000 women screened in the preceding two years, 80 underwent amniocentesis and 16 were found to have telltale abnormalities of the amniotic fluid. As it turned out, one of the 16 abnormal readings involved an unaffected fetus, which again pointed out the danger that a certain fraction of normal babies might be aborted without genuine cause.

Prolife groups object to mass AFP testing, just as they oppose all prenatal screening, because they believe it can only lead to more abortions. Disability rights organizations, such as the Spina Bifida Association of America, fear that a campaign to stamp out neural-tube defects will have a negative effect on the self-image of living myelomeningocele victims. For all these reasons the Food and Drug Administration delayed for three years its approval of AFP testing "kits," prepackaged assay systems that a number of American pharmaceutical houses wanted to market to hospitals and clinics around the country. Early in 1984 the FDA finally approved them. But there is still a debate over whether to distribute the kits to individual doctors' offices.

Despite the outcry, mass AFP screening has been introduced quietly in several U.S. communities, where it appears to be functioning very well. Programs are currently in place in Los Angeles, Baltimore, Chapel Hill, North Carolina, New Haven, Connecticut, Boston, Providence, Vermont, and Long Island. The state of Maine has been sponsoring a mass AFP screening program since 1978. It is conducted by the Foundation for Blood Research in Scarborough, a suburb of Portland. Women pay $20 for the initial serum test, which they may take in their doctor's office. The blood sample is then sent to the foundation, which runs it through analysis. If there is a positive reading, the foundation sets into motion its counseling services to help the woman through the anxious period while she is undergoing ultrasound and amniocentesis.

"The program has been quite successful. We are continuing to gain acceptance," says Dr. James Haddow, founder and director of the foundation. Haddow says that 6,000 women a year use the service, approximately 40 percent of all the pregnant women in Maine. He said that since the program started, it has detected 17 cases of anencephaly, 7 cases of open spina bifida, and 14 abdominal-wall defects. The vast majority of these babies were aborted. Figures supplied by Haddow indicate that it costs the Maine program $51,000, counting medical fees, for every two cases of neural-tube defect it catches. This is balanced against the $275,000 that the Spina Bifida Association of America estimates it costs to raise a myelomeningocele victim over a lifetime.

Haddow thinks the concept of mass AFP testing will gain gradual acceptance in the United States, and he hopes to see a time when the majority of pregnant women undergo the procedure. This would significantly reduce the incidence of spina bifida and each year spare thousands of families profound sorrow. But Haddow has one worry. "I am bothered by the total decentralization of testing in America. This has to be performed under expert supervision; you can't do it casually. It's not like a blood sugar test."

For sheer drama, none of the breakthroughs in the prevention and treatment of birth defects can rival medicine's attempt to operate on fetuses while they are still inside the uterus. At eight treatment centers around the United States, doctors are learning how to alleviate potentially fatal conditions by inserting therapeutic instruments into the womb. And they are preparing for the day, in the near future, when they will achieve the ultimate dream—temporarily removing the fetus from the uterus to repair a defect directly.

The two conditions most amenable to fetal surgery at present are congenital hydrocephalus and urinary-tract obstruction. Both ailments are caused by an abnormal accumulation of fluid, and threaten the fetus with death or severe impairment if the pressure is not relieved. In fetal hydrocephalus the cerebrospinal fluid starts to build up inside the ventricles of the brain; if the condition is not corrected before the 29th week of gestation, it will cause lasting brain damage. Repair, though, is exquisitely difficult. The fetus cannot be seen in the flesh; instead it must be visualized indirectly by means of a high-resolution ultrasound machine. Nor is it a stable target, for it bobs and weaves in its sea of amniotic fluid. The surgeon's job, then, is to pierce with a needle a living creature about the size of a telephone receiver, a creature that the doctor cannot actually see and that is floating around like a cork. After first anesthetizing the mother and administering Demerol to the fetus to reduce its movements, the physician inserts a hollow hypodermic needle through the mother's abdominal wall and into the child's brain. The needle, which is a foot long and almost as thick as a pencil, enters through the right, or less dominant, hemisphere of the brain in order to minimize damage to cerebral tissues. Using a plunger mechanism, the doctor then pushes a small plastic "shunt," or catheter, through the needle so that one end is inside the swollen ventricle and the other end is outside the body. The needle is then withdrawn, and for the rest of the pregnancy, the cerebrospinal fluid will be able to drain through the shunt into the amniotic sac.

Bladder obstruction is treated in the same manner, although it is done a little earlier in pregnancy. Whereas the hydrocephalus repair is generally carried out around the 25th week, the urinary procedure is done as early as the 20th week, in hopes of preventing permanent kidney damage. The needle is inserted in the bladder and again a shunt is implanted, enabling the obstructed urine to drain into the amniotic sac. A surgical team at the University of California, San Francisco, recently reported success in 19 of 26 cases of urinary obstruction.

A third condition, diaphragmatic hernia, is also a candidate, at least in principle, for fetal surgery. In this case, the abdominal organs bulge into the child's chest cavity through an abnormal opening in the diaphragm, preventing growth of the lungs. Repair requires an incision in the uterus and partial removal of the fetus. The procedure has not yet been tried in humans, but it has been successful in rhesus monkeys and sheep.

In its four-year history, fetal surgery has been attempted only a few dozen times. It is a highly experimental procedure, shrouded in controversy. Even the doctors who perform the surgery concede its risks and urge caution in expanding its frontiers. "Fetal surgery is the most exciting thing happening in obstetrics. It is also the most ethically troublesome and the most medically uncharted," says Dr. Richard Depp, who along with his colleague James T. Brown has conducted a number of intrauterine repairs at Chicago's Northwestern Memorial Hospital.

Doubts prevail for a number of reasons. Anytime one disturbs the uterus, one risks triggering premature labor. Here is where the animal experiments do not apply well to human experience. A monkey's uterus is usually limp; it can absorb a great deal of handling without going into early contractions. But the human uterus, once touched, tends to expel its contents. As a result, large doses of prostaglandin synthetase inhibitors, drugs that depress uterine contraction, must be administered before fetal surgery. And we can't predict the quality of life the survivors are going to experience. Some will have incurred serious internal damage by the time their conditions are diagnosed. What lasting effect this will have on their lives will not be known for several years. A urinary obstruction could so damage the kidneys, for example, that the survivor may develop end-stage renal disease and have to be placed on an artificial-kidney machine. Finally, for fetal surgery outside the womb to succeed, surgeons are going to have to solve the problem of how to keep the fetus from taking air into its lungs. "Once they breathe, it's all over," says Chicago's Dr. Brown. "You can't put their heads back in the amniotic fluid. They'll drown."

Nevertheless, the potential of prenatal surgery is vast. It may one day be routine to repair many disorders before birth, and surgeons may be assisted by various facts of fetal life. For one thing, the fetus has a poorly developed immune system. It is believed, therefore, that bone grafts and organ transplants can be performed without the risk of rejection. Even more astounding is the possibility that the fetus has the power to regenerate missing or incomplete body parts. This view is based on an observation made several years ago on a monkey fetus, whose fingers, severed early in pregnancy, later on in gestation grew back completely. This finding leads some doctors to believe that poorly formed limbs and other defective fetal structures may be induced to fill out normally prior to delivery.

But fetal surgery poses important ethical questions that must be answered. If fetuses become surgical patients, then it stands to reason that we will have to accord them "person" status. As patients, they will have a set of rights like anybody else. A paradox will then be created because society permits the abortion of fetuses at the same gestational age. Another issue revolves around whether the mother can be forced to undergo fetal surgery in the interest of her baby. Are parents under an obligation to submit to invasive procedures to prevent the suffering of their children? Following that logic, would children born with defects that might have been repaired by fetal surgery have just cause to sue their parents or obstetrician later in life for nonfeasance?

There seems to be an irreducible quantity of ethical chaos in the natural world, and it never goes away. It just keeps taking a different form. In this respect, it is like the insect population. Whatever brilliant means we devise for eradicating the weevil, mosquito, or medfly, more resistant strains of these hardy creatures inevitably return to plague us. So it is with ethical conflict. Any attempt to solve current moral dilemmas only breeds newer and increasingly stubborn ones down the road. "Poor man," wrote William Faulkner. "Poor mankind."

14

Conclusions

I think I always suspected that Mike was different, from the day he first came home from the hospital. It may have been the way he looked; his eyes lacked sparkle, his face was disturbingly lax, as though everything was not pulled together tight. Or maybe it was his nature, which seemed more peaceful than is usual for newborns. Of course, I may be crediting myself with too much prescience, looking now at things through the prism of hindsight. We certainly did not know until much later that there was anything really wrong with Mike.

It is hard to say exactly when we did know. Such awareness blooms like an inverse flower, from the outside in, with dreams and expectations folding in on themselves as each developmental milestone passes unmet. Mike was late sitting up. He was late standing up. He reached the ripe age of 18 months before he learned to walk. There is never any specific day on which you know a child is mentally impaired. You just . . . know.

I remember all too clearly the day Mike took his first step. In my mind's eye I see the entire family crowded around him, cheering him on. Someone has hold of him by a rope, which has been tied under his arms as a kind of harness to keep him standing. My mother is kneeling in front of him holding out a small toy, urging him to come to her, while I, the dutiful 12-year-old brother, am standing beside him ready in case he should fall. And once again I see him put his foot out and stumble forward. It was the smallest of attainments, but to us it was like a walk on the moon.

Mike's early childhood was a medical blur. My parents dragged him to a series of doctors with German-sounding names, and however many specialists they consulted was the number of diagnoses they received. He was brain damaged. He was hyperactive. He was dyslexic, dysfunctional, aphasiac, ataxic, and perceptually impaired. He would outgrow it. He would never outgrow it. He would be capable of independent living someday. He would require a lifetime of institutionalization. One day, after several years of trying to get answers, my mother took Mike to a children's neurologist with a reputation that inspired awe on several continents. The doctor administered a battery of tests. Then he sat back, looking vaguely baffled. At length, he remarked, "You know, Mrs. Lyon, he has an unusually large head." My mother, who had reached the end of her tether after so many years of testing, felt like giggling insanely. This legendary man of medicine, this avatar, had applied the sum of his knowledge and skill, and all he could say to her was that Mike had an unusually large head. She felt offended by the implication that Mike, who has a normal-sized head, was something of a monster, and she felt cheated by so unscientific a diagnosis. But, more than anything else, she was struck by the fact that the doctor himself was the possessor of a head that seemed to dwarf the rest of his body. Unable to restrain herself, she blurted, "Doctor, forgive me, but you have the largest head I've ever seen. With a little luck, maybe he can become a neurologist." With that, she snatched my brother's hand and was off. That was the last time she ever took him to a doctor.

To this day, I cannot tell you exactly what is wrong with Mike. It has always defied explanation. But he has severe limitations and will forever need supervision. He can read and write in a primitive way, but he has no concept of numbers. He has little common sense and would stand in the rain for hours if so instructed. In general, he functions at about the level of a 10-year-old.

For the first few years of his life, Mike lived at home, at great emotional cost to my parents. Though his daily needs demanded a significant amount of attention, it was as a constant symbol of lost potential that he became more than my mother could bear. With considerable mixed feelings, my parents placed Mike in a residential facility in Wisconsin shortly after his eighth birthday. Later, he lived in facilities in Colorado and New York. His contact with the family was confined to the two or three trips a year that we made to him, short visits that only added to his sense of isolation from those he loved, and the annual trek home he made at Christmas, traveling at the tender mercies of airline stewardesses. Today he is 30 years old. He lives in an institution not far from my home. It is a place that provides lifetime care, where the residents live in cottages, work in sheltered environments, and are kept motivated by a system of "cottage justice," in which they are rewarded for good behavior with tokens and punished for bad behavior with restrictions. I visit him whenever I can.

It was easy over the years not to take Mike seriously as a three-dimensional person. Part of this I attribute to the permanent separation of our lives. But, as I am ashamed to admit, it owes more to my preconceptions of a mentally disabled individual. I tended to think of Mike as lacking any significant interior life, any passions, hopes, resentments, or cares, since he seldom articulated anything of that kind. To me, he was a bland person with a flat exterior, a papier-mâché man of seemingly little ambition or sexuality. But this was only an illusion, as I was to find out.

Mike has a magical belief that if he leaves some of his possessions at our house, he is not really living permanently away from home. For this reason, he once came to visit at Christmas loaded down with an immense overseas bag filled with personal goods. He asked me to store it for him, ostensibly because they wouldn't let him keep it at "school," as he refers to his institution. For months the bag lay in the attic, untouched, until one day I was conducting one of those periodic inventories we make of the clutter of our lives. The bag caught my attention, and I began to go through it. Mostly, it contained odds and ends: a transistor radio that was missing batteries, a few erratically shaped things with glitter on them that Mike had made in a handicraft class, some 45 rpm records, a photo album with family pictures in it, a souvenir program from an outing to the Ringling Brothers Circus, a couple of ribbons for participating in the Special Olympics, and a stack of spiral notebooks. I opened one of the notebooks and received a shock. There, in Mike's tortured printing, was a diary of sorts. I couldn't believe it—that he would feel the need to record the daily events of his life. It was a literary impulse I would have thought beyond him. More amazing, however, were the contents of the diary itself. As I turned page after page, there stood revealed inner thoughts such as I would never have ascribed to anyone as uncomplicated as Mike. For two hours I sat in the attic transfixed. As Samuel Pepys had taken us into the mind of 17th-century man, so was my brother taking me into the mind of the mentally disabled.

Here was pride: "I got everry singeal token today four being good."

And career aspiration: "I would like to have the jobe of helpeing on the foode truck with John W——"

And penitence: "I am verry verry sorry sorry four what I did towardes you, Miss Jarvis and Mr. Haas [supervisors]."

And hope: "And I would like two gaine the privilleges backe of takeing a bath on the north weing and allso on the south weing and answerring the cottage telephone and allso would like to gaine the privilleges backe of carrying my own cigerettes."

Each day contained a careful tally of the good-behavior tokens he had received, red ones in one column, blue ones in another. Side by side were glum accounts of the restrictions he had incurred. There were comments on the weather and a note that he had spent the day "runnening eairendes."

What most astonished me were his expressions of emotion, such as this lascivious fantasy:

"Maybe Mike Lyon and Jane S. wille like to go to screwing out in back of the cottage."

And this profound piece of resentment, which I could scarcely believe from my meek and placid brother:

"No I will note serve any of my restrictiones any moorre at all four you Miss Joanes, and Miss Collins lookes like a big fate froge and she allso crockes like one and allso shie can go to healle and shie can allso suck dick and that meanes my peanes allso."

Suddenly, I had to perceive Mike in a different light. He had an inner sensibility, a thought life rich in its variety, if not in its experience. He had a street vocabulary of considerable breadth, and he had sexual daydreams. The public has many misconceptions about the sexuality of the mentally disabled. In the mythology, they either are portrayed as rapists, hulking brutes ready to defile people's innocent daughters, or they are presumed to be completely asexual, immune to the lusts and need for romance that occupy the normal population. Yet, here was my brother, contemplating a perfectly ordinary assignation alfresco.

That day marked a turning point in my relationship with Mike. I have since spent a substantial amount of time getting to know him all over again, learning to talk to him on a deeper level. What I have discovered is at once enlightening and distressing. I have found, for example, that he knows all too well how stultifying his life is and that it fills him with bitterness. He has a deep-seated longing to live outside the institution, preferably with his family, but otherwise on his own. He recoils when he hears the word *retarded* and feels keenly the gulf that separates him from other people.

"Why do some people get to live outside and us kids here have to live inside?" he asks me.

"I don't know, Mike."

"Is it because they're, you know, not as, you know, smart as other people?"

"Could be, Mike."

"Am I . . . like that?"

I cannot speak.

One night on the telephone not long ago Mike informed me that he had asked his supervisor whether he could enroll in a nearby college.

"Why?" I asked.

" 'Cause if I go to college maybe I could get a job reading books like you."

"I'm not reading a book. I'm writing a book."

"Oh."

"Anyway, what would you study if you went to college?"

"Oh, things."

"Like what?"

"Well, uh . . . biology, I guess."

"Biology? Do you know what biology is?"

"Well, no I don't. I just heard of it is all."

"Biology is the study of all living things."

"You mean like animals?"

"Sure. And plants."

"Plants? Why say that? Plants aren't alive, are they?"

"Of course, they're alive."

"Oh, man."

When I got married recently, Mike was strangely sour for a while, until I got him to admit that it was because he would like to get married, too, and live in a house like ours. He doesn't really understand why he cannot.

Mike is acutely responsive to incentives. About two years ago he was moved into an adult living center where he shares a compound with nine other people, enjoying such amenities as a bathroom of his own, his own closet, a desk, a dresser, and the privilege of staying up till midnight. His self-image improved overnight. Then, last month, he was given a prestigious job in the facility's new training center, where the better-functioning residents are groomed for possible day jobs off-grounds. He has been walking on air ever since. But I know it will wear off soon, as it always has before, if he doesn't realize his twin goals of working and living on the outside. Because this is impossible, I fear he is in for a terrible letdown.

Being around Mike has made me intensely aware of the fact that his existence is without any of the basic human fulfillments. Neither love nor marriage leavens the loneliness of his days and nights. Freedom and mobility will never be his. The satisfaction that comes from holding a responsible job is always going to elude him. This is not to say he doesn't know the pleasure of work. He has tasks to perform and does them well. Still, he is conscious of the qualitative difference between the occupations he is suited for and those that engage the rest of us. He was once assigned to spend the day putting nuts and bolts together and filling glass jars with them. A stripe on the glass told him how high he had to fill each jar. He hated the job with a single-minded passion, both for its monotony and for its lack of challenge, but above all for its obvious triviality compared with what other people do for a living. Mike tends not to appreciate what he can do; he only frets over the things he can't do. In that sense, he is very much like the rest of us.

All right, one might argue, his life has little purpose. But does life really require a purpose? Perhaps the simple joy of being alive is enough. I don't have an answer for that argument, but, using myself as a frame of reference, I know that I would not want to live my entire life in confinement, subject to rewards and punishments like a laboratory creature and deprived of the most pleasurable human experiences. I would not want to be separated from my family at the age of eight and to face the possibility that someday, if I outlive those close to me, I will be alone and defenseless among strangers.

My concern for Mike's plight has in turn made me question the wisdom of a policy of aggressively treating all newborns, regardless of the extent of their disabilities. My brother's life has acquired momentum, and I would never suggest that he hasn't the right to complete it. But it is not the sort of life that we would desire for our loved ones. And when one sees the kind of existence that is being preserved for the most direly affected children, it is difficult to understand how we can even speak of a "right" to such a life. It seems more fitting to speak of a right to a dignified death.

In the fall of 1983 an infant girl was found abandoned in a restroom wastebasket at Boise State University in Idaho. Baby Ashley, as her nurses christened her, was 12 weeks premature and weighed approximately 1,000 grams. Doctors at Boise's St. Luke's Regional Medical Center placed her on a ventilator. Not long afterward, she was found to be suffering from hydranencephaly, a severe brain disorder in which both cerebral hemispheres fail to develop and are replaced with a membraneous sac filled with cerebrospinal fluid. Hydranencephalic children typically have only a brain stem, permitting the maintenance of certain motor reflexes, such as heartbeat and swallowing, but portending no future intellectual function. Since there were no parents to approve a discontinuation of life support, Ashley's doctors were forced to go to court to ask permission. The child, they contended, was an infant analogue of Karen Ann Quinlan. She had no chance of ever becoming a thinking, feeling individual, they said, citing as evidence a CAT scan of her head, which revealed virtually no brain matter. It showed only the luminous ring of her skull, like a halo. But prolife forces and disability rights activists mounted a strong campaign to keep Ashley alive. They flew a Connecticut couple in to testify about their own experience in adopting 12 handicapped children, among them a four-year-old boy with hydranencephaly. The child had no intellect, the couple conceded, but he could smile and respond to a stroke on the cheek. They urged, therefore, that everything possible be done to preserve Ashley's life. Apparently impressed, a juvenile-court judge ordered the ventilator kept on. Ashley finally died on December 7, 1983, 73 days after her birth.

After two months of being forced to support a life against her clinical judgment, the child's doctor spoke out at a postmortem press conference. "Somebody along the way has missed the fact that there is a time for people to die," she commented acidly. "There is a time for us and babies as well. . . ."

In the final analysis, there are but two strong arguments to be made for keeping a child like Ashley alive. The first is that it is in the child's best interests to do so. The second is that it is in society's best interests; that is, it is important that we affirm our respect for life. Proponents of the second view would contend that to allow someone to die using quality-of-life criteria necessitates a judgment that one form of human existence is better than another, and that it thus opens the door to discriminating among people on the basis of whose life has the greatest social value. How soon, these proponents ask, before the judgment that there is "such a thing as a life not worthy to be lived" ushers in the era of genocide so vividly portrayed by Dr. Leo Alexander in his chronicle of Nazi war crimes? This "slippery slope" proposition, high-minded though it may be, in essence requires that we keep a child alive in order to satisfy an abstraction. Do we really want to force someone to endure a life that may be painful, dreadfully unpleasant, or devoid of cognitive experience because of *society*'s need to ascribe larger value to it or because of *society*'s desire to insulate itself from some projected evil?

It seems to me we are on more humane ground when we base our treatment decisions on what is in the child's best interest. This, of course, is not the end of the matter, because what is best for the child is often far from clear. But we are at least on the right track when we make compassion for the child our sole standard.

I hope my brother will forgive me for exposing his personal life to public scrutiny. I have cited his example because the exercise of compassion requires seeing the congenitally impaired as they are, as human beings of flesh and blood with difficult, dreary lives. Too often, in the debate over the withholding of treatment from defective newborns, the children come to be discussed in a strangely disembodied way, as if they were subordinate to the larger issue. At times, unreality takes over completely, and disabilities of the most grievous kind are sanitized so that they sould less devastating than they really are. We are told that a Baby Ashley will be capable of smiling if caressed on the cheek. We are told that a Baby Jane Doe may not be completely bedridden and may at least be vaguely aware of her surroundings. The implication is that minimal lives do not have to be bad and can even be enjoyable and fulfilling. But to test the nobility of these sentiments we have only to reflect on whether we would wish to experience such a life. Chances are, most of us would not. Why then do we ask the congenitally impaired to endure more suffering, pain, and endless boredom than we would want for ourselves?

Only when we can put ourselves in the place of an individual with severe birth defects can we begin to see that it may occasionally be a kindness to let a child die, rather than to expend maximum medical effort to perpetuate his or her life. This assertion has nothing to do with the social value of the child. It is not meant to imply that any youngster's life is not *worthy* to be lived. Instead, it is predicated on the belief that some lives are not *worthwhile* to be lived, that they are so ridden with pain, distress, and ennui that they may be of negative value to their owner.

If we accept the premise that there are children whose best interests lie in an early death, we are presented with an even more difficult question. How do we determine what level of suffering or deprivation warrants a decision to withhold or withdraw life support?

Such a question cannot be answered categorically. There is no suitable set of guidelines that can be worked out in advance, owing to the unique nature of each child's diagnosis and prognosis. Some physicians, it is true, have attempted to draft broad, preconceived treatment criteria, as did England's John Lorber in the case of spina bifida, but putting such concepts down on paper has always seemed to me to be arbitrary, inflexible, and mean-spirited. Decisions as momentous as those concerning whether a child should live or die are best made on an individual basis, taking into account the special circumstances of a given youngster's condition. The complexities of the question demand that the decision maker possess qualities of sensitivity, solicitude, wisdom, and mercy, along with an intimate knowledge of the patient's case. It follows, then, that the identity of the decision maker is every bit as important as the question of how the decision is made, for the two are inextricably tied.

It is my opinion that such judgments are properly the province of a child's mother and father. Obviously, there are many people who disagree with this view, and not without compelling reasons. But it is useful to study the alternatives to parental discretion. We might, for example, disqualify parents altogether and assign the decision to physicians. Doctors constitute a priest caste in our culture; it might be consistent with the vast authority they already enjoy for us to empower them to decree who shall live and who shall die. But this is a moral, not a scientific, judgment, and doctors bring to it no special expertise. Besides, it is not likely that doctors would welcome this license if it were extended to them.

A second alternative is to allow government bureaucrats to make the choice. This is impractical. Governmental officials have even less competence than doctors to make moral choices, and the mechanism by which they might enter a case has been proven to be ponderous and disruptive.

The courts? Judges have some experience at making ethical decisions, but their medical knowledge is limited. Furthermore, the time required to bring a case before the bench lobbies against it as a solution to a medical crisis.

Of course, those who purport to defend the rights of handicapped children advocate yet a fourth alternative, namely, the refusal to allow any human agency to decide. According to this view, the lives of all defective children are to be prolonged by all possible means, without regard to the quality of life. The appeal of such a dictum, which the Baby Doe regulations came uncomfortably close to embracing, is that it avoids the sin of *jus vitae necisque;* it grants no one the power of life or death over anyone else. It all seems very godly. The child's destiny is preprogrammed, and to all appearances no mortal has made a choice. In reality, though, a decision *has* been made, a decision to preserve life, no matter what the cost.

Each of these alternatives has serious drawbacks. In my view, all are less desirable than the acceptance of the primacy of parents as decision makers. This is not to say there aren't flaws in even this solution. Parents may put their own self-interest ahead of the interests of their child. They may be unduly influenced by a physician. They may make their decision while in a state of high anxiety. Nevertheless, the strengths they bring to the decision-making process seem, on balance, to outweigh the weaknesses. Parents have a profound bond of blood with the infant, giving them an attachment that no third party can ever have. Isn't it reasonable to assume that most of them will select the treatment option that inflicts the least amount of harm on their baby?

Before the birth of our daughter, I had long pondered the question of how I would react if a child of mine were born with serious problems. Would I be revolted by imperfection? Would I be negligent and selfish? As it happened, I received the unwelcome opportunity to find out. When our baby was delivered, doctors at first suspected she had sustained neurological damage on her left side. This later proved to be untrue, but for a period of some 48 hours both my wife and I experienced an agony beyond description. Throughout that uncertain time, we visualized our daughter growing up with a seriously diminished use of her left arm and leg and potentially suffering other deficits as well. But not once did we feel less love for her. Her affliction became our affliction, and I cannot imagine having made any medical decision that would have been to her detriment, no matter what the degree of her abnormalities.

We do live in the real world, however, and there are going to be parents who will refuse to authorize surgery that would be clearly beneficial to their impaired child. There will also be callous doctors who, perhaps because of a bias against the malformed, will recommend letting a child die in disregard of its best interests. The issue is, are there enough safeguards built into the current decision-making process to avert abuses? Some people in the medical community believe that the recent establishment of hospital ethics committees as instruments of review can provide this needed check. The decisions of physicians and parents would be subject to scrutiny and possible censure. How much prerogative ethics committees would ideally have remains to be determined, as the concept evolves. It is difficult to envision granting them absolute authority. Families and treating physicians would accept that prospect no more readily than were a Baby Doe squad to impose its judgment. Yet, not to allow the committees at least some control would reduce them to being a pointless sham.

It is true that such review boards do nothing to standardize the care of handicapped newborns—and it is the desire for such standardization that has prompted the great controversy of the recent past. In a society of laws, an island of self-regulation, such as the neonatal nursery has proven to be, is bound to provoke opposition in many quarters. But, as we have seen, throwing laws at an ethical problem, the way big government might throw money at a social problem, is sometimes a cumbersome and intrusive way of dealing with matters. For example, the law recently passed by Congress equating medical nontreatment with child abuse is poor legislation on several counts. If I understand "child abuse" correctly, it refers to hostile and injurious treatment of a youngster, not to the benevolent desire to protect one's child from a life of great distress. In addition, the law, by depending on a loose network of designated informers to apprise state agencies of such "abuse," seems unenforceable and open to serious misapplication. The law should be repealed. A responsible self-policing system may be the best solution that we can hope for.

If government wishes to enter the picture more directly, it can play an invaluable role—that of improving the lives of disabled children and their families. If we wish to encourage parents to raise severely disabled children, then we must provide financial and emotional support well beyond current levels. At the moment, we have created a disincentive, rather than an incentive, for parents to choose life. Amending the situation will require a tremendous commitment of money and human resources. But if we shirk the obligation, we will lose much of our moral leverage to tell parents what to do. It is they, after all, who will have to bear the long-range consequences of a decision to give maximum treatment to their child.

There will never be an entirely satisfactory solution to the problem of defective newborns. We will always face the unsettling fact that we have in our hands a sacred trust, the destinies of those who cannot speak for themselves. As with any such patients, of whatever age and mental capacity, one must take care not to sacrifice their lives to expediency. But neither should we forget the fundamental ideals of compassion that represent the very soul of medicine. Through the ages, healers have sought new treatments and technologies. But ever since the first primeval practitioner discovered the first medicinal herb, the goal has been the same—the welfare of the patient. Merely because we have progressed to some new frontier of technology is no reason to abandon that goal.

The sanctity-of-life principle derives from the same moral tradition as our concept of mercy. Is it not in the best spirit of that tradition that we temper the one with the other? We can embody these ideals best by not insisting that physicians invariably perpetuate lives that are painful or dolorous, and by allowing parents the freedom to decide what is and is not an acceptable life for their child, using the human heart as their guide.

Notes

1 "Baby Doe"

P. 21—The details of the Bloomington Baby Doe case were compiled from interviews conducted between June 1983 and February 1984. Those consulted include, in alphabetical order, Judge John Baker; Lawrence Brodeur; Roland Kohr, chief administrator of Bloomington Hospital; Andrew Mallor; Linda McCabe; Taleatha McIntosh; Dr. Walter Owens; Dr. John Pless; Dr. James Schaffer; Maudleine Starbuck; Bonnie Stuart; Ron Waicukauski, Monroe County prosecutor; and Dana Watters.

P. 36—In Re: The Matter of Baby Doe, Monroe County Juvenile Court, JV8204-038A.

Pp. 40–41—N. Fost, "Putting Hospitals on Notice," *Hastings Center Report* 12, no. 4 (Aug. 1982): 5–8.

P. 41—*Bloomington Herald-Telephone*, May 19, 1982.

P. 41—*Louisville Courier-Journal*, May 19, 1982.

Pp. 42–43—J. Strain, "The American Academy of Pediatrics Comments on the 'Baby Doe II' Regulations," *New England Journal of Medicine* 309 (1983): 443–444; author's interviews.

P. 44—American Academy of Pediatrics v. Heckler, No. 83-0774, U.S. District Court, D.C., Apr. 14, 1983.

P. 45—C. E. Koop to author, press conference, Apr. 6, 1984. HHS itself wrote, in the Jan. 12, 1984, *Federal Register*, p. 1642, "The Department strongly disputes the accounts of these investigations provided by personnel affiliated with the two hospitals. . . . Contrary to these reports, both of these investigations [Strong Memorial Hospital and Vanderbilt University Hospital] were conducted very expeditiously and professionally, and every effort was made to minimize any disruption to the hospitals." HHS went on to issue a point-by-point rebuttal of the charges in the affidavits—indicating, for example, that the Baby Doe squad spent only 11 hours at Vanderbilt Hospital, not 18, and that "at no time during the investigation did hospital personnel complain to [the Office of Civil Rights] that the investigation was disrupting patient care."

P. 46—Telephone interview with A. L. Washburn, Apr. 25, 1984.

Pp. 46–49—The People of the State of N.Y. on relation of A. L. Washburn, Jr., against Stony Brook Hosp. and the State Univ. of N.Y. at Stony Brook. From the transcript, pp. 32, 46, 47, 53, 141, 174, 217, 218, 220, 225, 226–27, 236, 238.

P. 49—Weber v. Stony Brook Hosp. 467 NYS 2d 685 (1983).

P. 50—Weber v. Stony Brook Hosp. 465 NE 2d 1186 (1983).

Pp. 50–51—K. Kerr, in *Newsday*, Oct. 29, 1983; ibid., Oct. 27, 1983.

Pp. 51–52—M. Chambers, in *New York Times*, Nov. 6, 1983.

P. 52—Editorial, *Wall Street Journal*, Oct. 31, 1983.

P. 52—Editorial, *New York Times*, Nov. 11, 1983.

P. 52—Koop, on CBS's "Face the Nation," Nov. 6, 1983.

P. 52—U.S. v. Univ. Hosp. of State Univ. of N.Y. at Stony Brook, 575 F. Supp. 607 (1983).

Pp. 52–53—U.S. v. Univ. Hosp., State Univ. of N.Y. at Stony Brook, U.S. Court of

Appeals, for the Second Circuit, Docket No. 83-6343 (1984).

P. 55—G. Newman to author, Apr. 25, 1984.

2 Infanticide

P. 59—C. E. Koop, L. Schnaufer, and A. M. Broennle, in *Pediatrics* 54 (1974): 558–64.

P. 60—*International Clearinghouse for Birth Defects Monitoring Systems, Annual Reports,* 1980, 1981.

Pp. 62–65—J. Warkany, in *Journal of Chronic Diseases* 10 (1959): 84–95. I am indebted to Dr. Warkany for his painstaking account.

Pp. 62–63—M. Piers, *Infanticide: Past and Present* (New York: W. W. Norton, 1978), 67–69.

Pp. 63–64—W. Langer, "Infanticide: A Historical Survey," *History of Childhood Quarterly* 1 (1974): 353–65.

P. 64—J. Locke, *An Essay Concerning Human Understanding,* bk. 3, chap. 6, sec. 23.

P. 64—*The Collected Works of Ambroise Paré,* trans. T. Johnson (Pound Ridge, N.Y.: Milford House, 1968), 961–1026.

Pp. 70–71—"Report of the Joseph P. Kennedy Foundation International Symposium on Human Rights, Retardation, and Research, Oct. 16, 1971."

Pp. 71–72—R. S. Duff and A. G. M. Campbell, "Moral and Ethical Dilemmas in the Special-Care Nursery," *New England Journal of Medicine* 289 (1973): 890–94.

Pp. 72–73—A. Shaw, "Dilemmas of 'Informed Consent' in Children," *New England Journal of Medicine* 289 (1973): 885–94.

P. 73—J. Lorber, "Results of Treatment of Myelomeningocele," *Developmental Medicine and Child Neurology* 13 (1971): 300.

P. 74—Maine Medical Center v. Houle, No. 74-145 Superior Court, Cumberland, Maine, Feb. 14, 1974.

P. 74—Application of Cicero, 421 N.Y.S. 2d 965 (1979).

Pp. 74–75—In re Phillip B., 92 Cal. App. 3d 796, 156 Cal. Reporter 48 (1979).

P. 75—In Re B. (A Minor) (Court of Appeal), *Weekly Law Reports,* Nov. 27, 1981.

P. 76—Koop, in Associated Press story, July 1, 1983.

P. 76—L. Alexander, "Medical Science under Dictatorship," *New England Journal of Medicine* 241 (1949): 39–47.

Pp. 77–78—A. Shaw, J. Randolph, and B. Manard, "Ethical Issues in Pediatric Surgery: A National Survey of Pediatricians and Pediatric Surgeons," *Pediatrics* 60, Supp. (1977): 588.

P. 78—"Treating the Defective Newborn: A Survey of Physicians' Attitudes," *Hastings Center Report* 6 (Apr. 1976): 2.

P. 78—I. Todres et al., "Pediatricians' Attitudes Affecting Decision-Making in Defective Newborns," *Pediatrics* 60 (1977): 197–201.

P. 78—Gallup poll, reported in *Chicago Sun-Times,* June 2, 1983.

P. 79—J. Paris, "Terminating Treatment for Newborns: A Theological Perspective," *Law, Medicine, and Health Care* 10 (June 1982): 120–24.

3 Born Too Soon

Pp. 80–82—On-site research at a major midwestern children's hospital.

Pp. 86–88—On-site research at a major midwestern children's hospital.

Pp. 88–90—See J. H. Comroe, Jr., "Premature Science and Immature Lungs," in *Retrospectroscope: Insights into Medical Discovery* (Menlo Park, Calif.: Von Gehr Press, 1977), 140–79. Dr. Comroe provides a fascinating and witty account of this respiratory research, for which I am much indebted.

P. 90—K. von Neergaard, "New Notions on a Fundamental Principle of Respiratory Mechanics: The Retractile Force of the Lung, Dependent on the Surface Tension in the Alveoli," *Z Gesamte Exp Med* 66 (1929): 373–94. English translation in "Pulmonary and Respiratory Physiology," *Benchmark Papers in Human Physiology,* ed. J. H. Comroe, Jr., pt. 1 (Stroudsburg, Pa.: Dowden, Hutchinson & Ross, 1976), 214–34.

Pp. 90–91—C. Macklin, "The Pulmonary Alveolar Mucoid Film and the Pneumocytes," *Lancet* 1 (1954): 1099–1104.

P. 91—R. E. Pattle, "Properties, Function, and Origin of the Alveolar Lining Layer, *Nature* 175 (1955): 1125–26.

P. 91—J. Clements, "Dependence of Pressure-Volume Characteristics of Lungs on Intrinsic Surface Active Material," *American Journal of Physiology* 187 (1956): 592.

P. 91—M. E. Avery and J. Mead, "Surface Properties in Relation to Atelectasis and Hyaline Membrane Disease," *American Journal of Diseases of Children* 97 (1959): 517–23.

P. 92—F. Adams et al., "Effects of Tracheal Instillation of Natural Surfactant in Premature Lambs," *Pediatric Research* 12 (1978): 841–48.

P. 92—*Medical World News*, May 14, 1979, pp. 10–11.

P. 92—J. A. Smyth et al., "Hyaline Membrane Disease Treated with Bovine Surfactant," *Pediatrics* 71 (1983): 913.

Pp. 92–93—M. Hallman et al., "Isolation of Human Surfactant from Amniotic Fluid and a Pilot Study of Its Efficacy in Respiratory Distress Syndrome," *Pediatrics* 71 (1983): 473–82.

P. 93—G. Gregory et al., "Continuous Positive Airway Pressure with Spontaneous Respiration: A New Method of Increasing Arterial Oxygenation in Respiratory Distress Syndrome," *Pediatric Research* 4 (1970): 469; G. Gregory et al., "Treatment of the Idiopathic Respiratory Distress Syndrome with Continuous Positive Airway Pressure," *New England Journal of Medicine* 284 (1971): 1332–40.

Pp. 94–96—W. Silverman, "Incubator-Baby Side Shows," *Pediatrics* 64 (1979): 127–40; A. J. Liebling, "Profiles: Patron of the Premies," *New Yorker*, June 3, 1939; L. J. Butterfield, "The Incubator Doctor in Denver: A Medical Missing Link" (privately published by the Denver Westerners).

P. 94—B. Tuchman, *The Guns of August* (New York: Macmillan, 1962), 30.

Pp. 96–97—On-site research at a major midwestern children's hospital.

P. 98—T. Terry, in *American Journal of Ophthalmology* 25 (1942): 203.

P. 98—M. Crosse and P. Evans, "Prevention of Retrolental Fibroplasia," *Archives of Ophthalmology* 48 (1952): 83–87; A. Patz, L. Hoeck, and E. De La Cruz, "Studies on Effect of High Oxygen Administration in Retrolental Fibroplasia: Nursery Observations," *American Journal of Ophthalmology* 35 (1952): 1248–53.

P. 99—R. J. Cremer, P. W. Perryman, and D. H. Richards, "Influence of Light on the Hyperbilirubinaemia of Infants," *Lancet* 1 (1958): 1094–97.

Pp. 101–2—L. Gluck, M. V. Kulovich, and R. C. Borer, Jr., "Diagnosis of the Respiratory Distress Syndrome by Amniocentesis," *American Journal of Obstetrics and Gynecology* 109 (1971): 440–45.

P. 102—J. Clements et al., "Assessment of the Risk of the Respiratory Distress Syndrome by a Rapid Test for Surfactant in Amniotic Fluid," *New England Journal of Medicine* 286 (1972): 1077–81.

P. 102—G. Liggins and R. Howie, "A Controlled Trial of Antepartum Glucocorticoid Treatment for Prevention of the Respiratory Distress Syndrome in Premature Infants," *Pediatrics* 50 (1972): 515–25; William Tooley, "Telling It Like It Was," *American Review of Respiratory Diseases* 115, supp. (1977): 19–28.

P. 105—L. Papile, G. Munsick-Bruno, and A. Schaefer, "Relationship of Cerebral Intraventricular Hemorrhage and Early Childhood Neurologic Handicaps," *Journal of Pediatrics* 103 (1983): 1273–76.

P. 106—J. Perlman, J. McMenamin, and J. Volpe, "Fluctuating Cerebral Blood-Flow Velocity in Respiratory Distress Syndrome, *New England Journal of Medicine* 309 (1983): 204–8.

Pp. 108–9—On-site research at a major midwestern children's hospital.

4 The Dark Side of Progress

P. 112—R. Nickel, F. Bennett, and F. Lamson, "School Performance of Children with Birth Weight of 1000 G or Less," *American Journal of Diseases of Children* 136 (1982): 105.

P. 112—A. Rothberg et al., "Infants Weighing 1,000 Grams or Less at Birth: Developmental Outcome for Ventilated and Nonventilated Infants," *Pediatrics* 71 (1983): 599.

Pp. 112–13—R. Cohen et al., "Favorable Results of Neonatal Intensive Care for Very

Low-Birthweight Infants," *Pediatrics* 69 (1982): 621–25.

P. 113—A. Teberg et al., "Infants with Birth Weight under 1500 G: Physical, Neurological, and Developmental Outcome," *Critical Care Medicine* 10 (1982): 10–14.

P. 113—H. Knobloch et al., "Considerations in Evaluating Changes in Outcome for Infants Weighing Less Than 1,501 Grams," *Pediatrics* 69 (1982): 285–95.

P. 113—M. Ruiz et al., "Early Development of Infants of Birth Weight Less Than 1,000 Grams with Reference to Mechanical Ventilation in Newborn Period," *Pediatrics* 68 (1981): 330–34.

P. 113—J. Driscoll, Jr., et al., "Mortality and Morbidity in Infants Less Than 1,001 Grams Birth Weight," *Pediatrics* 69 (1982): 21–26.

P. 113—S. Britton, P. Fitzhardinge, and S. Ashby, "Is Intensive Care Justified for Infants Weighing Less Than 801 Gm at Birth?" *Journal of Pediatrics* 99 (1981): 937–42.

P. 115—P. Budetti et al., *The Implications of Cost-Effectiveness Analysis of Medical Technology*, Background Paper no. 2, Case Studies of Medical Technologies no. 10: "The Costs and Effectiveness of Neonatal Intensive Care" (Washington, D.C.: Office of Technology Assessment, 1981), 23.

P. 115—C. Phibbs, "Charges for Level III Neonatal Intensive Care in California" (paper prepared for the Maternal and Infant Health section of the Department of Health Services, State of California, 1981).

P. 115—M. Boyle et al., "Economic Evaluation of Neonatal Intensive Care of Very Low-Birthweight Infants," *New England Journal of Medicine* 308 (1983): 1330–37.

Pp. 115–16—S. Schechner, "For the 1980s: How Small Is Too Small?" *Clinics in Perinatology* 7 (1980): 135–43.

Pp. 116–17—F. Bennett, N. Robinson, and C. Sells, "Growth and Development of Infants Weighing Less Than 800 Grams at Birth," *Pediatrics* 71 (1983): 319–27.

P. 118—Driscoll et al., "Mortality and Morbidity," 25.

P. 118—Cohen et al., "Favorable Results," 625.

P. 120—R. Phibbs to author, Aug. 11, 1983.

P. 121—P. and R. Stinson, *The Long Dying of Baby Andrew* (Boston: Atlantic / Little, Brown, 1983).

Pp. 121–22—From author's observations and interviews, Feb. and July 1983.

Pp. 122–24—Author's interviews, Nov. 1982–Aug. 1983.

Pp. 125–26—W. Silverman, "Mismatched Attitudes about Neonatal Death," *Hastings Center Report* 11, no. 6 (Dec. 1981): 12–16.

P. 129—J. Henahan, "80 Percent of Preemies in Follow-up Essentially Normal by Age 2," *Medical Tribune* 20 (Sept. 1979): 1–20.

P. 130—A. Jameton to author, Jan. 1983.

5 Birth Defects

P. 134–35—*International Clearinghouse for Birth Defects Monitoring Systems, Annual Report*, 1981.

Pp. 136–37—R. W. Smithells, S. Sheppard, and C. J. Schorah, "Possible Prevention of Neural-Tube Defects by Preconceptual Vitamin Supplementation," *Lancet*, Feb. 16, 1980, pp. 339–40; K. M. Laurence et al., "Double-Blind Randomised Controlled Trial of Folate Treatment before Conception to Prevent Recurrence of Neural-Tube Defects," *British Medical Journal* 282 (1981): 1509–11.

P. 140—D. Murphy, "The Outcome of 625 Pregnancies in Women Subjected to Pelvic Radium or Roentgen Irradiation," *American Journal of Obstetrics and Gynecology* 18 (1929): 179–87.

P. 140—F. Hale, "The Relationship of Vitamin A to Anopthalmos in Pigs," *American Journal of Ophthalmology* 18 (1935): 1087–92.

Pp. 140–41—J. Warkany and R. Nelson, "Appearance of Skeletal Abnormalities in the Offspring of Rats Reared on a Deficient Diet," *Science* 92 (1940): 383–84.

P. 141—C. Swan et al., "Congenital Defects in Infants Following Infectuous Diseases during Pregnancy," *Medical Journal of Australia* 2 (Sept. 11, 1943): 201–10.

P. 145—Estimations of occurrence from H. Kalter and J. Warkany, "Congenital Malformations," *New England Journal of Medicine* 308 (1983): 424–29 and 491–96.

Pp. 150–51—M. Schwartz et al., "Down's Syndrome in Adults: Brain Metabolism," *Science* 221 (1983): 781–83.

P. 151—G. Smith, P. Feldman, and G. Smith, "The Incidence of Down's Syndrome in Three Counties in Southern Illinois during the Years 1974–1978," *Illinois Medical Journal* 164 (Aug. 1983): 101–3.

Pp. 156–58—C. Norman, "Vietnam's Herbicide Legacy," *Science* 219 (1983): 1196–97; F. Wilcox, *Waiting for an Army to Die: The Tragedy of Agent Orange* (New York: Random House, 1983), 51–52; A. Lipson, letter to *New England Journal of Medicine* 309 (1983): 491.

Pp. 159–60—G. Oakley to author, Sept. 1983.

Pp. 160–61—Telephone interview with J. Madell; telephone interviews with Colorado public health officials, July 1984.

P. 161—M. G. Kovar, "Health Status of U.S. Children and Use of Medical Care," *Public Health Reports* 97 (Jan.–Feb. 1982): 3–14; interview with P. Newacheck and P. Budetti, Aug. 1983.

6 Suffer the Children

Pp. 163–64—From author's observations and interviews, Dec. 1982.

Pp. 169–74—Author's observations and interviews, July 1983–Sept. 1984; family names have been changed.

Pp. 174–78—S. West, telephone interviews with author, Nov. 1982 and June 1983.

Pp. 178–81—Author's observations and interviews, July 1983.

Pp. 183–84—J. Lorber, "Results of Treatment of Myelomeningocele," *Developmental Medicine and Child Neurology* 13 (1971): 300; Lorber, "Results of Selective Treatment of Spina Bifida Cystica," *Archives of Disease in Childhood* 56 (1981): 822; Lorber, "Early Results of Selective Treatment of Spina Bifida Cystica," *British Medical Journal* 4 (1973): 204.

Pp. 184–85—D. Shurtleff et al., "Myelodysplasia: Decision for Death or Disability," *New England Journal of Medicine* 291 (1974): 1005–10; telephone interview with David Shurtleff, Sept. 13, 1984.

P. 185—R. Gross et al., "Early Management and Decision Making for the Treatment of Myelomeningocele," *Pediatrics* 72 (1983): 450–57.

P. 186—J. Freeman, "The Shortsighted Treatment of Myelomeningocele: A Long-Term Case Report," *Pediatrics* 53 (1974): 311.

Pp. 186–87—Interview with David McLone, Nov. 1982.

7 The Law and Handicapped Newborns

Pp. 190–91—In the Interest of Jeff & Scott Mueller, Minors, No. 81J300 and 81J301, Circuit Court, Danville, Ill., May 1981.

P. 191—*Philadelphia Inquirer*, June 12, 1981.

P. 191—In the Interest of Jeff & Scott Mueller, Circuit Court, Danville, Ill., July 1981.

P. 192—Interview with J. Raffensperger, Dec. 1982.

P. 192—Telephone interview with E. Litak, Jan. 1984.

Pp. 192–93—"Acquittal of Paediatrician Charged after Death of Infant with Down Syndrome," *Lancet*, Nov. 14, 1981, pp. 1101–2.

P. 194—C. Damme, "Infanticide: The Worth of an Infant under the Law," *Medical History* 22 (1978): 1–24.

P. 195—Griswold v. Connecticut, 381 U.S. 479 (1965).

P. 195—Eisenstadt v. Baird, 405 U.S. 438 (1972).

P. 195—Roe v. Wade, 410 U.S. 113 (1973).

P. 196—Curlender v. Bio-Science Laboratories, 106 Cal. App. 3d 811, 165 Cal. Reporter 477 (1980).

P. 196—Turpin v. Sortini, 174 Cal. Reporter 128 (1981).

P. 197—Regina v. Senior, 1 Q.B. 283 (1899).

P. 197—People ex rel. Wallace v. Labrenz, 411 Ill. 618 (1952).

P. 197—*New York Times*, Sept. 22, 1983.

Pp. 197–98—Custody of a Minor, Mass. 393 N.E. 2d 836.

P. 198–Prince v. Massachusetts, 321 U.S. 158, 166 (1944).

Pp. 198–99—Originally in the *Pacific News Service,* Jan. 1978, quoted in F. Schaeffer and C. Koop, *Whatever Happened to the Human Race?* (Good News, 1983).

Pp. 199–200—Maine Medical Center v. Houle, No. 74-145, Superior Court, Cumberland, Maine, Feb. 14, 1974.

P. 200—In the Matter of Kerri Ann McNulty, No. 1960 (Probate Court Essex Co., Mass., Feb. 15, 1978.)

Pp. 201–2—In re Quinlan, 70 N.J. 10, 355 A2d 647 (1976).

P. 203—*Time,* Apr. 11, 1983.

P. 203—A. Morris, "Law, Morality, and Euthanasia for the Severely Defective Child," *Infanticide and the Value of Life,* ed. Marvin Kohl (Buffalo: Prometheus Books, 1978).

P. 217—Eichner v. Dillon, 52 N.Y. 2d 363 (1981).

Pp. 203–5—Supt. of Belchertown State School v. Saikewicz, 373 Mass. 728 (1977).

Pp. 205–6—In the Matter of John Storar, 52 N.Y. 2d 363, 420 N.E. 2d 64 (1981).

P. 207—Satz v. Perlmutter, 379 So. 2d 359 (1980).

P. 207—President's Commission for the Study of Ethical Problems in Medicine, *Deciding to Forego Life-Sustaining Treatment* (Washington, D.C.: GPO, 1983), 83.

Pp. 208–9—In re Phillip B., 92 Cal. App. 3d 796, 156 Cal. Reporter 48 (1979).

P. 209—J. Robertson, "Legal Aspects of Withholding Medical Treatment from Handicapped Children," in *Infanticide and the Handicapped Newborn,* ed. Horan and Delahoyde (Provo: Brigham Young Univ. Press, 1982), 26.

P. 209—R. Lindsey, in *New York Times,* Oct. 10, 1983.

P. 211—American Academy of Pediatrics, "Guidelines for Infant Bioethics Committees" (released Apr. 1984).

P. 211—American Academy of Pediatrics Committee on Bioethics, "Treatment of Critically Ill Newborns," *Pediatrics* 72 (1983): 566.

8 Sanctity of Life vs. Quality of Life

Pp. 214–15—J. Bresnahan, interview with author, Dec. 1982.

P. 215—S. Toulmin, "How Medicine Saved the Life of Ethics," *Perspectives in Biology and Medicine* 25 (1982): 736–50.

Pp. 215–16—L. J. Dunn, interview with author, Dec. 1982.

P. 216—P. Ramsey, *Ethics at the Edges of Life* (New Haven: Yale Univ. Press, 1978), 188.

Pp. 216–17—P. Singer, in *New York Review of Books,* Mar. 1, 1984.

P. 217—E. Diamond, "Treatment versus Nontreatment for the Handicapped Newborn," in *Infanticide and the Handicapped Newborn,* ed. Horan and Delahoyde (Provo: Brigham Young Univ. Press, 1982).

Pp. 217–18—R. McCormick, "The Quality of Life, the Sanctity of Life," *Hastings Center Report* 8, no. 1 (Feb. 1978): 30–36.

P. 218—J. Fletcher, *Humanhood: Essays in Biomedical Ethics* (Buffalo: Prometheus Books, 1979).

P. 218—T. Murray and A. Caplan, *Which Babies Shall Live: Humanistic Dimensions of the Care of Imperiled Newborns* (Clifton, N.J.: Humana Press, 1985).

P. 220—E. Cassel, "The Nature of Suffering and the Goals of Medicine," *New England Journal of Medicine* 306 (1982): 639–45.

P. 220—J. Donnelly, "Suffering: A Christian View," in *Infanticide and the Value of Life,* ed. M. Kohl (Buffalo: Prometheus Books, 1978), 164.

Pp. 220–21—A. Jonsen et al., "Critical Issues in Newborn Intensive Care: A Conference Report and Policy Proposal," *Pediatrics* 55 (1975): 756–68.

Pp. 221–22—A. Jonsen, interview with author, Aug. 11, 1983.

P. 222—President's Commission for the Study of Ethical Problems in Medicine, *Deciding to Forego Lifesaving Treatment* (Washington, D.C.: GPO, 1983), 218–19.

P. 223—R. McCormick, "To Save or Let Die: The Dilemma of Modern Medicine," *Journal of the American Medical Association* 229 (1974): 172–76.

Pp. 223–24—J. Paris, "Terminating Treatment for Newborns: A Theological Perspective," *Law, Medicine, and Health Care* 10 (June 1982): 122.

Pp. 224–25—A. Shaw, "Who Should Die and Who Should Decide?" in *Infanticide and the Value of Life*, 105–6.

P. 225—R. Brandt, "Defective Newborns and the Morality of Termination," in *Infanticide and the Value of Life*, 49.

P. 227—M. Tooley, *Abortion and Infanticide* (Oxford: Oxford Univ. Press, 1983).

Pp. 227–28—H. T. Engelhardt, "Some Persons Are Humans, Some Humans Are Persons, and the World Is What We Persons Make of It," in *Philosophical Medical Ethics: Its Nature and Significance*, ed. S. Spicker and H. T. Engelhardt (Dordrecht, Holland: D. Reidel, 1975), 183–93.

P. 228—P. Singer, "Sanctity of Life or Quality of Life" (a commentary), *Pediatrics* 72 (1983): 128–29.

P. 229—Fletcher, *Humanhood*, 7–18, 140–47, and 4.

Pp. 230–31—W. Bartholome, remark to author, Univ. of Illinois medical conference, Nov. 4, 1983.

Pp. 231–32—R. Weir, *Selective Treatment of Handicapped Newborns* (New York: Oxford Univ. Press, 1984), 205–8 and 221.

P. 233—P. Foot, "Euthanasia," in *Medicine and Moral Philosophy*, ed. M. Cohen, T. Nagel, and T. Scanlon (Princeton: Princeton Univ. Press, 1982), 303.

P. 233—Foot, "Euthanasia," 300.

P. 233—N. Fost, lecture at Northwestern Univ. medical conference, Dec. 16, 1983.

Pp. 233–34—M. Angell, "Handicapped Children: Baby Doe and Uncle Sam," *New England Journal of Medicine* 309 (1983): 659–61.

P. 235—R. Veatch, *A Theory of Medical Ethics* (New York: Basic Books, 1981), 161–63.

P. 236—A. Jonsen, "Do No Harm: Axiom of Medical Ethics," in *Philosophical Medical Ethics*, 27–41.

P. 236—H. T. Engelhardt, "Euthanasia and Children: The Injury of Continued Existence," *Journal of Pediatrics* 83 (1973): 170–71.

P. 236—J. Bresnahan, interview with author, Jan. 13, 1984.

9 Families in Distress

Pp. 237–40—From author's interviews, June 1983–Sept. 1984; family names have been changed.

P. 242—F. Idriss, interview with author, Dec. 1982.

Pp. 242–43—J. Bresnahan, interview with author, Dec. 1982.

P. 243—A. J. Solnit and M. H. Stark, "Mourning and the Birth of a Defective Child," *Psychoanalytical Study of the Child* 16 (1961): 523–37.

Pp. 244–45—M. Klaus and J. Kennell, "Caring for Parents of Infant with Congenital Malformation," in *Maternal-Infant Bonding* (St. Louis: C. V. Mosby, 1976), 167–208; J. Kennell and M. Klaus, *Bonding: The Beginnings of Parent-Infant Attachment* (St. Louis: New American Library, 1983), 140–61.

Pp. 245–48—From author's interviews, Dec. 1982–Aug. 1984.

P. 248—M. Trout, "Birth of a Sick or Handicapped Infant: Impact on the Family," *Child Welfare* 62 (1983): 337–48.

Pp. 248–52—From author's interviews, Feb. 1983; family names have been changed.

Pp. 252–53—A. Jonsen, interview with author, Aug. 11, 1983.

P. 253—From interviews with state adoption officials, with particular appreciation to Gary Morgan, of the Illinois Department of Children and Family Services.

Pp. 254–55—P. Gluck et al., "Pediatric Nursing Homes: Implications of the Massachusetts Experience for Residential Care of Multiply Handicapped Children," *New England Journal of Medicine* 309 (1983): 640–46.

Pp. 255–56—Author's research at Misericordia Home; interview with Sister Rosemary Connelly, July 1983.

10 Shortchanging the Disabled

Pp. 259–60—Figures from Karen Brock, of Social Security Administration; telephone interviews with Thomas Berkshire, aide to Gov. James Thompson, of Illinois, and Robert Granzier, director of Illinois Dept. of Rehabilitative Services, Jan. 1984.

P. 261—Fred Weintraub, lobbyist for Council of Exceptional Children, Washington, D.C., telephone interview, Jan. 1984.

Pp. 261–62—*Chicago Tribune,* Sept. 15, 1983.

P. 262—Estimate of children who lost Medicaid coverage comes from Children's Defense Fund of Washington, D.C.

P. 263—Telephone interview with Jane West, legislative assistant to Sen. Lowell Weicker, May 22, 1984.

Pp. 263–64—Report of loss of insurance coverage from telephone interview with Leonard Mosely, of Illinois Division of Services to Crippled Children, Jan. 1984.

Pp. 264–66—From telephone interviews with directors of state crippled children's, maternal and child health, and Medicaid agencies, Jan., Feb., and May 1984.

P. 265—*Chicago Sun-Times,* Oct. 20, 1983.

Pp. 266–67—From Children's Defense Fund white paper entitled "Children and Federal Health Care Cuts," prepared by S. Rosenbaum and J. Weitz; and telephone interview with S. Rosenbaum, Jan. 1984.

Pp. 268–69—A. Webb, telephone interview, Jan, 1984; L. Park, telephone interview, Jan. 1984.

P. 269—E. Page-El, telephone interview, Jan. 1984.

P. 270—J. Butler, telephone interview, Sept. 1983.

Pp. 270–71—L. Barber, telephone interview, Jan. 1984.

Pp. 273–75—C. Frame, interview with author, Jan. 1984.

P. 276—E. Bilotti, telephone interviews, Feb. 1984.

P. 277—E. C. Gilchrist, in *Neurodevelopmental Problems in Early Childhood,* ed. C. M. Drillien, M. B. Drummond (Great Britain: Blackwell Scientific Publications, 1977), 200–213.

Pp. 278–79—For a good, if rather critical, analysis of the Swedish system, see A. Ratza, "Community-Based Attendant Services in Sweden: Description and Reflections," *Rehabilitation World* (Summer / Fall 1982): 12–15.

11 The High Cost of Saving Babies

P. 281—W. Kirkley, "Fetal Survival—What Price?" *American Journal of Obstetrics and Gynecology* 137 (1980): 873–75.

P. 281—T. Swanson, "Economics of Mongolism," *Annals of the New York Academy of Sciences* 171 (1970): 679–83.

P. 281—*Source Book of Health Insurance Data, 1980–1981,* prepared by the Health Insurance Institute, Washington, D.C., p. 74.

P. 284—*Utilization of Short-Stay Hospitals,* Data from the National Health Survey, ser. 13, no. 60 (Washington, D.C.: National Center for Health Statistics), 35.

P. 284—Mortality figures from tables furnished by the National Center for Health Statistics.

P. 284—Catastrophic illness figure from *Source Book of Health Insurance Data, 1980–1981,* p. 73.

Pp. 284–85—Hospital cost figures from survey undertaken by author.

P. 285—The figure of $2.65 billion is based on an estimate made by Dr. P. Budetti and P. McManus, which amounted to $1.5 billion in 1978 dollars (see note to chap. 4, p. 115). I have adjusted the total for inflation. The figures for hospitalization and out-patient treatment of birth-impaired individuals are based on estimates made by P. Ma and F. Piazza in "Cost of Treating Birth Defects in State Crippled Children's Services, 1975," *Public Health Reports* 94 (Sept.–Oct. 1979): 420–24. Again, I have adjusted for inflation.

P. 286—*Source Book of Health Insurance Data, 1980–1981,* p. 53, chart based on HHS projections published in *Public Health Reports,* Sept.–Oct., 1978.

P. 286—A. Milunsky, *The Prenatal Diagnosis of Hereditary Disorders* (Springfield, Ill.: Charles C. Thomas, 1973), 160–70.

Pp. 286–87—M. Chapalain, "Perinatality: French Cost-Benefit Studies and Decisions on Handicap and Prevention," in *Major Mental Handicap: Methods and Costs of Prevention*, Ciba Foundation Symposium no. 59 (Amsterdam: Elsevier Scientific Publishing Co., 1978), 193–203.

P. 287—Budetti et al. (see note to chap. 4, p. 115), 42.

Pp. 287–88—Boyle et al. (see note to chap. 4, p. 115).

Pp. 289–90—E. Frederick, interview with author, Nov. 1982.

P. 290—S. Hupfeld, telephone interview, Aug. 1983.

Pp. 290–91—L. Butterfield, interview with author, Aug. 1983.

P. 291—D. Rothman, telephone interview with author, Jan. 1983.

Pp. 291–92—S. Rosenbaum and J. Weitz, "Children and Federal Health Care Cuts" (white paper prepared for the Children's Defense Fund), 9.

12 The Handicapped Speak

Pp. 294–97—From author's interviews, Dec. 1982–Aug. 1984.

P. 298—P. Graham and M. Rutter, "Organic Brain Dysfunction and Child Psychiatric Disorder," *British Medical Journal* 3 (1968): 695–700.

P. 299—M. Mahler, F. Pine and A. Bergman, *The Psychological Birth of the Human Infant: Symbiosis and Individuation* (New York: Basic Books, 1975).

P. 300—R. Prall, "The Physically Handicapped Child," in *Behavior Pathology of Childhood and Adolescence*, ed. Sidney Copel (New York: Basic Books, 1973), 354–86.

P. 300—B. Bettelheim, "How Do You Help a Child Who Has a Physical Handicap?" *Ladies Home Journal*, Sept. 1972, pp. 34–35.

P. 300—J. Schulman, interview with author, Nov. 1982.

P. 300—P. Pinkerton, "Parental Acceptance of the Handicapped Child," *Developmental Medicine and Child Neurology* 12 (1970): 207–12.

Pp. 301–2—E. Poznanski, "Emotional Issues in Raising Handicapped Children," *Rehabilitation Literature* 34 (Nov. 1973): 322–26.

P. 302—N. Josefowitz, in *Maternal-Infant Bonding*, ed. M. Klaus and J. Kennell (St. Louis: C. V. Mosby, 1976), 167–208.

Pp. 302–3—F. Macgregor, "Some Psycho-Social Problems Associated with Facial Deformities," *American Sociological Review* 16 (1951): 629–38.

P. 303—J. Phillips and L. Whitaker, "The Social Effects of Craniofacial Deformity and Its Correction," *Cleft Palate Journal* 16 (Jan. 1979): 7–15.

Pp. 303–4—A. Fineman, "Ego Development in Children with Congenital Defects of the Genitourinary System," *American Journal of Orthopsychiatry* 29 (1959): 110–18.

P. 305—The Insight Team of the *Sunday Times* of London, *Suffer the Children: The Story of Thalidomide* (New York: Viking, 1979); "Thalidomide Victims Now Grown, Thriving," Jon Van interviews Dr. Ernst Marquardt of Heidelberg, *Chicago Tribune*, Sept. 28, 1982.

Pp. 305–8—From author's interviews, Jan. 1983; family names have been changed.

P. 308—B. Castree and J. H. Walker, "The Young Adult with Spina Bifida," *British Medical Journal* 283 (1981): 1040–42.

Pp. 308–9—A. Garson, Jr., R. Williams, Jr., and J. Reckless, "Long-Term Follow-up of Patients with Tetralogy of Fallot: Physical Health and Psychopathology," *Journal of Pediatrics* 85 (1974): 429–33.

P. 309—Poznanski, "Emotional Issues."

P. 309—*Chicago Tribune*, Dec. 17, 1983.

P. 311—Sworn declaration of Elizabeth Bouvia, filed in Riverside Superior Court Oct. 27, 1983, docket no. 159780; *New York Times*, Oct. 29, 1983; *Riverside Press-Enterprise*, reprinted in *Chicago Tribune*, Feb. 8, 1984.

P. 312—J. Robertson, "Involuntary Euthanasia of Defective Newborns: A Legal Analysis," *Stanford Law Review* 27 (1975): 254.

13 What the Future Holds

Pp. 316–17—V. Kidd et al., "Prenatal Diagnosis of Alpha 1-Antitrypsin Deficiency by Direct Analysis of the Mutation Site in the Gene," *New England Journal of Medicine* 310 (1984): 639–42; S. Woo et al., "Cloned Human Phenylalanine Hydroxylase Gene

Allows Prenatal Diagnosis and Carrier Detection of Classical Phenylketonuria," *Nature* 306 (1983): 151–55.

P. 319—J. F. Gusella et al., "A Polymorphic DNA Marker Genetically Linked to Huntington's Disease," *Nature* 306 (1983): 234–38.

P. 320—A. Miller et al., "A Transmissible Retrovirus Expressing Human HPRT: Gene Transfer into Cells Deficient in HPRT," *Proceedings of the National Academy of Sciences* 80 (1983): 4709–13.

Pp. 320–21—A. Roach et al., "Characterization of Cloned cDNA Representing Rat Myelin Basic Protein: Absence of Expression in Brain of Shiverer Mutant Mice," *Cell* 34 (1983): 799–806.

P. 321—T. Ley et al., "5-azacytidine Selectively Increases Gamma-Globin Synthesis in a Patient with Beta-Thalassemia," *New England Journal of Medicine* 307 (1982): 1469–75.

P. 324—P. Layde, S. Von Allmen, and G. Oakley, Jr., "Maternal Serum Alpha-Fetoprotein Screening: A Cost-Benefit Analysis," *American Journal of Public Health* 69 (1979): 566–73.

P. 325—M. Bennett et al., "Some Problems of Alpha-fetoprotein Screening," *Lancet*, Dec. 16, 1978, pp. 1296–97.

P. 326—J. Haddow, telephone interview with author, Feb. 1984.

P. 327—R. Depp, interview with author, Dec. 1982.

P. 328—J. Brown, interview with author, Dec. 1982.

14 Conclusions

Pp. 335–36—*Idaho Statesman*, Oct. 16 and Dec. 10, 1983.

Select Bibliography

Annas, G. "Baby Doe Redux: Doctors as Child Abusers." *Hastings Center Report* 13, no. 5 (Oct. 1983): 26–27.

Bridge, P., and M. Bridge. "The Brief Life and Death of Christopher Bridge." *Hastings Center Report* 11, no. 6 (Dec. 1981): 17–19.

Comroe, J. H., Jr. "Premature Science and Immature Lungs." In *Retrospectroscope: Insights into Medical Discovery.* Menlo Park, Calif.: Von Gehr Press, 1977, 140–79.

Damme, C. "Infanticide: The Worth of an Infant under the Law." *Medical History* 22 (1978): 1–24.

Darling, R. "Parents, Physicians, and Spina Bifida," *Hastings Center Report* 7, no. 4 (Aug. 1977): 10–14.

Duff, R. S., and A. G. M. Campbell. "Moral and Ethical Dilemmas in the Special-Care Nursery." *New England Journal of Medicine* 289 (1973): 890–94. The watershed article that initiated open debate in the medical community.

Fost, N. "Putting Hospitals on Notice." *Hastings Center Report* 12, no. 4 (Aug. 1982): 5–8.

Fletcher, J. *Humanhood: Essays in Biomedical Ethics.* Buffalo: Prometheus Books, 1979.

Gustafson, J. M. "Mongolism, Parental Desires, and the Right to Life." *Perspectives in Biology and Medicine* 16 (Summer 1973): 529. A highly personal exploration of the question of letting Down's children die.

Holder, A. R. "Parents, Courts, and Refusal of Treatment." *Journal of Pediatrics* 104 (1983): 515–21. A legal analysis.

Horan, D., and M. Delahoyde, eds. *Infanticide and the Handicapped Newborn.* Provo: Brigham Young Univ. Press, 1982. Essays from a prolife point of view.

Jonsen, A., et al. "Critical Issues in Newborn Intensive Care: A Conference Report and Policy Proposal." *Pediatrics* 55 (1975): 312–34.

Jonsen, A., and M. Garland. *Ethics of Newborn Intensive Care.* San Francisco: Univ. of California Press, 1976.

Kohl, M., ed. *Infanticide and the Value of Life.* Buffalo: Prometheus Books, 1978. A provocative collection of essays, mostly pro-nontreatment.

McAuliffe, K., and S. McAuliffe. "Keeping Up with the Genetic Revolution." *New York Times Magazine,* Nov. 6, 1983. A highly readable account of DNA research.

McCormick, R. "To Save or Let Die: The Dilemma of Modern Medicine." *Journal of the American Medical Association* 229 (1974): 174.

Mellin, G., and M. Katzenstein. "The Saga of Thalidomide." *New England Journal of Medicine* 267 (1962): 1181–91 and 1238–43.

Ramsey, P. *Ethics at the Edges of Life.* New Haven: Yale Univ. Press, 1978.

Reich, W., and D. Ost, eds. *Encyclopedia of Bioethics.* New York: Free Press, 1978.

Robertson, J. A. "Involuntary Euthanasia of Defective Newborns: A Legal Analysis." *Stanford Law Review* 27 (1975): 213–69. An excellent and incisive analysis of the issue.

———. "Dilemma in Danville." *Hastings Center Report* 11, no. 5 (Oct. 1981): 5–8.

———. *The Rights of the Critically Ill.* New York: Bantam, 1983.

Silverman, W. *Retrolental Fibroplasia: A Modern Parable*. New York: Grune & Stratton, 1980.

———. "Mismatched Attitudes about Neonatal Death." *Hastings Center Report* 11, no. 6 (Dec. 1981): 12–16.

Singer, P., *Practical Ethics*. New York: Cambridge Univ. Press, 1979.

Stinson, R., and P. Stinson. *The Long Dying of Baby Andrew*. Boston: Atlantic / Little, Brown, 1983.

Strong, C. "The Tiniest Newborns." *Hastings Center Report* 13, no. 1 (Feb. 1983): 14–19.

Swinyard, C. *Decision Making and the Defective Newborn*. Springfield, Ill.: Charles C Thomas, 1978.

Taub, S. "Withholding Treatment from Defective Newborns." *Law, Medicine, and Health Care* 10 (Feb. 1982): 4–10.

Tooley, M. *Abortion and Infanticide*. Oxford: Oxford Univ. Press, 1983.

Vaux, K. *Who Shall Live?* Philadelphia: Fortress Press, 1970.

———. *Biomedical Ethics*. New York: Harper & Row, 1974.

Warkany, J. *Congenital Malformations*. Chicago: Year Book Medical Publishers, 1971. An exhaustive description of known birth defects.

Weber, L. J. *Who Shall Live? The Dilemma of Severely Handicapped Children and Its Meaning for Other Moral Questions*. New York: Paulist Press, 1976.

Weir, R. *Selective Nontreatment of Handicapped Newborns*. New York: Oxford Univ. Press, 1984. A comprehensive review of all schools of thought.

Zachary, R. "Life with Spina Bifida." *British Medical Journal* 2 (1977): 1461.

Index